Carrie stood near ~~~~~~~~~~~~~~~~~~~ ea at
JFK Airport becaus~~~~~~~~~~~~~~~~~~~. But
she stood off to the side, knowing that, unlike the reunions of others around her, theirs would not be joyous.
It would not mark the beginning of new friendship or
an exciting summer holiday or a memorable adventure
of youth.

It was a reunion because of a tragedy. And it was a
reunion with a man Carrie had vowed never to see
again— a man who was returning at a moment's notice
to be with Megan, as he always did when Megan needed
him. Megan needed him now. And Megan needed Carrie, too. Megan needed both of them. And they had
come.

Once, they had all been friends.

The door from the customs area opened. As Carrie
had expected, he was the first one through. In that moment, looking across the room into the tired, worried
blue eyes she knew so well, Carrie realized that together
they would forget everything but the friendship they'd
once shared, until this terrible ordeal was over.

As she waited for him to work his way through the
crowd, Carrie's heart pounded and her mind flooded
with memories of the first time he had smiled at her,
that autumn evening seven years before. So much had
happened in those seven years, so many memories between that lovely, long-ago evening and the tragedy that
reunited them now . . .

ROOM- MATES

KATHERINE STONE

ZEBRA BOOKS
KENSINGTON PUBLISHING CORP.

ZEBRA BOOKS are published by

Kensington Publishing Corp.
850 Third Avenue
New York, NY 10022

20   19   18   17   16   15

Printed in the United States of America

To Gary, because a promise is a promise.

Prologue

"Pan American Flight 167 from Paris is now arriving at Gate 34."

His plane has landed, Carrie thought uneasily, her heart suddenly racing. Until she heard the arrival announcement, she had avoided thinking about seeing him again. There had been too much else to worry about. But now, with the arrival of his flight, Carrie realized how difficult it would be, how unprepared she really was.

In a few moments, she would see him. It wouldn't take long for him to clear customs. He would be off the plane quickly from the first class cabin. He wouldn't have any luggage, nothing to slow him down. He probably hadn't even checked out of his hotel in Paris. As soon as he had received the message—Carrie's message that Megan needed him—he had taken the next plane from Paris to New York.

Carrie waited outside the crowded customs area at John F. Kennedy International Airport. She stood near the door where the arriving passengers would exit once they had cleared customs, but she remained slightly apart from the crowd of people already gathered directly in front of the door to await the incoming travelers.

Small, excited children were closest to the door. Their impatience to greet grandparents from the "old country" or a father home on leave frequently erupted into jumping, running, giggling, and squealing. Behind the row of active children were the families pressing to catch the first glimpse

7

of a teenage son or daughter returning from a school year abroad or meet a visiting European teenager who would spend the summer in America with them. Behind the families were the tour group leaders busily displaying signs, organizing porters, reviewing client lists, and preparing vouchers.

School was out on both sides of the Atlantic. It was summer; time to travel, to explore new cultures, to meet new people. The migration across the Atlantic, in both directions, was brisk, enthusiastic, excited. The mood of the people in the customs area reflected the energy and enthusiasm for the summer season that had just begun.

Carrie was only vaguely aware of the buoyant, energized mood of the customs area, and even less aware of the stares, occasionally directed her way by the other people in the area. Of course they recognized her. Her soft strawberry blond curls, her bright blue eyes, her ready smile, her easy laugh were known to millions. Usually, she greeted the inevitable autograph seekers with gracious surprise. Today, no one even approached her. Today, her fans saw the fatigue and worry in her eyes and correctly sensed the tension and turmoil beneath her usual serenity.

Today, she needed her privacy.

Carrie stood near the door because she didn't want to miss him, but she stood off to the side, knowing that, unlike the reunions of others around her, theirs would not be joyous. It would not mark the beginning of new friendship or an exciting super holiday or a memorable adventure of youth.

It was a reunion because of a tragedy. And it was a reunion with a man Carrie had vowed never to see again—a man who was returning at a moment's notice to be with Megan, as he always did when Megan needed him. But now Megan needed both of them, and they had come.

Once, they had all been friends. For now, for the moment, Carrie had to remember the friendship and forget the recent bitter, hateful words and the pain. When it was over—as soon as it was over—they could go their separate ways. Again. *Forever.*

Can I do it? Carrie wondered. Can I forget what we have said to each other? What we have done to each other? Remembering the friendship, remembering the innocent beginning, remembering *more* than the friendship . . . It was harder, more painful, than remembering the hatred and bitterness.

I have to do it, Carrie thought. *We* have to do it. For Megan. No matter how difficult.

The door from the customs area opened. As Carrie had expected, he was the first one through. As soon as she saw him and felt the rush of unsummoned emotions, Carrie knew how difficult it would be. He paused at the door, his eyes calmly searching the area for her, finding her almost immediately. He looked at her over the row of lively children, beyond the eager families and the busy tour guides. Their eyes met, and held, tentatively, for a moment.

In that moment, looking across the room into the tired, worried blue eyes she knew so well, Carrie realized that they could—*would*—do it. They would forget everything but the friendship for as long as this horrible ordeal lasted. It would be difficult, but they would do it, together. She saw in his eyes an acknowledgment that he knew how hard it would be, for both of them. And she saw a promise that he would try.

Before his eyes left hers, before he started to move toward her, he smiled. A tired, awkward, inquiring smile. A smile that asked a question and required an answer: Will you try, too?

Carrie smiled slightly in return, controlling the rush of emotions with difficulty. Yes, she would try.

As she waited for him to work his way through the crowd, Carrie's heart pounded and her mind flooded with memories of the first time he had smiled at her, that autumn evening seven years before. So much had happened in those seven years, so many memories between that lovely, long ago evening and the tragedy that reunited them now.

Carrie's reverie was interrupted when he reached her, finally, and said, gently, "Hello, Caroline."

Part One

Chapter One

"Here we are, Carrie. Lagunita Hall." Stephen grinned as he watched his sister's eyes widen.

"Hurry and park!" Carrie's fingers wrapped tightly around the door handle. Her mouth was dry and her stomach fluttered.

She was *here*. Finally. Here in California. Here at Stanford. But, most importantly, here at Lagunita Hall. Lagunita Hall, the dormitory for freshman women at Stanford for over a century. Her mother had lived here. And her grandmother. Carrie had been raised on wonderful, romantic stories about Lagunita Hall. Her parents had met at a "parlour party" at Lagunita. Carrie knew that story, and a hundred others.

Carrie knew about the Stanford traditions—the bonfire before the big game, the famous ax, the menu for Sunday evening dinner listing chicken, spinach lasagna, fresh San Francisco sourdough rolls, and pumpkin pie, the Lagunita song, the Lagunita pledge. And she knew the secret of Lagunita Hall—the weeping willow whose branches provided easy access to the balcony and whose drooping leaves allowed privacy for clandestine meetings.

Carrie had loved the stories of happy times that her mother and grandmother had told her. She had longed for the day when she, too, would live at Lagunita Hall and have adventures of her own.

13

And now she was here.

Carrie stared at the immense bulk of old red brick and white shutters covered with strands of ivy, parched brown by another summer of California sun. Today a banner stretched across the front of the building: *Welcome - Class of '74.* The daisy-studded front lawn was crowded with a colorful array of people, posters, displays, suitcases, and tables with signs that read: "Register here: A-H"; "Stanford Pre-Medical Society"; "Stanford Drama Club"; "Students Against Vietnam War"; "The Stanford *Daily*"; "R.O.T.C."; "Orientation Week Activities Center." Lagunita Hall had seen this all before—the hubbub of Freshman Week—and gave the comforting appearance, for those who loved it as Carrie did, of a kind, slightly bemused grandparent.

Miraculously, but with luck and finesse typical of him, Stephen managed to create a parking space in Lagunita's already full parking lot. Carrie opened the car door before the engine was off, but waited for Stephen before walking toward the crowd. The excitement and impatience that had boarded the plane with her in Boston six hours earlier and had progressively intensified as her destination had approached, suddenly, inexplicably abandoned her. In its wake lay an uncomfortable mixture of apprehension and exhaustion. Carrie realized that without Stephen she would be unable to negotiate the mechanics of registering, of finding her room, of carrying her luggage. In fact, she realized as she tried unsuccessfully to subdue her pounding heart and fortify her rubbery legs, without Stephen she would be unable to move from this spot.

It was more than a little disquieting. Carrie made a mental note to add another name to her "In College I Will Learn to Become Independent From" list. In addition to her parents and her lifelong friends, she would have to add Stephen. But not today. Not now.

"Carrie, let's find out where your room is before we unload your luggage. If you're in the east wing it will be easier to drive the car around."

Carrie nodded, mute. The effort of speech seemed overwhelming and she had no confidence that a sound would be made even if she tried. Stephen peered into his sister's light blue eyes, correctly interpreted the tentative smile she gave him, put his arm around her shoulders, and guided her unerringly toward the table with the sign that read: "Registration R-Z."

Confidence bolstered slightly by Stephen's arm and the ease with which she was able to register, Carrie weaved slowly among the tables, collecting fliers and information brochures to be carefully read later. Every student group was represented: the drama club, pre-law society, debate team, women's field hockey team, the yearbook staff, Students for a Democratic Society . . .

"What group do they represent?" Carrie whispered to Stephen and indicated with her eyes a group of shirtless, tan men who carried no posters or fliers, yet created an undeniable presence. They stood in the middle of the lawn, laughing, talking, casually tossing a football, but mostly watching the activity.

"They, my dear little sister," Stephen replied as he waved amiably to the group, "represent . . . me . . . us . . . the Stanford men. They are inspecting the new crop of Stanford dollies!" Stephen tried to look sheepish but was obviously pleased with the look of outrage mixed with excitement on his sister's face.

"Stephen, that's awful!" Carrie wished that she had spent more time with her airplane-limp hair before they had left the San Francisco airport.

"I know, just *awful*. Listen, they're my friends. Why don't we go talk to them?"

"Stephen, no. No!" It was a whispered hiss.

"Okay, okay. You're so funny—I mean strange." Stephen gave her a quick squeeze and continued to guide her through the crowd. Carrie caught the glance of a woman in the throng, a look of admiration, which was of course, for Stephen.

It had been a long time since Carrie had been with Stephen in a group of strangers; she had forgotten the effect that his appearance usually caused. She looked at him carefully, as if for the first time, and noted that he was more handsome than ever. His tall, slender body had taken a new shape, broad shoulders tapering to a narrow waist, finely muscled arms and legs. Two years of rowing on the varsity crew, Carrie thought. His jet black hair, closely cropped around his aristocratic face during prep school, now curled softly over his ears, around his face, onto his neck. His skin was browned from the California sun. His green eyes sparkled under his long, dark lashes as he stared quizzically at her.

"What are you staring at?"

"You. I've hardly seen you in two years. You look so . . ." Carrie paused. She couldn't say "handsome" to her brother. "Uh, older. You know, more mature. In a good way. More muscles."

"And you are still my cute, adorable little sister."

Carrie's third floor dormitory room had a view of the lake and its own balcony. It was a three-room suite. The door from the corridor opened into a large central room that contained a bed, a sofa, a desk, several chairs, a window seat, and the suite's only telephone. The two smaller rooms were located on either side of the central room.

The door to the suite was wide open, but the room was empty. However, the wall was covered with colorful posters: "Ashland Shakespeare Festival—1970"; "The Jefferson Airplane"; "The Doors"; "Cream"; "The Beatles"; "Janis Joplin"; "Monterey Jazz Festival—1968"; *"Private Lives*—Mibu Community Theater Company, 1969." Mounds of brightly colored clothes lay on the bed and white ruffled curtains framed the window. It was obvious that at least one of Carrie's roommates had arrived. And whoever she was, she had claimed the large center room and, with it, the telephone, the window seat, and an apparent waiver of privacy. Both of the side bedrooms were unoccupied.

Carrie selected the one that gave her an unobstructed view of Lake Lagunita.

Carrie looked at her small, sterile room and sighed. "I'll be glad when my trunk arrives. This room needs some color. Maybe I can borrow some posters from my roommate."

"Truth or no, this room will fill up soon enough with souvenirs, if I know you. Also, they make very colorful textbooks these days . . ." Stephen tried to cheer her up. He knew that she was exhausted and probably more than little disappointed in Lagunita Hall. It was impossible for the antiquated building with its shoe-worn carpet, its cracked, gray-yellow walls, and its musty smell to live up to his sister's expectations. In time, he knew, she would love Lagunita Hall, its bulky comfort, its archaic charm, the warmth of the friendships she would make there. But it would take time. For now she would be disappointed, just as he had been. But she couldn't admit it, just as he hadn't.

"Hello there! Anybody home?" Before Stephen or Carrie answered, she appeared at Carrie's doorway. For a long, startled moment, none of them spoke. Finally it was Megan, used to the gasping silence that her presence often produced.

"Hi, I'm Megan. You must be one of my roommates. But who are *you?*"

Megan smiled briefly at Carrie, then engaged in a long, leisurely, less than wholesome perusal of Stephen. She leaned provocatively against the doorjamb. She wore short yellow shorts, an emerald green T-shirt with "OPHELIA" lettered across the front, and a rainbow-colored scarf tied loosely around her mane of golden hair. Her long, tanned legs tapered delicately to fine-boned ankles. She wore sandals with two-inch heels. Her eyes, appraising Stephen with undisguised interest, were cornflower blue. They sparkled with obvious approval at what they saw.

Carrie was speechless. Megan was beautiful, dazzling. Carrie's friends, all of whom had gone to Radcliffe, Vassar, or Smith, had warned her about the "competition" at Stanford. They had heard about the notorious Stanford dollies, those beautiful, liberal, Southern California blondes.

Carrie looked at Stephen for help. A blush had deepened his tan for a moment, but he had recovered quickly and was enjoying immensely the game that he was playing with Megan. He returned her stare with one of his own. Carrie felt like an intruder, an unwilling, uneasy witness to an intimate, personal moment.

"I'm Carrie Richards. This is my brother, Stephen." The embarrassment in Carrie's voice jarred Stephen and Megan out of their nonverbal flirtation. Megan offered her long, slender hand to Carrie and then to Stephen.

"Welcome," Megan purred. "I'm so glad that everyone is beginning to arrive. I've been here since yesterday and, frankly, it's been a bit boring. I applied the first-come-first-served rule and chose the center room for myself. You don't mind, I hope?" Megan didn't make it sound as if it would matter even if Carrie did care. In fact, Carrie preferred the privacy of her own, smaller room. Besides, it seemed appropriate for Megan to have the showcase room.

"No. I don't mind at all. I love the way you've decorated it. It's so bright and cheery." Carrie looked forlornly at her room. Drab. It was drab compared to Megan's, just as she herself was drab by comparison. Carrie was uncomfortably conscious of her heavier-than-stylish body, her too-short hair, and her fair, untannable skin.

I should have stayed back East, she thought. There she could do what she'd done for years, covering her weight with acceptably bulky, warm sweaters, wool skirts, down jackets. There, she could protect her delicate skin from the weather with scarves and gloves. Here, if Megan and Stephen were any indication, one wore just enough light cotton clothing to be decent. Carrie suddenly felt terribly discouraged. Even her brother had adopted the sunny West Coast life-style. He might love his "cute, adorable" sister, but it was abundantly obvious that he expected "women" to look like Megan. She noticed, with panic, that Stephen was about to leave.

"I've got crew practice, Carrie. I'll call you this evening." He paused and looked at Megan for a long moment. "See ya, Megan."

Carrie wanted to be alone. First, she would cry. Then, she would calmly decide how to explain to Stephen, her parents, and even Megan, that this West Coast adventure had really been a big mistake; how she belonged with her friends, people like herself, at Radcliffe. They would understand. It was painfully obvious that she was terribly out of place; that she would never fit in.

But Megan had no intention of leaving Carrie alone.

"Good-looking brother, Carrie. What year is he?" Megan stretched out on the blue-and-white-striped mattress on Carrie's narrow, unmade bed.

"Junior." How could she get Megan to leave? Couldn't Megan see that she was upset? Surely her terse answer and the fact that she was staring at the floor would tell Megan something.

Miraculously Megan jumped up.

"C'mon. Let's go into my room. This room is too small. Besides, I really have to put away my clothes."

Carrie sat in the alcove by the window in Megan's room. The late afternoon autumn sun cast a copper sheen on Lake Lagunita. The lake was flat calm. Two sailboats with colorful but motionless sails rocked idly as their crews drank beer and splashed in the water. Carrie couldn't hear their laughter, but she sensed it—sleek, tan bodies, laughing, flirting. Beyond the lake, four cows grazed on the green-brown hill, their eating undisturbed by the activity at the lake—oblivious, tranquil, fat.

Fat. I'm not really *fat*, Carrie thought. Just plump. But compared to Megan . . . Carrie watched in misery as Megan hung up sundresses, short cotton skirts, scant tops, all in bright, vivid colors.

"Tell me about yourself, Carrie. Is it just Carrie?"

"Carrie, short for Caroline. Everyone calls me Carrie. There's not much to tell. I'm from Boston. I came here because my parents went to college here. And, of course, Stephen." And I hate it here, she wanted to say, but instead added, "I don't know yet what my major will be. I like to write, so, maybe journalism. How about you?"

"I'm from Malibu. I'm an actress." Megan did not say, "I want to be an actress," or even "I am going to be an actress." She said, as a simple matter of fact, that she was an actress. "My father has some notion about me being a well-educated actress. So here I am. I only do theater work, and this school does have a wonderful English department, so at least I can really study Shakespeare, *et al.*"

"You acted in high school?" Carrie was amazed by Megan's confidence.

"School plays, of course. But those don't really count, do they? No, I've worked in theater for years. Mostly summer stock. This summer I was with the Ashland Shakespeare Festival. That's why I have this T-shirt. I was Ophelia. I also understudied Juliet. I did two matinee performances. A blond Juliet—not very Italian. It drove the director crazy, but I refused to wear a wig. My hair was perfect for Ophelia, of course. I wore wildflowers that we picked right there in the meadow. It was a wonderful summer." Megan sighed and bounced onto her bed, now no longer covered with clothes.

"You must be very good." Carrie's depression was waning. This was what college was about, meeting interesting, talented people.

"Ha!" Megan laughed and ran her long, tan fingers through her silky blond hair. "I'm lucky. I've had the obvious young-pretty-girl parts. It's been deceptively easy, as my director, Ian Knight, reminded me constantly this summer. To be really good, as I plan to be, requires discipline and training. That's why I'm not complaining too much about coming to college. I'm going to work with Ian again next summer—in New York!"

Megan paused to properly emphasize the significance of performing in New York. Then she continued, "If I work hard this year, reading plays, understanding the characters, experimenting with different emotions, Ian has promised to try me in some more challenging roles."

Their conversation was abruptly suspended by the arrival of their other roommate.

Beth carried only a small, blue leather purse, perfectly color coordinated with her linen suit and leather shoes. Her luggage, also blue leather, was carried by two fraternity men. Beth paused as she entered the room, pointedly double checked the number above the door, nonverbally registered her annoyance that the center room had already been taken, and led the two men, who grinned and winked at Megan and Carrie, into the remaining small bedroom.

"Do you think she'll tip them?" Megan whispered to Carrie. Carrie shrugged and giggled.

The men passed back through the center room, gave a friendly wave, and left. Carrie and Megan waited, casting conspiratorial glances at each other as they listened to the noises from the other room. They heard Beth open the suitcases, wash her hands, and hang something in the closet. Finally she reentered Megan's room.

When she spoke, her soft, slow Southern voice caught Megan and Carrie by surprise.

"I'm Beth. I'm from Houston."

"I'm Megan. This is Carrie. Houston?"

"That's right. Why?" Beth stood quietly without fidgeting. Carrie was certain that Beth could, and doubtless did, balance a book on her head for hours. Her dark brown hair curled perfectly and symmetrically at her shoulders. Beth didn't look hot or tired. Her cream-colored silk blouse and blue linen skirt had a just-pressed look. Her hair hadn't wilted; her makeup hadn't smudged. Even her pearls looked polished. Fastidious, perfectly groomed, and, Carrie decided, pretty—a southern belle prettiness, with high-arched eyebrows, large, depthless brown eyes, small, straight nose,

21

heart-shaped mouth, ample breasts, petite waist. Determination and energy in a deceptively delicate package.

"I have never known anyone from Houston. I love your accent! I must learn it," Megan said enthusiastically.

"Megan's an actress," Carrie explained.

Beth looked neither impressed nor interested.

"Right. And I have never played a character from the South. This will give me a chance to really learn the accent. Who knows? Maybe I'll get to do Blanche in *Streetcar*." Beth's expression made Megan stop short of announcing her plan to make recordings of Beth's voice.

"Well, I am going to unpack, make my bed, and take a nap. I will be awake by five-thirty if you all want to go to dinner together." Clearly, the subject of her accent was one that Beth had no intention of discussing. She was, apparently, willing to be seen in public with her roommates, at least for their first night at Stanford.

Beth must not know anyone else at Stanford, Carrie and Megan concluded, giggling, after Beth shut the door.

"Carrie, darlin', have you all ever taken a nap in your life, much less at the moment you arrive at college?" Megan whispered. Her Southern accent was already remarkably good.

"Not unless I'm sick. But for Beth it must fall under the category of beauty rest. She is beautiful, don't you think?"

Megan looked startled, then nodded.

"I guess so. It's just that she's so much not my type. I just have the urge to muss up her hair, or make her swear. Or even just make her really laugh. Carrie, I hope I can prevent myself from trying to provoke her—the temptation will be so strong. You'll have to keep me under control. I do love her accent, though. C'mon, you all, let's go do some exploring so sleeping beauty can nap."

An hour earlier, Carrie had decided to leave Stanford as soon as possible. Now, she wouldn't have left for anything. She was intrigued by her two roommates. Already, she felt comfortable with Megan. And she looked forward to getting to know—trying to get to know—Beth. Her role in the inevitable clashes between Beth and Megan would be necessary and challenging. As Carrie walked through the battered front doorway of Lagunita Hall into the fading rays of the autumn sun, she felt proud of the sleek, tan blonde beside her, excited about the year that was about to unfold, and forgot for a moment her own too-thick waist and jiggly thighs.

Chapter Two

"How's Sister Carrie? All tucked in?" Jake knew that Stephen had been anxious about Carrie's arrival. The anxiety had been unspoken, but after two years of rooming together, they had learned to sense each other's worries. Jake had an uncanny ability not only to sense Stephen's worry but to guess, with remarkable accuracy, the likely cause. Stephen, likewise, could tell when Jake was troubled; but he never knew the cause. And, unlike Stephen, Jake was unwilling to discuss his problem or ask for help.

"I had to go to crew practice, so I got her into the dormitory and left. She seemed a little depressed. New things are often a letdown, especially for Carrie. She has such grand expectations." Stephen grimaced.

"She'd either be mindless or totally unimaginative if her expectations were always met. And I doubt she is either, if she's anything like her brother."

"But that's just it, Jake. She isn't like me at all. She has been so protected, so coddled all her life—by me and by my parents. She's warm, friendly, and funny, but so naive. She is totally unprepared for anyone or anything that isn't sweetness and light. Her toughness has never been tested. I just don't know if she's a survivor." Stephen paused. "It was almost pathetic to watch Carrie's reaction to one of her roommates. Of course, Megan is in a league by herself."

24

"Megan? Not *the* Megan? At least I think that's the name everyone has been talking about since the *Frosh Book* came out. Let's see. Page six, I think." Jake leafed through the *Frosh Book*. It was the photo album of the entering freshman class. It accounted for the flurry of calls for "blind dates" during the first few weeks of Autumn Quarter. Jake handed the book to Stephen, opened to page six.

"That's Megan, all right. Carrie's roommate. This picture doesn't even begin to do her justice. She actually seemed pleasant enough, but it's going to be hard for Carrie. The phone will be continually ringing for Megan." Stephen sighed. "I didn't meet her other roommate."

"Why don't we have Carrie over for Sunday dinner? I think that's the first night they don't have a planned orientation function. I would really like to meet her." Stephen knew that Jake meant it. Carrie would have two older brothers if she needed them.

For the five days of Orientation Week, the freshmen were immersed in planned activities: campus tours, study technique workshops, meetings with academic advisers, panel discussions by upperclassmen, a barbecue, an afternoon at the beach, an evening in San Francisco, and, finally, registration for classes. By the end of Orientation Week, every freshman could reliably find the post office, the bookstore, the library, the classrooms, the gymnasium. They learned and, after a few tentative attempts, became comfortable using the nicknames for the main buildings and landmarks on campus: Stanford Memorial Church—"Mem Chu," Hoover Tower—"Hoo Tow," and Tresidder Memorial Student Union—"Tres Mem Stu U".

"Tres Mem Stu U to you, Mem Chu!" Megan whispered, giggling to Carrie during the campus tour. Then she added, "You all!"

Megan's academic adviser was "totally worthless, no

creative streak whatsoever." Carrie's adviser was "very nice, very helpful." Beth's was "conceptually naive."

"Conceptually naive?" Megan asked, perfectly imitating Beth's accent.

"Unsophisticated about the relationship of applied mathematics and physics to aeronautics." Beth looked serious and concerned.

"Whaaaaat?"

Carrie knew, but had decided not to mention to Megan, that Beth was a mathematics major and that her dream was to work for NASA in the space program.

"I'll explain it to you later, Megan," Carrie said quietly.

"Explain it to me now."

Beth explained, with support from Carrie. As she spoke, Beth became more animated than Megan had ever seen her—more animated and more genuine.

Somewhere, underneath that candy-coated shell, is a determined, smart woman, Megan thought. She said, "I'm impressed Beth, really. Damned impressed." Megan liked to watch Beth's reaction when she swore. Beth never registered shock, but would, if sufficiently provoked, look annoyed. It was a wonderful, haughty look. In addition to learning Beth's accent, Megan was trying to master some of Beth's expressions.

"Well, darlin', why don't you all just land that li'l ol' spaceship on the moon," Megan said to Carrie after Beth left. But despite this teasing, Megan was impressed. In spite of herself, she respected and admired Beth's brains and determination.

Carrie liked Beth. She didn't understand her, and was even a little afraid of her. But she liked her. And Beth seemed to like Carrie. The conflict came, predictably, between Megan and Beth, and tested Carrie's friendship with both of them.

"She's so *obvious,* Carrie. No restraint. No decorum. Megan is simply not a lady. It's not her fault. Her Hollywood producer father, no real mother, growing up in California. Still, she makes no effort."

"I like Megan, Beth. She's open and honest. And she's very funny." Carrie remembered somewhat sheepishly that some of Megan's funniest moments were her imitations of Beth. Carrie sighed. "I wish you two could be friends."

"I know you do, because you want everyone to be happy. That is what's so wonderful about you, Carrie. But it's unrealistic. Megan and I can't be friends. But, we can agree not to make you choose sides. It is amazing to me that she doesn't offend you, though. At least not yet."

Stephen invited Carrie to have Sunday dinner with him and Jake at the end of Orientation Week. Sunday dinners were special, boasting cloth napkins, candlelight, five courses, reserved seating, jackets and ties and party dresses. Carrie responded enthusiastically to the invitation and asked if she could bring her two roommates.

Carrie, Megan, and Beth walked across campus together to Stephen's dormitory, Carrie flanked by her two roommates. Megan wore a blue and white sundress, a puka-shell necklace, sandals without nylons, and a fragrant gardenia over her left ear. She walked with a buoyancy that was gazelle-graceful and sent a message of robust health and limitless energy. Her long, soft, golden curls coiled and uncoiled with each step, and her hair glittered in the fading rays of the autumn sun.

Beth strolled evenly beside Carrie. Her dark brown hair was brushed off her forehead and into a perfect, gentle flip at her shoulders. A narrow yellow ribbon held her hair back from her face. Beth had chosen a yellow-and-white dress with a fitted bodice and full skirt, and had carefully draped a white cashmere sweater over her shoulders. She wore, as she always did, lipstick, mascara, cultured pearl earrings and necklace, nylons, and Bal à Versailles perfume.

Unlike Beth and Megan, who were preoccupied with

maintaining their attitudes of civilized contempt toward each other, Carrie was acutely aware of the reaction they caused. She noted the low whisper from a passing bicyclist, the nudge and nod between two men studying under a palm tree, the unconcealed stares of other co-eds. Carrie wondered if they all thought it was strange that she was part of the trio. Did they ask, "But did you see the one in the middle," then laugh? Carrie shook away the thought.

Stephen and Jake were waiting in the lobby of their dormitory. Carrie gave Stephen a kiss on the cheek, then noticed Jake and blushed. Carrie had heard about Stephen's enigmatic roommate for two years. Because Jake had invariably declined invitations to visit their family during vacations, she had never met him. But Carrie felt she knew him because Stephen spoke of him often.

Jake Easton. Three years older than Stephen. What had he done before starting college? He had never said. He was from West Virginia. Stephen guessed that the Eastons were an old, wealthy family and that Jake didn't need to go to college, didn't need to prepare himself to make a living. Stephen liked his theory, but it had some holes. It didn't adequately explain why Jake never talked about his family, his youth, his life before coming to Stanford. And it didn't adequately explain why Jake studied so hard and took his education so seriously. Stephen concluded, with no help from Jake, that Jake was a true scholar, dedicated to learning for its own sake. And as for his steadfast unwillingness to discuss his past, that was simply part of Jake's very private personality.

Because of what Stephen had told Carrie, she had been prepared to meet a dilettante; a charming, carefree playboy; a blond Stephen; a male Megan. Carrie couldn't believe that the quiet, restrained man standing next to Stephen was Jake. He was a "man"; despite his tanned, wrinkle-free face and medium-length, sun-blond hair, he looked older. A look of age borne of what? Wisdom? Experience? Pain?

Jake's dark blue eyes twinkled with warmth and recognition in a response to Carrie's glance, and his lips turned up into a smile. But it wasn't the joyous, confident, trouble-free look that typified Stephen and Megan. It was a look from someone whose life had not been so easy. Where she had expected ebullience, Carrie saw reserve and restraint. Or was she simply misreading sparkle as intensity and maturity as wisdom borne of pain?

Carrie glanced swiftly at Megan and Beth. Their faces reflected nothing but obvious pleasure and approval of Carrie's handsome brother and his equally handsome roommate. Carrie turned her attention to Stephen and Beth.

Carrie had purposely told Stephen very little about Beth. She knew that he would be impressed. Beth was much more his type than Megan, despite the obvious flirting they had done when they met. As Beth herself had said, she was a lady. And, Carrie knew, that mattered to Stephen. Beneath the California tan and easy, casual life-style he had adopted, things like that mattered a great deal to Stephen. Carrie watched Beth blush as Stephen's green eyes flickered at her with approval. Then Stephen's eyes rested a moment on Carrie with concern, curiosity.

"You are such a nice brother. I'm fine!" Carrie said, having correctly interpteted the meaning of his look as, How are you, little sister? Then she whispered, "What do you think of Beth?"

"I think the three most gorgeous girls at Stanford all live in the same room," Stephen said.

Carrie smiled. Then she glanced over at Jake again. He was greeting Megan and Beth. Polite, gracious. Carrie looked at them all—Stephen, Beth, Megan, and Jake—and made a promise to herself. It was a promise she had made a hundred times before, but never so seriously. This time she knew she could keep it. Carrie looked at Jake. This time she *would* keep it. Maybe they wouldn't be the three most beautiful girls on campus, but at least they could be the two most beautiful and their not-so-bad roommate. At that moment Jake approached her and the promise became etched in stone.

"Hi, Caroline. Welcome to Stanford." It was as if he were welcoming her to his estate. Maybe that wasn't pain in his eyes. Maybe Jake had the eyes of the very wealthy; eyes full, not of pain, but of boredom, eyes that had seen everything, possessed everything, and, finally, discarded everything. Perhaps the passion for knowledge was the only thing left. Emotions flooded Carrie—unexpected, confusing emotions. Anger. Pity. How could she feel so strongly about someone she hadn't even met? It was silly! Carrie smiled and looked bravely into his dark blue eyes.

"Thank you. I'm glad to be here. Everyone calls me Carrie."

"I know. But Caroline suits you."

Carrie didn't have the courage to ask him what he meant. They walked into the large dining room together, without speaking.

During dinner, Carrie said very little, but she enjoyed listening to the conversations of Stephen and Beth on her right and Jake and Megan on her left.

"What's your major, Stephen?" Beth spoke so softly that Stephen had to lean toward her to hear.

"I'm in pre-law."

"Will you stay here for Law School? I guess it's too early to know for sure."

"No. I want to practice in Massachusetts. So I plan to get my degree in Boston." Which meant Harvard Law School. Beth acknowledged his ambition with a slow, meaningful smile.

"Tell Stephen your major, Beth," Megan chided from across the table and winked at Carrie, who frowned. Beth appeared unruffled.

"I'm not really sure. There are so many courses that look interesting. It's hard to decide. Perhaps you could make some suggestions, Stephen." Beth actually looked helpless and fragile, and successfully avoided Megan's glare and

Carrie's look of bewilderment. They both knew how carefully Beth had mapped out her entire four year curriculum, quarter by quarter—physics, calculus, engineering, chemistry—and how begrudgingly she had included the required "inconsequential" courses such as freshman English, western civilization, anthropology, philosophy.

Carrie was certain that Stephen would have been impressed and intrigued had he known Beth's real plan. But it was clear that Stephen was also intrigued with Beth's helplessness.

"Well, sure," Stephen said. "There really are some do-and don't-miss courses."

Megan looked at Carrie, rolled her eyes, impatiently ran her fingers through her silky hair, and turned her attention to Jake. Unlike Stephen, who was mesmerized by Beth, Jake had observed the interplay between Beth and Megan and was amused.

"Do you have a major, Megan?"

"Why, yes, I do. Jake." Megan batted her eyes and spoke in her best Southern accent. "I am a double major in pre-med and pre-law with a minor in physical chemistry."

Megan glanced at Stephen and Beth, but they were absorbed in a discussion of a sociology course, a subject that she knew Beth would dismiss as "trivial."

Jake laughed. It was a deep, genuine laugh. Carrie looked at him. He looked like the laugh sounded—amused and untroubled.

"Your accent is very good," he whispered.

"Why thank you, suh. You have just a touch of a drawl yourself."

"Now I'm impressed even more. Most people miss it. But you're right. West Virginia."

"And there's something else about your voice. Your diction is so crisp and clear. It's a trained voice. Like an actor's. Or the speech of a foreigner trained to speak English. But since no one teaches English with a drawl, you must be an actor. Right?"

Carrie watched Jake as Megan spoke. The relaxed, happy look gave way momentarily to the troubled, serious one. His eyes narrowed slightly, but he recovered quickly. It all happened in a second, so that when it was over and he looked relaxed again, Carrie wondered if it had all been her imagination. No, something Megan said had disturbed him. Carrie was sure of it.

"No, I'm not an actor. This is just a voice. What about you? You must be a linguist."

Jake steered the conversation away from himself. That's what Stephen had said—he never talks about himself. But why? Something to hide? A game of the idle rich? And that troubled look; fleeting, but real.

"I am the actress." Megan explained her plans to Jake, as she had to Carrie. Jake's attention focused on Megan, her enthusiasm and energy. In so doing he focused away from himself; he seemed relaxed. Or was it relieved? Carrie wondered.

"Would you consider doing a play, Jake? Your voice is so good and you would have such presence on stage. I've already checked. The Drama Club is doing *The Importance of Being Earnest* this quarter. I want to do Gwendolyn, but I'm afraid they'll give me Cecily. You would be a marvelous Earnest." It was, apparently, a forgone conclusion that Megan would be one of the female leads. Jake found her confidence amusing but not offensive.

"Sure of yourself, aren't you?"

"What?" Megan reflected a moment on what she had said, then smiled. "You have to be confident. But, the truth is, I'm good. I'll get a part. The unknown that remains is, will you be my leading man?"

"In the play, no." Jake paused. Megan blushed. It was apparently the effect that Jake had planned. He came to her rescue quickly. "I will, however, be happy to help you rehearse your lines."

"I'll take you up on that offer, you know. And you may

regret it. I'm a good actress, but I lack discipline and training, such as in learning lines."

Jake said nothing, but he smiled.

"Why didn't you tell us about Stephen?" Beth asked. They sat in Megan's room after returning from dinner.

"Tell you what about him?" Carrie asked innocently.

"That he's handsome, intelligent, kind, gentlemanly . . ."

"She didn't need to tell us, because I had already met him." Megan interjected.

"They why didn't *you* tell me?"

"Why should I? Actually, I should have told Stephen about you. Warned him about Miss Astronaut!" Megan glared, remembering.

"I am not planning to be an astronaut. There is nothing wrong with a lady's being a bit vague about her career. Besides," Beth added hastily when she saw the unsympathetic looks of her roommates, "plans can change. Stephen actually told me about some courses that I may add to my schedule. Does he have a girlfriend?" Beth tried to sound casual as she asked the question.

"Stephen has girlfriends from time to time, but nobody serious at the moment—at least that I know about. I'm really glad that you like him, Beth," Carrie said and looked pointedly at Megan.

"I like him, Carrie," Megan answered the unspoken question. "He's gorgeous and nice. But he's not my type. He couldn't possibly be both Beth's type and my type, could he? I like him, but it seems that he is Beth's."

Carrie was satisfied. They both liked Stephen. Even though they didn't like each other, they both liked Carrie and they both liked Stephen. That meant they could do things as a group—Stephen, Beth, Megan, Carrie, and Jake. Jake . . .

"What did you think of Jake?" Carrie asked offhandedly. How could she ask if they had seen what she had seen?

33

"Nice. Very handsome! Diamond in the rough. That makes him interesting." Megan expected no argument from her succinct appraisal. But Beth disagreed.

"Diamond in the rough! He's so polished he glitters. And he knows it. Vain, arrogant . . ." Beth pulled up short. She did not want to offend Carrie. Jake was, after all, Stephen's roommate and, for reasons Beth couldn't understand, Stephen's best friend. She didn't want her negative impressions of Jake to influence Stephen's feelings about her.

"He's not really vain or arrogant. That's all a ruse, a camouflage covering his seriousness and sensitivity," Megan argued back. She reflected a moment then added, "I suspect he is vain sexually. But I bet he has reason to be. I have the feeling he is damned good."

Megan observed with pleasure that her remark had made Beth gasp. She also noted that Carrie blushed.

"What do you think of him, Carrie?"

"I don't know," Carrie said honestly. "I just don't know."

And Beth and Megan don't know, either, Carrie thought. But Megan will find out. And I'll learn about him second-hand.

Carrie remembered her promise to herself, and her plan. She looked at her two roommates, her new friends.

"Beth, Megan, I need your help." Carrie's tone made them look at her with surprise and attention. "I'm sure that it has not escaped your notice that I am hardly thin." Carrie smiled weakly. It wasn't really funny, but it wasn't life and death, either. It was just very important to her.

Beth and Megan weren't smiling. They looked concerned.

"Seeing you both, being here . . . for the first time in my life I really want to look good. As good as I can, that is. So, first I need to lose weight. And after that, do something with my hair, my clothes. Everything! Would you . . . do you think you could help?"

"Of course we'll help." For the first time since they'd met, Beth and Megan were in agreement.

"This is going to be fun. What do you want us to do?" Megan sounded enthusiastic.

"Well, for now, just be supportive. You know, encourage me. Don't tempt me to break my diet. But also don't nag or make me feel guilty if I lapse occasionally. I really want to lose the weight. For the first time in years of halfhearted dieting, I really believe that I can do it. Because for the first time in my life it seems important for me to look my best."

"Of course you can do it. And you are going to look great. You have a perfect complexion, big, innocent eyes, and beautiful hair. It's naturally curly, isn't it?"

"Yes, naturally curly. Not as curly as Stephen's, though." Carrie smiled gratefully at Megan and patted her close-cropped strawberry-blond locks.

"You wouldn't want it as curly as Stephen's. We're not going for the Little Orphan Annie look. We're going for glamour. So let it grow and we'll see how it looks."

"Okay, coach!" Carrie hoped that Megan's enthusiasm in overhauling her would last throughout the long, boring weeks of dieting that lay ahead.

"I hope you plan to do this sensibly, Carrie. Eat the right foods. No crash dieting." Beth looked stern.

"Don't worry," Carrie said. But she had no intention of being sensible. Her plan was to eat as little as possible, to lose as much weight as quickly as she could. She was as impatient as Megan to see the new Carrie.

"Oh, another thing," she continued carefully, "I want to surprise Stephen. I don't want him to know I'm dieting until I've lost enough weight for it to be noticeable. Then we can have them—Stephen and Jake—over for Sunday dinner here. So promise not to tell Stephen, or Jake."

Beth and Megan agreed, but Beth's disappointment was obvious.

"That means you may not see Stephen for weeks!"

"That means you all may not see Stephen for weeks, you mean," Megan said.

35

"Beth, you can see Stephen, of course. Just don't tell him. I guess it does mean not bringing him to the room."

"Really, Carrie, don't you think Stephen will want to see you? You two seem so close."

"I'll just talk to him on the phone a lot. He's really busy with crew practice and his studies. And I'll be busy with my classes. I think it would be fun to surprise him. That is, assuming I actually look better. What if I don't?" Carrie wrinkled her nose.

"Don't worry, babe. You've got all the right raw material. You'll look terrific."

The next day, Carrie found two gift-wrapped packages on her bed. The first, from Megan, was a pair of emerald green shorts and a matching emerald green, blue, and yellow halter top. The size on the label seemed optimistic, even to Carrie. The other package, from Beth, contained, predictably, sensible diet aids: a bottle of vitamins, a calorie guide, a tape measure, graph paper, and a small box of gold paper stars. Carrie smiled. How typical of each of them.

On the floor, tied in a large red ribbon, was a white bathroom scale with a gift card that read: "To Carrie, from both of us. Good luck!"

Chapter Three

The first few days of Carrie's diet were deceptively easy. She was too busy with classes and too nervous about studying to be hungry. Her heart pounded and her stomach churned with excitement and apprehension. She spent hours in the bookstore, buying the required texts, carefully selecting purchases from the long lists of "suggested reading," and buying colorful notebooks, pens, pencils, and index cards for each class. Carrie also bought Stanford book covers, a cardinal-colored Stanford sweatshirt, note cards with scenes from campus, a Stanford pennant, and a tote bag. To add color to her room, she bought a red wastebasket with the Stanford logo: a block *S* with an evergreen tree growing through it.

"I think this is what they call school spirit," Megan teased when she walked into Carrie's room. "It's too bad that the school color clashes so miserably with your hair. And it's not too good with mine. Actually, Beth would look wonderful dressed in cardinal, but I don't think she would be caught dead in a Stanford sweatshirt!"

Carrie took neat, careful, complete notes in class. In the evening she studied these and made additional notes from reading assignments. Megan and Beth approached their studies with comparable seriousness, and they fell into a comfortable routine. The tension between Beth and Megan eased slightly; they were preoccupied with their studies and unified in their determination to help Carrie. Beth's course load was so heavy that Megan actually felt sorry for her and even took care to keep their room and the hallway outside their room quiet during Beth's inevitable afternoon nap. Beth usually studied past midnight and woke up before six. Megan and Carrie rarely saw her after dinner.

Lagunita Hall fell into a routine of its own. Between seven and ten o'clock every night, the corridors were quiet, except for the frequent sound of ringing telephones behind the closed doors. Everyone was in her room, ostensibly studying, but, often, waiting for a special phone call. At ten o'clock precisely, the dormitory switchboard closed, calls were disconnected, and no further calls were received until seven in the morning when the switchboard reopened.

By five minutes past ten, the corridors bustled with activity. Friends congregated in the corridors and in each other's rooms to excitedly share news of the special call that had come, or to commiserate and analyze why he hadn't called.

By ten thirty, the smell of freshly popped, buttered popcorn filled the corridors. The quiet was replaced by animated conversation, laughter, and music. It was an uninterrupted time—the switchboard was closed—to share secrets, to make friends, to pierce each other's ears, to give a friend a permanent, to learn a new dance step, to unwind. Megan and Carrie joined the nightly study break often. Beth never did.

Megan, Beth, and Carrie conformed to the study period between seven and ten. Their room was quiet, except for the frequent phone calls. It was fortunate that the phone was in Megan's room; she didn't mind the frequent interruption. And, most of the calls were for her.

For awhile, as the upperclassmen worked their way through the *Frosh Book,* there were an equal number of calls for Beth. Unlike Megan, Beth resented the interruption. Her studies were too important to be jeopardized by something so trivial.

"Who is it?" Beth would ask Megan irritably.

Megan would provide the name. It was never anyone that Beth knew; occasionally, it was someone who had already called Megan, unaware that the two were roommates. There was only one person Beth wanted to talk to, and he called frequently, but always spoke only to his sister.

"Tell him I'm not here," Beth would say.

"Then he'll just call back later," Megan said, finally annoyed after several evenings of fending off her calls and Beth's.

"Oh," Beth answered, her mind mostly focused on a physics problem.

"Why don't I tell them, all of them, except *you know who* . . ." Megan paused, pleased to see that she had gotten Beth's attention. It obviously irritated Beth that Megan knew she was hoping Stephen would call for her. It was even worse that, because Megan always answered the phone, she knew that Stephen hadn't called. Megan continued, "Why don't I tell them that you're engaged?"

"Because I'm not."

"Okay. I'll tell them you have a social disease," Megan taunted.

"No! Megan!" Beth hissed.

"You have a social disease, Beth. You are antisocial."

They glowered at each other for a moment.

"All right, Megan. Please just tell them that I am already involved," Beth said, finally. It was true. She was involved—with her studies.

Megan took her own calls from the upperclassmen with amusement. She had copies of the Stanford *Quad,* the school's yearbook, by the telephone, so she could have the same advantage as the caller, she could study *his* picture. Occasionally, she would accept an invitation for a date. Mostly, using the same purposely vague excuse she gave for Beth, Megan would sigh theatrically and tell them that she was involved.

Megan talked frequently and at length, despite the fact that they lived in Connecticut, to Ian Knight and his wife, Margaret. Megan told them, enthusiastically, and in entertaining detail, about her reactions to Stanford, about her roommates, about her classes. The first time Carrie overheard part of Megan's conversation, she assumed that Megan was talking to her parents.

"My parents?" Megan asked. She looked confused for a moment, then thoughtful. She said, "I guess Ian and Margaret are like family to me. Like what family should be. A combination of parents and older brother and sister. We are pretty close."

Carrie talked almost nightly to Stephen. She never talked to Jake. She wondered if Megan had talked to Jake.

And Megan wondered, idly, when Jake would decide to call.

One night, Beth walked into Megan's room. She looked perplexed. Megan was lying on her bed memorizing lines for her upcoming audition for *The Importance of Being Earnest;* Carrie was studying in her room, but as usual, the adjoining door was open.

"Megan? Carrie? I'm sorry to bother you, but I could use your help. Just for a couple of minutes."

"Of course. What's wrong?" Carrie appeared immediately in the doorway. It was so unlike Beth to ask for help of any kind.

"It's a stupid chemistry problem. I just can't figure out why there isn't striec hindrance." Beth shrugged her shoulders and made a face.

"Whaaat? Beth, you look like it's the end of the world!" Megan controlled her urge to laugh because Beth looked so upset.

"It's just so frustrating. I've been working on the problem for hours. I just can't visualize it correctly."

"So how can we help?" Carrie asked.

40

"Just come into my room for a minute."

Carrie and Megan followed Beth into her room and were astounded by what they saw. Beth's room, usually as neat and orderly as Beth herself, was strewn with books and pillows. Carrie couldn't believe that Beth had actually put her beautiful silk pillows on the floor.

"This is the molecule," Beth explained, casually gesturing at the books and pillows. "Now, Carrie, if you could stand over there. And Megan over here."

Beth narrowed her eyes, like an interior decorator trying to visualize the perfect placement of a piece of furniture.

"Okay, now Carrie, please walk around these books. And Megan, walk around those pillows."

Carrie and Megan followed Beth's instructions. Beth sat on her bed, her brow furrowed, concentrating. She gave them each several different paths to follow. Finally, she clapped her hands and smiled.

"That's it. That's how it can be done! Thank you." Beth got up. Clearly Megan and Carrie were now excused; the mission had been accomplished.

"Wait a minute," Megan said. "Just for the record, what were we?"

"Oh. You were electrons." Beth sounded surprised. It hadn't occurred to her that Megan and Carrie hadn't understood the problem.

"Electrons? I've never played an electron before. When I win my first Tony and I have to reflect on my career, I'll tell them about the challenge of playing an electron. Such a tricky accent, you know!"

The second week of Carrie's diet was much harder. Her nervous energy had somewhat dissipated, and the anxious, churning feeling in her stomach was replaced by a more familiar one—the uncomfortable ache of hunger. She lost five pounds the first week, then held steady at that plateau for four frustrating days. Her slightly smaller body, her

41

looser clothes, and her determination helped her survive the gnawing hunger and frustration. Once, in a moment of generalized discouragement, she lapsed into one of her favorites—a large package of Fig Newtons.

Beth and Megan were effusive in their praise, although when Beth looked up from her studies long enough to notice how little Carrie ate, she voiced skepticism about the sensibility of Carrie's method.

By the end of the third week, the change was noticeable. Carrie had lost thirteen pounds and looked gaunt to her roommates. The dieting had become easy because she wasn't really dieting. Instead, she was simply not eating. The decision to eat nothing was easier than deciding how much—how little—she could eat each day. If she ate nothing at all, she would lose the most amount of weight in the least amount of time. If she ate anything—even a few bites of chicken, or carrots, or even lettuce—it would slow down the rate of weight loss.

Carrie had made the decision to eat nothing at the beginning of the third week. By the middle of that week, the ache of hunger had vanished, replaced by nausea at the sight or thought of food. Carrie continued to go to dinner with Megan and Beth. She slowly sipped a cup of hot tea, rearranged the food on her plate, and ate nothing. Every night, she took an orange from the dessert tray to eat in her room. But she never ate it.

Carrie knew the radical diet might not be healthy. She promised herself she would start eating if she noticed any deleterious effects. But she didn't notice any. In fact, she had more energy and required less sleep. And her mind was clearer and her senses sharper than they had ever been.

Toward the end of the fourth week of Carrie's diet, after she had lost twenty pounds, Beth decided that it was time to call Stephen. She did not regard the phone call as a violation of the rule that women never telephone men. This was an exceptional situation. It was a call she had to make for medical reasons.

"Stephen? This is Beth."

"Hi, Beth. How are you?" If Stephen was surprised, his voice didn't reveal it. He was used to calls from women, although it did seem out of character for Beth. It was a bit of a coincidence, in fact, for he had been planning to call her.

"I'm fine. Stephen, when was the last time you saw Carrie?" Beth knew the answer perfectly well. That Sunday dinner. Carrie's plan to keep Stephen at bay by frequent phone calls had worked.

"I guess not since you came over for dinner. Three or four weeks ago. But I've spoken to her often. She sounds fine. Why?" Stephen sounded worried.

"Well, she's been avoiding you because she's been on a diet. She wanted to surprise you with the results. But I'm getting worried. She has lost a lot of weight and barely eats anything."

"Carrie? Really?" Good for her, Stephen thought.

"Stephen, an orange and three cups of tea doesn't seem adequate, does it?"

"What, for breakfast?"

"For the entire day, Stephen. That's all she eats. And I think she has to force herself to eat the orange. There's a name for it, you know."

"Anorexia nervosa. Of course I know," Stephen snapped. He was irritated at himself for not checking on Carrie in person. But she had sounded so happy.

"I think that you, and Jake, of course, should come here for dinner this Sunday."

"Of course. We'll be there. And Beth, I'm sorry I snapped. I really do thank you for calling." Beth was very relieved that he had added that.

"I hope you aren't angry, Carrie. You look so good, I thought it was time," Beth explained.

"Is Jake coming, too?"

"Well, I invited them both."

"I'm not angry, Beth. But this means I have to find something to wear that fits. Do you want to go shopping with me?"

Beth and Carrie found an ivory and lavender dress with a fitted bodice and slightly flared skirt. It was nicely tailored, no frills, no ruffles, no little-girl look.

"Simple elegance," Megan had said, inwardly admiring Beth's perfect taste. It was Beth who had insisted on the dress. Megan would have chosen flamboyant colors and low neckline and it would have been all wrong. It would have clashed with Carrie's aristocratic, peaceful beauty.

Beth also insisted that Carrie wear *her* pearls and a few drops of *her* Bal à Versailles. Megan insisted, with agreement from Beth, in moderation, on mascara and a suggestion of blue eye shadow. They were all very pleased with the result. Carrie's stomach churned, an anxious fluttering that she hadn't felt for weeks.

Stephen barely recognized his transformed little sister. Her high cheekbones, previously hidden by baby fat, her sapphire blue eyes, larger and clearer than he had remembered them, her delicate, straight nose and her full lips gave her a slightly haunting, undeniably womanly look.

"Carrie. You are absolutely beautiful."

Carrie responded with a soft smile and a guttural laugh. Even those had changed. The smile was enigmatic, alluring. The laugh was throaty. But the eyes were merry, as always.

"I have shed a bit of my well-insulated cocoon, haven't I? I still have about ten pounds to go, but the hard part is over."

"I don't think you should lose one more pound. You look terrific." Then Stephen remembered Beth's concerned phone call and added, "In fact, I hear that you've been eating practically nothing. That isn't very healthy."

Stephen tried to sound stern, but the attempt was halfhearted. He had never seen his sister look healthier or more radiant. He was very proud of her.

"Oh, Stephen. The anorexia nervosa nonsense. This is willpower, you see, not psychosis. For the first time in my life I've actually succeeded at this. I don't count the calories in toothpaste, so don't worry. Just be happy for me. It feels great," Carrie said, a little uneasily. Recently she *had* wondered about the caloric content of toothpaste.

She smiled and hugged him. He returned her hug and was struck by the boniness, her prominent ribs, her small waist. She felt fragile.

"I am proud of you. Very. Shall we go down to dinner?"

"Is Jake coming?"

"Sure. He's waiting in the lobby. In case I had to give you the big brother to little sister anorexia talk. I do plan to keep my eyes on you, though. Someone has to protect you from all the lecherous men on this campus!"

Jake, Megan, and Beth stood by the huge marble fireplace in the living room of Lagunita Hall. Megan and Jake were chatting and Beth nervously watched for Stephen and Carrie to appear.

"Here they come," she said. Beth was relieved to see that Steven looked relaxed and calm; she had been afraid that he might be annoyed at not having been told about Carrie's diet even sooner.

For the first time, Beth noticed the family resemblance: high cheekbones, ample lips, straight, narrow nose, strong jaw. Remarkable, Beth mused, that such similar features can be so elegant and feminine in Carrie and so strong and masculine in Stephen. Megan and Jake stopped talking and watched Stephen and Carrie approach. Megan was beaming. She nudged Jake.

"So, what do you think?"

"Beautiful." He smiled as Carrie approached. "You look lovely, Caroline." As they walked into the dining room, Jake whispered to Carrie, "Very lovely."

Carrie managed to eat nothing, despite Stephen's watchful eye. She was too excited to eat. She artfully rearranged her chicken and rice to give the illusion that she had eaten

45

everything but the bones and skin. She smiled at Jake and said nothing. Jake smiled back as he talked with Megan.

"When are the auditions for your play?"

"Tomorrow at two. Why don't you come and watch? I wouldn't mind. In fact, I do better with an audience." Megan's long fingers rested gently on Jake's bare forearm. Carrie watched, envious of Megan's ability to be so relaxed and natural. Megan found Jake attractive and she was letting him know it. It looked so easy. Carrie sighed. It just isn't my style, she thought.

"I have a political science seminar tomorrow at two."

"Great! That means you'll be at the audition!" Megan tilted her head toward him.

"No, but I promise to be there opening night."

"I still wish you would try out for Earnest."

The following morning, Megan walked into Carrie's room and sat on her bed. Carrie was brushing her hair, her back to Megan. Megan's presence didn't surprise Carrie, since they both had Western Civilization at nine o'clock and often walked to class together. After a few moments, Carrie realized that Megan wasn't speaking. That was surprising.

Curious, Carrie turned to look at Megan. It was the first time that Carrie had ever seen Megan look worried.

"Megan, what's wrong?"

"You. Me. Us."

"What?"

"Jake says you're starving and could get really sick, and I've just been watching you, egging you on."

"Jake?" Carrie whispered, horrified. She remembered the serious conversation between Jake and Megan that had taken place in a remote corner of the living room last night, after dinner. It never occurred to Carrie that they could be talking about her. "What does Jake know?"

"He seems to know quite a lot about starvation. I have no idea why he knows, but he seems knowledgeable."

Another of Jake's scholarly pursuits? Starvation? Carrie wondered.

"What did he say?" she asked quietly, tentatively. Carrie didn't want to hear that Jake didn't like how she looked, or that he thought she was crazy. Carrie sat down, shaken.

"He thinks you look gorgeous, of course," Megan said quickly, sensing for the first time that how Carrie looked in Jake's eyes, what he thought of her, was very important to Carrie. Jake might even be the reason Carrie was doing this. "You are gorgeous. But he says from the texture and color of the skin, and from the amount of weight you've lost, you must have gone for days at a time without eating anything."

Megan stopped and looked at Carrie. Carrie returned Megan's gaze. Her large, innocent eyes looked sad, and not so innocent.

"I told him," Megan continued, "that I have had dinner with you every night. That I've seen you eat. He asked me to estimate how much you ate last night. After I told him, he told me that you ate nothing. Absolutely nothing. Is that true, Carrie?"

"Megan, I feel fine," Carrie said defensively, avoiding an answer to Megan's question. Her mind reeled. Jake had noticed. No one else had noticed, but Jake had. But that wasn't what she had wanted him to notice. "I am healthy, full of energy, doing well in my classes . . ."

"Jake said that's part of the starvation syndrome," Megan interrupted, using the terms Jake had used last night. "For awhile, you feel that way. But it's a feeling, not reality. Your body isn't really strong. In fact, it's weak. Your brain is actually starving for glucose and your muscles begin to break down to provide glucose for your brain."

"Does Jake think I have anorexia nervosa?" Carrie asked anxiously.

"No! Of course not. No one does. We just think that

you've gotten so caught up in your diet, and been so successful with it, that you may not be able to tell that your health is suffering."

"But I feel fine," Carrie protested. "It's *my* brain and *my* body. I know how I feel."

Megan waited a few moments. She knew Jake was right. He had even accurately predicted Carrie's reaction, her outrage. Megan had to convince Carrie, just as Jake had convinced her. She had to frighten Carrie about the seriousness of what she was doing, just as Jake had frightened her. Jake had told Megan that if she couldn't get Carrie to eat in the next twenty-four hours, he would talk to Stephen about having Carrie hospitalized. Megan couldn't tell Carrie that. It had become quite obvious in the past few minutes that Carrie was extremely sensitive about Jake's opinion of her.

In the next few moments, Megan devised a plan. She wished there were time to clear it with Jake, but there wasn't.

"Okay, Carrie, you say your brain is fine. I admit, you seem perfectly fine to me. So, how about your body? You say it's strong, full of energy. Jake says it's probably dangerously weak," Megan said carefully.

Dangerously weak. Carrie shuddered, not at the meaning of the words, but at the fact that Jake had said them. What did he think of her?

"How can we test it?" Megan asked quietly.

Carrie shrugged.

"Well," Megan began, "I know that you have a tennis racket. So do I. Why don't we play some tennis?"

"Okay," Carrie agreed. She had no choice. "When?"

"How about before lunch. At eleven?"

"Okay. I'll meet you here."

After rallying for five minutes, Megan walked to the center of the court. Carrie joined her. It was Megan, not Carrie, who was out of breath. Megan had gotten a workout; Carrie had hardly moved.

"You're good, Carrie," Megan said between breaths, "too good for me."

"Thanks," Carrie said, hoping the test was over. "I have always played pretty well, taught at the local club, played on school teams. But I was always too slow to be really good, because of my weight. Now, today, I feel much quicker."

"Maybe you should sign up for the advanced tennis class. Maybe you should even try out for the team." What am I suggesting? Megan wondered. If Jake is right, Carrie couldn't play tennis for five minutes with anyone who was good. Megan remembered, grimly, that she had to convince Carrie of that.

"Let's run a couple of laps around the track," Megan said.

"Why?"

"You know why. C'mon."

Carrie couldn't refuse the challenge, but she was worried. Even the minimal effort she had exerted during the rallies with Megan had made her heart race and her head feel light.

"Okay."

Megan set the pace. For the first half lap, they ran together.

Then, without warning, Carrie fell to the ground, gasping for breath. Her heart raced, a delicate, fluttering sensation, not a strong, effective heartbeat. She couldn't speak, her eyes blurred, waves of nausea swept through her body. She had trouble remaining conscious. Her body shook uncontrollably.

"Carrie" Megan screamed, rushing to her gasping, trembling friend. Carrie didn't seem to recognize her; her eyes didn't focus. She didn't, or couldn't, speak. Megan put her arms around Carrie and felt the weak, rapid pulse and the cold, clammy skin. "Carrie, please, talk to me!"

In a few moments, moments that seemed like hours to both of them, Carrie's breathing slowed. Finally, tentatively, she spoke.

"Megan . . ."

"Carrie, are you all right?" Megan looked into Carrie's eyes and, with great relief, saw recognition in them.

"I don't know what happened. I thought I was going to die. I couldn't control anything . . . my breathing, my speech, the shaking . . ." Carrie stopped abruptly. The effort involved in speaking made her weak.

"You're starving, honey. Your body and brain are starving. Don't you see?" Megan pleaded, her fear surfacing. This had been her idea, and it had almost been disastrous. What if . . . ? Megan shook her gently and repeated, "Don't you see?"

Carrie nodded, slowly, exhausted. Then she began to cry.

"I felt fine. I really did," she protested weakly.

"I know. But you just didn't have any reserve energy."

"What do I do now?" Carrie asked helplessly. It was hard to think. Harder to make decisions.

"Eat!" Megan exclaimed and squeezed her. "And I don't mean that you should gain back any weight. I just mean that you should eat sensibly. And, when you're stronger, start toning those weak muscles. I really think you should enroll in that tennis class."

Carrie nodded. She still felt woozy. She didn't think she could stand up, not yet. But she understood Megan's words. And she would remember what had happened.

Carrie and Megan sat on the grass beside the track for forty-five minutes. Megan chattered, now giddy with relief, while they waited for Carrie's strength to return, enough to walk back to Lagunita Hall.

"After we get back," Megan said buoyantly as it became clear that Carrie would be all right, "we'll have lunch. Then, you rest and I'll go to my audition. Then I'll come back and I'll tell you about the audition over high tea. Then, we'll do dinner!"

Carrie smiled. "You're a dear friend, Megan."

* * *

Just before her audition, Megan informed the director that she was only auditioning for the part of Gwendolyn and that she would not accept the role of Cecily if offered. The director, a professor in the drama department, listened to Megan's announcement. At first, he was surprised. She was a stereotypical Cecily. Then he was annoyed. And, finally, he was bored. Another egocentric co-ed. She probably had all the lead roles in high school and actually believes that she has talent, he thought, yawning. He glanced at the roster: Megan Chase.

Well, Miss Megan Chase, you're about to make the transition from big fish in small pond to tiny fish in ocean.

He smiled slightly, slumped back in his chair, and mentally began to prepare his scathing critique of the audition that was about to begin. He didn't like arrogant would-be actors. And his dislike was justified, he felt, they rarely had enough talent to make it worth dealing with their egos.

Megan had memorized the scene. She didn't even hold the script. Instead of reading the part, she performed it, lived it, became Gwendolyn. She owned the stage, gesturing with her long, graceful fingers, tossing her golden hair, speaking with character and emotion. Megan didn't rush; it was a time to be savored. The pace was critical—a short pause here for emphasis; a longer one, later, to prove her control.

The director leaned forward in his chair. The usual backstage hubbub hushed. Everyone was watching Megan, mesmerized.

She is actually making Gwendolyn interesting, the director thought. Strong, but feminine. A Gwendolyn with personality. Surely not what Wilde had intended. And yet Megan was performing the lines that Wilde had written. And giving them her own, enchanting interpretation.

And then it was over. The theater was silent. Megan stood in the center of the stage, facing the director, waiting.

"The part of Gwendolyn, Miss uh"—he glanced at his roster—"Chase, is yours." His voice sounded calm, but that was because he was an actor with some talent of his own. He was terribly excited. He couldn't wait to direct this young woman.

"Thank you." Megan's voice was comparably contained. She nodded, as if approving his decision. As she walked past the six other women who had been waiting their turns to audition, it didn't occur to Megan that it wasn't fair that they hadn't even been given a chance at the part.

That evening, Jake called Megan to check on Carrie. He was angry about what had happened but relieved that Carrie was all right and seemed convinced that her dieting had been too rigorous. After they stopped discussing Carrie, Megan told Jake that she had won the part of Gwendolyn and reminded Jake of his promise to help her learn her lines.

"I know you'll be strict with me. I know you won't let me peek at lines that I should know."

"Not likely."

"And there'll be no distractions. Just serious line learning." Megan had ample experience with "help" from men who would rehearse a few lines and then become more interested in creating new dialogue with Megan than rehashing the carefully chosen words of the playwright.

"Naturally."

As the weeks passed, it was Megan, not Jake, who violated the strictly business agreement. She counted on her meetings with Jake as a time to vent her frustrations, unabashedly report her successes, and share her innermost secrets and fears. Jake listened with interest and responded with a perfect blend of concern and irreverence. He teased her about the silliness of most of her rampages. And he quietly understood her fears about loneliness and death.

"Jake, sometimes I am so afraid of dying. Of being gone forever. No more mind. No more consciousness. It would be like those millions of years before I was born."

"But those weren't painful years, or frightening years."

"Of course not. Because I had never yet lived. But now,

the thought of giving it all up. Forever. If only I could believe that I would be up on a soft, fleecy cloud, watching it all. But I don't believe that. I believe that there is only an empty void, very black, very cold. Forever." Megan shivered involuntarily.

"I think," Jake said slowly, almost to himself, "that when death comes, if it is a natural death, that it is not frightening. I think that it is peaceful. And maybe, even, welcome."

One evening Megan suggested that they rehearse outside. It was an unusually warm October in Palo Alto.

"Let's go for a walk and find some nice, grassy spot. It's such a beautiful evening. I've even packed some supplies." Megan nodded her head toward a bulging forest green knapsack. Jake lifted it and swung it effortlessly over his shoulder.

"Supplies? This is heavy. What . . . ?"

"You'll see. It's a surprise."

They walked in silence in the balmy autumn night air. The twilight sky was pink and orange; a single star twinkled. The air smelled of eucalyptus. Crickets chattered. They walked along the eucalyptus lined lane toward the riding stables and golf course. The trees, still full of leaves, obscured the fading sunlight.

"It's getting dark and sinister. 'This is the forest primeval . . .' " Megan whispered and pulled her sweater more snugly around her shoulders.

Jake stopped, looking up at the trees dripping with weblike moss that were silhouetted against the pink sky. Then he looked at Megan.

"No, it's getting enchanted."

The path through the forest ended at the eighteenth green of the golf course. Two golf carts sped away in the distance.

"This looks like a nice spot," Megan said tentatively, still slightly shaken by Jake's comment. "There's a blanket in the knapsack."

Jake handed the knapsack to her to unpack.

"I brought champagne. To celebrate. I mean, since we

have dress rehearsals for the next four nights and open this weekend, I thought this might be our last time. I brought candles, too, so you can read your lines. Except you know Earnest's lines better than that idiot Roger does. Oh, real champagne glasses. Crystal. Never travel without them." Megan stopped short. Jake was staring at her with a look of surprise mixed with amusement.

"I'm babbling, aren't I? And I haven't even had a sip of champagne." Megan handed him the unopened bottle.

"Yes, you are." Jake paused. He carefully directed the cork toward the woods and pried it off. He filled the two glasses and handed one to Megan, then asked, "Why?"

"Nervous about the play, maybe?"

"Unlikely."

"Nervous about being with you in this isolated, enchanted forest?" Megan stared into her already empty glass.

"Apparently, but why? Why nervous?" Jake refilled the glass.

Megan sat down on the blanket, ran her fingers through her hair, and closed her eyes. The cool breeze felt good against her flushed cheeks. The champagne made her feel happy and daring. She tossed her head back and looked up at Jake.

"Why haven't you ever tried to kiss me, or anything?"

"Because you made it crystal clear in the beginning that you didn't want me to."

"Meaning otherwise you might have?"

"Meaning otherwise I would have."

"Do you always do what women want you to do? Or don't want you to do?"

"Only the ones I care about."

"Are there lots? Of ones you care about?"

"No, not many." He sat down beside her, reached for a candle and his copy of the play. Megan was lying on her back staring at the now starry orange-black sky. "Shall we begin?"

"Begin?" Megan sat up. Her head spun and she had to pause before speaking. "I thought . . ."

She sputtered and stopped. Jake's expression was one of mock surprise.

"You thought what?" he asked softly and pulled her toward him. Megan quivered as his mouth met hers and his hand gently touched her face. She pressed her body against his and felt the taut muscles and the hidden strength. It was a long, warm, champagne-flavored kiss. When Jake pulled away to look at her, his eyes were clouded with desire. It was a look that Megan had seen before. But it had never made her tremble as it did now.

Then Jake blinked, and the look was gone. His eyes were clear again, twinkling as they teased.

"Now we practice your lines."

"Beast!"

With great effort Megan forced herself to concentrate on the play, not on Jake. They lay on their backs on the blanket, not touching. The candle flickered in the soft breeze. Jake slipped effortlessly into his usual role of taskmaster, feeding her cue lines, waiting in patient silence for her to deliver her lines correctly.

As if the kiss had never happened, Megan thought. She had a worse thought. What if it hadn't mattered to him?

When they finished rehearsing, Jake turned to her, pulled her body against his, and kissed her. He kissed her face, her mouth, her neck, her hair. She felt his heart pounding, so forcefully that it felt as if it were inside her. He moved his hands gently under her blouse, cool, controlled, experienced hands that explored her back, and, in time, found her breasts. Megan pressed closer and ran her long, slender fingers around his neck, into his soft, fine hair, down his slightly damp back. She reached to stroke his right thigh. His body tensed. The rhythm was broken. He reached for her hand, brought it to his mouth, and kissed it.

"Jake?"

"It's nothing, Megan." He kissed her deeply. In moments

they were moving together again. Two sleek, healthy bodies driven by desire, molding perfectly.

"Make love to me, Jake."

"Megan," Jake murmured. Then he pulled himself away to look at her. "Is it safe?"

Megan's inability to return his gaze answered his question.

"No? I have nothing with me. Next time, darling."

"Next time? When will there be a next time as perfect as this?" Megan's voice betrayed the half-mocking pout that Jake could have seen if the candle hadn't flickered out. Disappointment mingled with excitement.

"Next time will be more perfect. Why don't we come back here after the opening night performance?"

"Yes, let's do. That would be perfect."

Chapter Four

Elizabeth Louise Thompson knew that she was beautiful. Not pretty or cute or handsome—beautiful. Thick dark brown hair with red-gold highlights, depthless brown eyes framed in long, dark lashes, perfect pearl white teeth, full red lips. The eyes sparkled and the lips smiled coyly or pouted seductively, by instinct. They were co-conspirators in a game of nature that Beth didn't want to play.

Not that Beth minded being beautiful. Not really. She loved perfect beautiful things. But as she grew older and her mind filled with questions, her beauty became an obstacle because no one would listen to her. All they wanted to do was look at her, admire her, flirt with her, touch her. They wanted to possess her, to own that beauty.

No one made any effort to know her—the Beth inside the beautiful shell. When they looked they saw perfection. Why bother to look any further? In junior high school, Beth yearned for acne, braces, glasses, obesity, and a friend—someone who would be her friend in spite of how she looked, not because of how she looked. In junior high school Beth was "most popular." Everyone wanted to be her friend. She was terribly lonely.

Beth was a genius. She didn't know it; she just knew that she was different. No one knew it. If anyone had known, it would have been considered a problem. Among

Houston's social elite, among the oil-rich multimillionaires like Beth's father, only one thing mattered for a woman: she had to be beautiful. Beautiful and gracious, like Beth, was even better. But brains? A liability at best. Certainly unnecessary, and, if used, frankly unattractive.

As a little girl, Beth never played dolls or house. In fact, she never played. Whenever possible she retreated to her huge room in the east wing of the family mansion and read. Beth didn't like fiction. Beth didn't care about Heidi or Dorothy or Alice. She had no interest in fantasy places like Oz or Wonderland. Or the Swiss Alps, for that matter.

Beth's interest was in science, in the world around her. She wanted to understand how things worked and why they worked—flowers and humans and television sets and animals and galaxies. She read about astronomy, botany, physiology, biology, mechanics. Each question that she answered led to more questions, more reading, more answers. And more questions. In time, her interest became directed and it evolved into an obsession. Beth wanted to understand space. She wanted to understand it and conquer it.

Beth told no one of her obsession. It was her secret, private and forbidden. She didn't play house or dolls, but she substituted these trivial activities with socially acceptable alternatives, playing the piano and riding horses. She could do both of these by herself. They didn't interfere with her thinking. And they required training and discipline. Beth became an accomplished pianist and won blue ribbons for her riding.

Beth loved a few things: her science books, the stars, the piano, her horse. Beth hated many things: trivial conversations, giggling silly girls, giggling silly boys, poor taste. But the thing she hated the most was being touched.

In grade school the boys tugged at her long, thick braids and ran off giggling. In junior high school they laughed nervously and tried to bump into her while they were talking. In high school, they just wanted to touch her. Everyone wanted to touch her, not just the boys. Beth volunteered to work at the community hospital, to talk to patients, to cheer them up. They all wanted to touch her, to touch her beautiful, young, healthy skin with their sallow, withered, sick hands. Beth quit after two days.

In high school, she tried to find someone to talk to. She sought out the smart, ugly, bespectacled boys in her science classes. In her presence, they became mute. And when she persisted, they became like all the others, flirting pathetically, trying to touch her. Beth hated them all—the stupid girls who denied their minds and wanted to be touched; the boys who only wanted to touch her.

Beth's graciousness, her manners, her impeccable taste were as inbred as her beauty. No matter how much she hurt, how much she hated, how much she ached to tell someone her secrets and her dreams, it never showed. She suffered silently while her eyes flashed, her lip seduced, and her body beckoned with sensual gracefulness.

Beth's high school science teacher, Mr. Hamilton, may not have guessed Beth's inner turmoil, but he correctly assessed her intelligence and potential. At the beginning of her senior year, he scheduled a meeting with her. Beth was skeptical. Mr. Hamilton was a ponderous, absentminded old man, but still a man, and by age sixteen Beth's hatred and distrust extended to all males. He might try to touch her. Beth kept the appointment because politeness demanded it.

"Elizabeth. What are your plans for next year?"

"Well, sir. Meet a nice boy. Get married. Have children. Give lovely lawn parties in the summer." Beth was purring, but inside she ached. She thought of her mother. Beth's beauty had come from her and, Beth suspected, so had her brains. But it was impossible to tell. Her mother's mind had been pruned and shaped so expertly that its only apparent function was the planning of social events. Sometimes Beth saw something in her mother's eyes that made her fear for her own sanity.

Mr. Hamilton was staring at her. His face reddened. He

gnawed at his lip. Something inside him was coming to a boil.

"Bullshit!" he finally spat.

Instinctively Beth looked shocked and startled. Then she began to laugh, a genuine, unladylike laugh from deep in her soul.

"Bullshit. You're right, Mr. Hamilton. *Bullshit!"*

Beth told him her dreams. They weren't even plans, because until then she hadn't known how to escape. Mr. Hamilton took her dreams and made them into plans for her.

He wanted her to go to M.I.T., to get the most rigorous, pure science training possible. Beth's father vetoed M.I.T. outright. And he vetoed Radcliffe—"smells too strongly of braininess." They settled on Stanford; it was socially acceptable. Mr. Hamilton was satisfied. Beth was ecstatic.

Beth glided amiably through her senior year. No one could hurt her anymore. She could escape. She would escape. She even allowed herself to be entered in the Miss Texas Beauty Pageant. It was a nostalgic concession to her father. Unbeknownst to Beth, J.T. Thompson was praying that his daughter would win the Texas pageant and the Miss America pageant and abandon the college idea altogether.

Beth almost did win. Until the final interview she was ahead in the judges' scoring. She played the piano flawlessly. She won the bathing suit contest and tied with another girl in the evening gown competition.

But on the question, "Where do you derive your inspiration, Miss Thompson?" Beth faltered. She false-started several times, sputtered, and finally lied unconvincingly, "From my wonderful parents, my teachers, my friends." Beth smiled shakily.

She had wanted to say, "From the stars, the moon, Mr. Hamilton, Albert Einstein, my horse . . ."

The judges could forgive the awkwardness. She was human after all. But they could not forgive or forget the incredible omission that she made. Beth hadn't mentioned

God. Not even in passing. It was unbelievable and unforgivable.

Elizabeth Louise Thompson was first runner-up in the Miss Texas Pageant. And since the new Miss Texas was in excellent health and remained so, Beth never competed for Miss America and began Stanford, as scheduled, five months later.

To Beth, Stanford was a means to an end. She would learn the tools she needed to get a job at NASA. And once she had her foot in the door, she would show them. And the people at NASA would be people like herself—dedicated, driven, obsessed. She could trust them.

Stanford was the first step. In the months of planning of anticipating the year to come, Beth never spent one minute thinking about the people that she would meet. It never occurred to her that she might, after all the lonely years that had come before, make a friend. She was accustomed to solitude, comfortable with it. And J.T. had promised to send her horse to Palo Alto once Beth got settled.

Beth liked Carrie instantly. Beth had never liked anyone instantly before. In fact, Beth had liked very few people at all, ever. Her instant dislike for Megan was typical of her usual reaction to strangers.

Carrie was undemanding, nonpossessive, and interested. She didn't want to own Beth, or Beth's beauty. She didn't want to touch Beth. She didn't want to compete with Beth. Carrie wanted for Beth what she wanted for all of them—happiness. Happiness and harmony.

Had someone described Carrie to Beth, Beth would have dismissed her as an insipid Pollyanna. It would have been hard for Beth to imagine that someone could be so unselfish and have any personality at all. But there was something about Carrie; she was genuine, loving, peaceful, content.

In anyone else, especially anyone else with Carrie's intelligence, Beth would have been extremely critical of the contentment. Beth and Megan were obsessed with their careers, driven to achieve excellence. Carrie's only goal seemed to be happiness for herself and for others.

But, of course, there was more. There was something that propelled Carrie from deep inside, something that made her stop eating and lose weight and transform her outer self into a beautiful reflection of her inner being. Carrie was a peaceful, ethereal, sublime beauty, unthreatened and nonthreatening.

Beth's first surprise at Stanford was that she had a friend. A true friend. The second surprise shook the foundations of Beth's carefully constructed fortress between herself and the rest of the world.

The second surprise was Stephen. Carrie's brother. Again the reaction was instant, but different.

Effortlessly, Stephen gave her something she had always wanted. He talked to her, he listened to her, he admired her mind, and he didn't try to touch her. Beth wanted from Stephen what she had never wanted before—she wanted him to touch her.

In the weeks between the dinner at Lagunita Hall and the opening night of *The Importance of Being Earnest,* Beth fell in love with Stephen.

Stephen called the night after the dinner at Lagunita Hall.

"Hello, Stephen," Megan said. "I'll go get Carrie. She's just across the hall."

"Megan," Stephen said quickly before she put the phone down. "Is Beth there?"

"Beth?"

"Yes."

"Sure, just a sec." Megan smiled. She knew Beth would be thrilled; it made Megan happy. Megan was in a magnanimous mood. It had been a remarkable day. She had watched Carrie eat two meals, she had won the role of Gwendolyn, and Jake had agreed to help her learn her lines. Besides, it was inevitable. Beth and Stephen were perfectly suited.

Megan tapped on Beth's closed door before entering.

Then, in a singsong using her best Southern accent, she called, "Miss Scarlett, it's you know who-oo."

"What?"

"It's Rhe-ett. Rhett Butler."

"Megan," Beth said sternly.

Megan smiled sweetly. "It's Stephen. If you're busy . . ."

"I'm not busy."

The telephone had a long cord. Beth was able to return to her room and close the door.

"Hello?"

"Hi, Beth. It's Stephen."

"Stephen, hello."

"I wanted to thank you for having us to dinner last night, and for telling me about Carrie's diet." Something about talking to Beth inspired politeness.

"You're most welcome, Stephen. I enjoyed seeing you all."

A silence followed. Beth's pearl white teeth played with her lower lip.

"I wonder," Stephen began. It already sounded stilted. He had done this so many times. It had never been difficult before. He stared again. "Would you like to go to a movie with me next Saturday night? They're having a film festival at Mem Aud . . . uh . . . Memorial Auditorium. I'm not sure what will be showing. But it should be good."

"I'd love to, Stephen."

"Great. I'll call you on Thursday to arrange the time. Maybe we can have dinner, too?"

"That would be wonderful."

"Good." Stephen paused. Usually, he had no trouble talking on the telephone, but, with Beth, it was virtually impossible. She was so polite and proper. He had no idea what she was really thinking.

Beth was like that in person, too; a beautiful doll with impeccable manners. But, in person, there were glimpses of the other layers of Beth, the intriguing layers beneath the perfect veneer. When he was with her, he could watch her sultry eyes flash, her delicate eyebrows furrow, her full lips curl in amusement. Over the phone, Beth had no personality, or, at best, a predictable one.

"Good," Stephen repeated. Then be asked, "Is my little sister around?"

Carrie had returned and Beth signaled her to the phone. Before Stephen could speak, Carrie reassured him that she had already started a sensible diet.

"I guess I had overdone it a bit," Carrie said. "Jake was right."

"Jake?" Stephen asked, surprised.

Good, Carrie thought, relieved. Jake hadn't even mentioned it to Stephen. It confirmed what Megan had said, that none of this had affected Jake's opinion of her. He was only concerned that Carrie had unwittingly, naively, jeopardized her health. Jake had been right, and now it was over. Resolved.

The film festival selection of the week was Ingmar Bergman's *The Seventh Seal.* Stephen had second thoughts when he saw the title. Was it appropriate for Beth? Would it be too harsh, too grim, too depressing?

"No, Stephen, I would like to see it," she said smoothly when he called her Thursday night.

"Really?" How could he tell?

"Yes!" A trace of energy in her voice—the real Beth. "Yes. It's a classic and I've never seen it. I like Bergman. I would truly like to see the film."

Stephen watched Beth watching *The Seventh Seal,* her huge brown eyes focused intently on the screen, reacting, unselfconsciously, to the action of the film. Beth never flinched or covered her eyes. When it was over, she looked at Stephen, smiled, and said, "Very, very interesting."

Stephen wondered if it was a polite platitude or a genuine appraisal. Later, over a pizza, he found out. Beth animatedly discussed the symbols used in the movie and expanded on some aspects with her not inconsiderable knowledge of Ingmar Bergman and his work.

"I can't believe you know so much about him, Beth," Stephen said, amazed.

Beth was quiet. Was Stephen being critical? Was she being too opinionated, too aggressive? Beth didn't know. Her only attempts at open, honest communication had been with Carrie. Beth trusted Carrie. Beth hoped, desperately, that she could trust Carrie's brother.

"Hey," Stephen said, peering into her downcast brown eyes, "that was a compliment, you know." Stephen repeated the question. "How do you know so much about Bergman?"

"I read a lot," she said simply, honestly. "I always have."

"You are so full of surprises."

"I don't mean to be."

"Another compliment."

"Oh," Beth said, then almost giggled. "I'm not used to this."

"To what?"

"Talking. Saying what you think, what you know. Saying what you mean."

"I like hearing what you think. What you really think, not what you're supposed to think, or say."

"It's an old habit," Beth said thoughtfully.

"Worth breaking. At least, with me."

That night, Beth told Stephen about her real career plans, her carefully designed program of courses that left no time for sociology or English literature. He teased her for her silliness about not telling him from the start. He laughed, then she laughed. It felt so good to laugh, with a man, about something they both thought was funny.

When he walked her back to Lagunita Hall that night, Stephen wondered if he should kiss her. He wanted to. She was so beautiful, so sensuous. He was just beginning to learn about the real Beth, the Beth of many surprises, the Beth who wanted to trust him. He didn't want to frighten her away. There was plenty of time.

Instead of kissing her, he asked her to go out with him the next weekend.

"That would be wonderful, Stephen," she said, lapsing involuntarily into her gracious Southern manners voice.

"Meaning what?" Stephen teased.

"Oh!" Beth laughed. "Meaning, yes, Stephen. I would love to."

Stephen decided they should go to the UCLA-Stanford football game Saturday afternoon, then, after the game, to a barbecue with other members of the crew at a farmhouse in the hills. If Beth could handle *The Seventh Seal,* she could handle a football game. Besides, he learned more about her when she was slightly off guard. It made her more natural, less encumbered by her defenses.

"Is that okay?" he asked over the phone.

"Are you testing me, Stephen?" she asked lightly.

"No! Well, maybe. I'm not testing you by taking you to the game. But I do want you to tell me if you would prefer not to go."

"I want to go."

Carrie and Megan were in Megan's room when Beth returned the phone to the desk beside Megan's bed.

"What should I wear to a football game?" she asked casually, looking at Carrie.

"You're not going to a football game!" Megan exclaimed.

"Of course I am. Why not?"

"It just doesn't seem like you. Have you ever been to one?" Megan asked.

"Yes, of course. My father owns one of the biggest boxes at the Astrodome in Houston. I believe he owned a part of the Oilers for awhile."

"Oh," Megan said pleasantly. "You win this one, Beth."

"You should wear something cardinal red and white, Beth," Carrie interjected. "Everyone in the student section does."

Cardinal was a beautiful color on Beth, although she had never worn a piece of cardinal red clothing before. She bought a slightly flared red skirt and wore a matching ribbon in her hair.

"You look like a cheerleader!" Carrie exclaimed moments before Stephen arrived to get Beth.

"Oh, no," Beth said wistfully.

"Beth, it was a compliment," Carrie declared quickly.

"Oh!" Beth smiled. Then she said in a gentle tone that Carrie had never heard her use before, "You sound like your brother."

Stephen told her she looked beautiful; there was no possibility of misinterpretation.

Beth and Stephen sat pressed together on the crowded bleachers. Beth loved the closeness, feeling his warmth, leaning even closer to hear his words over the noise.

At first, Stephen explained things to her, about the game, about certain plays. Beth listened seriously, nodded, and watched the action on the field intently. As the game progressed and the crowd noise increased, it was almost impossible to talk. At halftime, they watched the antics of the notoriously unorthodox, funny, talented Stanford Marching Band. Beth laughed at the clever routines and nodded appreciatively at their music.

Toward the end of the fourth quarter, on a critical play, a penalty flag was thrown.

"What happened?" Stephen asked his friends sitting nearby. "I didn't see the penalty. Did anybody?"

"I think it was clipping," Beth said.

"What did you say?" Stephen looked at her in amazement!

"I said"—Beth spoke into his ear—"I think it was clipping. Against UCLA. At least, that's what it looked like to me." Beth shrugged.

A few moments later, the referee gave the signal by touching behind his knee—clipping, against UCLA.

Impulsively, Stephen put his arms around Beth and pulled her face close to his. "Beth, you are incredible."

Their cheeks touched briefly before Stephen released his hold and turned his attention to the final moments of the game. Beth wanted to keep touching him. She wondered if he would mind if she put her hands around his bare, muscled forearm. The thought, and the memory of the brief embrace and his words, preoccupied her for the rest of the game.

In the car, as they drove to the farmhouse in the hills behind the campus, he asked, "Why didn't you tell me you knew so much about football?"

"It's not so much. Besides, you never asked." Beth bristled slightly.

"Why do you know so much? You didn't learn that from reading."

"When I was little, I sometimes watched the games with my father, to be with him. When I was older, I went to the games. It was expected."

"But you must like it. You watched so intently."

"Not really. But it's more interesting if you know the rules and the strategy, don't you think? Otherwise, it would be boring. A waste of time."

"You seemed pretty involved with the game today," Stephen pressed.

"I was. It was an exciting game. It was terrific that we won."

"Do you ever yell or cheer?" Stephen's voice teased gently.

Beth laughed. "I'm not from another planet, you know. Do you think they only make good ol' *boys* down Texas way?" Beth deepened her accent.

"Don't tell me."

"Yes sir, deep down, way deep inside every Southern lady, is just a plain, fun lovin', good ol' gal."

Stephen's fellow crew members watched Stephen's date with considerable curiosity. Beth was so different from Stephen's other dates. Some recognized her from the *Frosh*

Book. Some had even called her, but had gotten no farther than her protective roommate.

They talked to her, flirting with her. Instinctively, as she had done hundreds of times, as she had been trained and bred to do, Beth flirted back. But, unlike all the other times, at parties and barbecues in Texas, when she had loathed the attentions of the young men and had loathed the young men for being attentive, Beth enjoyed herself. Her trust and admiration of Stephen spilled over to his friends. In the past few weeks, she had even become tolerant of men who had approached her on campus, in the bookstore, after class, in the library. Annoyance had been replaced by amusement. Beth had told them, pleasantly, that she was "involved."

Because of Stephen, Beth felt safe.

After dinner, there was dancing on the porch of the farmhouse. Stephen waited until a slow song was played, then he asked Beth to dance. He led her, by the hand, to a far, dark, private corner of the porch.

For an awkward moment, Beth wasn't sure where to put her hands. Stephen rescued her. He put her arms around his neck, then he put his arms around her waist. They moved slowly to the music, swaying gently, their bodies moving together, pressing together.

Stephen's lips found hers while they danced, without breaking the rhythm. He kissed her deeply, her warm mouth eagerly responding to him. Beth closed her eyes, felt the warmth and sexuality of his body, the strength of his arms around her, his safe, depthless mouth that wanted hers. She was inside him, part of him. There was nothing else, no one else.

Stephen realized that the song had ended before Beth did. Wordlessly, he took her hand and led her down the porch stairs. The night was balmy, lighted by a yellow harvest moon. Silently, they walked around the side of the farmhouse. As soon as they were out of sight of the others, Stephen kissed her again.

First, he kissed her mouth. Then, as he began to kiss her

cheeks, her nose, her face, her neck, Beth's lips found his, forcing them to return to hers. Surprised, Stephen pulled back a minute, smiled into her beautiful, seductive eyes, and whispered, "Okay." Then he began kissing her, kissing her mouth, the way she wanted him to.

Beth couldn't think. Her mind and body were taken over by unbelievable feelings—Stephen's kiss, the warmth of his mouth, the desire of his tongue and his body for her, the security of his arms around her, the softness of his lips, the power of his hands, the rhythm of his body. The rhythm of her body.

As they kissed, Stephen stroked her cheeks, her hair, her long ivory neck, his hand slowly, inevitably moving toward her breast. Stephen felt her body stiffen. Quickly he removed his hand and looked at her, seriously. Beth's brow furrowed slightly with worry, not anger. What would Stephen think of her? Would *he* be angry?

"Sorry," they said to each other in unison. It helped. They relaxed.

"I'm the one who's sorry, Beth. You shouldn't apologize to me."

"Oh. You're not angry?"

"Angry? No. Of course not." Stephen held her close to him and talked softly into her ear. His breath was warm, moist. It made Beth tremble. "We won't do anything you don't want to."

"You don't mind?"

"No," he said gently, nibbling her ear. "I could kiss you forever."

"Then do, please."

Two days before the opening night performance of *The Importance of Being Earnest,* Megan went to the student health center.

"May I help you?" the receptionist asked.

Megan glanced around the waiting area. She instantly

recognized two other students from Lagunita Hall. Megan waved cheerfully and said seriously to the receptionist, "I would like to see a gynecologist."

Megan filled out the medical history form. It took very little time; she had always been completely healthy—robust health.

The gynecologist, a pleasant woman of fifty, responded calmly to Megan's request for birth control pills.

"Why The Pill, Megan?" she asked.

Why not? Megan wondered but said, "I thought it was the most reliable and the easiest."

Megan had never given much thought to birth control. She considered it the man's responsibility. If he didn't have protection, she wouldn't make love to him. It simply hadn't mattered that much to her. Until now. Until Jake. Now, she decided, it was her responsibility to make certain they could make love whenever they wanted to.

"It is easy and reliable. But, birth control pills are hormones. They may have effects other than preventing conception."

"Dangerous effects?" Megan asked.

"Sometimes the effects can be dangerous, yes. For example, high blood pressure, abnormal blood clotting, even strokes. Sometimes the effects are just troublesome, such as weight gain, nausea, lethargy, acne. The Pill is a relatively new type of medication. We, the medical community, don't yet have long-term data. We have no idea, yet, what effects there might be from taking The Pill for ten, twenty, or thirty years. The effects could be good, bad, or indifferent."

"I had no idea," Megan said slowly. She took such great care of her health. She didn't want to jeopardize the carefully achieved, disciplined balance that gave her her radiant looks and her limitless energy. "Can some women take The Pill with no effects?"

"Oh yes."

"Can you predict?"

"No. You, for example, are the picture of health. Your

71

blood pressure and heart rate are quite normal. But that doesn't mean you wouldn't have problems." The doctor paused. She had this conversation almost daily. Most girls shrugged off the possible risks and opted for the ease and freedom of The Pill.

Megan seemed to take the warnings more seriously.

"Megan, I am not trying to talk you out of birth control. I have not asked you about your relationship with the young man and have no intention of doing so. That's your business. I do favor birth control, in general, because the potential health risks and emotional damage of an unwanted pregnancy far outweigh the risks of birth control, even The Pill."

"So what do you suggest?" Megan asked.

"For a casual relationship, I recommend the diaphragm. It can be inserted well in advance, so it doesn't interfere with spontaneity. I will occasionally prescribe The Pill, on a trial basis with close follow up, especially for couples who are living together or are married."

"I guess I should try the diaphragm, then," Megan said.

"Fine," the doctor replied. "If it isn't satisfactory for you, or if the relationship becomes more permanent and you would like to try The Pill, I'll make a note on your chart that we have already discussed the risks and precautions. That way, you can come back and get a prescription."

Megan got front row seats for the opening night performance of her play for Carrie, Beth, Stephen, and Jake. It was her play; Megan's performance of Gwendolyn stole the show. Jake and Carrie watched their friend proudly. Beth and Stephen were wide-eyed; Megan's performance was stylish, talented, and professional. What they saw was hard to reconcile with their mutual, largely negative opinion of Megan.

After the play, they assembled backstage with a euphoric Megan. They all were genuinely effusive in their praise.

"You were truly sensational, Megan," Stephen said.

"Thank you, Stephen. I thought this actress business would be a bit too frivolous and unimportant for you." Megan smiled, but her eyes delivered a challenge: Don't deny it. You think my career is trivial compared to your grand plan of becoming Harvard Law School's most famous graduate!

Stephen frowned, blushed, and then angrily glowered back.

"Of course it's frivolous and inconsequential, Megan, but that doesn't mean that you don't do it well." The venom in his voice surprised them all.

Carrie gasped. Jake and Megan looked startled. Beth suppressed, somewhat unsuccessfully, a smug grin.

A long, silent moment followed, tense with emotions that none of them understood.

"Megan could choose any career she wants. She has chosen to be a great actress. And she will be," Carrie said finally, defiantly. Her friendship with Megan had not faltered, despite Beth's obvious dislike of Megan and despite Megan's friendship with Jake.

It wasn't Megan's fault that Jake was attracted to her, not Carrie, just as Carrie herself had no control over what happened to her whenever she saw Jake. She could not control how her heart pounded noisily, how she became mute when be spoke to her, how her body ached all those evenings when he and Megan rehearsed together. She overheard them from her room—Megan's giggles, Jake's reserved laugh, the quiet of a serious conversation, Jake's comforting voice.

But Carrie's envy of Megan translated into admiration, not dislike. Megan was her dear, trusted friend.

"Loyal Caroline. What a friend you are to Megan!" Jake smiled at Carrie, then stared with obvious, uncharacteristic disapproval at Stephen.

"She started it, Jake. She threw the first taunt," Stephen said flatly.

Jake's response was prevented by the arrival of the director, who insinuated himself between Stephen and Jake.

He carried an armful of long-stemmed red roses, which he presented flamboyantly to Megan.

"Never in the history of *Earnest* has Gwendolyn been the star of the show. It's lucky Oscar Wilde never saw this production. You were truly brilliant, my dear."

He was too elated to notice the general tone of the group or to detect that he had intruded on an argument. The interruption provided an opportunity for Beth and Stephen to leave.

"Carrie, I'm walking Beth back to the dorm. Do you want to come?"

Carrie was angry with Stephen but knew that Jake and Megan wanted to be alone. She nodded silently to Stephen and waved good-bye to Megan, who was smiling vaguely in response to the director's commentary on her performance. As usual, Carrie couldn't make herself look at Jake; she was too shy. And she was afraid that he might be able to tell how she felt, and that would make her feel even more foolish.

"Carrie, I'm sorry," Stephen said as soon as they were out of Megan's earshot. "I just lost my temper."

"You barely know Megan. How could you have built up so much resentment?"

"I don't have built-up resentment. But her confidence is a bit much. She is so arrogant. It annoys me."

"I think you're even wrong about that, Stephen. Megan's really warm and sensitive and as unsure of herself as anyone. She tries very hard to seem positive and optimistic. Maybe she tries too hard. Maybe she's really very insecure—" Carrie stopped short, surprised at what she had said and suddenly aware that Beth was listening with considerable interest. Carrie added quickly, "Anyway, she's my friend and I expect you to be nice to her."

"God, Jake, why did I do that?"
"Tell me." Jake's voice was flat.

"It was Beth I was taunting. Through Stephen. He seems to be the spokesman for the duo."

"I don't think that Stephen and Beth are a duo."

"Really? They seem the perfect match—fastidious, rigid, hypercritical, goal oriented, insensitive . . . Shall I go on?"

"You're talking about Beth. Remember, I know Stephen. That is not a fair description of him."

"But it is fair of Beth?"

"I admit that I am not particularly fond of Beth." Jake's expression conveyed the extent of his lack of fondness.

"So why does Stephen like her so much?"

"I'm not sure that he does. I don't know how he feels."

"I am most sorry that this put you and Stephen at odds."

"So am I."

By the time Megan changed and was ready to leave theater, it was raining. Huge, cold drops splashed on her face and the wind tangled her hair. She was being punished.

"Since the final curtain, this night has been a washout. So much for the eighteenth green. It's probably just as well. I get the feeling that you would just as soon not be with me." Megan's voice was tired, discouraged. She leaned against a Corinthian pillar, out of the rain, shoulders slumped.

"I want to be with you," Jake said quietly, without emotion.

Megan straightened and waited, barely breathing.

"There's a cabin at the beach. It belongs to a friend. I have the keys and a guarantee of privacy. We'll have to take your car—I've lent mine out for the weekend."

"Okay. The keys are in my room. This will give me a chance to talk to Carrie. I'll tell her it's an all-night cast party."

Megan knew how Carrie felt about Jake, even though Carrie never mentioned it. And Megan sensed that Jake knew, too, and that they both wanted to protect Carrie from the intimacies of their relationship. Neither Jake nor Megan wanted to hurt Carrie.

While he waited for Megan in the lobby at Lagunita Hall, Jake telephoned Stephen. In more than two years as room-mates, there had been a few disagreements. But they had been intellectual, political, philosophical arguments, not personal, emotional ones. And there had never been anger, until tonight. The anger had come so unexpectedly and with such venom.

"Stephen, it's Jake. I'm not sure why or how it happened, but I am sorry that it did."

"It wasn't what she said, but how she said it. Something snapped. I have never lost control like that before."

"She's sorry. I think she was so high from her success that she wasn't thinking . . ."

"Maybe. Something. I don't know. I'm still not over the kind of sick feeling."

"I know. I worry about Carrie. Megan is talking to her now. Carrie wants everything to be perfect, harmonious, all the time. She wants us all to be friends."

"When did you get to know my little sister so well?"

Jake hesitated. "I don't know her well. Just from what you've said." Jake took a deep breath and sighed audibly. "Anyway, I'm sorry it happened. I just wanted to clear the air as soon as possible."

"Thanks. I'm the one who's sorry. I was the one who lost control."

Jake drove. The rain fell in thick, wet walls and the wind blew in violent gusts through the valley. The car shuddered and slipped on the wet, black road. Jake drove carefully but decisively. Neither of them spoke. In the car, before they had left, Jake had kissed her and held her briefly, tightly.

Now, in the darkness of the night, in the violence of the storm, and in the stern, concentrated silence of her prospective lover, Megan felt unspeakably frightened and alone.

This was the death void that she instinctively knew existed. The empty, lonely, violent eternity that she dreaded so desperately.

Megan grasped the armrest and squeezed until her knuckles were white and her fingers were numb. She wanted to touch Jake, to feel his warmth, his aliveness, but she didn't dare break his concentration on the treacherous, narrow road. If she could just lay her hand on his thigh.

But she hadn't been allowed to touch there before.

"You okay?" Jake didn't eke his eyes off the road.

Megan almost wept with relief at the sound of his normal, slightly strained voice.

"Yes . . . now."

"We're almost to the coast. The cabin is just a mile north. Not much longer." Megan thought she saw him smile in the darkness.

Then they were there—the warm cabin, the fire Jake built in the brick fireplace, the fine brandy she sipped slowly. The horror of the storm and the darkness were forgotten. The cabin was a safe, cozy refuge, full of life and warmth and light. Megan wondered who the cabin belonged to. It was clear that Jake knew it well, had been there before. With whom? she wondered.

"I have to tell you about my leg. So you won't be surprised." Jake stared into the fire. "When I was young I had a bad accident. I fell out of a tree and broke my femur, my thigh bone. Shattered it, really. It was an open fracture, which means that the skin was broken down to the bone. As a result, it became badly infected. I was in the hospital for a long time. Lots of surgery. It's a good result, actually. I didn't lose my leg and it's about the same length as my other leg. I don't even limp unless I overdo. It's totally healed, but it looks bad. Very bad. Distorted."

Jake turned around and looked at Megan.

Megan looked down into her almost empty glass of brandy; she couldn't return his gaze. Her mind was reeling, not from the words but from his voice. It didn't sound like

Jake. It was a carefully rehearsed speech. Memorized. Word perfect. And, Megan realized, undeniably false.

Jake was lying! She was certain of it. But why? What could matter so much that he couldn't tell her? She had trusted him with so many confidences; why couldn't he trust her? Someday she would make him tell her.

But not tonight. Tonight she wanted him. She had already almost ruined the evening once. She had no intention of testing his patience by accusing him of lying. Still, it bothered her. She took a final gulp of brandy and washed the worry away.

"Let me see."

Jake frowned, then slowly undressed, apparently unembarrassed despite the description he had given her. He has nothing to be ashamed of, Megan thought as she eyed, anxiously, his tan, naked torso, well muscled, perfectly shaped, sensual.

Then Jake stepped out of his slacks and Megan gasped. The tan stopped at his waistline. Below, his skin was chalk white—pale, unhealthy; skin hidden too long from the sun. And the white legs—one perfectly shaped, finely muscled, artfully tapered, like an alabaster statue. And the other, muscled below the knee, but no more than bone tightly wrapped in purple scar tissue for most of the thigh. One overdeveloped muscle tracked from his hip to his knee, its hyper-trophied bulges stretching the fibers to the scar tissue. That grotesque muscle enabled him, somehow, to walk. And without a limp.

It must have taken years of training, years of pain, frustration, and patience. And the result was a blend of Jake's determination and the workmanship of many clever doctors. But was this really their best effort? Was this the best modern medicine could do? It would have been a macabre joke if it hadn't been the leg of a handsome young man. A perfect specimen for a museum of medical curiosities, if it hadn't been Jake's leg. Jake and the Elephant man, side by side. Megan shuddered, angry at herself for the thought.

Megan ran her fingers through her hair, tossed her mane, cocked her head, and gestured at the underwear that Jake still wore.

"I'm waiting." Her voice was low.

Without speaking, Jake took her hand and led her into the bedroom. Slowly he undressed her, pausing to kiss each new area of exposed flesh—her graceful neck, the softness of her shoulders, her firm breasts, her flat stomach, her long, tapered legs. Megan trembled at his touch, involuntarily moving toward him, answering his warm, probing kisses with her body, urging his body to join hers. Quickly.

Jake sensed her urgency; it matched his own need for her. They made love with an energy that left Megan breathless and excited. And wanting more. Jake held her afterward, stroking her silky golden hair, not speaking, staring into her eyes. Speaking to her with his eyes. Megan saw, in Jake's intense blue eyes, lust and pleasure and desire.

Megan sent him a message through her eyes: I want you, again. Now.

Jake smiled. He kissed her, watching her as he kissed her, as he made love to her, again. Megan quivered at his touch and at his gaze, flooded with sensations of pleasure and a curious, exciting aching. The sensations were new, powerful, demanding. Megan followed the commands of her body and Jake's eyes. The feelings weren't safe or comfortable, but insistent, relentless, inevitably leading to an explosion that left her not with a familiar aching but with something new: a powerful sense of freedom and wholeness.

Afterward, Megan lay in Jake's arms, exhausted, satisfied, and with a knowledge that the satisfaction would demand renewal.

Megan put her head on Jake's flat, firm stomach, then slowly moved to his thigh. She felt the huge muscle, bulging, straining to be free of its too tightly wrapped covering—an angry organ, tense, trapped. Under the muscle, alive with palpable energy and curtailed strength, was the bone, hard, cold, skeletal . . . dead. Megan forced herself not to withdraw from the lifeless, vividly anatomic structure that lay exposed, unadorned by soft cushions of fat and muscle.

But this isn't dead bone, she thought. This is Jake. Part of alive, passionate Jake. Megan nestled her head in the angle of his legs. She pressed her forehead against the muscle of his leg and slowly, gently, kissed the length of the cold, irregular bone.

After a few moments, Jake pulled her back to him, and they made love for a third time. Quietly, tenderly, and, still, wordlessly.

Megan was awakened by warmth and light in her eyes, the morning sun filtering through the loosely woven curtains in the bedroom. She was alone in bed. The cabin was silent.

"Jake?" No reply. The cabin was empty. Megan walked out onto the porch.

The sapphire blue ocean glittered in the early morning sun. Unmenacing waves lapped languidly on the kelp-strewn beach. The air had a just-washed freshness—crisp, clean, pure. The storm, so violent, so destructive, so evil, had left in its wake a new world—bright, peaceful, perfect.

Jake must be at the beach, she thought. She showered, dressed, and stumbled gracefully down the narrow, winding path to the beach.

She saw him in the distance, sitting on the smooth, white sand, his long arms resting casually over his flexed khaki slacks. Jake stared at the ocean, lost in thought, unaware that he was no longer alone.

As she approached, unobserved, Megan caught a glimpse of Jake's expression—sad, thoughtful. In pain? It was a fleeting glimpse, because he soon sensed her presence, turned, and smiled.

"Good morning," Megan said quietly. Those were the

first words either had spoken since he had stood before her, almost naked, in front of the fire. She suddenly felt awkward, unsure. She sat on the sand a few feet away from him.

"Good morning." Jake took her hand and pulled her beside him. He put his arms around her and began to kiss her.

He caught a strand of her long, blond hair in his mouth and pulled away for a moment to free it. Megan saw the look in his eyes. She knew its meaning; she had learned it last night.

Gently, he lowered her onto her back on the sand and began to unbutton her blouse.

"Jake!" Megan sat up.

"What?" he whispered against her throat.

"We can't make love here!"

"We can't?" Jake gave a cursory glance at the empty beach. "Why not?"

Megan smiled, tossed her mane of golden hair, lay back down on the sand, and extended her arms to him. Why not?

They made love under the just-warm November sun, their naked flesh caressed by the cool, gentle sea breeze, the rhythm of their lovemaking the rhythm of nature—the quiet, lapping rhythm of the ocean waves.

Megan had never felt so pure.

Chapter Five

The Monday following opening night a bouquet of white roses and forget-me-nots was delivered to the lobby desk at Lagunita Hall for Miss Megan Chase. The on-duty freshman receptionist rang the room immediately. Beth was alone and in need of a study break. And curious. And, for reasons she couldn't pinpoint, worried. Who would send flowers to Megan? Almost anyone, especially following her great success as Gwendolyn. Still . . .

"I'll be right down to pick them up."

The bouquet was lovely—delicate, ethereal, graceful—and obviously made especially for Megan. The envelope was, maddeningly, sealed. The handwriting surely belonged to the florist. Beth's curiosity would have to wait. She placed the flowers on Megan's bedside table. It was almost noon. Carrie and Megan would be returning from class soon.

"Megan, look!" Carrie spotted the flowers as they entered the room. "They're beautiful."

Megan looked startled, then puzzled. She held back a moment, then smiled. Jake, of course, for their wonderful weekend. But how did he know?

Carrie handed the envelope to Megan. Carrie knew they were probably from Jake. But the new Carrie, the Carrie who had been forced to face reality opening night, could handle it. She accepted the fact of Megan and Jake.

Megan opened the envelope uneasily. Beth leaned against her door jamb and held her breath.

"To an unforgettable performance (yours), and a regrettable (forgettable?) performance (mine). I am truly sorry. Stephen."

Megan read the note twice, then folded it in half and then in half again. It took a few moments for her to realize that Carrie and Beth were waiting.

"From Stephen." Megan shrugged and laughed nervously.

Carrie smiled. Beth retreated. Megan glowered at the bouquet. Forget-me-nots. But he couldn't possibly know. She had never told anyone.

Megan picked at lunch, snapped at her roommates, and sulked all afternoon, glaring at the bouquet. Finally her irritability became unbearable even to her. There was no point guessing. She would have to find out. She walked briskly across campus, remembering.

Forget-me-nots. Her flower. Her own private symbol of hope, of strength, of resilience . . .

Megan was five when her mother abandoned them, Megan and her father. Megan's mother returned to her native Sweden, to the modeling and acting career that had been abruptly suspended when she met, and fell in love with, Robert Chase. She left them both, her husband and her daughter, without looking back.

"Your mother was so young," Megan's father explained to her years later. Too young to have understood the pain that she caused us or the pain she herself would feel. "Besides," he told his beautiful daughter who was an exact image of the woman he had loved so deeply, "I would never have let her take you away from me."

Megan's father consoled himself by working to the point of exhaustion. Already in great demand as one of Hollywood's bright, innovative directors, Robert found more than enough work to keep him totally preoccupied. He turned over the care of his five-year-old daughter to nannies, housekeepers, and expensive private schools.

That spring, abandoned by her mother and forgotten by her father, Megan spent her days playing, by herself, in the magnificent garden of her father's home in Beverly Hills. Megan created her own world, populated by many interesting characters, all played by Megan herself. The shrubs and flowers in the beautiful garden were an integral part of her make-believe world. They had names and personalities. As spring became summer, Megan watched them grow and blossom under her nurturing, loving care.

Megan had a favorite flower, a delicate turquoise and violet flower that grew in cracks in the cement and in the shadows of the roses, azaleas, and rhododendrons. Megan's flower looked fragile and pretty, but it was the most resilient, most courageous of them all. It could be crushed by a rainstorm, or a careless foot, but in two days it would be upright again, stretching for the sun.

One day, one of the gardeners started to pull the flowers from the cracks in the cement.

"What are you doing?" Megan asked in horror.

"It's a weed."

"No! It isn't. It's a beautiful flower."

The gardener smiled at her. He knew how rough life had been for the golden-haired little girl. He admired her spirit.

"Do you want me to leave it?" he asked.

"Yes! Please!" Megan exclaimed. Then she asked, thoughtfully, "Does it have a name?"

"It's called a forget-me-not."

Forget-me-not. It was her flower. And it was she. She would survive, as it had survived, reaching for the sun, even in the most difficult situations. And she would not be forgotten—ever again.

Five-year-old Megan Chase made a vow. She would never tell anyone; it was her secret.

And now, fifteen years later, Stephen Richards had sent her a bouquet of forget-me-nots.

The door to Jake and Stephen's room was closed, but

Megan heard their voices. She knocked. Stephen answered the door.

"How did you know?" Angry, accusatory. How dare you know!

"You're very welcome." Stephen forced a smile. Anger rushed through his body as it had two nights before. But this time he would control it.

"Megan, what's going on?" Jake casually positioned himself between Megan and Stephen.

"I sent her a bouquet of flowers. Apparently an unpopular gesture." Stephen's voice was ice cold.

"But you sent me forget-me-nots . . . Why?" Megan's voice was soft, pleading.

What an actress! Stephen thought. He took a deep breath. Control, he reminded himself.

Why had he sent forget-me-nots? True, in all of his years of dating, of proms, of girlfriends, of thank-yous, and of apologies, Stephen had sent many flowers. But he had never before sent forget-me-nots. And this hadn't been a whimsical decision. In fact, it had been difficult to find a florist who had forget-me-nots. Forget-me-nots seemed right for Megan. Wild, but somehow delicate and fragile. Pretty. Megan's were eyes blue-violet. And the name . . .

"They seemed like you. Stephen shrugged. In a moment he would be apologizing again, but for what?

"Megan—" Jake began, but he was interrupted.

Megan broke the tension as quickly as she had created it. She tossed her head and walked toward Stephen, smiling, her long, graceful hand outstretched.

"I am sorry for making a fuss. It was nice of you. I apologize for being a brat, then and now."

Stephen shook her hand, tentatively. He arched an eyebrow at Jake, who shrugged. Jake had no intention of trying to explain Megan and her moods, even though he was beginning to understand them. But he could rescue Stephen.

"Megan, this behavior must be a result of hypoglycemia. Why don't I take you for a drive along El Camino and find you something to eat." Jake looked at her meaningfully. The look meant, Come with me; I want you.

They never stopped for hamburgers. Jake drove directly to the Colonial Inn, a tidy white motel with wrought-iron railings and cotton-print curtains. It would become their favorite place to be together when they didn't have time, or couldn't wait, to drive to the cabin at San Gregorio.

Most women who entered college in the fall of 1970 were virgins, by choice; indeed, by acclamation. They held the firm, uncontested view that they would be virgins until their wedding night. It was not even a debatable issue.

To Megan, virginity was something to get over, like braces or the measles, something that you needed to have for awhile, though you were better off after it was gone. Megan had gotten over virginity four years before she entered Stanford, on a balmy summer night at a beach party in Malibu. The man was ten years her senior, a handsome, arrogant, box-office attraction who was starring in one of her father's pictures. Megan didn't like him or *it*, but the next day she felt wonderful, free, and something else—powerful. She had the power to give pleasure, if she chose to.

Megan chose to often. Not because she enjoyed sex—it worried her a bit that she didn't—but because of the power. Because she was in control. She enjoyed teasing, eventually relenting, and watching their faces. She didn't hate them, but she envied them a little. Why didn't it feel as wonderful for her as it obviously did for them? Megan had to be content with the power and the game. She felt very little until Jake.

Then Megan knew what had driven men to her; she knew the feeling of pleasure and the demands of that pleasure to be renewed. She enjoyed making love with Jake. She loved the way they moved together, intuitively, without limits or barriers. Nothing was wrong; everything was possible. Free. She loved being with him, making love with him; and she loved the quiet conversations they had afterward.

It was an addiction, Megan admitted when she made herself think about it, a fun, wonderful, exciting addiction. Her body made demands and only Jake could satisfy them. They got together somewhere, somehow, almost daily, and when they missed a day because of exams, term papers, Megan's play, or because of sheer fatigue, Jake would often find a note in his mailbox at the campus post office.

"I cannot wait until tonight. Please skip your political science seminar, just this once. M."

He would put a note in her mailbox.

"The Middle East needs me."

And she would answer.

"Not as much as I do!"

And he would write in response.

"Meet me outside the classroom after the seminar."

Jake was a willing accomplice to Megan's demands but never at the expense of his studies. Willing and able—able to do with his hands, his lips, his eyes, his body, what no one had ever done to her before. Talented, sensuous hands. Gentle lips. Probing, intense eyes. In control. And inscrutable.

"What are you thinking?" Megan lay nestled in Jake's arms in their usual room in the Colonial Inn. It was two days before the Thanksgiving holidays. They would be apart for awhile.

Jake stroked her hair tenderly and smiled.

"How beautiful you are." It was an easy lie. It hadn't been what he had been thinking about then, but it was true. And he had thought it often.

At the moment Megan asked the question his thoughts had taken him, as they did too often and without being summoned, to another time, another afternoon, another woman. To a time of great pain and different joy.

Part Two

Chapter Six

Saigon . . . October, 1964

That afternoon, six years before, had been unbearably hot and humid, almost too hot to move, but the act of walking created a slight breeze on the breathless day. The humidity was just short of rain; rain would have been a blessing, but it was not to be.

It was a day that taunted them all, without mercy, an angry, tormented day, punishing them all for hating each other, for killing each other.

Jake and two other enlisted men were assigned patrol duty, to keep things "quiet and under control" in the back streets of Saigon. They walked slowly in their sweat-drenched, dark green fatigues; they carried submachine guns. The streets were crowded but strangely quiet. Except for the silence, it was business as usual: beggars, starving children, the goods of the market place, all embroidered in a colorful tapestry in which the common thread, woven throughout, was the dark green of the United States Army uniform.

Today the children didn't cry, the beggars gestured soundlessly with their flesh-bare arms, and the merchants didn't barter. It was, simply, too hot to speak.

Jake and his buddies walked up one side of a dirty street and down the other, through the market, back to an adjacent street, their paths repeatedly crisscrossing paths of other trios as armed patrols, providing a constant reminder of the military presence.

They were in the second hour of the eight-hour watch when "the incident" happened. It was incredible that they hadn't noticed him before; the heat, the silence, contrived to dull their normally acute senses. It was lucky that Jake noticed him when he did.

A black limousine from the diplomatic motor pool pulled to a stop at the curb just ahead of them. Reflexively, Jake and the others stopped, stood at attention, and waited, expecting to see a general, a diplomatic envoy, a visiting dignitary.

But who emerged, slowly, elegantly, *coolly,* was a beautiful young woman. Her coal black hair was curled into a sleek knot on the top of her perfectly shaped head; she wore a lavender linen dress with a white linen jacket, short white gloves, and pearls. She carried a wicker basket, overstuffed with bread and fruit.

They stared at her, a vision of loveliness and surely an illusion in the hell and horror of the world they knew. She stared back at them, her violet eyes sparkling in her beautiful, untroubled face. She proceeded, unconcerned, with her mission—to give the basket of food to a woman huddled in the dust with two small, thin, silent children.

Jake never knew what—a noise, a movement, an intuition—made him pull his mesmerized eyes away from her and look toward a shadow in an open doorway. In an instant the shadow took shape and meaning—a machine gun, aimed at her.

"Get down," he yelled. She froze, startled but unafraid. He grabbed her, pulling her down to a crouch beside him.

"What—" she whispered but was interrupted by the deafening sound of close range machine-gun fire. Her eyes filled with terror; her gloved fingers tightened around Jake's arm.

"Get into the car and keep down." Jake turned toward the car and saw that the chauffeur lay in her path, dead, in a pool of blood. She gasped and didn't move.

"C'mon, ma'am. *Now.*" Jake guided her firmly over the dead body; her white cloth pumps turned red and wet with blood. He shoved her into the back of the car, told her to lie on the floor, and closed the heavy car door.

The gunfire, which had started with the machine gun of the assassin and had been answered quickly by the guns of his buddies, ceased. Jake saw what the machine guns had done to the assassin; he hoped that she hadn't seen. The contents of the basket were strewn on the ground; already beggars were clambering for the precious food. The woman and the two children had vanished. The street was crowded with other patrols and curious citizens.

But "the incident" was over. All that remained was the bloody aftermath, the reports, the explanations and guesses, and a beautiful woman with white gloves and pearls and blood-soaked shoes lying on the floor of a chauffeurless car.

"I'd better get her outta here," Jake said and got into the car. "Don't get up yet, ma'am. You all right?" He didn't want her to see what he saw.

"Yes. Thank you." Even in her fright, the voice was rich and elegant and gracious. "Thank you very much."

Jake drove to the next street. It was deserted; its occupants had all rushed to the site of the murders. He told her to sit up and looked at her in the rearview mirror. Beautiful, frightened, and, now, sad.

"The chauffeur?"

"Dead, ma'am." Couldn't she tell? Maybe she hadn't looked as she stepped over his body. "Do I take you to the base?"

"Whatever is convenient for you. I had been at a tea at the base. There was leftover food. That's why I had a basket. He was driving me home. I didn't think . . ."

Didn't think is right, Jake thought. Still, it was just bad luck. It couldn't have been planned.

"Where d'ya live?"

She directed him unerringly to a residential area in the outskirts of the city. He had no idea that such houses, such wealth, existed anywhere, least of all in Saigon. She lived, as many officers' families lived, in houses that had been built by the French before the war. Her "home" was a mansion surrounded by a white brick wall topped by a spiked iron fence. A guard, dressed in fatigues, stood at the iron gate.

His hand moved to the trigger of his gun when he saw Jake instead of the chauffeur. He made Jake get out of the car and demanded identification and explanations. He was only satisfied after telephoning the base that Jake would do no harm to the general's wife.

"General's wife?" Jake asked.

"Yes. Didn't you even know who she was?"

"No. Just had to get her outta there."

"Jesus, you'll probably get a medal for this. Lucky bastard."

She stepped out of her blood-soaked shoes before she entered the house. Jake stood outside, waiting. For what? To be thanked again? To be dismissed? To be invited in?

To be spoken to, he realized. She hadn't spoken for awhile. She had been too silent during his explanations to the guard.

She turned toward him, her violet eyes liquid with tears, her lips trembling.

"Help me," she whispered.

Quickly, Jake took off his bloody, dirty boots and stepped onto the white marble floor of the house in stockinged feet. He put his hand below her elbow and guided her off the cold marble floor onto the thick cream rug in the living room. He steered her around a large planter to the sofa. She sat down, covered her face with her hands, and trembled.

Jake suppressed an impulse to sit down beside her and hold her. He was too hot, too sweaty, too dirty to touch her or her furniture. Tentatively he patted her trembling shoulder.

"Quite a shock, ma'am. You'll be okay."

She nodded—two beats—then shook her head.

"No, I'll never forget it. I am so stupid. I was just trying to help that poor woman and now . . . It's all my fault."

"You didn't mean no harm."

94

"Does that really matter?" She looked up at him. He shrugged. She wiped her eyes. "What's your name?"

"Jake." It caught him off guard. "I mean Private Easton, ma'am. Mrs. . . ."

"Julia. Call me Julia. You saved my life, Jake. You really did. He did mean to kill me, didn't he?" Julia's voice wavered.

"Maybe." Jake shrugged, but there was no uncertainty in his voice. Of course she was the target.

"Yes." She sounded calm. Julia stared at her hands for several moments, then asked, "How old are you, Jake?"

"Eighteen," he lied. It was a lie he had been living with for two years. In a month he really would be eighteen. It was hardly a lie anymore; still he hated to lie to her.

Julia arched an eyebrow. He looks older. He acts older, she thought. My God, I'm sixteen years older than he is.

She wanted to know all about him, this boy-man who had saved her life, someone whom she would normally dismiss out of hand because he was dirty and couldn't even speak English. Why doesn't he speak properly? she wondered. He looks so confident, handsome, controlled. Julia sighed. She wanted to know more about him, but she was too exhausted to ask. She had to rest, to recover for a moment. But she didn't want him to leave.

"I have to take a shower. To wash off . . ." she paused. She had to say it. "The blood. Then I need to lie down and rest and have a cup of tea. I need to have you stay a bit longer. I still don't feel safe."

It wasn't a question or an invitation; it was a command. Probably learned it from her husband, Jake thought and smiled. It would be fine to stay. But he felt uncomfortable. He had blood to wash off, too.

"There's a swimming pool out back. And a shower in the dressing room. If you'd like . . ."

"Sounds real good, ma'am."

* * *

95

Jake had forgotten the day's heat until he stepped from the air-conditioned house onto the patio. The cement burned his stockinged feet. He sprinted to a small building at one end of the courtyard and found a newly tiled shower, wash basin, toilet, several dressing rooms, towels, soap, sandals, and terry cloth robes.

He removed all his clothes and put them in a pile on the floor of the shower. As he washed himself, the clothes soaked in the soapy water. When he had finished scrubbing himself, he scrubbed his clothes. Red-brown water swirled through the drain and finally ran clear. He wrung out the clothes until they were barely damp; the sun would complete the drying in no time. He wrapped a towel around his waist and carried his clothes outside.

The day's heat enveloped him; it wouldn't be long before the aquamarine water of the pool would be irresistible. Jake hadn't seen any swimming trunks in the dressing room. But he was quite alone and probably would be for some time. Julia might sleep for hours. He could safely swim naked until his clothes dried. Then, with clean clothes, he could sit in the white living room.

The cool water on his warm skin reminded him of one of his few happy memories of home—swimming in the river on a hot summer day. He usually swam in jeans then. This felt much better. More free. A new pleasure.

From the coolness of the pool he looked around. The house was perched on top of a hill. The view from the courtyard was north, toward the lush green jungle. In another time it could have been paradise. Maybe it had been, once.

He floated lazily in the pool, getting out occasionally to check his clothes, to re-arrange the damp parts, warming himself quickly in the hot sun, diving back in the cool water. There was no measure of time in this protected world of sun and water and jungle. A unit of time was as long as a daydream or a memory or a fantasy. Jake had no idea how long he had been in the pool when Julia arrived.

"I heard splashing." Julia looked refreshed and back to

normal—cool, elegant, calm. Her black hair fell loosely around her face. She wore a short terry cloth robe over a black one-piece bathing suit.

"Problem here, ma'am." Jake smiled. "Couldn't find any trunks."

He shrugged. He was treading water in the center of the pool. It occurred to Julia that he didn't really consider this a problem but simply felt obliged to let her know.

"Oh." There were trunks in the house. Frank's trunks. Julia considered a moment and then said, lightly, "Oh, well. I'll just close my eyes when you get out of the pool."

Julia sat on the steps at the shallow end of the pool, in the water. Jake treaded water in the deep end, resting occasionally at the edge of the pool. They talked. Julie asked questions and Jake gave answers. For the first time in years, the answers he gave were honest. To her, of all people. A general's wife. But she, of all people, wouldn't turn him in. She couldn't. So he told her the truth.

About his home, in East Town, West Virginia, in a place called Appalachia. About his coal miner father whose lips turned blue by the time he was thirty-five, who took eight seconds to exhale his breath, then inhaled with desperate gasps because his brain needed oxygen; who couldn't fit more than three words in between breaths. About his mother, thin, tired, hunched, and sagging. She had always been that way, ever since Jake could remember—when he was four and she was twenty-one. There were sisters and brothers, nameless mouths to feed, diapers to change, toys and clothes to share. Jake was the oldest, the heir-apparent to the mine, the first one to drain the life out of his mother.

It was a fragmented, inarticulate story, bits and pieces connected with "ain'ts." But Julia heard beyond the grammar. She heard the story behind the words—the hopelessness, the hatred, the relentless deterioration.

How did he escape? She forced a thought to the back of her mind: was this life as an enlisted soldier in Vietnam

97

really an improvement at all? Or was this young man destined to spend his life in some form of hell?

"Why did you stop?" Julia realized that Jake had stopped speaking.

"Thought you might be bored."

"No. Tell me how you got away," she urged.

A church group had come. To help. They brought books that Jake couldn't read because he had never been taught, and they brought dreams. Jake listened and dreamed. And when they left, he went with them, as a stowaway in their truck. They discovered him when they got to Charleston. They didn't send him back; they knew it would kill him. They suggested that he join the army, knowing that it might kill him, too. But there weren't many choices.

"I was sixteen and couldn't read or write or add or nothin'," he explained.

"How did you get into the army?"

"Ma'am, no offense, but it ain't hard to join the army when there's a war on. They were real happy to see my big, healthy body. Don't need no brains to pull a trigger."

Julia shuddered, not because of the way he said it, but because she knew it was true.

Jake was silent again. That was the story, Julia mused. Illiterate coal miner's son saves life of blue-blood intellectual. She lives happily ever after with her husband, the general. And he . . . what? Dies in the jungle five miles north? Physically survives but goes crazy? Returns a "hero" from a war everyone already hates and becomes, like the war, an object of hatred? Out of desperation returns to the coal mine? A handsome man crippled by his tongue and his words. Julia thought of *Pygmalion*. I wonder . . .

"This ain't the end for me," he suddenly declared. Had he read her thoughts? "It can't be."

"What will you become?"

"Dunno. I want to go to college. To learn everything, then decide. I learn quick. But I still cain't read or talk right. I sorta hoped I'd learn some in the army."

So he was disappointed with the army. Julia was relieved. But he had set himself up for disappointment. The idea of going to college! He had never even gone to school. She wondered when in his life he would be forced to give up his dreams and what it would do to him. He was fighting for his life. And he had saved hers. Could she do anything to save his?

"Do you think you owe me?" He was reading her thoughts again. She looked at him. He returned her stare with his clear blue eyes. Serious, earnest. And, what was it? Confidence. The confidence of a survivor.

"You know that I do."

"Then . . ." He paused.

Julia waited. He could demand that she make love with him and she could call it even. Two moments of frenzy, emotion, and risk, different, but somehow similar. Or he could make much greater demands. She held her breath.

"You help me. Teach me to talk like you. Teach me to read. Teach me to write."

Julia flicked the water with her long ivory fingers, then looked at him and said carefully, "All right, Jake, I'll try."

"Okay! Let's start!" He began to get out of the pool, pushing his body out of the water effortlessly with his strong arms. Halfway out he added, casually, "Oh. Close your eyes."

It was a taunt, more articulate in tone than it ever could have been in words. It said, *Play this silly modesty game if you like, but I am unashamed of my body.*

Julia didn't even blink. She watched his perfectly formed body as he toweled off, wrapped the towel around his waist, and collected his hot, dry clothes. Before he went to the dressing room, he stopped beside her.

"Don't have to start today. With everything that's happened . . . husband home soon . . ."

"No, it's fine. In fact it will be good to keep my mind occupied. My husband will be away for at least three days."

"Who is your husband?"

Julia told him. It made him almost stand at attention and did make him seriously reconsider his proposal. Julia's husband wasn't *a* general, he was *the* general. But he was so much older than Julia.

"He leaves you here alone?"

"I have guards. You know that. I am perfectly safe. What happened today happened because I broke the rules. I'm safe if I stay here, or get chauffeured directly to the base and back."

She really believes she is safe, Jake thought. Doesn't it occur to her that guards and chauffeurs are easily overpowered? Julia was a target, the easiest kind—naive, defenseless, trusting.

Jake shuddered for her life the way, moments before, Julia had shuddered, deep inside, for his.

"Frank, he saved my life and do you know what he asked for in return? He asked simply for a right he should have had from the day he was born. He is over here fighting to get that right. He's risking his life to earn the right to be like everyone else. It makes me sick."

"Do you want to help him, Julia, or do you just feel obliged?" Frank asked gently.

"I want to, Frank. Wait until you meet him. You'll see why. You'll want to help him, too. You'll want to make sure that he never has to spend another day fighting in his life."

There, she had said it. Frank had been back for two days. They had discussed "the incident" over and over. They had discussed Julia's promise to help Jake. They had discussed what Frank wanted, to send Julia back to Washington. And now, finally, she said what she wanted—she wanted Jake to be safe.

Frank took a long moment to let Julia's words sink in. It was of a different magnitude than simply wanting to help an illiterate hick learn to read and write. This boy meant a great deal to Julia. How much? Frank wondered. He sighed and gazed at his beautiful young wife. He didn't doubt her love for him or her fidelity.

But he knew, too, that she was a woman of whims and fancies, a spoiled little girl. Spoiled by her father, Frank's best friend. And spoiled by Frank. Julia got what she wanted; she expected it. Frank adored spoiling her. But this request . . .

Of course it was in his power. Anything to do with this war was in his power. He could send the boy and Julia back to Washington tonight. Was she serious about this, or was it just a passing fancy?

"Did he ask for this?"

"No! He asked for what I told you, that I teach him. Nothing more. This is my idea and I haven't mentioned it to him." Because, Julia thought, Jake would not agree. It was part of his confidence; he was immortal.

"Do you think it's fair?" Frank knew the second he asked that it was unwise to ask his liberal wife if asking someone not to fight was fair.

"Fair? Fair is a meaningless word in the context of war. Or for that matter in any context that applies to Jake's life. He hasn't had one moment of 'fair' in seventeen years. But it is just and right and, please, you can do this, can't you?"

"You know I can. May I just wait until after I meet him? If I am going to transfer him to a non-combat status, I need to at least decide what he is qualified for. He has to be something other than favorite pupil and mascot of the general's wife." He kissed her. "He'll be here tomorrow?"

"Yes. He has guard duty tonight, all night. He'll be over for lessons in the afternoon and he'll stay for dinner. He has the weekend off, so he'll be here most of the weekend. There should be no more 'ain'ts' by Monday. I love you."

Before he met Jake, there was only one person in the world whom Frank truly loved: Julia. Once he met Jake, there were two. Within minutes of meeting Jake that evening, Frank knew that he would protect him. Somehow he would get Jake and Julia back to Washington soon. It had been unforgivably selfish of him to bring Julia to Vietnam. But she had insisted.

The telephone rang during dinner that evening. Frank returned after twenty minutes, looking deeply troubled.

"Darling?"

"Bad skirmish up north. Lots of casualties. I have to go to the base."

"I'll come with you, sir." Jake stood up.

"No!" Frank and Julia said in unison, startling each other and Jake with their vehemence.

"No, Jake. It doesn't involve this base. This is your weekend of liberty. Stay here. Take care of Julia. In the long run your weekend of lessons is much more important." If I have my way, and I intend to, this will be your last weekend in Vietnam, Frank thought but didn't voice it aloud.

"Yes sir. Thank you, sir." Jake smiled.

He would have willingly gone with Frank, Julia thought with horror.

"Call me, Frank. And be careful," Julia said.

"I'm safe, Julia. You know that."

The day after she agreed to teach Jake, Julia made several lengthy calls to the United States. To her friend Kate, who taught third grade. To Miss Willis, her English teacher at Bryn Mawr. To the Superintendent of Public Schools in Arlington, to find out how to get a high school diploma by mail. To her personal secretary, who was given the task of collecting, packing, and mailing the books, flash cards, equivalency examinations recommended by Kate, Miss Willis, and Superintendent Doyle. With these, Julia would develop a systematic program.

Until their arrival, she and Jake would work on the items that she found the most distasteful—the ain'ts, the cain'ts, the incomplete sentences, and ma'ams, and the ugly, thick accent.

Julia assumed that Jake despised his inability to speak as much as she did. But she was wrong. Jake regarded it as an obstacle in the way of what he wanted to do with his life, something he wanted to change as a means to an end, not because it was inherently wrong. When Julia would say how "awful" his accent was or how she "couldn't stand" the way he said something, he withdrew, became silent and less confident. It took longer for him to find the correct words and he would begin to call her "ma'am."

"Jake, when you think, when you daydream, do you do it in words?" Julia was curious. She was certain that locked behind the illiteracy, the verbal expression limited by a pitifully small vocabulary, was an intent, sensitive, imaginative mind. But how could she know? She had to teach him the words before he could tell her about his thoughts. But she knew what he was like, because his eyes, his graceful body, his strong hands, were so articulate . . .

"No, ma'am." Julia scowled at him. Jake was angry at her for insulting him again. He returned the scowl. "No, *ma'am* I think in pictures, like dreams."

"Images," Julia said, relieved. "Images."

"Images," Jake repeated. Julia made a rule that every time she used a word that Jake didn't know, he had to repeat it, pronouncing it exactly the way she did.

After Frank left for the base that night, Jake and Julia "worked," learning new words, mimicking Julia's voice, conjugal verbs until three in the morning. Frank had called at midnight.

"I have to stay at the base tonight. We really miscalculated on their numbers. How's the kid?"

"He's a quick learner." Julia smiled at "the kid," the man-boy whose eyes made her lose track for a moment and whose innocent, inadvertent touch as he leaned toward her to watch her write a word gave her goose bumps. Frank's description jerked her unceremoniously back to reality. A seventeen-year-old kid. But emotionally, Jake had never been a kid.

"I need a break."

It was mid-afternoon the next day. They had been working without a break for four hours. Frank had called to say he would be home for a late dinner. Julia stretched, catlike. Jake saw that she looked tired and felt a pang of guilt. Was this a fair demand? It must be boring for her, exhausting to be a drill sergeant. And yet, Julia giggled often enough, and her violet eyes sparkled. And she nudged him playfully when he did something correctly. She seemed to enjoy it.

"Okay." Jake did not want a break. He had accomplished more in the week he had known Julia than he had in seventeen years. She was the key that would unlock his life for him. He was impatient, but it was unfair and unwise to push Julia. He was dependent on her good will.

"How about a swim?" she asked.

"Sure." Jake stretched, too, and as he looked at Julia, his mind left the future and his goals and settled firmly on the moment. There had never been moments like this in his life, sipping iced tea, talking—or at least trying to—with a beautiful, exciting, intelligent woman, going for a swim with her. He would have moments like these in his new life, the life she was helping him begin.

"I guess I need some trunks."

"Really?" Julia tossed the question over her shoulder as he left the room.

Jake undressed, neatly folded his clothes, wrapped a towel around his waist, started toward the pool, and stopped. He sat down on the stool in the dressing room and buried his face in his hands.

Five minutes later he unwrapped the towel, folded it

neatly, and got dressed. He walked through the house to the master bedroom. The door was closed. He could hear her.

"Julia?" he whispered next to the door.

"Jake?" She opened the door. She was wearing the mid-thigh terry robe, buttoned shut. "I'm almost ready . . . Why are you dressed?"

Julia backed into the room and sat on the bed. Jake leaned against the door jamb.

"Had . . . I had an image. It scared me." Jake paused and stared at her with a look that she had never seen before in his crystal-clear blue eyes. But it was a look she recognized.

"Scared you?"

"Because I wanted it so bad." He looked down, then looked at her again. "So much."

"What?" She knew. She wanted it, too.

"You. You and me."

Julia swallowed hard; her mouth was dry. Her heart pounded. Underneath the robe, she was naked. But had she really thought it would happen? Or was it just a fantasy? But this wasn't fantasy. He was there, telling her he wanted her. But he was dressed.

"Yes," she whispered. Neither of them moved.

"I'm going now."

"Going? Where?"

"To the base. To think. I have to decide. You have to decide."

"No." Julia didn't want to think about it. She didn't want to think about making love to a seventeen-year-old. She didn't want to think about being unfaithful to the man she loved. She didn't want to think. She just wanted to feel her body against his. She just wanted him to speak to her with his hands and lips; to speak the passion that she knew was there but that he had no words to express.

The rules were different here. War changed the rules. She could have been murdered a week ago. War wasn't a time for making thoughtful, rational decisions. It was a time for living out passions and desires. She wanted Jake. She wanted him now.

"Don't go." Julia stretched her arms out to him, but he didn't move. She walked across the room. She touched his cheek and his neck.

He kissed her and her body trembled. He held her against his taut-muscled body, his lips softly, gently, pressing against hers. Over and over. She wanted more, was impatient for more. But she couldn't move; he held her too tightly.

"Julia. We have to think about it." Their lips touched as he spoke.

"I have thought about it," she lied.

"I haven't. Not about all of it." "Ramifications" was not a word in Jake's vocabulary. But the potential ramifications of sleeping with another man's wife, the general's wife, the woman on whom his future depended, cluttered his mind. He had to sort it out, to see where it fit in the set of rules that Jake had created for himself, rules that included fulfilling obligations, honoring commitments, and moving with caution. His plans were too important to risk for a moment of pleasure.

But if his feelings for Julia were as honest as he believed them to be, then it couldn't be wrong. Because at that time in his life, Jake believed that, above all, there could be love. And when there was love, there were no rules other than the directives of the heart.

"Jake, stay. It will be all right. I promise you." Why was she so desperate? Julia, who believed in fidelity, who had taunted many men and rejected them. Julia, who didn't believe in the passion of the moment. Julia, who had enjoyed the games she had played with men before she married Frank. But Jake wasn't playing and neither was she.

"It's mostly wrong. But if we both decide, then . . ."

It's lucky he speaks so well with his eyes, Julia thought. She understood what he meant, the seriousness of their decision. And it scared her. Now the image scared them both. She nodded and his lips brushed against her hair.

"I'll be back at ten. For dinner with you and Frank. And more lessons." He didn't balk at Frank's name.

For the rest of the day, Julia paced and fidgeted. She tried to devise lesson plans for Jake, but she couldn't concentrate. Finally, she made herself sit in the living room with no distractions and think. And, in time, she made her decision.

By ten-thirty she began to worry. Frank and Jake were both late, and neither had called. At eleven-thirty the phone rang. Julia answered it in the middle of the first ring.

"Julia, I'm sorry. All hell has broken loose. This was my first chance to call. Go ahead and eat if you haven't already. I'll be home within the hour." Frank sounded exhausted.

"Jake isn't here," Julia said very quietly.

"What? Where is he?" The worry in Frank's voice was contagious.

"He went back to the base about three. To rest. He was planning to return tonight. Frank . . . ?"

"His unit went into combat at six."

"Fighting at night?"

"No, but the enemy is only five miles north. We have to be in position by dawn." His voice trailed off. Fighting and casualties. Too many casualties. They had seriously underrated the ability of the Viet Cong to traverse dense jungle quickly. And now, they were paying dearly. And Jake.

"Did Jake have to go? He had liberty, didn't he?" Julia asked pleadingly, but she knew the answer. He didn't have to go, but he would go. In this circumstance, he would go.

"Where else could he be," Frank said wearily. It wasn't a question.

The fighting began just before dawn. A full moon and a single star still glowed in the pale gray sky.

It was a sound that Jake would always remember, like

the other sounds that would awaken him, sweat-soaked, for years to come—the soft thud of bullets hitting healthy muscled flesh; the louder thud of that flesh falling to the sodden earth; the sound of screaming men and the deafening noise of machine guns.

Those sounds were already indelibly etched in his memory, even before this day. This day, his last day in combat, a new memory was made. He heard the sound of his blood pulsing through his head. He heard the sound of his femur shattering, like a young tree, falling, splintering. And then, he heard his own screams, drowning out the other noises. The sound of his own screaming, the sound of his own pain.

Chapter Seven

Julia was allowed to visit Jake in the base hospital the day after he was injured. She walked into the hot, crowded open ward of the hospital with trepidation. Would Jake blame her for this? What had he decided in those few minutes before he went to combat?

She would probably never know. Their relationship—hers, Frank's and Jake's—had become clearly defined in the past twenty-four hours. She and Frank were his parents, his guardians. She would fly to Washington with him as soon as possible and be with him, like a mother, through the surgery that the doctors said was necessary, to pick pieces of shattered bone out of the flesh and to insert a metal bar into the marrow of his femur.

What had he decided? she wondered as she walked past bed after bed of sick, wounded, moaning young men. Would Jake be moaning with pain? She prayed not, it would make her guilt even worse.

He smiled as she approached. The cool, elegant vision whose life he had saved a week before was incongruous in this ugly setting of pain and death, as she had been on the streets of Saigon, and, as she had been then, oblivious to her incongruity, full of life and loveliness.

"I am so sorry!" she blurted out when she saw him, tears filling her eyes. Despite the smile and the still-clear blue eyes, he was in obvious pain. His skin was white and slightly damp; his fists were clenched under the sheets. She touched his face—it was cold and wet.

"It's not your fault," Jake said firmly.

Julia stared at him, trying to read his eyes. If he ever blamed her, he had now forgiven her. There was no anger or hatred in his eyes. But there was pain. And sadness. Julia wanted to hold him, like a mother holding her child. Instead she found one of his hands and held it.

"I guess we are scheduled to fly to Washington tomorrow."

"We?"

"Of course. And be prepared to learn. We have about twenty hours of flight time." She looked at his pale face and the muscles in his jaw reflexively contracting. He was in a great deal of pain. "That is, if you feel like it," Julia said softly and gently touched his damp forehead.

"Yes, ma'am!" Jake forced a smile.

Two hours before their scheduled landing in Washington, the intensity of Jake's pain suddenly increased. Until then, Jake and Julia had occupied themselves with "lessons," Jake's memory being only slightly blurred by the morphine that the army nurse administered to him at regular intervals.

The pain was new, sudden, severe. Julia saw it in his face immediately.

"What, Jake?"

"My leg. Something has happened. Call someone, please."

The airplane carried in its huge belly sixty wounded soldiers, four nurses, one doctor, and Julia. Throughout the flight the doctor and nurses were kept frantically busy with the medications, dressing changes, intravenous lines, and blood transfusions. Jake required relatively little nursing care; in fact, until then he had been the most stable patient on the plane. He was simply being sent home for definitive surgery. An eager orthopedic resident who had been lucky enough to escape duty in a combat zone would learn, from Jake, about the treachery of shrapnel in flesh. And the resident would learn the difficult but highly successful technique of intramedullary nailing, the surgical installation of a metal nail into the marrow of the femur to hold the healing bone fragments in line. Until that moment Jake had been a "routine" case, a bad open fracture but stable.

Julia walked from cot to cot until she found the doctor. He was ordering antibiotics for a soldier whose fever had climbed to one hundred four degrees. Julia looked at his tired, young face and felt two simultaneous emotions—panic and compassion. It was too much for one man to care for; he needed to rest. *But not until he took care of Jake!*

That the problem was serious was instantly apparent to Jake, Julia, the doctor, and the nurse as soon as the bandages were removed. The leg was swollen, tense with fluid. The color had gone from flesh pink to bruise purple. Brownish fluid stained the sterile dressings that the doctor removed. The skin was beginning to blister.

"When did the pain start?

"Five minutes ago."

"Maybe the morphine masked the pain," he murmured to the nurse. It was a comment Jake never forgot. Would the outcome have been different if he hadn't taken the morphine, if he had felt the muscles in his leg dying earlier than he had? In the months and years of pain that lay ahead, Jake would rarely take anything for relief.

"What is it, doctor?" Julia demanded. Panic had totally supplanted compassion. This man had to do something to help Jake, no matter how tired he was or how many other sick patients he had to care for.

At that moment the doctor was painfully aware that he was looking at the patient in the most serious condition on the plane.

He ordered penicillin, six million units, stat. And he put Jake on oxygen. Then he went to the cockpit.

He returned in twenty minutes; he looked more tired but, strangely, relieved. He had a plan.

"It's called clostridial myonecrosis," he began.

"Gas gangrene!" Julia hissed.

The doctor eyed her with renewed curiosity. It had been remarkable enough that she was on the flight, the incredibly beautiful young wife of the general personally caring for an illiterate enlisted man. Not only caring for, but obviously enjoying the interaction. The doctor had hoped, early on, to have a chance to speak with her, but it hadn't been possible. Now he had his chance, and she knew that clostridial myonecrosis was the same as gas gangrene.

"Yes. Gas gangrene. An infection of the muscles caused by a bacterium. The infection causes the muscles to die; that's what causes all the pain. The treatment . . ." He took his eyes off Julia. She was too beautiful, too worried, and too smart. In a moment she would start asking about his "chances." He focused on Jake. Jake's respirations had doubled; he was becoming septic. His blood pressure had probably dropped. He gestured for the nurse to check vital signs. But Jake's mental status was normal. His thought processes were clear. That was the eerie feature of the disease. He remembered learning about it in medical school; the patient knows his plight, understands that he is going to die, and accepts death peacefully. Jake did not look peaceful.

"The treatment is removal of the infected muscle—in a hyperbaric oxygen chamber if one is available. I have radioed ahead to Walter Reed. The operating room will be ready to operate, in the chamber, as soon as we arrive. I need to have you sign a consent for surgery now. It will save time."

"Can you give him something for pain?" Julia asked. It was more like an order.

"No!" the doctor and Jake said in unison.

"His blood pressure is too low," the doctor added.

* * *

The doctors removed all but one muscle from Jake's thigh. There was argument in the operating room about leaving that muscle. How could it possibly not be infected? Isn't it safer just to remove it?

"Easier to remove it now. But not necessarily dangerous to leave it. And if it is viable, maybe the boy can walk again. Sometime. We're going to leave it." Dr. Richard Phillips was the senior orthopedic surgeon. There was little point in arguing with Dr. Phillips. He was a cautious man, and he was usually right.

Jake was hospitalized for almost one year. He had multiple surgical procedures: the intramedullary nailing, skin grafts, tendon insertion of Dr. Phillips's "viable" muscle into the tibia. During that time he learned to walk, a new way, to read, to write. And to speak like a gentleman.

Julia was solely responsible for his beautiful speech, his elegant vocabulary, and his style of speaking. Once she was confident that he had the tools, Julia turned over the task of educating him—teaching him history, science, mathematics, geography, literature—to a variety of scholarly, expensive, and intrigued tutors.

Jake became a pet, everyone's pet. The nurses' favorite patient. Dr. Phillips's star—reportable—patient. Julia's unbelievably successful project. The tutors' favorite, most interesting pupil. Throughout the relentless daily lessons, Jake remained even tempered, pleasant, entertaining.

"He's a puppet, Julia. Your puppet, the doctors' puppet, the tutors' puppet. It is no good for him. He has to be allowed to develop something on his own. He is being smothered. His personality—his charming, boyish personality—is being smothered." It had been a year. Frank had been home for three months. In those months he had visited Jake frequently but, until that night in early June, he had never voiced any objections to Jake's care or the program Julia had planned for Jake.

"I had no idea you felt this way, Frank."

"I had a revelation today. We have to get him out of the hospital, give him a break from the lessons. Let him be."

Jake was released from the hospital the next day. Julia cried when she saw how happy he was. Frank was right. Julia canceled all lessons for the summer. Jake was on his own to learn whatever he wanted—to learn about living with his new, but damaged, body and his finely cultivated mind.

"Julia and I would like to have you live with us, son, but it's up to you. I know you're in need of some privacy. We have a pretty big house."

"Thank you, sir . . . Frank."

Jake moved into the first floor guest room of Frank and Julia's white colonial in Arlington. To Julia's amazement, Jake spent hours by himself, in his room and walking slowly, painfully, through the rose and lilac gardens on their estate.

"He has to find himself, to decide who he is and what he is going to be. He has to reconcile the new Jake with who and where he has been," Frank said. He was very proud of the young man that slowly emerged over the summer.

Julia didn't know how to behave. Jake no longer needed a drill sergeant or a mother. Julia didn't know what he needed and felt uncomfortable about approaching him. Jake had to be the initiator. He had to let her know how he planned to live the next phase of his life. She waited.

One evening at dinner in early July, Julia announced that she was going to the symphony.

"Alone?" Frank asked.

"You haven't suddenly become a symphony buff, after a half century of loathing have you?" she teased. Frank smiled and shook his head emphatically. Neither looked at Jake.

"It probably wouldn't surprise you to hear that I have never been to a symphony. If it's anything like the music that Julia plays whenever you're away, Frank, I think I'd enjoy it very much."

"You've listened to my music for one month, all day every day, and this is the first time you've mentioned it." Julia's

114

heart pounded. She wanted Jake to go to the concert with her.

"I think you would have known if I hadn't liked it." Jake smiled at her. A man's smile—a smile of appreciation.

Over the next three years, Jake and Julia spent many afternoons and evenings at galleries, operas, symphonies, the theatre. These were their shared passions. Jake's passion for the arts was instinctive. No one had taught him what artists, what musical pieces, what plays to love. He had his own taste—clear, definite, and invariably similar to Julia's.

I didn't teach him this, she thought, often. This is Jake, who he is, what he is. *And he is so much like me.*

Frank took Jake to see his passions—football, baseball, hockey, basketball. Jake had no instinctive interest in sports, but it hardly mattered. It was time with Frank, and that mattered a great deal. Jake idolized Frank. He admired Frank's honest patriotism, Frank's scrupulous fairness, Frank's uncanny intuition, Frank's unpretentious genius. Frank spoke little, but his words were important. Frank honored commitments, kept promises, always. And he deeply loved Julia. And Jake.

Frank also took Jake with him to the Pentagon. These trips were more than just an opportunity to be with Frank. It was a chance to meet government officials and military strategists, men like Stuart Dawson . . .

Jake and Julia and Frank lived together for three years as a family. Frank and Jake were father and son; Frank and Julia, husband and wife; but Jake and Julia . . .

Julia was mother, sister, friend, teacher, companion, and rival for Frank's attention. But, despite that day in Saigon, she was never Jake's lover. In all the time they spent together, they never discussed what would have happened if Jake's regiment hadn't gone into battle. They never asked what decision the other had made that afternoon—it didn't matter. Neither would betray Frank, not now, not in the "real world," not loving Frank the way they both did.

But the sexual tension was there. Though the fantasy had

remained in Saigon, the feelings had returned home with them. As Jake became a man, as he evolved before her eyes into the independent, thoughtful man that he was, Julia wanted him even more. And she wanted him to want her. In Saigon, a seventeen-year-old illiterate boy had wanted a glamorous, wealthy, well-educated older woman. It made sense. In Saigon Julia had been a symbol of the world Jake wanted for himself.

But now he was a handsome, well-educated man in his own right. The social and educational barriers had vanished. The issue was painfully simple and uncluttered—he was a man; she was a woman. Did he desire her? Did he want her, still?

Julia wondered, and it tormented her. She believed that Jake still wanted her. She caught him, in rare, unguarded moments, gazing at her with the sale expression in his clear blue eyes that she had seen that afternoon in Saigon.

But he never talked about it. They never talked about it. There was no point.

The unresolved and unresolvable sexual tension between them translated into irritability, taunting, and criticism. The situation was aggravated when Jake became identified as a highly desirable, eminently eligible bachelor.

Jake was the prize of the season among the upper echelons of Arlington society. It was presumed that he was a nephew—Frank's or Julia's, no one really knew. It didn't matter; the lineage on either side was blue-blooded and steeped in wealth. Mothers wanted him at debutante balls. Fathers wanted him in their sight, because they knew their daughters wanted him—in their silk-sheeted beds.

Jake obliged the daughters, discreetly, politely. He never fell in love with any of them, but he capably satisfied their needs for romance and lust. And when the affair was over, they parted, invariably, as friends. For the girls, the end was greeted with a mixture of sadness, romantic memories, and, strangely, relief. Their attraction to him was magnetic—uncontrollable and somewhat unsettling. They felt more comfortable when it was over.

Julia watched Jake's affairs with the Arlington socialites with an emotional medley of pride, jealousy, and anger—anger at herself for being jealous and anger at Jake for flaunting the affairs in front of her.

"They are so young," Jake said to her one evening before leaving for yet another garden party. He was trying to tell her that he preferred older women. Not any older women, just her.

"Your age," Julia snapped, irritated.

"I am not that age. I never have been."

"I imagine they are marvelous. Sexually, I mean. Sleek, nubile bodies," Julia taunted, not wanting an answer.

"Yes, of course. Truly marvelous. Eager. Willing. Unsullied. Unspoiled. Unused." Jake glared at her. Conversations like this were becoming more frequent and they angered her. How did she think he felt, living in a house where Julia shared her bed with Frank, not him? Julia had no right to chide him.

During those years, Jake and Julia had a few magic moments, unencumbered by taunting, jealousy, and competition—an outdoor concert in the spring in Washington, innocently holding hands strolling along cherry-tree-lined lanes or a rare quiet, thoughtful conversation about a play, a novel, a poem, a painting.

But as Jake became more fully formed as a handsome, sexual, confident, well-educated man, the tension between them increased. As a strong and independent man, Jake no longer needed Julia. But he needed other women.

Three months before the autumn of Jake's freshman year at Stanford, Frank was appointed Ambassador to France. In July, Frank and Julia flew to Paris. At the last moment Jake announced his intention to remain in Arlington for the summer. Frank's initial disappointment that Jake would not be accompanying them was quickly forgotten when he saw the effect it had on Julia. Frank arrived in Paris with his wife who seemed, miraculously, younger, happier, and more relaxed than she had been in the four years since Jake's injury.

Chapter Eight

"Hello?" Stephen could tell instantly that it was a long-distance call. He tensed involuntarily. Long-distance phone calls were like telegrams, bearers of bad tidings. It was several moments before the voice, small and distant, spoke.

"Jake?" it asked. It was not a voice Stephen recognized. Not a woman that he knew.

"This is Stephen."

"Is Jake there?' The voice became smaller, edged with panic. Frail.

Stephen handed the telephone to Jake with an expression that warned him that something was wrong.

"Hello."

"Jake!"

"Julia. What's wrong?"

"Frank is dead."

"No!" Jake's face drained of color. His eyes became damp. Stephen watched helplessly.

"Jake, I need you to be with me through this. I don't know if I can make it. Can you come?"

"Of course." His voice was soft, soft and gentle. "Where are you?"

"Paris, still. But we . . . I . . . Frank and I . . . Frank's body . . ." The voice stopped. Jake waited. In a few moments Julia spoke again. Flat, controlled. Barely controlled.

"The funeral will be in Arlington day after tomorrow. Can you meet me at the house tomorrow? I should be there by mid-afternoon."

"I will meet your plane."

"No. The State Department is handling all that. Please just be at home when I get there. Can you?" The panic was back in her voice.

"I will see you tomorrow."

Jake heard a faint "Thank-you" before the line went dead. Slowly he replaced the receiver and thought about what she had said. And what she hadn't said—how Frank had died; when Frank had died. Jake hadn't even told her how sorry he was. But that didn't need saying. They shared the love for Frank. And now they would share the grief.

Jake held his hand on the receiver for several moments, absorbed in his thoughts, oblivious to Stephen, who waited helplessly. Then Jake dialed the directory assistance operator and asked for the number of an airline. Then he depressed the disconnect button, redialed, and calmly made reservations for that evening's nonstop flight to Washington DC. First Class. Open return. Only after he hung up the phone and started to walk into his bedroom did he notice Stephen and realize that he had been waiting.

"My . . ." Jake hesitated. His voice was no longer strong or calm. "My father died. I have to go."

"I am so sorry," Stephen replied helplessly.

They had been roommates since they had enrolled at Stanford one and a half years before. Jake had never mentioned his family. Stephen had assumed that the family relations were strained, or, at least, distant. But Jake's obvious grief at his father's death indicated deep love and affection. Who was the young woman on the telephone? Stephen wondered. A sister that Jake had never mentioned? His voice had been so caring, loving, when he had spoken to her. Stephen was used to unanswered questions about his roommate's private life.

"What can I do, Jake? To help."

119

Jake looked startled, then grateful, at Stephen's offer. It continued to surprise him that someone like Stephen was such a loyal friend. Jake shrugged; suddenly he couldn't make any more plans or decisions.

"I will drive you to the airport," Stephen said definitely. "And I will let your instructors know that you will be away for awhile. Okay?" Stephen wanted to comfort Jake, to put his hand on his shoulder. But it wasn't possible. Not with Jake.

"Thank you," Jake whispered.

The next afternoon Julia walked into her elegant home in Arlington and into Jake's arms. She started crying as soon as she saw him and began to sob as he held her. Jake cried silently. Finally Julia's body stopped shaking and the sobs subsided. She rubbed her eyes and looked up at him, smiling weakly.

"Seeing you makes it more real. In Paris it was all protocol, politics, and arrangements. But here. In his home. With you. Without him. He should be here. I want him here." Julia started crying again.

"I know. I want him, too." Jake squeezed his eyes tightly in a vain attempt to fight back tears of his own.

"You must be exhausted," Jake said in a few moments, looking at her sunken black eyes and thin, drawn skin. "Will you try to rest?"

She nodded, turned, and started toward the master bedroom—her bedroom, hers and Frank's. She stopped; Jake watched her shoulders sag.

"I can't go in there alone," she whispered, her back to Jake. "Come with me."

Jake took her hand and led her along the French wallpapered corridor to the bedroom. Julia stopped at the door.

"I'm afraid."

"I know."

Jake sat on the antique French chaise longue in front of

the marble fireplace and waited while Julia changed. Finally she emerged from her dressing room, hair brushed, face washed, wearing a modest white cotton nightgown with long sleeves, pearl buttons, and a ruffled collar. She looked like a small child ready for bed.

"Shall I tuck you in?"

Julia smiled. Small, frail. And very pretty.

Jake smoothed the handmade quilt over her, touched her gently on her cheek, and turned to leave.

"Jake." She grabbed his arm. "Just hold me until I fall asleep. Please." She lifted the covers and motioned for him to join her. He took off his shoes, his slacks, his shirt, and lay beside her, holding her cuddled against him like a child. He stroked her gently, wordlessly. In moments they were both asleep.

They buried Frank the next day, a formal, impersonal ceremony attended by diplomats, politicians, military officers. Jake and Julia hated it. Frank, the Frank they knew, had been stolen from them, wrapped in pomp and circumstance, to be stored permanently in the realm of the famous dead—history.

That night, and the next, they lay together in Frank and Julia's bed, huddling like frightened children, hiding under the covers, afraid to come out.

On the third day after the funeral, Julia said, "The lawyers are coming tomorrow to read the will. After that you should go back to school."

Jake looked startled at the suddenness of Julia's decision that he should leave, and at the fact that she had made it without consulting him. Julia misinterpreted the cause of his surprise and smiled wryly. "You really should be here for the reading of the will."

Frank's estate was enormous because, like Julia, he had been born wealthy. And the wealth begat more wealth. According to Frank's last will and testament, the almost limitless wealth that was his legacy was to be divided equally between his beloved wife, Julia, and the man whom he would have chosen to have been his son, Jake.

Jake was stunned, speechless. After the lawyers left he said, "It's wrong, Julia. It should all be yours."

Julia laughed. For the first time since Frank's death, her light, bubbling laughter filled the room.

"Jake, darling. I don't need it. Before my father died, I had a small fortune. After he died, it became a huge fortune. I don't need a penny of Frank's money. But we discussed it and decided, purely to prevent gossip, that you and I should divide it. Both Frank and I wanted to give it all to you!"

Jake shook his head. "I don't know what to say."

Julia shrugged. Money was part of her life and always had been. She used it to get what she wanted when she wanted it. She became expert at managing money, investing, buying, selling. Julia knew how to make money make more money. She had shrewdness coupled with uncanny impulses. Like almost everything she did, Julia viewed it as a game, a challenge; and, as with most of her endeavors, she had mastered it effortlessly.

"It's only money," she said nonchalantly. It couldn't, for example, bring Frank back.

"It's freedom, Julia."

"It is true that with this inheritance, you will never have to work a day in your life. Neither will your children, or your grandchildren. I wonder what you'll do," Julia mused.

Jake was silent, but his mind was reeling. They spoke very little that evening and at bedtime Julia said, "You are leaving soon, aren't you?"

"Yes."

"Back to Stanford."

"Yes. Tomorrow or the day after. I should meet with someone about the estate."

"No rush. It will take a while to settle. And they'll find you, never doubt it. I'll tell you who to listen to, and if you want my advice . . ."

"Then I'll leave tomorrow. If you're okay?" He stared at her. She didn't return his gaze but nodded slowly.

"Just okay. But it's time to make the next move, whatever it is." Julia paused, then smiled. "Separate bedrooms, I suppose. I guess I need to know if I can sleep alone."

In the middle of the night she came to his bedroom. Jake was awake. He hadn't been asleep at all. He had been thinking—about his fortune, about his life, his plans. About Julia.

"Hi," she whispered.

"Hi." He pulled her to him, not as a father to a suffering child, but as a man to a woman. They were in his bed, not Frank's. And she had come to him.

He kissed her and she responded, as she had so many years before in Saigon. But, as in Saigon, their passion was encumbered, still, by Frank. They both knew it.

"Julia?" he whispered. She knew the question; he didn't have to ask it. And they both knew the answer.

She nodded, her cheek rubbing gently against his.

"Yes. It's too soon. Just hold me. I'm not going to practice sleeping by myself as long as you're still in the house. It's too great a luxury. Tomorrow, after you're gone . . ."

After you're gone too, she thought and pressed herself closer.

Five months after Frank's death, Julia flew to San Francisco to visit Jake. Unannounced. Unexpected. Uninvited. She spent the first evening by herself in her suite at the Fairmont.

The following day, she took a sixty-dollar taxi ride from the entrance of the Fairmont Hotel to the front door of Jake's dormitory at Stanford.

She knocked lightly on the door of Jake's room.

"Come in!" Stephen was studying at his desk with his back to the door. Interruptions were common. The intruder in fact, rarely knocked and immediately made his request known—can I borrow a book, class notes, slide rule, your car . . . ?

Stephen heard the door open and close quietly, but instead of hearing the usual request, there was silence. Curious, he spun around in his swivel desk chair.

When he saw her, he simultaneously gasped and stood up. Julia smiled.

"I'm sorry that I startled you. You must be Stephen." She walked toward him and extended a white-gloved hand. "I'm Julia."

Julia? Stephen's mind, blurred by Julia's unexpected and dazzling appearance, tried to focus. Who is Julia? It came to him in little bits—the distant voice on the phone the night Jake's father died; the long, late-night phone calls Jake made on the private line that he had had installed after his return from the funeral. A sister?

"Jake and I are friends." Julia settled the issue.

Julia had the clear advantage; she knew him, his name, and whatever Jake had chosen to tell her about him. And he knew nothing about her. And she had another advantage. On this eighty-degree day in May Julia was cool and calm in a white linen suit with a violet silk blouse and her jet black hair knotted elegantly on top of her head. Stephen, shirtless, shoeless, wearing only his Stanford crew trunks, felt hot and humid.

"Is Jake expecting you?"

"No, it's a surprise. Is he here?" A shadow of worry crossed her face.

"He's here, on campus. He has a political science seminar this afternoon. He'll be back in about two hours. I can go find him if you want me to."

"No, it wouldn't do to interrupt him."

She knew Jake well; that was clear. She knew that his studies were a top priority. Stephen wondered if she knew why Jake's studies were so important. He wondered, also, whether or not it would make a difference if Jake knew that Julia was waiting.

"I'll just wait if you don't mind." Julia glanced around the hot, stuffy dormitory room with its meager furnishings, decrepit sofa, rugless floor, parking lot view and marveled that Jake had not moved to an apartment off campus. She knew the reason, of course. Jake valued his friendship with Stephen and Stephen couldn't afford off-campus housing.

Besides, Julia thought, Jake doesn't want to be different. She smiled at the thought. As if Jake could ever be anything but different, unique. Remarkable. But maybe he could lose himself in the melting pot of the Stanford campus of the late sixties. Because they were all trying so hard to be unique and different, to make a statement amidst the flower children, acid heads, conscientious objectors, warmongers, Jake truly did not stand out. And there was something else that distinguished Jake from the other undergraduates. Jake was trying hard not to be noticed.

"In fact, maybe I'll just take a walk around campus."

Stephen eyed her skeptically.

"You're overdressed," he said.

"But this is it. My clothes are in my hotel in the city." And, she thought, this is my most casual outfit. Julia squinted her violet eyes at Stephen. "What I need is a pair of shorts just like the ones you're wearing. And a T-shirt. And a pair of sandals. Right?"

"That certainly would blend in well." She would still stand our. Stephen couldn't imagine her in shorts and a T-shirt.

"Is there a bookstore nearby?" Julia withdrew a fifty-dollar bill from her leather purse. "Would you be able to go buy something for me? Oh, but you're studying . . ."

"Really, I was just about to take a break. Too hot to study. So I can show you around, if you want."

Julia changed into the new purchases in Jake's room and emerged in moments, looking, Stephen thought, even more beautiful. Her black hair, now loose, hung halfway down her back, thick, black, with a slight curl. Her face radiated youth and flushed with pleasure at the coed pretext.

"I love my shorts!" She laughed. They were bright red with a large white *S* with a green tree overlying.

"They really are *you*," Stephen teased but was unable to hide his admiration.

They strolled around campus, drawing open stares, the handsome, dark-haired couple. Friends of Stephen's waved with obvious interest. After a tour of the Quad, Memorial Church, the undergraduate library, and White Plaza, they walked to Lake Lagunita and sat watching the swimmers, boaters, and would-be studiers using sun-warped books for pillows.

"This is really blissful. I wonder if Jake ever sits here, like this, and just enjoys the loveliness." It was a statement, but Stephen chose to answer.

"Jake is pretty serious. He studies hard. He's not really the playful type." He does stay out all night, though, and often leaves for the weekend, Stephen thought but didn't add. He had no idea if Jake spent those times alone or with someone. Just like Stephen had no idea about Julia.

"A man with a purpose," Julia said softly.

"Is he?" Stephen asked quickly, curious for information about his roommate.

"Perhaps. At least he appears to behave in a purposeful manner."

Stephen did a double take. It was a Jake-type answer, adroit, rhetorical, and totally nonrevealing. He realized then that in the hours they had spent together that afternoon Julia had learned a lot about him and he had learned nothing about Julia. And he was unlikely to learn anything, because she politely, graciously, expertly, kept her distance. Just like Jake.

Jake was in the room when they returned.

"Julia?" His voice sounded concerned, but when he saw her, relaxed, smiling, he knew that she hadn't come because of a problem. It was for another reason altogether.

"Jake! Hi. I just happened to be in the neighborhood." Julia stopped. Jake wasn't smiling. The look of worry had been replaced by something else. Anger? Not quite. Annoyance? Yes.

"I took Julia for a tour of the campus," Stephen interjected, sensing the inexplicable tension and trying to ease it.

"I hoped that you would be free this evening." Julia stared at Jake.

Jake shrugged noncommittally. He had plans to spend the weekend in Carmel. They were to leave in two hours. A casual relationship, but a nice one. He had been looking forward to the weekend with Susan. He had had no idea that Julia would decide to visit, without warning. Julia's decision, not his. And yet, it was Julia . . .

"Do you have a car?"

"No, there is a very happy taxi cab driver taking the night off in San Francisco." What was he thinking? "If you're busy, I can take a cab back."

"How long are you planning to stay?"

"Just for the weekend," Julia answered coldly.

Without another word, Jake went into his room and closed the door. Julia and Stephen waited in the sitting room in uneasy silence. They could hear Jake's voice speaking hesitantly into the telephone.

"Apparently he has other plans for the weekend," Julia stated the obvious finally. She sighed. Her surprise had backfired. It had never occurred to her that Jake would be unavailable. Since Frank's death, she had assumed that they were both waiting until the right time. Until enough time had passed. But Jake wasn't waiting. Or maybe she had waited too long.

Jake returned after ten minutes, carrying a small suitcase. "Let's go. Or do you want to change first?"

"Where are we going?"

"To your hotel then to dinner. I assume we have reservations somewhere?" He answered dryly. He was acquiescing to her plans, but his annoyance was plain. She had preempted his weekend.

"Yes," she whispered. Half whisper, half hiss. Julia

wished Stephen wasn't witnessing this. And yet, if his presence kept her under control, surely it was controlling Jake as well. The thought of Jake's uncontrolled rage made her shiver. Perhaps she should ask Stephen to join them. "I'll change at the hotel."

With great effort, Julia forced a smile and an effusion of thanks to Stephen for their splendid afternoon. Then she walked silently beside Jake to the parking lot. Had she been in the mood to speak to him, she would have teased him about his unpretentious car. Julia knew that he loved fine cars, as she had taught him to love fine, expensive quality in all things. But Jake treasured his anonymity even more. Nothing showy. It wasn't his style; at least not as a sophomore at Stanford.

They drove in silence, through the lovely residential streets of Palo Alto and Atherton, past carefully tended gardens bursting with color—fuchsia, yellow-orange, lilac. The heat of the day had receded slightly; the breeze was warm, gentle, fragrant. It was a perfect California spring evening. It could have been perfect, but Jake was spoiling it. Julia's anger grew.

"You bastard," she blurted out finally, startled by her own voice and its venom.

Jake's lips curled momentarily into a faint smile.

"It's a new set of rules, Julia."

"Meaning?"

"Jake's rules." He paused. "And Julia's rules. But not only Julia's rules. Not only Julia's whims."

"Give a man a little money—" She tried to tease, to lighten the mood. Jake interrupted sternly.

"It has nothing to do with money and you know it."

She knew it. It had to do with them, with a relationship that had begun years ago between a boy and a woman, a relationship that had defined boundaries, because of Frank. Until now. Frank was dead. The mourning was over. The woman was free. And the boy had become a man. A man with his own pride, his own standards, his own rules. And Julia had assumed Jake wanted her. *Assumed.* Julia's rules.

But Jake had never played by her rules, beginning with that dreadful day in Saigon when he had left her to think about what he wanted. And now she had flown to San Francisco because she wanted him, because the sadness and grief over Frank's death was no longer an obstacle. Because she was ready. It hadn't occurred to her that Jake might not be.

Julia lapsed into silence, berating herself for her foolishness.

Jake turned onto a wooded road and stopped the car. He stroked her cheek, then pulled her to him and kissed her. Julia's body trembled against his. He kissed her, not allowing her mouth to leave his. Finally he released her enough to look at her.

"I want you, Julia."

"I want you, too. As I always have."

"And now it's time?"

"Yes."

"You're certain?"

"Yes."

Jake kissed her briefly and restarted the car.

"Where are we going for dinner?" Jake asked lightly.

Julia started to name the restaurant, then smiled. "Wherever you like!"

Jake laughed. "Can the shrew be tamed?"

"You are a bastard," Julia teased, happy to have him back, happy for the repartee. Her eyes flashed.

"Who is she?

"What?"

"The other woman. The plans for the weekend." Julia hoped she hadn't pressed her advantage.

"Not funny. You made me do a very rude thing to a *nice, uncomplicated, undemanding* woman."

"You could have let me take a cab back to the hotel and spend the weekend alone."

"I should have. But I couldn't."

"Couldn't?"

"No."

"Because you want me?"

"Perhaps."

Julia curled against the door, facing him, smiling.

"Now what are you doing?"

"Purring."

"Gloating."

"No I am not." Julie's tone was serious. "I was so afraid this afternoon. That I had ruined everything. That you had changed."

"We have to be careful with each other, that's all. Very careful."

"Okay," Julie whispered.

Julie drew a few discreetly concealed stares as she and Jake crossed the elegant lobby of the Fairmont to the bank of elevators reserved for the suite floors. The doorman and concierge vividly remembered the woman who had left the hotel, by taxi, a few hours before. Now that same woman had returned, wearing red gym shorts, a light cotton T-shirt, complete with logo, her perfectly coiffed jet black hair now falling loosely around her face; it was a surprising, but still beautiful, transformation.

By the time they reached the elevators, Julia was giggling. Jake wasn't.

"Whoever taught you to be so stuffy?" she teased, then regretted the question as she realized its answer.

"Frank," Jake said quietly. He took her hand and said, 'Frank is a part of us. He always will be."

"I know," she said, relieved that Jake felt as she did—and that he had said it.

When they reached the top floor, Julia handed Jake the key to the suite. He opened the heavy oak door and followed her in.

"Very nice, Julia," he said after surveying the expensively, tastefully decorated living room with a spectacular view of San Francisco Bay. He noticed a bottle of champagne chilling beside the sofa, two crystal glasses, and caviar. He raised an eyebrow and looked at her, smiling slightly.

Julia shrugged. "I wasn't sure if I would have your company. But I hoped. I ordered your favorite, just in case. They were supposed to come at five, so the champagne should be chilled."

"Would you like some?" Jake asked, removing the champagne bottle and looking at the label. It was very expensive. The best.

"Help yourself. I think I'll take a shower."

"When and where is dinner?"

"The Blue Fox. At eight. But we don't have to," she added hastily.

"Go take your shower," Jake said amiably.

After Julia left, Jake checked the time: six o'clock. Then he made a phone call, walked through the master bedroom, and tapped lightly on the bathroom door. He heard the shower running. Julia couldn't hear him. He opened the door and walked in.

"Julia?" he called from the dressing area as he undressed.

"Jake!"

"May I join you?"

"Yes," Julia answered, startled. Jake's rules.

"Good," he said, as he walked toward the shower stall. "Did I ever tell you about my favorite fantasy about us in Saigon?"

"No," she answered just as he opened the shower door.

"My God, you are beautiful, Julia," he said, stepping into the shower. He put his arms around her naked, soapy body and pulled her against him. He put his lips to her ear and whispered, "Beautiful and slippery."

"Tell me about your favorite fantasy," Julia said weakly, unable to concentrate; the feeling of her own wet, naked body molding perfectly to his consumed her with desire.

"My favorite fantasy . . ." he began gently, with a sigh of pleasure—an articulate, unspoken acknowledgment of how wonderful it felt to him to be with her, their naked bodies fully touching, caressed by each other and the hot, enveloping water.

After his first three words, Jake paused to kiss her. It was a very long pause. Long enough for all the soap to wash away. Long enough for them to know what would follow. What must follow. Soon.

"Jake," Julia whispered as he kissed her, his soft lips discovering her, loving her, his warm, sensuous hands making her entire being tremble. "Oh, Jake."

"Julia, darling."

"I want you so much."

"You have me."

"I want all of you. Now."

Jake led her into the bedroom and made love to her tenderly, passionately, wanting to savor every precious moment, trying to make it last forever, but driven by a barely controllable need for her, as she herself was driven by her similarly demanding need for him. They had waited so long—years of wanting and wondering and doubting and dreaming; years of remembering a forbidden kiss and a hidden desire. Now the desire, the dreams, the needs, were fulfilled in a powerful, consuming union of pleasure and, afterward, peaceful, loving satisfaction.

After they made love the first time, they slept in each other's arms. They awakened, together, at nine.

"Uh-oh," Julia said when she noticed the time.

"What?"

"The Blue Fox."

"I canceled our reservations hours ago. We have champagne and caviar."

"And each other."

"And each other," he repeated and kissed her. "Nonetheless, I am going to bring the champagne and caviar in here."

"Then tell me about your favorite fantasy," she called after him as he left the room.

132

"My favorite fantasy," he said after pouring two glasses of champagne, "was that we made love, in the pool, at your house in Saigon. It was a very sensuous fantasy—hot yellow-gold sun, cool aquamarine water, long, leisurely hours of making love with you. Again and again."

"I like that part," Julia said softly. "Again and again."

The next morning, Jake asked, "Do you want to see San Francisco?"

"Well, sure, I guess," Julia replied tentatively. She didn't really want to leave the suite.

"This will be painless, Julia, and you will be able to answer questions honestly when your friends quiz you about your trip," Jake said cheerfully. He handed her a monogrammed terry-cloth bathrobe provided by the hotel. "Here, put this on."

Julia "saw" San Francisco from the windows of their suite. Jake pointed out the principal tourist attractions: the Golden Gate Bridge, Alcatraz, the Presidio, Fisherman's Wharf, Ghirardelli Square, Coit Tower, Golden Gate Park, Union Square, the cable cars.

"What a wonderful tour," Julia teased twenty minutes later when it was over.

"Is there anything else you would like to see?" he asked, pretending to be serious.

"Nothing."

"Good. Then there is absolutely no reason for us to leave this suite, is there?"

"None whatsoever. Ever."

"Are you really leaving tomorrow morning?" Jake asked. It was Sunday evening.

"Yes. Why?"

"Just toying with the concept of college student keeping mistress in Presidential Suite at the Fairmont."

"Mistress? Is that what I am?"

"You can be whatever you want," Jake answered seriously. Lover, girlfriend, wife, he added to himself.

Julia was silent, bursting with questions she was afraid to ask. What next? Where do we go from here? Do you want me as much as ever? As much as I want you? She waited.

"Do you have plans for the summer?"

"Plans?" she asked coyly, her heart pounding.

"I have no plans for an entire summer that begins in about four weeks."

"Really! How marvelous for you."

"Marvelous, yes. But here's the problem. If you stand someone up for a weekend, you know, cancel the whole weekend at the last minute"—Jake's expression was stern, worried, serious—"are you obliged to spend the summer with her?"

Jake paused. Julia held her breath. Her heart fluttered and ached. Slowly she shook her head.

"Or," Jake continued evenly, "do you make plans to spend the summer with the woman you love?" He stared at her.

"The woman you love," Julia whispered. "The woman who loves you."

They spoke daily over the next few weeks, making plans for their summer. As soon as the doctors had given Jake's leg its yearly checkup, they would fly to Monte Carlo and find a villa to use as their home base. They would travel to see their favorite operas in Vienna and Milan, cruise through Greece, spend a week at the fjords and two weeks in southern Wales. Every night their plans changed, because Julia thought of new, better adventures.

Two places were included on every itinerary—Paris and Monte Carlo. Julia had not returned to Paris since Frank's death. Paris had been their home for eighteen months. Julia knew that she had to return to Paris and to be there with Jake. She wanted to spend time in Monte Carlo because she wanted to buy a villa there, for herself.

Jake was a willing accomplice to all Julia's plans. He had spent the summer after his freshman year with Frank and Julia in Paris and was eager to return. He wanted to perfect his French. In reality, it mattered very little to him where they went as long as they were together.

The orthopedists and neurologists at Walter Reed Hospital performed their tests in a record three days and pronounced that Jake's leg was doing "remarkably well." When Jake arrived at the house in Arlington, he found Julia curled up in a large chair in the living room, staring into a glass of iced tea. They were scheduled to fly to Paris the following morning.

"What's wrong?"

"I'm not ready to leave yet. Let's just relax here and leave in a few days."

"Is it just because of Paris?" Jake sat on the arm of the chair and stroked her hair.

"No. It's because I don't want to share you with the rest of the world. Not yet. I just want us to be alone, private, for awhile. Is that all right?"

Jake smile and kissed the top of her head. "That's wonderful."

They rarely left the house. One by one plans were postponed and, eventually, canceled. They saw no one. Groceries were delivered. Julia taught Jake how to cook, but they made the meals together. It was a quiet, peaceful time. The taunting that had threatened to destroy their relationship the last time they had lived in the Arlington house, years before, had vanished. Their conversations were gentle, careful, serious; they read and discussed plays, books, and poetry, listened to music, talked, and made love.

One evening, toward the end of July, Jake asked, "Do you think we should at least go to Paris?"

"Are you getting restless?" Julia asked anxiously.

"No, you know that I am blissfully happy right here." Jake paused. "But I thought you wanted to go to Paris."

"Yes. I do. Sometime. But August in Paris is awful. No Parisiens. Hot. Desolate."

"Are you uncomfortable about being seen with me?" Jake's tone was serious.

"No! Don't think that for a second. I love you. I am proud to be with you. This all . . . us . . . would make Frank happy. I don't care what anyone else thinks anyway. Do you want to go out more?"

"No. I just wondered."

"The only reason that I don't want to leave here is because I am so happy—alone with you."

"And Paris?"

"We'll pretend we've gone. One week of speaking French, only. No exceptions. *D'accords?*"

Jake's aptitude for English was an aptitude for all languages. In his first two years at Stanford he had taken French and Italian and spoke both fluently. He and Julia spoke to each other, read to each other, in all three languages. That summer Jake began to teach himself Arabic and Hebrew. Julia didn't join in the enterprise, nor did he give her an adequate explanation for his interest in mastering so many languages.

"I think that being unable to express yourself for so many years, and then learning to speak, has made me intrigued with languages."

"That's a facile explanation. Hardly your style." Julia smiled. What was her purposeful man planning? He had no intention of telling her, yet. She would have to wait, to be patient. She was learning to be patient, learning to live by Jake's rules.

August passed quickly. Too quickly. The Thursday before Labor Day weekend Jake suggested that they go out for dinner, for the first time all summer. Julia readily agreed because she was curious. There had to be a reason. Jake was not a whimsical man.

Jake made reservations at Washington's most exclusive restaurant, the haunt of Washington's most famous, recognizable faces; a place where Julia knew everyone and everyone knew her. Jake's purpose became obvious as soon as he told her which restaurant. It was a test—to see if it really didn't matter to her to be seen with Jake, by her friends, by Frank's friends, in her city. But why? Why the test?

All the right people were there: Frank's friends, Julia's friends, parents of the debutantes that Jake had escorted, slept with, and never married. They all stopped by the table.

"Julia, darling, how are you? Where have you been?"

"Here. In Arlington. We—you remember Jake, don't you?—have had a very quiet summer . . ." Then she would smile at Jake with a look that left no doubt about their relationship or her love.

"So?" she asked as soon as they left the restaurant.

"So?"

"How did I do?"

"You passed with honors. Were you pretending?"

"No!"

"Good."

They drove in silence for awhile. Patience, Julia thought impatiently. Then she began to giggle.

"What?"

"What's going on? I can't stand it!"

"Nothing is going on."

Five minutes later Jake said, "I've come up with a plan to reunite Frank's estate."

"What a coincidence. So have I."

"Really?"

"Yes. I've made a new will. You get everything. Frank's plus mine."

"Not funny, Julia," Jake said angrily.

Julia looked startled.

Jake drove on in silence. This was not the right time. Julia was being infuriatingly flip. But he had to make plans.

They had to make plans. He stared at her until she looked serious.

"I want to marry you. I want you to marry me." Jake's rules. Julia's rules.

"Are you serious?" Julia asked reflexively, then stopped. He was serious. Deep inside she quivered.

"Yes. Of course I am. I love you. You love me. Don't you?"

"Yes. I do love you." More than I have ever loved anyone or anything, Julia thought, suddenly uneasy. "I love you very much."

"So, you will?" Jake's voice was eager.

Julia took a deep breath. When she spoke, finally, she spoke very slowly.

"Jake, I am so surprised. I never even thought about it. Everything is perfect as it is, isn't it?"

"Except that we aren't married. Except that I want to make plans to spend my life with you. Except that school starts in three weeks and I need to know if you will move to Palo Alto or if I should move to Washington. Other than that, perfect."

"Those plans don't really revolve around marriage, do they?"

"I want to marry you."

"You are serious, aren't you?"

"Yes!"

"I am an old woman."

"I know. I just feel sorry for you, I guess."

"I mean it. Thank God I'm not twice as old as you anymore."

"What?"

"In Saigon. You were seventeen. I was thirty-four. Twice as old." She wrinkled her wrinkle-free nose. "It was awful."

"This is silliness. I can't believe you would even notice age. You look about eighteen and act about ten. Especially now."

"It's not an inconsequential point, Jake. Anyway, I'm really flattered, honored that you asked me, but also very surprised. I have to think about it. Really."

They didn't discuss it for two days, but their minds were on little else. Julia was moody and preoccupied. Jake's patience and understanding disintegrated into anger the longer Julia deliberated.

Finally she decided.

"I can't."

"Can't? Won't. Don't want to. But not can't. You can do anything you want." Jake controlled his anger with difficulty.

"No. I can't. I cannot marry you. I love you, too much." Julia smiled. "I never believed that you could love someone too much to marry him—I thought it was a line for high fiction only—but it's true. It's really the reason."

"I don't believe it. It's a meaningless reason."

"No. It has meaning. It means I know it wouldn't work."

"Because . . ."

"Because of my age . . ." Julia waved off his protest. "Because of my need to dominate and the fact that you dominate me. Eventually I'd either shrivel or rebel. I care too much to rebel, so I'd shrivel and be miserable."

Jake waited for Julia to tell him the real reason.

"And because of Frank and Saigon and the guilt about all of that." She meant his leg and her unspoken belief that he had been punished for her desires. She sighed. "Too many memories. Too much history. I don't think I have the courage or energy to love as much as I love you. Not forever. Not as a spoken pledge."

It had been a painful revelation for Julia. It had forced her to look at herself. At her deep love for Jake. At her belief that they would, eventually, hurt each other. At her intention to avoid emotional pain. Frank's death had been too painful. She was simply unwilling to take the risk. She was, she finally admitted to herself, a coward. And a hedonist.

"But this summer love nest arrangement is just dandy. Do you have someone lined up for autumn when I'm back at school?" The sarcasm and anger in Jake's voice made her cry.

"I would love to believe that we could get married and be happy and that there would be no pain. Or that the pain would be worth it because of the happiness. But I don't believe it. Not now."

"And you are unwilling to take the risk."

"I can't. No, you're right. I won't."

Jake left the house. He returned the following morning. Julia was sitting in the kitchen drinking lukewarm, over-brewed coffee. They both had been awake all night and looked it.

"What do you want to do about us, Julia?" he asked gently, exhausted.

"I will always love you. I want us always to be part of each other's lives."

"As lovers?"

She nodded. "As everything. As we are now. Can't we just keep what we have? And change nothing?" she pleaded weakly.

"No. Life will change around us. We'll react to the change; change with it. If we're not together, we'll meet other people . . ." Jake paused. Was it a threat? No, just a fact.

Julia cried softly and nodded.

"You haven't slept."

"Have you?" She forced a weak smile.

"No, but I'm a child. Let me tuck you in."

Julia had no resistance left. Her thoughts were foggy and it hurt to keep her eyes open. Jake tucked the comforter over her and kissed her on the cheek.

"Sleep well, darling."

When Julia awoke, Jake was gone. His clothes. His books. He left no note. He was gone.

The next day, when she was rested, she analyzed her grief; she found loneliness, sadness, anger, and something else—relief. A huge responsibility had been lifted. She would always love him, and now she could. This gave her the freedom to do it, without the responsibility. She could live her life exactly as she pleased, without accountability to the intensely serious, purposeful young man that she loved.

By the next day, Julia felt very well. She knew that she would see him again, be with him again, make love to him again. But it would take time, for him. He would have to work through the pain and anger. But in the end, it would be best for both of them. She wanted to tell him, but she knew he wouldn't believe her. And she had no idea where to reach him.

Julia spent the week shopping and planning for her trip to Monte Carlo. She would go there to buy a villa. And then she would fly to Paris, to face that by herself. Julia felt strong and confident. But it bothered her, when she allowed herself to admit it, that Jake didn't call. He would call her again, someday. But she would have to wait. It would have to be his move. Jake's rules.

Jake spent the three weeks before school started at the beach house at San Gregorio that he had inherited from Frank. He read, listened to music, went to plays and operas in San Francisco, and thought about Julia. He remembered her words and tried, unsuccessfully, to understand their meaning. He tried to hate her, but it was not possible.

Finally, he made peace with it. It wasn't the end of the relationship, it would just continue in a way that he wouldn't have chosen, but could live with. Julia's rules. In a few months, he would call her.

Three weeks later Jake left Julia's house in Arlington, he and Stephen entertained Carrie, Beth, and Megan at the first Sunday candlelight dinner of the new school year. Two months later, Jake took Megan to the house at San Gregorio.

Part Three

Chapter Nine

Stanford, California . . . November, 1970

By the middle of November, the peace among the roommates that had been disrupted by the opening night fiasco was finally restored. Megan and Beth declared a truce at Carrie's insistence. Megan spent more time away from the room. She was secretive about her whereabouts, her frequent weekends away, but Beth and Carrie assumed that she was with someone. And Carrie assumed that it was Jake.

Beth's concern about the significance of the bouquet that Stephen sent to Megan was short-lived. It was, Beth decided, a gentlemanly gesture, nothing more. As the weeks passed, Beth became more confident about Stephen's feelings for her. Because of Stephen, Beth was happy, more tolerant, more social. Occasionally, Beth even joined the ten o'clock dormitory study breaks and the frequent corridor parties.

At the party following the last mid-term, Megan and Carrie began singing their favorite songs from musicals, starting with *My Fair Lady.*

"I wish someone knew how to play the piano," Megan said. "We could go to the living room, invite the rest of the dorm, and sing all night!"

"I play the piano," Beth said calmly.

"You do, Beth?" Carrie asked. "Can you play these songs?"

"I can play any song that I've heard," Beth answered simply, honestly.

"Let's go!"

It became a tradition, every Thursday night from ten until twelve—the Lagunita Hall sing-along and pajama party. Beth's repertoire was extensive: musicals, ballads, folk songs, traditional love songs. Beth played not only the melody, but also the harmony and bass.

"Both hands, all fingers, all songs!" Carrie observed proudly.

"This isn't hard, Carrie," Beth said privately to Carrie, slightly embarrassed but mostly pleased with the image she had at Lagunita Hall. She was admired for something she did well, for something she enjoyed doing.

"It would be for anyone else. We never even knew you played."

"This isn't really playing. It's fun. What I really play, what I like to play the most, is classical music. But it takes hours of practice every day. I just haven't had the time," Beth said wistfully.

Beth's repertoire expanded quickly to meet the demands of her audience.

"Do you know 'Light My Fire,' Beth?"

" 'Light My Fire,' " Beth repeated weakly, shaking her head.

"The Doors, Beth," Megan said, as if telling Beth the name of the group would enlighten her. Then she explained, "Beth isn't heavily into acid rock. Yet."

"If I heard it, I could play it," Beth offered.

After that, Beth agreed to learn, by listening to records, three or more new songs a week, time permitting. Suggested titles were submitted to Megan, who selected the ones most frequently requested. By the end of autumn quarter, Beth could play selections from The Beatles, the Rolling Stones, the Doors, Cream, Janis Joplin, Jefferson Airplane, the Grateful Dead, Crosby, Stills, Nash, and Young, and Country Joe and the Fish. Beth considered this a trivial accomplishment, except that it was fun, she made friends, she laughed. It felt good.

Stephen's respect for Beth grew. He respected her quick mind, her careful, honest opinions, her values, her talent. And, he respected her sexual standards, as difficult as it was for both of them.

Carrie adhered carefully to her "sensible" diet and even lost five additional pounds. Stephen insisted that she was too thin, but Beth and Megan agreed that she was just right. Carrie enrolled in the advanced tennis class and had already received strong hints that she should try out for the freshman tennis team.

No one noticed the change in Carrie. It happened after opening night—because of opening night. It was nothing anyone would notice; nothing anyone could see. The change was deep inside her, a feeling only she knew about. She had told no one. But she had underestimated Michael . . .

Michael Jenkins leaned casually against the edge of the large oak desk and faced his class of twenty students. Freshman English was required for all Stanford students. Within any given class one could expect a spectrum of enthusiasm and talent ranging from boredom verging on illiteracy to eager, prosaic verbosity. True talent was, indeed, rare. But this year, only his second at Stanford, Michael had a student with talent.

He glanced at the stack of papers that sat on the desk, the most recent class assignment. He had read and reread the essay on the top of the stack. It was an intensely personal statement about loneliness, disillusionment, and pain; emotional but not maudlin; sad but ultimately optimistic and hopeful. And laced delicately throughout, there was humor. It was a masterpiece. Michael had struggled with the urge to read it to the class, as he had wanted to do with other essays she had written. But, as he had done before, he had decided against it.

As the students filed past the desk to collect their essays, Michael took Carrie's off the top of the stack and held it. When she approached, he gestured to her with the hand that held her essay. As he watched her characteristically tranquil expression turn immediately to comprehension and, then, to apprehension, he regretted, for a moment, his decision to speak with her.

Michael encouraged his students to write about themselves, their impressions of college, their confrontations with new philosophies, ideologies, social pressures. Most of the students wrote about issues such as Vietnam, virginity, marijuana, acid rock music, existentialism, Timothy Leary, Ginger Baker, or Richard Nixon. But Carrie wrote about life, about love, about expectations, about disappointment and disillusionment. Instead of chronicling her reaction to all the new outside influences as the other students did, Carrie wrote about struggles and conflicts within herself. Her writing was personal, sensitive, sometimes happy, sometimes tormented, always compelling.

For two months, Michael had been a silent witness to her remarkable diary. He spent hours writing careful comments, some critical, some ecstatic, on each piece; and on each he urged her to make an appointment to meet with him. But she never had and it was almost Thanksgiving; the quarter was almost over. He had hoped that she would initiate a meeting, had given her every opportunity to do so, but since she hadn't, he decided to force the issue.

When Carrie realized that he was holding her essay—that essay—she panicked. I should have thrown it away, she thought. It was stupid to turn it in. But he kept telling us he wanted honesty . . .

It was about that night—opening night of Megan's play and closing night for the "old," trusting, naive, optimistic Carrie. It had been a small moment in her life, but an irrevocable one. In it, she had learned about envy and anger and betrayal and hatred. She had hated them all that night— Stephen and Beth for their smugness; Megan for her insatiable vanity; and even Jake, for wanting Megan. Carrie had hated them all for making her hate them, for making her feel hatred for the first time in her life.

The moment had passed, purged in part by the words she had furiously pressed onto the pages that now lay firmly, threateningly, in Michael's hand. By daybreak, the anger and hatred had subsided, leaving in their wake a wisdom borne of sadness. No one noticed the change in Carrie, but, overnight, she had grown up.

She should never have even kept that rainy night's tirade of words and emotions, much less shown it to anyone. She realized now that she had done it as a challenge to Michael Jenkins and his incessant urging that they write from the heart. She had given him the heartfelt honesty he wanted, and now she had to steel herself for yet another aftershock of that unforgettable night.

"Sorry." She smiled and reached for the pages. "I got a bit carried away."

But it wasn't going to be that easy. The pages remained in Michael's grip.

"Caroline."

"Carrie," she corrected immediately. Only Jake and her high school English teacher, Miss Gray, called her Caroline.

"Carrie." Michael sighed. This wasn't going to be easy. He felt her tugging to get away. "May I buy you a cup of coffee? Are you free now?"

Carrie was caught off guard. She hadn't learned to say no, to make excuses to men. It had never really been an issue. Megan and Beth had warned her that, the way she looked, she would have to learn strategies for avoiding situations that she wanted to avoid. She did not want to have coffee with Michael Jenkins. But she was free and admitted it.

Michael found a table for two in a remote corner of the student union cafeteria. Carrie sipped tea and eyed the essay—her essay—that he had put, folded length-wise, in the pocket of his corduroy jacket. He drank black coffee and ate a piece of lemon meringue pie.

"Would you like something to eat?" he had asked as they walked through the cafeteria line. "Not still dieting, I trust?"

"I'm amazed you knew about my diet!" The first few weeks of Freshman English had been a lecture series held in a large auditorium. The class had not broken into the small seminar groups until after the lecture series was complete. By the first class led by Michael Jenkins, Carrie had already lost twenty-five pounds and was, even by her critical standards, thin.

"Oh, well, I remembered seeing you during Orientation Week, at the barbecue," Michael had explained in the midst of paying the cashier and steering himself and Carrie through the crowded cafeteria.

"Really?" Carrie asked after they sat down. She was embarrassed that he had noticed her and wondered what he had thought. Poor, pale, fat girl, no doubt. Carrie resented the fact that anyone had felt sorry for her, especially, she realized, Michael. "A fatter version."

"A different version. A different cover, that is. The same book."

Carrie stared at him suspiciously. Was he to be trusted, this would-be scholar at whom she had thrust her innermost feelings for the past two months? He knew too much about her. And now, with no coaxing, it seemed that he was planning to psychoanalyze her. Carrie felt a moment of fear. Since her discovery that life wasn't entirely nice and beautiful, she had become more skeptical. Was he crazy? *Psychopathic English teacher murders coed.* Surely psychopaths came in all different covers—big, handsome, relaxed, with steady brown eyes and an easy smile, would be a cunning disguise indeed. Carrie's willingness to trust was past history.

"Meaning?" She was surprised at the accusatory tone of her voice. Michael looked startled.

"Meaning I don't remember you because of how you looked." He wanted to add, You didn't look bad then, by

150

the way, but he sensed that it was safer to avoid obvious flattery. "I remembered you because of how you acted. Mid-position between participant and observer. Comfortable in that position. Everyone else needed to be clearly within the group. Or clearly away from it. But you seemed quite content to be in between. Not lonely. Not aloof. Unlike the others . . . they were all trying, some pathetically and frantically, to prove something." Michael stopped abruptly. He was embarrassing her.

"I don't remember feeling comfortable," Carrie murmured.

"Or uncomfortable?" Michael smiled. He was not succeeding in putting her at ease. He decided to eat his pie very slowly; good manners would dictate that she couldn't leave until he was through. And Carrie was a well-mannered lady.

"No." She smiled and shrugged. "I didn't feel uncomfortable either."

They were silent for awhile, then both drew the breath anticipatory to speaking at the same moment. Michael's words came first.

"This essay is wonderful, Carrie." He fumbled for the paper and handed it to her. "You are very talented. Gifted. I admit that I have tricked you into this meeting because I wanted to talk to you. To meet you. Do you plan a career as a writer?"

"I haven't thought about it. This is really the first time I have written anything so personal. This quarter, I mean. And it's because, as you know"—she blushed, but relaxed; he wasn't planning to murder her—"it's been a time of considerable personal upheaval. I appreciate, and I know the other students do, too, that you let us write about our feelings. My roommates have spent the past two months analyzing *Heart of Darkness.*"

"That's next quarter. I've learned from experience that Freshman English—in fact no class Autumn Quarter—has a freshman's undivided attention. Too much, as you say, upheaval. Too much newness, too many decisions. Too many choices. So I let my students ventilate, discover, up-heave on paper. They feel better and I am in the unique position of having their attention." He smiled at her. It was a beautiful smile.

"Well, you're very smart. You certainly got my undivided attention, or, at least, my undivided emotion."

"I hope that you will stay in my seminar next quarter. I don't want you to be scared away by what you wrote, and I read, this quarter. *Or* because I am telling you that you have talent and *that* scares you." He watched her, like a parent cleverly anticipating his child's every excuse. Carrie had planned to change seminars. It was obvious. "We'll see how you do with *Heart of Darkness.*"

"I think we may find that my 'talent,' as you call it, may be limited to the writing of my personal diary." Carrie grimaced.

"Then so be it. You can turn pre-med, like everyone else on this campus. But stick with me for one more quarter, will you? I'm not a writer myself, but I think I'm a pretty good critic."

He was right. He was an insightful, constructive critic. But Carrie was too shy to tell him. Instead she said, "You're not a writer . . . ?" She left the "Then what are you?" unsaid.

"I'm not your kind of writer. I am a journalist of sorts. Concrete, factual, unemotional chronicler of data."

"Then what are you doing here?" Carrie laughed.

"Long story." Michael pushed at his lemon meringue pie and reported the facts of his life to her. Unemotionally. Factually. Like a journalist. Born: Long Island, twenty-eight years ago. The usual prep schools. Harvard, degree in English. Graduate school, Columbia, in journalism. Oh, yes, in there somewhere a marriage. And, sometime later, a divorce. No children. And then the inevitable dilemma of the professional student—take a deep breath and plunge into the real world or continue in the cloistered, protected life of academia.

"You've chosen academia."

"No, this is a calculated detour, a glimpse at life in the West. Then back to New York as a working journalist."

"When?" It was a polite question. Carrie didn't even wonder if its answer would ever matter to her.

"Next year." Vague enough.

It became a standing joke between them, a bond that could recall the past, the exciting, happy beginning of their relationship, because Michael claimed and would remind her of it, gently chiding, that Carrie had asked him for their first date.

"But it wasn't supposed to be a date!" she would always reply, laughing.

A week after their first talk, Michael walked out of the classroom with her. They both pulled up short as they saw what had happened while they had been in class. The mid-morning sky had turned grey-black, rain already flooded the shallow pathways, and thunder rumbled just over the hill.

"This had better stop by tonight," Carrie said, almost to herself.

"Plans?" Michael asked politely.

"Oh. Yes. We're going up to the city. To the Fillmore. To hear some bands. Apparently it's usual to have to get there a couple of hours early and stand outside until the doors open." She grimaced.

"I know. Who's playing?" Michael asked with interest.

"Let's see. The Doors. Jefferson Airplane. Those are the main ones." Carrie had never been to a rock concert and she couldn't wait. She loved the music that blared from almost every room in the dormitory. Carrie moved easily to the beat, could study to it, dress to it, exercise to it, and dance—in the privacy of Megan's room—to it.

"That's enough! Who's going?"

"All the roommates—Stephen, Jake, Megan, Beth."

Michael had read between the lines of Carrie's writing enough to know that there would be two couples and Carrie.

And Carrie would handle it graciously, but it would be hard for her.

"You need a sixth person," he said bluntly.

"Oh! Well, sure . . . do you want to come?"

In the matter of the technicality, who asked whom, indeed, Carrie had asked Michael.

The rain continued into the evening. Huddling, in pairs, was essential, if pleasant. It was lucky that Michael had joined them. He eased Carrie's discomfort at their sudden, enforced closeness by talking, offering entertaining, carefully edited anecdotes about his life—a life, it seemed to Carrie, packed with marvelous experiences, free of trauma and uncertainty. But that was merely because Michael was a skilled editor and journalist; he chose his anecdotes carefully. He did not, for example, elaborate on his "no harm, no foul" marriage, or on Sara, his ex-wife.

Michael and Sara met in a literature class during their junior year at Harvard. They became inseparable, best friends with common interests: politics, literature, theatre, and rugby. They played the same word games: Dictionary, Botticelli, Twenty Questions, Scrabble. They loved rhetoric and debate. They loved the tortuous, clever arguments their bright, inquisitive minds could devise. They agreed on most issues but wholeheartedly enjoyed the game and art of clever intellectual discussions. They made each other laugh. Life became easy, comfortable, secure. They were almost oblivious to the rest of the world. They were their own, self-sufficient unit—*saraandmichael.*

They were married the weekend following graduation, in a ceremony they had written, attended by their families and a few Dictionary-playing friends.

And on his wedding day, Michael thought, This is a happy but not joyous occasion. The thought troubled him and it festered.

Michael and Sara made their new home in New York City.

Michael studied journalism at Columbia. Sara worked as a copy editor for a medical publishing company and wrote short stories. Sara was intrigued by her work, learned as she edited, and was happy with her marriage. She awoke each morning eager for the day to start. She attributed Michael's periods of gloominess, when she noticed them, to the stresses of graduate school and career worries. It did not occur to her that he could be unhappy with their marriage.

They didn't laugh as much as they once had, true enough, but, Sara reasoned, these were more serious times. They had to tend to the business of becoming responsible, independent adults. And they didn't make love much; but they never really had. And as long as there had been touching and hugging, it hadn't mattered. By the end of their first year of marriage, Sara noticed that the hugging and touching had almost stopped.

Eventually Michael told her. He wasn't happy with their marriage. Something was missing. No, he didn't know what. But he had known it for a long time. It wasn't her fault. It, whatever *it* was, had never really been there. Of course he loved her. No, there was nothing she could do, except to agree to a divorce. He had to be free.

It took two months for Sara to believe him, two months of physical separation interspersed with painful conversations, tears, pleading, late-night emotional telephone calls. Michael was relentless in his determination to end the marriage; the more Sara pushed, the more resolute and ruthless he became. Michael was desperate. So was Sara. Eventually, he won.

At the same time it became clear to Sara that Michael was serious, something else became abundantly clear: it was her fault. Her sleep-deprived, food-deprived, thought-battered mind reached this conclusion. And it found a solution: suicide. It made sense. She was unloved, unlovable, and had squandered the love of a wonderful man.

Sara proceeded in the way that truly suicidal people do. She told no one; indeed, her new cheeriness was received with great relief by her coworkers and Michael. She gave away her possessions, mostly to charity, but she packed a box for Michael to pick up, afterward and she made careful plans.

Sara had learned a lot from her work. She knew about barbiturate overdose, about epilepsy, about overworked interns, about neurologists, about emergency rooms.

Getting the pills, getting enough to be lethal, was surprisingly easy. She began collecting them on Friday evening, anticipating that she would have enough by Sunday night. But the combination of her honest, intelligent face, her careful preparation, including the name of a neurologist in Boston, and three tired, gullible, or simply compassionate interns—Sara felt guilty, briefly, for duping them—resulted in three large bottles of phenobarbital by Saturday afternoon.

It had been too simple.

"I have idiopathic epilepsy. Well controlled with phenobarbital. I can't take Dilantin because my gums get swollen." At this point, Sara smiled, showing the doctor how upsetting swollen gums would be to her rather nice mouth. She carefully avoided the correct medical term, gingival hyperplasia, because she gathered, correctly, that doctors were skeptical of patients who knew the right terms.

"Anyway, I came here a month ago and until this week I expected to be returning to Boston. But now I have a great job. Of course, I'll need to find a neurologist here. On Monday I'll phone Dr. Buckley, my neurologist in Boston, and have him refer me to someone. But in the meantime I'm out of my phenobarbital. I only need enough to last through the weekend . . ."

Each doctor had given her a one-month supply. One even gave her two refills on the prescription. And they all recommended local neurologists to her. They all welcomed her to come back if they could be of further help to her. They were all so nice and young and helpful.

Sara's guilt was assuaged by the knowledge that the doctors would never know what she had done. She had given a false name and address when she checked in, she paid the hospital and pharmacy bills in full, in cash, before she left, and she would discard the bottles with the doctors' names on them. They would never know. They would continue to be kind and compassionate; and someone who really did have epilepsy and really did need a prescription for phenobarbital would get it from them.

It bothered Sara a little that she was twenty-four hours ahead of schedule. She would be another day dead when they missed her at work on Monday. And they might not investigate until Tuesday. She decided it didn't matter.

She poured the capsules into a small bowl in her apartment and threw the empty bottles in a trash can two blocks away. She bought a bottle of cognac. She sat on her neatly made bed and looked with satisfaction at her neat, virtually empty, clean apartment. Then, she started to drink.

Sara hadn't eaten for two days and had only slept briefly the day before. Nervous energy and irrational determination had propelled her to this point. Then the cognac took over; it made her giggle. She hallucinated. She became mesmerized with the capsules.

One final game of Scrabble, she thought, with the capsules. She spelled words with them. The first word: *MICHAEL*. To the *M* she added *OTHER*. Then she added six more letters: *F, U, C . . .* Through the *A* in *MICHAEL* she ran *BASTARD*. She ran out of capsules before she ran out of pejorative words to attach to her husband's name. But she was happy with the result; she wanted to take a picture of it. But she had given away her camera. Why? Oh, yes, because . . .

Sara stared at the words she had spelled with the capsules and laughed. Kill herself for that? For him? The warmth of the cognac gave her power.

Maybe I could become a doctor. I know so much about medicine. Perhaps I should write medical mystery stories. Sara smiled and lay down on top of the bed, on top of the capsules, and fell asleep.

When she awoke twenty-four hours later, Sara collected the capsules, saving the ones that hadn't been crushed. She opened them, emptying the lethal powder into the toilet and saving the shells. She strung the empty capsules, end to end, making a necklace long enough to loop around her neck three times. She would wear it in the years to come as a reminder of her folly and of her strength. And she would receive many compliments on the unique necklace—it was the era of beads and necklaces and drugs and pills.

Sara put on the necklace and telephoned Michael.

"Hi. I just wanted to let you know that I'll file for divorce in the morning. It should be quick and easy. It's best to just get it over with." Her voice was calm; she felt calm.

"Okay. Fine." Michael sounded tentative. It was what he wanted, even though he didn't know why. Sara's voice, confident and cheerful, made him sad.

The next day, after she met with an attorney, Sara began the first in a series of successful medical mysteries.

Michael escaped to Stanford. In search of "It." The magic. The spark. "It" had to exist, somewhere.

Chapter Ten

Jake thought of Julia, often, that fall. But he didn't try to reach her until Thanksgiving. He had declined Megan's invitation to spend the Thanksgiving weekend at her father's beach house at Malibu. Stephen, Beth, and Carrie were going.

Jake didn't analyze why he had said no, but as he dialed Julia's unlisted number, a number she had installed because of him, he knew the answer. He wanted to be alone and he wanted to talk to Julia.

The telephone rang five times. It was unlikely she would be home on Thanksgiving day. It was likely, in fact, she would be in Europe. It might not even be her telephone number anymore . . .

Six. Seven.

"Jake?" she answered. When the phone rang, Julia had stared at it, paralyzed. She had not yet had the heart to disconnect it. It was the phone for calls from Jake; he was the only person who had the number. All her other calls came through her answering service, as messages. She insisted that her service call her only in an emergency. On the rare occasions that her service called her, it was a different telephone number. It had to be Jake. Or a wrong number . . .

"Hi."

"Hi." Relief pulsed through her. She had almost given up.

159

She had resisted the almost uncontrollable urge to call or to write or to visit him. At last, her patience had paid off.

"Happy Thanksgiving."

"Thanks."

"How are you?"

"I'm fine, Jake. Gadding about, as usual. Keeping busy." She paused. "I've missed you."

"I've missed you, too."

Julia finally interrupted the long silence that followed.

"I bought a villa in Monte Carlo."

"You wanted to do that."

"Yes. And I found a perfect one. High on a hill over-looking the Mediterranean. Commanding view but totally private."

"Sounds lovely."

Silence. Again, Julia broke it.

"Why did you call?"

"Because I've missed you. To tell you I still don't understand, and I've tried to, but I can live with it. The way you want it."

"Do you mean it?"

"Yes."

Julia hesitated.

"Are you coming to Washington at Christmas break?"

"I've already gotten the reminder from the hospital. EMG, NCV, the usual lineup of tests."

"Then what?"

"No plans." Is that why I'm calling her, he wondered, because I want to see her? If that was the reason, it was subconscious, but as the idea crystallized, he wanted it more. "Why?"

"Would you like to come to the villa for Christmas?"

"Are you having a group?"

"No. I was just going by myself. I have to be in Paris by New Year's Eve for the parties."

"Paris?"

"Yes. It's okay. I was there this fall. I can handle it."

Silence. The ball is in your court, Jake, Julia thought, and waited.

"I'd like to come. Very much."

Stephen found Jake studying in their room when he returned from the Thanksgiving weekend at Malibu.

"I hope you didn't spend the weekend studying."

"No. I had a good Thanksgiving. How was the trip?"

"Megan's father is a rather prominent producer. Nice fellow actually. Unbelievable house." Stephen wondered if Jake would have been impressed. "Megan has a very young stepmother who is, according to Megan, a 'very minor starlet from another galaxy.' "

"You all got along? Including you and Megan?"

"Yes. She was all right. I never said she wasn't a talented entertainer. In fact, that's what I said that got me into such trouble, as you recall. She would like you to call her, by the way."

Stephen had almost forgotten. Megan had said, casually, as he dropped them off at Lagunita Hall, "Oh, Stephen, have Jake give me a call when he has a chance."

Carrie answered the phone.

"Hi. Caroline? This is Jake. I hear you had a nice weekend."

"It was wonderful. It's too bad you couldn't have come with us."

"I'm sorry I missed it." He paused. "Megan wanted me to call. Is she there?"

Carrie handed the phone to Megan and left the room.

"I'm going crazy," Megan whispered into the phone.

"Not your kind of group?"

"No, it was fine, actually. But I am going through withdrawal. I haven't been with you for five days."

Jake laughed. "Megan, you are so good for my ego."

"I don't care about your ego right now. What are you going to do about my body?"

161

"What do you suggest?" he teased. He glanced at his watch. It was still early.

When Megan didn't answer, Jake assumed that she was no longer alone.

"I will pick you up in half an hour. Okay?"

"Sure, thanks," Megan answered cheerfully, dispassionately, as Beth passed through the room.

It rained that year during the last few weeks of Winter Quarter. All day, every day. The grey-black sky scowled defiantly at the soggy earth. Tempers shortened. There was little to do but study. And, during study breaks, the choices were talking or eating, or talking on the telephone to Michael, Jake, or Stephen. And there was only one telephone, and little privacy.

"I can't stand this rain!" Megan announced, hourly.

Beth resented the rain because she enjoyed sitting by the lake talking to Stephen on sunny days.

Carrie thought it was cozy but didn't dare mention it.

"Do you realize that if it's raining here it must be snowing in the mountains? I can't believe I didn't think of this before!" Megan said gaily at the end of one solid week of rain.

Without further explanation but with the familiar gleam of an idea in her blue eyes, she ordered Beth off the phone and made a long distance call. Within thirty minutes, it was settled. They could use her father's lodge at Lake Tahoe. They all would go—Jake, Megan, Stephen, Beth, Carrie, and Michael.

"Will your father be there?" Carrie asked quietly.

"What? Oh. I see. Who will chaperone us?" Megan didn't understand Carrie's brand of morality, but she tried to respect it. "Well . . . we'll chaperone ourselves. It's a lodge, Carrie. Lots of bedrooms. We'll each have our own room, how's that?"

"I don't know . . ." Carrie had her own worries. About Michael. About saying no to Michael. She would have to

162

make it clear to him before they left, because inviting him to go to a lodge in the mountains for a weekend sounded wicked. And obvious. But Carrie didn't want to go without Michael. That would be difficult. Maybe she and Beth could share a room.

They all went in Michael's van, loaded with food, skis, and textbooks. Megan organized it all; she planned menus, bought food, checked on road conditions, waited anxiously in the lobby of Lagunita Hall for the key to arrive by special delivery, and forgot all about the dreariness of the rain.

Stephen and Jake agreed to go on the condition that periods of uninterrupted study would be allowed. Both had taken heavy course loads Winter Quarter. Jake would study while the others skied; only he and Megan knew that, because of his leg, it would be impossible for him even to try to ski.

The "lodge" was a lakeside mansion elegantly renovated in a rustic style, with old brick fireplace, heavy-beam ceilings, natural-wood-paneled walls, the smell of cedar, beautifully furnished with comfortable overstuffed chairs and sofas, throw rugs, and cushions.

Beth and Carrie found a bedroom with twin beds and its own bathroom complete with an oversized bathtub. Jake, Stephen, and Michael each selected a private room with a double bed, and Megan chose a room a discreet distance away from Jake's.

The morning after they arrived, they all went skiing except Jake. When they returned, Michael and Stephen were carrying Megan into the lodge. Her ankle was taped. Carrie followed them in, carrying a pair of crutches.

"She was showing off," Carrie smilingly explained to Jake under her breath. "She really is a fabulous skier."

"I was a fabulous skier. Now my career is tragically, prematurely ended!" Megan lapsed into theatrics, feigning a faint and eventually giggling. "This is so stupid. How can I go to the casino tonight?"

"You can't," Jake and Stephen replied in unison.

163

"Ice and elevation for you tonight, Megan," Jake said firmly. "I'll stay here with you."

The idea of being alone with Jake in the lodge soothed any pain or self-pity she was feeling, until Megan realized how unfair it was.

"No Jake, you've been cooped up here all day. And you've been looking forward to playing poker. I'm perfectly safe here and I have lots of studying to do. Just put me in front of a roaring fire with a little wine and my books and I'll be totally happy."

The matter seemed settled. After dinner they helped Megan arrange herself in front of the fire in her pale yellow down bathrobe with a lamb's wool blanket over her lap and her bad ankle outstretched on a leather footstool.

"This is very cozy," Megan purred. "I don't even feel jealous about missing the casino." She waved dramatically at them as they bundled themselves in parkas, ski caps, gloves, and after-ski boots.

At the door, Stephen paused, then took off his parka and said, "I think I'll stay here after all. I'm feeling guilty about my studies." Stephen didn't think it was safe to leave Megan alone in the lodge.

Beth looked bewildered; it would be too obvious for her to stay. It would declare that her interest in the casino had been feigned and that she didn't want to be with Carrie, Jake, and Michael. The tone of Stephen's voice did not invite argument, resistance, or company.

The others left. Without speaking to Megan, Stephen gathered his books and sat in a chair on the opposite side of the fire. After an hour, Stephen walked to the table beside Megan's chair and poured himself a glass of wine. Silently, he refilled Megan's wine glass and returned to his chair.

Megan began to giggle.

"Do you know what this reminds me of?" she asked, eyes flashing.

"No." Stephen did not want to get into an argument with her. For months their relationship had been civil, polite if ingenuine. They had both made an effort. More than once Stephen had felt the unexpected, uncomfortable rush of anger at something that she said, but he had controlled it.

"Do you want to know?" She was taunting him.

"Sure," Stephen said flatly, staring at his wine.

"Have you read *The French Lieutenant's Woman?*"

"You know I have. It was required reading for Contemporary Literature. You were in my class, remember?" Stephen wasn't in the mood for playing games with Megan.

"I didn't know if you had actually *read* it." Megan smiled sweetly.

Stephen stared at her, marveling at his control.

"Anyway, this reminds me of the scene when the woman—what was her name—had sprained her ankle and was sitting in front of the fire. And he—this wine has really gone to my head; I can't remember his name either—comes and . . ." Megan shrugged. "I guess I live my life as a series of scenes. Sorry to interrupt you." Megan looked back at her book.

A few moments later, Stephen stood in front of her, blocking the fire's warmth. He stared down at her until she looked up. When she returned his gaze, she was startled and intrigued and excited. And a little frightened.

"Miss Woodruff," Stephen said. He knelt down and looked at her ankle. "I fear you are injured. Shall I fetch a doctor?"

The actress in Megan didn't miss a beat, even though her heart did. The words came easily; she remembered the name without thinking about remembering.

"Mr. Smithson. I thought I should never see you again." Demure, shy, virginal.

Stephen put his large, strong hands over her small, neatly folded ones.

"I had to see you again."

"I am so glad."

They then forgot any facsimile of the words. Stephen touched her face, then kissed her. Megan kissed him back.

She ran her fingers through his fine, black, curly hair and watched his passionate, determined green eyes.

He carried her into his bedroom and began to make love to her. Slowly, gently, carefully.

He thinks I'm a virgin, Megan realized. Or is he still playacting? Sarah Woodruff was a virgin, but Smithson didn't know it. She would play the part. At that moment, for the first time in her life, Megan wished that it were true, that she could be his and his alone.

Afterward, he held her, stroking her golden hair tentatively.

"Megan," he whispered.

"Mr. Smithson!" Megan regretted it the moment she spoke. She felt Stephen's body tense. He wasn't acting, but was she?

"Stephen, this is so strange."

"Are you hurt?" he asked anxiously.

He believes that I was a virgin, Megan thought. How did Jake explain all those nights and weekends he spent away from their room? Of course, Jake never felt the need to explain anything, and Stephen would never ask. Could he really be that naive? He *was* Carrie's brother. It seemed important to Stephen.

"No." She would never tell him. "I mean this is strange that this happened. Did you know that it was going to?"

"No. But then it just seemed inevitable. And right . . ."

"And wonderful," Megan offered quietly.

"And wonderful." Stephen kissed her again and whispered her name.

"I thought you hated me," Megan teased later, after they had made love again. She curled against him, confused, forcing herself not to think about Jake, Beth, Carrie, her own past.

"Hmmm. I wonder where all that is now." It troubled him. The emotion he was feeling now was as strong and surprising as the anger she had made him feel before. He had finally been able to control the anger. But this new emotion, the needing, the wanting, the sharing, felt too good to try to suppress. But it could control him. "I never hated you. You just made me very angry. And I made you angry, too."

"From now on, maybe we can just make each other very happy."

"Darling Megan . . .

Megan emerged from her own room the next morning looking rested and radiant. The limp was almost gone.

"Good morning. How was the casino?"

Beth and Carrie were making pancakes and bacon and Jake was stoking the fire. He didn't turn to look at her, but his back stiffened when he heard her voice. She noticed his reaction. Had Stephen told him? She looked quickly around the room for Stephen. He wasn't there.

"The casino was great fun. Jake won quite a bit of money playing poker," Carrie said.

Jake still faced the fire, poking at a stubborn log.

"Where are Michael and Stephen?" Megan asked innocently.

"Loading the van. They think we should be ready to leave as soon as we get back from skiing. To avoid the traffic."

"Stephen seems eager to get back," Jake said flatly into the fire.

Megan walked over to him and crouched down beside him. It hurt her ankle so she stood up.

"Will you walk to the lake with me? In case I trip again?"

Jake nodded. They walked in silence for five minutes.

"What?" Megan finally demanded. He could only know if Stephen had told him. And that seemed unlikely.

"You tell me."

"Apparently I don't have to. I can't believe that Stephen did."

"No. He didn't have to. It's pretty obvious, Megan."

"From him?" Megan unsuccessfully suppressed pleasure at the thought that last night had visibly changed Stephen.

"From both of you. Two cats stuffed to capacity with canaries. The feathers are everywhere."

"You are really behaving strangely."

"What do you want? Righteous indignation? Anger at the inevitable?"

"Inevitable?" Megan asked, incredulous.

"Of course. It's been a charged relationship from the moment you met. Until now, the feelings have been strong but misguided. Hopefully now you can make something good of it."

"So you think it's real? That last night was just a beginning?"

"Yes." Jake was surprised. "Don't you?"

"Yes," she said softly and realized then how much it mattered to her.

They walked in silence and stood at the edge of the icebound lake. The wind was ice cold.

Megan looked up at him. The freezing wind whipped his face.

"What about us?"

"Us?"

"In all these months we never talked about us. How we felt about each other." She paused. "And now it's over."

"And not in need of a postmortem," Jake said flatly into the wind.

"But did you care? Do you care that it's over?" Why am I pushing him? It isn't fair. It doesn't matter anymore. Had it ever mattered to him? She stared at his profile, his windwatery eyes, his cold-reddened cheeks. And she couldn't tell.

Finally he said, simply, "I'll miss you, Megan. I'll miss us."

Megan and Stephen tried, somewhat unsuccessfully, to hide their feelings until they returned to campus. Beth correctly guessed most of it during the ride back to Stanford from Lake Tahoe. Carrie noticed Jake's silence but didn't put it into context until that evening when Megan told her.

"I am in love with your brother, Carrie."

"You are a sensational actress, Megan. I almost believed you."

"It's true. It just happened last night. I mean it just all made sense last night."

"Sense?"

"All the fighting. Thinking we hated each other. Just emotions in need of direction. And we found the direction last night."

"Does Beth know?" Carrie asked immediately, worried. Then, she added quietly, "Does Jake know?"

At the same time, across campus, Stephen knocked on Jake's door. Jake had never seen him so obviously happy and excited.

"You and Megan are good friends, aren't you?"

Jake was taken aback at the question. Did Stephen really not know that they had been lovers? It was possible, of course, because Jake had never mentioned it. But Carrie had guessed immediately and they had tried to hide it from her.

"Yes. Good friends."

"I think I'm in love with her," Stephen said proudly.

He never needs to know, Jake vowed. He would tell Megan never to mention it either.

"That's wonderful." Jake's enthusiasm was genuine. He and Megan had been great lovers and good friends. But they had not been in love with each other.

"You don't seem surprised."

"She told me this morning."

"That we are in love? Really?"

"Words to that effect." Jake marveled at his roommate's ecstasy. Naive, unspoiled, pure. Jake hoped that it would last. That Stephen and Megan could make it last.

* * *

The next morning Jake made it a point to meet Megan after her eight o'clock class.

"We have to talk."

"Okay." Megan looked at his untroubled face. He's not here to do a postmortem on "us" after all, she thought.

"Stephen doesn't know about us. I don't think he ever needs to."

"I agree. Thank you."

"The other thing is that I would like to offer him—both of you—the cabin at San Gregorio. To use whenever you like. To live there if you want." Jake knew that Stephen couldn't afford to pay for motel rooms and they needed a private place.

"I thought it belonged to a friend of yours!"

"It's on permanent loan. Anyway, I thought I should check with you before I made the offer."

"Because we spent time there."

"Right."

"You are amazing. We'd love the cabin. Why are you doing this?"

"Because I care about both of you."

"You do care!"

"I told you I would miss you."

Stephen called Beth that evening. As usual, Megan answered the phone.

"Stephen!" She had been anxiously waiting to hear from him.

"Hi," he said gently. "Megan, I have to talk to Beth. To try to explain."

"I know. Okay. When can I see you?"

"I'll call you right back, after I've spoken with Beth. But I may need to see her tonight. All right?"

Beth said she didn't want to see him. It wasn't necessary; she understood perfectly.

Beth spoke to Stephen in the gracious, uninterpretable Southern voice he hadn't heard for six months. He wanted to see her, to talk to her, to preserve, even at the end, the honesty and respect. He wanted to convince her that it had nothing to do with her. There was just something between him and Megan; something he couldn't explain; something he couldn't ignore.

But Beth refused to meet with him, refused to discuss it.

"There is no need to explain, Stephen. I understand."

"How can you understand, Beth? I don't understand it myself."

"Well, it's happened. That's really all there is to say. Goodbye, Stephen."

Beth understood one thing: Megan had done this to her. It was Megan's fault. Megan's, not Stephen's. Beth hated Megan. She didn't hate Stephen. She couldn't.

In the weeks that followed, weeks of pain and torment for Beth, the loneliness that had been her lifelong companion, until Stephen, returned. The icy, civilized barriers that effectively protected, and distanced, Beth from the rest of the world reappeared. Beth retreated. She canceled the Thursday evening singalongs. She said that her studies prevented her from continuing. But it wasn't true; it simply didn't matter to her anymore to laugh, to have friends.

Beth refused to let Megan see her pain. She had too much pride. Beth tried to behave as if nothing had happened, nothing of consequence. But that spring the room was like an armed camp. There was no laughter, no teasing, no chatter. Just polite hostility.

Carrie knew that Stephen had never been so happy; she had never seen him so much in love. Megan was transformed, too. Her arrogance vanished and was replaced by a genuine, unselfish concern for the man she loved. She was even careful to protect Beth from the details of her relationship with Stephen. Megan didn't want to hurt Beth,

171

or anyone. All Megan wanted was to be with Stephen, in their own private world.

Beth and Carrie continued to be friends. Beth didn't tell Carrie how she felt, how much she hurt. Carrie knew, even though Beth didn't tell her, because Carrie knew what it felt like when the man you cared about chose to be with someone else. And, for both Beth and Carrie, the other woman was the same: Megan.

Chapter Eleven

Jake stared in disbelief at the letter that lay on his desk. He had read it once; he couldn't face reading it again.

My darling Jake,

By the time this reaches you I will be Countess Jean-Phillipe Pinot. I have known him forever. He's fiftyish, attractive—the typical French Count (but not boring). He's divorced, in need of "legitimate" companionship. I was tiring of the gossip, and the loneliness, so I agreed to marry him. The usual pre-nuptial agreements, of course!

Jake, I know you'll be angry and disgusted. And you won't understand. But this is what I need now . . .

The letter was five pages long, in Julia's elegant script. She alternated paragraphs of general chatter with serious attempts to explain her decision and pleas that he would at least try to understand.

If Jake heard the knock on the door, its significance didn't register. His mind was blurred with anger, bombarded with facts that didn't mesh: Christmas in Monte Carlo five months before had been perfect; Julia's determination to avoid "the demands and commitments of marriage"; their tentative plans to spend the summer together. But this explained why Julia had cried so bitterly when they parted in December. December . . . it had been perfect . . .

They spent eight days at Julia's villa, an exotic hideaway partially hidden by a colorful mantle of bougainvilleas and wisteria and fragrant with the smell of lilacs. The villa overlooked the Mediterranean. From it, one had a commanding view of the principality of Monaco—the Palace of the Grimaldis, the Monte Carlo Casino, the Oceanographic Museum, the Sporting Club, the Monte Carlo Golf Course, and the fabulous yacht basin, cluttered with the world's most spectacular yachts.

Jake and Julia made love, talked quietly, and read, lapsing effortlessly into the pattern of the previous summer. They felt no urge to leave their fabulous, private, peaceful retreat, despite the lure of the charming, beautiful, lively jewel of the Cote d'Azur, Monte Carlo.

The tourists left Monte Carlo during the holidays, to return to their own homes. In their stead, Monte Carlo saw, and welcomed, a different group of people, people who could spend their holidays anywhere in the world, yet chose Monte Carlo. They wanted to celebrate with their friends, people like themselves—rich, powerful, discriminating people.

The usual richness and vitality of Monte Carlo was enhanced by the festivity of the holiday season and the anticipated influx of its very special guests. Lavish, colorful decorations festooned the narrow, winding streets. Glamorous galas were held all night, every night.

Julia insisted—it was a matter of etiquette—that she and Jake attend one party, a fabulous formal ball held in a private salon of the Monte Carlo Casino, a party for the truly elite, hosted by the Prince and Princess. Julia knew most of the invited guests, a spectacular blend of royalty, heads of state, limitless wealth, fame, and power. They knew Julia. And they were interested in her handsome young escort.

Julia rested her slender, bejeweled hand elegantly, but possessively, on Jake's tuxedoed shoulder as she, and others, watched him play baccarat. Play, and win. Julia alone knew that Jake had never played before, but that he had studied a book that afternoon about the rules and strategy of the game. With that, Jake looked like an expert, calm, confident, and successful.

Except for the party, and a brief tour of Monte Carlo because it was Jake's first trip, Jake and Julia didn't leave the villa. They didn't discuss Jake's marriage proposal or Julia's refusal; they carefully avoided discussing anything that could disrupt their happiness at being together again.

Jake wondered at Julia's insistence that she had to go to Paris, alone, for the New Year's celebrations. But it didn't worry him. Undoubtedly, it was another matter of etiquette, a promise she had made before she knew they would be together. Jake didn't worry, because he knew how Julia felt about him. There could be no doubt.

Julia was so sad when they parted in the Charles de Gaulle Airport in Paris; she, to take a taxi to the George V Hotel in Paris, he, to return to Stanford. He remembered the surprising flow of tears from her beautiful, violet eyes.

Carrie knocked again on Jake and Stephen's dormitory room door. This knock was louder, more impatient. She was out of breath and late.

"Stephen?" Carrie turned the doorknob and walked into the room. It was empty, but the connecting door to Jake's room was ajar. On impulse, Carrie walked to the door.

Jake was sitting at his desk, totally absorbed. It was obvious that he hadn't heard her. Carrie hesitated, then whispered.

"Jake?"

He spun around, startled.

"Caroline. I didn't hear you." Was it her imagination or did he rearrange the papers on his desk? The movement of his hands drew Carrie's attention to the desk, to an envelope, torn open, as if in haste, pale blue with matching pale blue paper, five or six sheets. An important, absorbing letter. To

Jake, from whom? Not from Megan. But maybe an explanation of why Jake had seemed genuinely pleased about Stephen and Megan. Maybe there had always been someone else, someone other than Megan. Another mystery about Jake.

"I was supposed to meet Stephen and Megan here. To go to the rally."

It was one of many of the springtime peace rallies protesting the Vietnam War. Peace rally, speeches, live bands, singing, dancing, and celebration of life in Frost Amphitheater. All proceeds went to the antiwar movement.

"They left. They waited for you and then decided you'd all gotten your signals crossed. They just left." He watched Carrie's reaction, typically calm. The thought of going by herself to the rally didn't bother her. Then she looked at Jake and smiled.

"I'll wait for you. We can walk over together." It started out as a positive statement and ended as a shy question.

"I'm not going." He didn't hold her gaze.

"Not going?" Her eyes widened, and she stared at him, incredulous, curious.

"No." Firm. With an edge. Of what? Impatience. Defensiveness. It was clear that he had no intention of explaining.

"Why not?"

"I can't," Jake said softly, carefully controlling his voice.

"Can't. Oh, I see. You're busy. Too busy to take time to protest this despicable, immoral war. Or is it just beneath you, too undignified, to go to a rally, to mingle with the commoners?" Carrie stopped abruptly because she was so frightened by the angry expression on Jake's face.

"You don't know what you're talking about, Caroline," Jake said evenly, his lips taut.

"That our government, our army is over there slaughtering thousands of innocent people because of some fanatical idea that it's in their best interest? I know that. And I know that it's wrong. Criminal." Carrie's own anger gave her courage.

"That," Jake said slowly, "young American men, boys re-

176

ally, younger than you, Caroline, are dying so that people like you can spend a lovely May afternoon in the California sun singing, dancing, and cheering the intellectuals who tell you that this war is immoral. Dumb boys, who couldn't escape the horror by going to college. And poor boys, who weren't rich enough to buy escape. They don't all believe in what they're doing. But many do. They believe that their freedom, and yours, is worth the cost of their young lives. They are dying so that you can get dressed up in practically nothing on a beautiful sunny day and feel free and righteous and pure."

Carrie was wearing the green short shorts and matching halter top that Megan had given her on the first day of her diet, in the size that had seemed unrealistic, ever. The clothes fit perfectly now and Carrie had actually begun to feel comfortable in the brief outfit because she knew it looked so good on her. Comfortable until a few moments ago. *Practically nothing.* Jake's words were cruel and he had no right . . .

"What the hell game are you playing now, Jake? You feel guilty for your own privileged position so you're creating some patriotic camouflage to justify the abomination in Vietnam? It won't work, Jake. It's a cheap, intellectual game that isn't even as honest as spending an upbeat day in the sun. But it is so typical of you. You have to feel superior. You won't allow yourself to stoop to the level of the masses, even if the masses are supposedly your friends. You really are an arrogant snob."

As she spoke, a flicker of pain, the pain that she had glimpsed before, crossed Jake's face. It passed quickly and was replaced by a look she couldn't interpret. The anger, for the moment, had vanished. Carrie waited. Jake sighed.

"So be it," he whispered. She barely heard him. The fight was over. Jake had retreated. Carrie felt raw and exposed. And not ready to let it go.

"I don't know why any American would willingly go to a place like that. Unless he's a psychopathic killer."

"I told you why they go. Some don't have a choice; they go because they have to go. And they become patriots. Some even choose to go."

"No sane human being would choose to kill another human being," Carrie said as a statement of fact. It was the doctrine of the day, believed and lived on college campuses in the early seventies. It was against the laws of nature to kill. If another human being intended to kill you, you need only to talk to him, human to human, brother to brother, and he would understand. If a robber held a gun to your head and demanded your money or your life, the doctrine recommended with absolute confidence of success that you could offer the robber half of your money and you would part as brothers, with a feeling of the oneness of humankind.

Carrie subscribed to this doctrine wholeheartedly; indeed, it coincided with her basic beliefs in the goodness of life. No one ever mentioned the more fundamental laws of nature, self-preservation and survival of the fittest. Or the human foibles of power and greed.

"You just don't understand," Jake said reluctantly. He didn't want to be the one to shatter her lovely fantasy. It would be shattered eventually, as she grew older, as she saw some of the inescapable ugliness of life.

"And you do understand?"

"Yes."

"How?" she challenged. She had never spoken to Jake like this. She was usually too shy to speak to him at all.

Jake paused. "Because I have been there."

"Where?" Worry crept into her voice. Was she about to learn something that she didn't want to know?

"Vietnam."

"No you haven't." She didn't want to believe it. "Oh, I see, before the war.

"During the war. In the war."

"As a specialist," she said quickly.

"I enlisted." His heart was pounding. It was inevitable now. Inevitably destructive to both of them. He had vowed to tell no one. It was part of someone else's life; he had almost convinced himself. But that was his fantasy. It was part of his life then, now, and forever. Inescapable. Inevitable. A shadow. A twilight shadow—long, dark inseparable.

"But you didn't fight," Carrie pleaded. "You never killed anyone."

Jake said nothing. There was nothing he could say.

Carrie began to tremble. Her body shuddered and she let out a cry.

"I don't believe it. It isn't true. Not you!" She shook her head and swayed.

Quickly Jake's arms were around her. He guided her to his bed and sat beside her, holding her, gently and tentatively at first, then, because she buried her tear-damp face into his chest, he folded his arms tightly around her.

As he tenderly stroked her hair with his long, strong hands, unsummoned thoughts bombarded her mind. Killer's hands; murderer's hands. How many men had he killed? How many women? How many children? Had he killed them with those hands that were stroking her so gently? She felt his lips kiss her hair, pressing slowly, firmly, interspersed with murmurs, "Caroline, darling, don't cry. I am so sorry. Please don't cry."

The gentleness of his touch, the unexpected softness of his lips, the tone of his whispers erased all thoughts and consumed Carrie with a curious, powerful sense of wanting. She had felt it, in small bits, since she had first met Jake, but now the urgent, aching feelings were crystallized into clear, powerful desire.

She wanted him to touch her and kiss her and hold her. Without thinking, but guided without hesitation by the power of her desire, Carrie turned her face toward his. She saw in his eyes what must have been a reflection of her own—pleasure. Consuming. Demanding. Commanding.

Their lips met and Carrie was enveloped by the taste of him, the warmth of him, the feel of him. He pulled her close. She would remember later, vaguely but undeniably, that there was something about his leg. As she lay curled against his warm, alive body, there was one part that was cold, lifeless. She barely noticed at the time, but later it became a vivid, troublesome part of her memory of that afternoon.

They lay on his bed, fully clothed, for several hours. Kissing, holding, wordlessly afraid to let go. When Jake drew away from her even a little, the horrible thoughts rushed back and she began to cry silently. When he kissed her tears and her mouth, the thoughts vanished. Exhausted and confused, Carrie slept, finally, in his arms.

Jake heard the outside door to the room open and was off the bed quickly. He tucked the blanket over Carrie and whispered, "Stay here."

Megan, Stephen, and Michael stood in the entry room, flushed with sun, alcohol, and the exhilaration of the afternoon.

"Did Carrie ever come by?"

"Yes. In fact she's here. Asleep on my bed, I think. She felt ill. I suggested that she rest a while before going to the rally. She's been here the whole time."

"Is she all right?" Michael asked, concerned.

"I'm okay." It was Carrie who answered. She stood in the doorway, the blanket wrapped around her. "I feel better now. I had a nice nap."

"You both missed a great rally—" Stephen began, but Carrie interrupted.

"No big deal. There will be others. I think I'll head back to Lagunita. I have some studying to do." Carrie slid the blanket off her shoulders and handed it to Jake. "Thank you."

Without another word, or even a glance at Michael, she left the room. She had to get away from all of them. She had learned something else when she walked past Jake's desk. The letter, obviously written by a woman, began, "My darling Jake . . ."

Carrie had to get away, to think, to write, to try to understand the incomprehensible facts and feelings of the afternoon.

* * *

Carrie didn't see Jake for two weeks. He didn't call. Carrie told Michael that she couldn't spend the summer with him in New York. It meant that she wasn't ready to make a long-term commitment to him; that she didn't think their relationship would work.

"It's hackneyed, Carrie," Michael said finally, after they had discussed and analyzed to the point of exhaustion, "but I hope that we can be friends. I want to be your friend. I am your friend. Always."

Carrie didn't tell Michael, or anyone, about what had happened with Jake. For the next two weeks Carrie ate little, slept fitfully, and wrote slow, careful words carved from her soul.

When they saw each other again it was by accident. Carrie awoke at five. The predawn sky was pearly grey. She decided to go for a walk. She loved the silent early-morning campus. It was an empty stage that, in hours, would be cluttered with activity, and the grand buildings, the dewy grass, and the sturdy, rustling palms would be lost in the backdrop of a thousand actors. She loved the hours when the scene was set but the players were absent, when she could hear the sound of the fountain without a symphony of voices, bicycle bells, radios, cars. The fountain had a wonderful voice of its own, musical, chattering. She sat there often in the early morning, listening.

This morning her place was already taken. He turned as he heard her approach and stood up when he recognized her.

"Caroline?"

"Jake!" she whispered. "What are you doing at my fountain?"

"I could ask you the same question."

"But I've never seen you here before."

"True. This is not my usual time. I admit it."

Jake's nightmares usually forced him out of bed about two. He would pace the campus and sit by the fountain for several hours, then return to his room to try to sleep. This particular night he had been up at two and had decided not to return to his bed; he knew it would be useless.

They listened to the fountain, then, finally, both spoke at once.

Carrie laughed. It helped them both.

"How are you? Studying for finals?" Jake asked.

"Thinking about studying for finals!" Carrie said. Thinking about you . . .

"Are you going to New York for the summer?"

"With Michael? No. That wasn't meant to be. I think he's glad to be going back. To start his career in journalism." She paused. "I am going to be teaching tennis at a club in Boston. I've done that before, in high school. What are you going to do?"

"Stay out here. Take classes at Berkeley. Read."

Another silence.

Carrie wanted to leave. This meeting had been an accident. He hadn't wanted to see her. He hadn't called. As much as she had wanted him to call, wanted to see him, this didn't feel right.

She straightened up and extended her hand, cold from the morning air.

"Well, if I don't see you again this year, I hope you have a nice summer."

Jake took her cold extended hand and covered it with both of his hands.

"Caroline, I have wanted to call you, to apologize."

"Why haven't you?" Carrie asked quietly, holding her breath.

"Because I didn't want you to misunderstand, to misinterpret."

To think that you care about me, Carrie thought miserably. She tried to pull away, but he held her hand firmly.

"How do you think I interpreted what happened?" she asked.

"In a generous and gracious way. In a positive way. You may have even forgotten the facts, or forgiven them."

"Is that so bad?" Carrie asked. It was true.

"Not for me. It means that you are still willing to speak with me. Maybe, to be my friend. But it's bad for you, because you may have forgotten how fundamentally different we are. How unhappy it makes you to think of what I have done with my life." He paused. "I should never have kissed you."

Carrie listened carefully. What had he said? That they could be friends. Platonic friends. She wanted to be Jake's friend. If that were truly possible . . .

"What do you want?" she asked hesitantly.

"I want to take my painfully thin little friend to dine with me at one of San Francisco's finest restaurants."

"Dine?" Carrie asked, smiling.

"Yes, I think that will be my project—to teach you the fine art of dining. We'll start now and pick up again next fall. Okay?"

"Yes!"

Jake spent the summer at the cabin in San Gregorio. He had a telephone installed. It didn't ring all summer. No one even knew that he was there. He used it to make dinner and theatre reservations, for himself, in San Francisco. He planned to leave it connected for Stephen and Megan.

Jake took a heavy load of classes at Berkeley: spoken Chinese, spoken Japanese, political history of the Middle East, Shakespeare. He studied in the library and ate meals in the sidewalk cafes on Telegraph Avenue. Even during the summer term, the campus at Berkeley was a hub of political activity. The antiwar activists congregated frequently; rallies of some sort were a daily occurrence.

Telegraph Avenue was populated by "flower children,"

who were in the early seventies already beginning to show signs of wilting. Dissolute, expressionless faces supported by phlegmatic bodies ambled through the streets without apparent aim. The smell of marijuana was pervasive, marijuana and wilting bodies. And the aroma of pizza, espresso, and incense.

The Avenue was patrolled by Hell's Angels, stewing in their black leather jackets under the hot summer sun. Tourists scurried in and out of shops, buying beads, candles, incense, and posters, taking pictures of the flower children and the Hell's Angels, tourists en route to or from Disneyland, taking in yet another tourist attraction—the counterculture of the Bay Area.

Jake attracted very little attention, an uninterestingly normal-appearing specimen. He spoke to no one in his classes and rebuffed several advances made by a rather pretty coed in his spoken Chinese course. Jake had no urge for conversation or company. He spent little time thinking about his personal life. He focused relentlessly on his studies, the perfection of the languages and an understanding of the politics. And he marveled at the genius of William Shakespeare.

Jake moved back to campus the week before Labor Day. He had agreed to be a counselor for one of the dormitories, the senior student available to guide, counsel, and help the lowerclassmen. With the job came a large, private room with sitting area, bedroom, refrigerator, and, even, a view of the lake. His solitary summer made him glad that he had opted for a single room, but he had second thoughts about the dormitory. Perhaps he should have found an apartment off campus.

He was surprised to find two letters in his mailbox at the campus post office. The first, postmarked July 29th in Geneva, was from Julia. Jake tossed it, unopened, into a wastebasket. The other letter, postmarked July 18th in Boston, was in a hand that he didn't recognize. Small, neat, legible, not flashy like Julia's. He turned the envelope over: Caroline Richards.

Jake walked across White Plaza to the fountain and sat down. It was almost dusk. The campus, on the eve of Labor Day weekend, was deserted. In the fading sunlight he read the letter.

Dear Jake,

You said that you were spending the summer in Palo Alto. So, hopefully, this will reach you.

I wanted you to know how much I enjoyed our dinner together, "dining" in San Francisco. It was a sensational restaurant and a lovely evening. Thank you.

Stephen and Megan are subsidizing the commuter trains between New York and Hartford in a big way. Stephen is enjoying clerking at the law office. Megan is living at Pinehaven—Ian and Margaret Knight's estate in Connecticut (doesn't that sound lovely?). She has the lead in Ian's new play and is thrilled that he now considers her a "serious" actress. I think she attributes her metamorphosis in large part to the coaching you gave her with Gwendolyn. We are planning a family trip to New York in August to see the play. It's "off, off, off, off" Broadway, as Megan points out constantly. But it is New York. And the reviews are very good.

My job at THE CLUB—that's Brentwood Heights Lawn Tennis and Golf Club—has been going well.

How are you? I hope you are well and happy.

Thank you again for dinner.

Carrie (Caroline!)

Jake smiled as he read it. It was typically Caroline—honest, straightforward, thoughtful, mentioning herself only in passing, unspoiled. He hoped she was happy, too. He had seen her unhappy, made her unhappy, that afternoon last spring. It was a memory he would never forget. He would never forget any of the memories of Caroline: dinner that first Sunday, dinner a month later with a thinner Caroline,

185

opening night of *Earnest,* the concert at the Fillmore, the weekend at Lake Tahoe, the morning at the fountain, their dinner in San Francisco. The memories were clear and vivid. And the thought of her filled him with peace.

That night he telephoned Boston. Stephen answered the phone.

"Hello."

"Stephen? It's Jake."

"Jake! A voice from the past. We'd almost decided to place bets on when and if you'd surface."

"I have surfaced. When are you and Megan arriving?"

"Next Wednesday. That will give us plenty of time to settle in the cabin before school starts. Is the cabin still available?"

"Yes, of course. In fact I've been there this summer. There are a few improvements—telephone, dishwasher, washer and dryer. It's really quite civilized."

"And it's really ours?"

"Yes. My friend likes the idea of happy, non-destructive tenants." Jake shifted the subject swiftly. "Why don't I meet you at the airport?"

"That would be great."

"When are you arriving?"

"I'll go look at the tickets. Here, talk to Megan."

"Hi Jake!"

"How are you?"

"Wonderful. Really wonderful. It has been a perfect summer. And I'm even looking forward to school."

"Because of Stephen."

"Yes. And the cabin. We are desperate to really be together. That's the only part that has been a bit . . . uh . . . tricky."

"How was your play?"

"How did you know I got a part?"

"When did you ever not get a part?"

"Thanks. That's nice. It was a true, tough role. Lots of emotions. Lots of changes. It was really good for me to do.

I wonder what they're planning to do on campus this fall. Have you seen any notices?"

"You really are relentless. Why don't you just nest with Stephen this quarter?"

"I will. But I have to act."

Before Jake could answer, Stephen was back.

"She has to act, Jake. Apparently this obsession is the real thing." Stephen's voice gently teased and was full of pride. "Crazy. Anyway, here's the flight information. This is really nice of you."

"My pleasure," Jake said and wrote down the information. "How's Caroline?" he asked casually.

"Fine."

"Is she there?"

"No, she's at the club, as usual. She had a match of some sort at nine tonight. She should be back soon."

"Is she coming out with you and Megan?"

"No, but she'll be out a week early for orientation. And, I think, to try out for the tennis team."

"That good?"

"Yes. Really. She's really gotten good." Stephen was very proud of both of his women.

"Well, see you Wednesday."

"Okay. Thanks for calling."

"Sure."

Jake depressed the lever, looked at the name Carrie had written in her letter, and dialed directory assistance. Then he dialed again.

"Brentwood Club. May I help you?"

"Yes. I am trying to reach Caroline Richards. Is she off the court?" Jake realized how little he knew about tennis, tennis terms, length of tennis matches, and people who answered telephones at tennis clubs.

"Just one moment, I'll page."

Jake was put on hold before he could reply.

In a few moments she answered.

"This is Carrie." She didn't sound surprised to get a telephone call. In fact, she got many, arranging matches and lessons.

"This is Jake. I hope you were done with your match."

"Yes. Just finished," she answered mechanically, her mind reeling, her heart pounding. *Jake.* How had he found her? Why was he calling? "Jake, is everything all right?"

"Of course."

"Where are you?" He sounded far away.

"Stanford. I've been here all summer, but I didn't check my mail until today."

"Oh." Her foolish letter.

"So I just got your letter."

"You didn't have to call!"

"I wanted you to know that I just got it. I didn't want you to think that I'd gotten it and not answered."

"That's nice of you." Carrie had taken the call in the pro shop. Even at ten at night it was busy. The lighted courts stayed open until one in the morning. She wanted to be alone to talk to him, but she couldn't be. "How are you? How was your summer?"

"Fine. Very productive. I hear your tennis is spectacular."

"That's my brother. But it has improved."

The more he heard her voice, the more he wanted to talk to her. He sensed that it was awkward for her to talk at the club. He almost asked if he could call her back later, when she was at home. But he had nothing else to say. He just wanted to hear her voice, her joyful, optimistic reporting of life as she saw it.

"Jake, are you still there?"

"Yes. I was thinking. When do you return to campus?" She told him.

"Would you like to dine with me again? We have a lot of eating to do before we deplete San Francisco's supply of fine restaurants."

"I'd love to."

"How about the night after you get back?"

"Perfect."

188

"Where are you living this year?"

"In Lagunita again. With Beth. We have a double room."

"I'll call you the night you return, to finalize plans."

"Proper attire and so on." Carrie laughed gaily, her heart still galloping.

"That sort of thing. Talk to you then."

"Okay."

Beth . . . , Jake mused after he hung up the phone. He had almost forgotten about Beth in just three months. He wondered how hard it would be for Carrie to room with Beth and spend time with Stephen and Megan. Forgettable, hostile Beth. How she would hate the idea of being forgotten!

Part Four

Chapter Twelve

Stanford, California . . . September, 1971

As Jake walked into Lagunita Hall to pick up Carrie, he held the front door open for a dark-haired woman wearing jeans and carrying a large, apparently heavy box. She tossed a strand of her thick, tousled hair off her forehead and looked at him.

"Thank you, Jake." The unmistakable drawl.

"Beth! Here let me carry that. You can show me the way to your room. I'm here to get Caroline."

Beth relinquished the box reluctantly. She want Jake's help. Seeing Jake caused the horrible memories to return. Jake was Stephen's best friend. Jake had never liked Beth, and he had always liked Megan. Had Jake's opinion of her influenced Stephen?

"I didn't recognize you."

"Deep down us Texans are all a little bit country," she said flatly, ending the conversation.

She looks better, Jake thought. But still, inside, cold, intractable Beth. Forgettable Beth, he thought and suppressed a smile.

They found Carrie pacing in the room. Her summer of endless exercise made her restless in this, the withdrawal period. She had excess energy, an urge to be constantly moving. It had been, she had realized as she sat restlessly on the six-hour plane flight the day before, a summer without thought or introspection. She had exercised daily to the point of exhaustion, then slept, then exercised again to exhaustion. Except for the silly letter to Jake, she hadn't written a word.

During the school year, her writing had been her escape. That summer, exercise had been. But the writing had been an effort of pain and hope and emotion and soul. The exercise had been, simply, a drug—mindless, numbing. It had been a total escape. And it had been so peaceful, so fulfilling, so harmonious, so even. She had felt no need to write, to purge her soul, to explore the aches, because there were no aches.

In the instant that she saw Jake, Carrie remembered why she had written and why she had ached. And her finely tuned athlete's heart, which calmly pumped a leisurely fifty heartfuls of blood per minute, suddenly pounded in her chest, crashing to get out, uncontrolled and uncontrollable. That was why she wrote. He was why.

"Hello Caroline."

Carrie giggled on cue. "Jake."

"Are you ready?" He wanted to be rid of Beth and alone with Carrie.

"Don't you think that Beth looks marvelous?" Carrie asked as they walked down the corridor.

"Beth looks better. Not marvelous. Beauty is as beauty does." He paused and looked at her. "You look marvelous."

"I am awfully healthy and fit."

"Sleek."

Carrie blushed.

"You look well, too." She stopped. He really didn't look well. He looked haunted and tired and tense. The tan was merely an illusion of health.

"From studying outside, in the sun."

"Studying. That's right. You said you were going to take courses at Berkeley. You really are determined, aren't you?"

"They offer some courses that we don't have here."

"Such as?" Carrie pressed. Why was he always so secretive?

"Marijuana 101. It's a different world on Telegraph Avenue. We really are cloistered here." Jake smiled. Carrie dropped the subject of Jake's summer.

Jake loved listening to Carrie. She always had a series of amusing, interesting anecdotes. And, he realized, unlike Megan and Julia, Carrie herself was never the focal point of the anecdote. It was never an anecdote about her; it was a life event at which she happened to be present. Carrie was an insightful observer and a talented reporter. Over dinner, she talked, and he listened, enchanted, happy for the first time in months.

"I'm chattering, as always."

"I'm not complaining. Tell me about the club," he urged.

Midway through a story about a spoiled, temperamental, rich child, Carrie stopped and peered at him across the table. His face was muted by candlelight.

"You are rich, aren't you?" She asked point-blank.

"What kind of question is that?"

"Direct. Are you?"

Jake smiled. "As a matter of fact, I am rich."

"Aha!"

"But I was never a spoiled rich child, so I won't take offense at your story."

"Are you personally rich, or is your family rich?"

"I am personally rich. Why, don't tell me you are a gold digger?" Jake looked amused.

How many questions could she ask before he withdrew, became silent? What did she want to know the most—everything. Who are you? Why did you go to Vietnam? Why are you so driven? Did you love Megan? How did you feel when Megan fell in love with Stephen? Did you care? What do you care about? What makes you look so sad? What is wrong with your leg? Who writes "My darling Jake" to you?

The possible questions darted through her mind. She couldn't even choose one to ask. She smiled back at him, her eyes sparkling.

"You are very funny," he said.

"Funny?" He's changing the subject, she thought.

"Different, unique."

"Strange?"

"In a different, unique, delightful way."

"You treat me like an amusing child. Entertaining, but not to be reckoned with." There was a slight edge to her voice. He was in control again, as usual. It was infuriating.

"I don't know about reckoning with. But I do take you seriously, Caroline."

They ate in silence for awhile. Then Carrie's humor and bravado got a second wind.

"You own the cabin, don't you?"

His surprised look gave her the answer.

"Don't tell them."

"Okay." Carrie liked keeping Jake's secrets.

"You're very good at this, you know."

"At what?"

"Interrogation. The art of surprise. Clever guesses."

"I like to know a little about my dinner companions."

"You know a lot about this dinner companion," Jake said seriously. Was it a warning?

Carrie started to protest that she knew nothing about him, then stopped. Maybe she did know a lot compared to what he usually told people.

"I'm not trying to be coy about my past. I just can't see that it matters. Wouldn't it be better—for both of us—if you didn't know about Vietnam?"

"But it's all part of you. Of who you are and what you are. You are a product of your past."

God help me if I am, Jake thought. "But one can escape from his past. Or at least try."

In a few moments, Carrie lapsed back into humorous anecdotes. She could make him laugh. When Jake laughed it made her feel wonderful. It was a deep, easy laugh.

After dinner they walked along Fisherman's Wharf. He walked beside her, not touching. Occasionally he would touch her arm, to guide her.

"I love the boats. Do you have a yacht?"

He laughed. "No, I do not."

"An airplane?"

"No."

"And you call yourself rich?" she teased.

"Yes." Jake laughed again. "Very."

He said good night to her at the dormitory door.

"Thank you for dining with me, Caroline," he said, standing at a distance from her.

Carrie smiled and nodded and went inside, confused, elated, restless, as she always was whenever she was with him.

Carrie liked Beth's new looks. Beth looked casual and natural, and, Carrie thought, more beautiful. She learned quickly that the inner Beth hadn't changed. If anything, her bitterness about Stephen and Megan and her summer working at NASA had made her even tougher, more intense. And the veneer of gracious manners had almost disappeared. Beth's coldness and contempt were nearer the surface than ever, along with an honest acknowledgment of what mattered to her—Carrie, her own career, Carrie's brother.

Beth had returned to Houston in June and had gone immediately to the personnel office at NASA. She oversold her skills and her experience, but not her potential. She did the selling to a man. She got a job. Because of my looks, Beth thought smugly, but I'll show them.

It was a low-level job, but Beth advanced quickly. She made it clear to the most senior person at the job site that she regarded this summer as an apprenticeship. This was going to be her career; she didn't care how long or how hard she had to work.

Within a week, Beth changed her looks. At work, she looked like a worker. She wore slacks, rolled up her sleeves, wore no makeup, and casually pulled her hair off her eyes with a large barrette. She worked side by side with men who admired her brain. They also noticed her beauty, but they correctly interpreted her iciness. They wondered about this beautiful woman whose beauty was greatest at the end of a long day, a tired, bewitching beauty that, in fatigue, revealed a deeper, carefully hidden torment.

Beth was tormented. She hated Megan with passion and energy that scared her. She did not hate Stephen. She loved him and always would. He had simply been duped by Megan. Crafty, clever Megan. In her most irrational moments, Beth convinced herself that Megan had taken Stephen away purely to spite her.

Beth didn't blame anyone but Megan. She also believed that Megan would become bored soon enough, ready for a new challenge, and that she would toss Stephen aside like an old toy. It troubled Beth that Stephen could be so foolish, because, until then, he had seemed perfect. He was so unlike all the other men that Beth had met. But apparently even he had a weak spot—he could be manipulated by an unscrupulous woman.

Beth would be there when Megan was through with Stephen. She only prayed that it would be soon. Beth missed him so much. If it went on too long, if he allowed it to go on too long, she might even begin to hate him. That was what tormented her the most. What if, after all, Stephen was just one of them? What if she ended up having to hate Stephen?

What Beth learned that summer at NASA jolted her perception of reality. She learned that there were men who could admire her mind. For the first time in her life she actually approved of her own looks, her no-nonsense, trouble-free short hair, her makeup-free face, her blue jeans, her carefully clipped fingernails. For the first time in her life, her body was not an enemy; it didn't betray her by attracting annoying attention.

Beth learned that hatred, her hatred for Megan, was as sustaining as love. Her thoughts were as preoccupied with revenge as they had been occupied with passion for Stephen. She also learned that computers were an essential tool for her future. Computers were the future. The sooner she mastered computers, the better. Her mathematical mind was able to solve most complicated problems with time and a slide rule. She could instruct a computer to solve the problem in a fraction of the time. The computer was a new challenge, a clever, multi-potent adversary, which, if she could master its language, would become an indispensable ally.

When Beth returned to Stanford, she enrolled in two advanced computer courses. She convinced the professors that her experience at NASA should exempt her from the introductory course requirements. In truth, she had very little experience, but she was impatient to learn the more challenging aspects of writing computer programs.

Beth was the only woman in either class. The classes were small seminars; most of the students were enrolled in both classes. For the first time in her life, Beth was intellectually in over her head. She simply didn't know the basics of computer language and the textbooks all took basic knowledge as a given.

Beth needed help. She decided that it would be best to hire one of the other students to tutor her. If she asked a professor to help her, he might make her drop the class.

Her classmates were a homogeneous-looking group of spectacled, serious, nonathletic eggheads. Male equivalents of what she should have looked like. She liked them all, in principle, for their brains and their apparent lack of interest in her. She finally selected a tall, slender blond with tousled hair and wire-rimmed glasses. He always asked what she considered to be pertinent questions in class, had the answers when questioned, and, at rest, his mouth curved amiably into a smile.

"John?" Beth had followed him for a distance away from the classroom. He spun around.

"Yes? Uh, I don't know your name."

"Beth. I was wondering if I could talk to you for a minute about the classes." Beth stopped. John was laughing at her.

"Sorry. I cannot believe your accent. It's strange enough to have a woman in the classes, but a Southern belle!"

"I'm a Texan."

"You never say anything in class. I just had imagined a different voice." John was enjoying himself.

"If you say 'wow' or 'neat,' I'm leaving."

"I admit it, in some ways I am the 'wow' and 'neat' type, but I usually save that kind of enthusiasm for ideas, not accents. Besides, *you* called this meeting." He was taunting her and for some reason she wasn't annoyed. Perhaps because he was so clearly testing her mind but not flirting.

"Right." A term from the summer. "I wondered if I could pay you to teach me some of the basics of computer language. I feel a little behind in the class."

"A little?"

"A lot"

"Have you ever taken a computer course before?"

"Not exactly."

"Do you realize how many courses the rest of us have taken? Don't you think it's a little nervy just to sashay into an upper-level course?"

"I am a little nervy." Beth paused. "I am also very smart. I have the right kind of mind for this. I learn quickly. I don't think it will take long—"

"You are saying it won't take you long to make up three years of courses?"

Beth shrugged. "I've done a lot of reading. All you have to do is answer my questions. There are just some concepts I don't understand." She paused. "I'll pay you fifty dollars an hour."

John threw back his head and laughed. It was a pleasant laugh. "Fifty dollars an hour?"

John had worked all his life; he had a part-time job at Stanford. He had never made more than five dollars an hour. He wondered if it was all a joke—her presence in class, this conversation, her offer. If so, it was a pretty funny one. If not, she was a remarkable woman. He looked at her serious dark eyes; they weren't laughing. Not even a twinkle.

"If you can teach me what I need to know, it's worth that much money to me."

"If I can teach you what you need to know, in a reasonable amount of time, then you can pay me."

Finding a time proved difficult. John worked at the campus coffeehouse, waiting tables and playing the guitar. He was entitled to short breaks each hour.

"We can talk during your breaks. I'll just get a table and keep ordering coffee and studying."

"You're kidding!"

"No. I'll be there tonight at nine. I'll have my questions written out."

During his first break, John walked over to her table, barely able to suppress his amusement. She sat in a corner table, peering over her books in the dimly lit room. She was the only person there alone and the only one studying. But she seemed oblivious to the noise, the smoke, the poor lighting, the smell of marijuana, and the conversations of other students.

"Okay. Ask away."

Alter the second question John knew that everything Beth had said was true. She had the right kind of mind; she had done the reading. And, worst of all, she would learn it quickly. Already she was asking about ideas that many of them had asked about, some only after months of study, some not at all. The ones who never knew to ask the questions that Beth was asking would never truly conquer the computer. But she would. She was asking the same questions that John had asked, long before his classmates. Question after question reminded him vividly of his own learning and his own thrill at finding the answers. It excited him to explain the answers to her, because when she understood, her reaction was as his had been—joyous, triumphant, powerful.

Most of the people who worked in the coffeehouse performed as well as waited tables. John played the guitar and sang, ballads and folk songs popularized by the singers of the sixties and early seventies: Joan Baez, Judy Collins, Peter, Paul, and Mary, Bob Dylan. The first night Beth was there, John asked her what she thought.

"About what?"

"My singing." John knew he had a pleasant, strong singing voice.

"Your . . . ?" Beth looked confused. She hadn't noticed; she had been studying. The next night she listened and was impressed. She thought wistfully about her piano playing. It had been so long since she had really played. Even this summer, at home, she hadn't had time to practice.

Beth came to the coffeehouse at nine, five nights in a row. Five nights in a row John's employer had to remind John when his breaks were over. The coffeehouse manager was intrigued. Beth and John huddled together, close but not intimate, one talking seriously, the other listening intently and nodding, then the roles reversing. Occasionally they wrote on sheets of paper. Occasionally they smiled. She always listened when he sang.

They're planning something, he finally decided. Like a bank robbery. Bonnie and Clyde of the coffeehouse set. He liked John. Over the years he had been a reliable, hard worker and a popular entertainer, always punctual, always pleasant. So, his goading was gentle; every hour he went to their table, feeling like an intruder, and tapped John on the shoulder.

By the end of the first night, John knew that in a few hours of concentrated work they could succeed at Beth's goal. It was silly to drag those hours out into bits and pieces at work. Silly but wonderful. Normally, John used those hours to think, to make plans, to solve problems as he mechanically did his work. But with Beth there, he looked forward to going to work.

By the end of the first week, he and Beth could discuss concepts at a level that was challenging to him. He discussed ideas with her that he had never discussed with his classmates, because they weren't ready or because he didn't trust them. The frustration of the constant interruption while he was working became too great. They arranged to meet in the evening, before work, for dinner at the Student Union Building.

At the end of the second week, Beth gave him five hundred dollars in cash. They both knew that she had caught up with the rest of the class. Indeed, the evening tutorials had become discussions of the ideas and problem assigned in class.

"What's this?" John asked innocently when she handed him the envelope.

"Five hundred dollars. I didn't count all the hours in the coffeehouse when we weren't talking." She sounded almost apologetic.

"I'm not taking it."

"We made a deal. You really helped me. If it hadn't been for you, I might have had to give up." In the two weeks he had known her, despite the fact that they had not spent one minute in personal conversation, John had learned about Beth's determination.

"Well, but it has been fun. It took you about five minutes to catch up, so pay me ten dollars. The rest of the time I learned as much from you as you did from me." John didn't know anyone who could give away five hundred dollars. He hated to imagine what Beth would have to go without to make up for it.

"No, John. We had a deal." She hesitated. "I really can afford it. You just saved me at least a year of tuition. I'll probably be able to graduate a year early. So, take it." She shoved the envelope at him. He took it because he didn't want to make her angry.

"When I'm a millionaire I'll pay you back, with interest."

"A millionaire?"

"Multi actually. Yes. I have a plan." He hesitated, debating something with himself. "Someday I'll tell you about it."

John hadn't told anyone about his plan. He hadn't ever told anyone that he planned to be a millionaire. But as he thought about it later, he made a decision. He would tell Beth about it someday. He would like to have her opinion. Their minds worked alike. He knew that she would take it seriously and that she would tell him honestly what she thought.

Chapter Thirteen

Within a week of her return to campus that fall, once she and Stephen had settled into the cabin at San Gregorio, Megan went to the student health center to request a prescription for birth control pills. Megan decided that she now fell into the category that the doctor had mentioned—a serious, permanent relationship. The gynecologist Megan had seen was not in; however, she had left clear notes on Megan's chart that enabled Megan to get the prescription.

Megan auditioned for, and won, the lead in the campus production of *Cat On A Hot Tin Roof.* It was a challenging, emotionally exhausting role. It gave Megan a chance to test her—Beth's—Southern accent.

Megan devoted her spare time to making the perfect "nest" for herself and Stephen, her energy and her love for Stephen and their life together apparently limitless. Megan hung new blue and white curtains and made a quilt for their bed. She planted the window boxes with small azalea bushes interspersed with forget-me-nots.

"Forget-me-nots?" Stephen asked when he saw Megan's latest cheerful embellishment to their home.

She told him, then, what she had never told anyone, about the frightened, lonely five-year-old girl with her private world of flowers and forget-me-nots. Stephen held her hand as she spoke, gazing lovingly into her eyes.

"You are my forget-me-not. My precious, forever, forget-me-not," he said quietly when she finished.

"And you are my darling Stefano," Megan said. Stefano, her private, intimate nickname for Stephen, her gorgeous Roman god with black curly hair, sensuous green eyes, and a perfectly sculpted body. Her wonderful lover. Her dearest friend.

Megan and Stephen sat on the deck of the cabin at San Gregorio watching the autumn sun set over the vast blue-gray ocean. Below, on the beach, a young mother played tag with her two children. Stephen and Megan watched them frolic in the still-warm sand, could hear their joyous laughter, their shrieks of delight.

"What beautiful children," Megan said. "So happy. So free. No worries. That's how our children will be."

"Our children?" Stephen asked, surprised.

Megan turned to him, her blue eyes sparkling. "Yes! Our beautiful little children." She stopped suddenly, detecting a flicker of worry in Stephen's face. "You do want children, don't you?"

"I guess. Yes. *Someday,"* he said thoughtfully. Then he held her hand to his lips and said, "But right now, all I want, all I can ever imagine wanting, is you. You. Forever."

In November, Megan started having terrible headaches. They made her cry, from pain and frustration. Stephen told her that she was pushing too hard. But, even when she rested, she couldn't completely control them. Stephen's concern deepened and finally he enlisted Jake's help.

"She won't see a doctor. I'm afraid it's something serious."

"She's probably afraid, too," Jake offered. He knew Megan and her fear of death.

Stephen nodded. "Will you speak to her? It's becoming a battered issue with us. We've come to an impasse."

"Sure."

Jake made an appointment for Megan at the Palo Alto Clinic with a neurologist. He had called Dr. Phillips in Bethesda, described the symptoms, and made an appointment with a specialist. Then he made a mid-morning coffee date with Megan. They met in front of the Student Union.

"Let's go somewhere else. I have my car."

Megan wasn't surprised. She and Jake had spent a lot of time off campus. They had enjoyed getting away.

Jake drove directly to the clinic and parked in the lot.

Megan understood immediately and pressed herself resolutely into the car seat.

"You goddamned goody two shoes."

"We're not playing games here, Megan. I've had some people pull some strings to get you in this soon. This doctor is usually booked for months in advance.

"Does Stephen know you did this?"

"No. He asked for my help though. I knew if I told him, he'd tell you and you would balk."

"I'm balking now."

"Don't be a child. And don't you dare make a fool of me." She had never been ordered by Jake before. It was clear that she had no choice. She opened the car door slowly.

"You bastard."

The headaches disappeared within one month of the appointment. Megan told no one why they resolved, but reassured everyone that it had been "ridiculous, really nothing." Her own relief and the return of her good health were so apparent that they confirmed what she said—there was nothing wrong with her.

* * *

Jake took Carrie to dinner in San Francisco every other week that fall. They were easy, happy times. Carrie abandoned her obsession to find out about Jake's past. She didn't want to jeopardize their growing friendship. It was enough, because it was all she had, just to be with him. On his terms.

Jake's terms: no touching; no kiss, even a brotherly one. Off-limits topics: Jake's past; Jake's future; Jake. Fair topics: anything about Carrie. Was she dating? "Not really." Why not? "No one interesting. Too busy." Was she writing? "Yes." Did she want him to read what she wrote? "No!"

One evening he took her to the theater before dinner. It was the repertory's production of Shaw's *Man and Superman*. Carrie watched Jake's face during the performance— transfixed, mesmerized, peaceful.

"You really enjoy theater," she said afterward.

"Yes, I do. But I prefer opera."

"Opera!"

"Have you seen much opera?"

"None." Carrie giggled.

"Caroline, what do they teach you in Boston? I'll take you to an opera in the spring. I think you'll like it."

The day after he received his acceptance to Harvard Law School, in December, Stephen and Megan announced their engagement. They planned a June wedding. They would be married the day after Stephen's graduation in the small chapel in Memorial Church. Carrie would be the maid of honor. Jake would be the best man.

"White roses and forget-me-nots everywhere!" Megan announced over lunch the next day. "Carrie, we have to start looking, soon, for our dresses. Let's make the guest list right now. Let's see, your family, my family, Jake's family."

"Jake's family?"

"Sure. I mean they'll be here for his graduation anyway."

"That's right. I guess they will be."

"And Ian and Margaret, of course." Ian Knight, Megan's

208

director, the man who was shaping her career. Ian and Margaret, Megan's surrogate family, her dear friends. Carrie was eager to meet them. "I'm sure they'll come out from Connecticut."

"And Beth?"

"No, not Beth. She wouldn't come anyway. She still thinks I stole Stephen from her. She doesn't understand that he was never hers."

It was true. It had become increasingly difficult for Carrie to juggle her friendships with Megan and Beth. Beth refused to hear anything about Megan and Stephen. Carrie had hoped the wedding announcement would end Beth's anger, but it only made it worse.

"Poor Stephen," Beth had said with venom. Then she had added, confidently, "The wedding will never happen."

"It *will* happen, Beth. They are really in love. I wish you could accept that."

"Megan is in love with Megan. Period. She is enjoying the role of being in love with Stephen. But she'll tire of it, Carrie. Long before June."

By unspoken agreement, John and Beth met twice weekly. Beth drank iced tea, watched John eat his cafeteria dinner, and they discussed computers, science, aeronautics. They never spoke about their personal lives, although John made occasional attempts to find out about Beth.

"I discovered something interesting the other day."

"Yes?"

"I saw your picture in the *Frosh Book*."

"Oh." Uninterested.

"From Southern belle to . . ." John hesitated. To what? Truculent beauty.

"Cowgirl," Beth said.

"Hardly. So, why the change?"

Beth looked surprised. "To avoid attention, of course. So people—*men*—would leave me alone."

"If it's working, it's not because of the way you look. You do a fairly good job of projecting . . ." Again he paused. He was never sure how far to push her.

"Contempt," Beth offered.

"That's a good word. You never give anybody a break."

"Wrong. I just don't give everybody a break. Most people are so trivial. So uncritical. I don't trust uncritical people. Except Carrie, of course."

"Contempt is looming larger as the correct adjective."

Beth smiled. "John, you are no goody-goody yourself. You are probably as critical as I am."

"I don't deny it."

Beth was silent for awhile. Then she said, "You know that song that you sing, with the line about the great relief of having you to talk to?"

John nodded.

"It makes me think of you. It is so comfortable . . ." Beth stopped short. Her clear brown eyes clouded, opaqued by an emotion that horrified John. But they weren't looking at John. They followed a couple passing by the window, a handsome black-haired man with a beautiful golden blond woman, holding hands, laughing. John didn't recognize them, but he watched Beth and learned something about her. This woman with the brilliant mind and sharp tongue and incredible natural sensuality had been wounded deeply. And the wound was still wide open, raw, exposed, unhealed. And, perhaps, unhealing.

Beth sighed and looked at the table.

"If looks could kill," John said carefully, "those two would be history."

"Wrong." Beth managed a half smile. "My aim is better than that. Only one of them would be history."

John waited for her to say more. He wanted to press her. What had happened to "the great relief of having you to talk to"? he wondered. But he waited too long. Beth looked at her watch.

"I have to go."

* * *

Letters arrived from Julia. Jake threw them all away, unopened. One evening in February, just as he was leaving to get Carrie for their dinner in the city, a telegram arrived.

Jean-Phillipe spending Easter holidays with children. I can't face them. Meet me at the villa . . . please. Love Julia.

Jake crumpled the yellow paper in a ball and threw it angrily on the floor. In a rage he drove to Carrie's dormitory.

Carrie opened the door immediately to his knock. She looked radiant—fresh, unspoiled, eager to be with him, happy to see him.

"Is Beth here?" he asked without saying hello.

"No. Jake, what's wrong?" Carrie backed into the room. He followed her and shut the door.

"It's no good. We can't go out tonight, Caroline. Something has come up." He had his hand on the doorknob.

"Are you okay?" Her voice was tentative and sad. But despite her disappointment, she was worried about him. He couldn't bear to look at her.

"I'm okay. I'm sorry. It's just something I have to deal with now. Tonight. I won't be good company until I sort it out." Jake was restless to leave. He hated the hurt on Carrie's face.

"I'm your friend, you know. It wouldn't hurt you to tell me what's wrong. Maybe I could help."

He was tempted to tell her everything. About the adultery he would have committed in Saigon if he hadn't been wounded. About the adultery he was thinking about now. That was the worst part—he was seriously thinking about going to Julia. To be with her while her husband was with his children.

He thought about telling Carrie right then about the kind of man he was. To put them both out of the misery that their hopeless friendship would bring them. To end it. Because Carrie would never understand. She could learn all that she would ever need to know about him in a few moments and she would be disgusted.

And it would be over.

Jake paused. He didn't have the courage to tell her. He didn't have the courage to lose her.

Jake drove aimlessly for an hour, then drove to the cabin at San Gregorio. For once in his life, he needed to talk, to ask for advice. He wanted to tell Stephen about Vietnam and Julia and Carrie. He couldn't make sense of his emotions on his own.

He pounded on the cabin door.

"Who is it?"

"It's me, Megan. Jake."

She opened the door quickly. Her face was flushed, her eyes puffy. Tear-swollen eyes. He smelled Scotch on her breath.

"Where's Stephen?" he demanded, choosing to avoid commenting on her obvious distress.

"In Boston, finding us a place to live, meeting with some lawyers about a summer job."

"Damn!"

"What's your problem?" Megan snarled.

"Nothing that wouldn't be helped by some of that Scotch. What's yours?" he asked idly. Jake wasn't in the mood for a Megan tailspin. He poured himself a large glass of Scotch and began drinking.

They glowered at each other and drank. Finally Megan began to giggle.

"I hate you. You are so smug."

"I hate you, too." Jake smiled.

"Have you ever felt so consumed by someone else that you were afraid of losing yourself? Never mind; of course you haven't."

"Maybe," Jake answered seriously. Maybe before. Maybe now. Maybe that was his great fear. "I think you're going through the usual pre-nuptial cold feet."

"What about doing something you believe is wrong because you care more about what the other person wants than your own self-respect?" It was carefully worded.

"Spell it out to me, Megan." This wasn't the usual theatrical Megan tailspin. It was something quite specific.

"I can't!"

"Great. Gosh, it's been nice visiting with you." Jake got up to leave.

Megan stepped in front of the door and, when he tried to pass, she kissed him. Jake kissed her back.

"We always had chemistry, didn't we?" he murmured.

"Make love to me, Jake. For old times' sake."

"It's not old times, Megan. You are about to marry my best friend."

"It's not like having an affair. What we have started long before I fell in love with Stephen. And it's different from the love I have for Stephen. It's something else, but it's real, and it will always be there. And besides, it doesn't count."

"Doesn't count?"

"I'm not being unfaithful to Stephen."

"Really? Whose rules are those?"

"Those are *the* rules."

"Megan's rules. Maybe Jake's rules." Certainly Julia's rules. "But not Stephen's." Or Carrie's.

Megan started to cry. "I know. It's just—"

"It's just that you need something. What, Megan? What is wrong?"

Megan shook her head. "I can't tell you. Not yet. Oh, I am so tired and confused."

"Why don't I put you in bed—to sleep. This may all be better in the morning."

* * *

Jake thought about the telegram he would send to Julia in the morning: Not in a million years. He drove toward Lagunita Hall. It was one-thirty in the morning. He just wanted to drive by.

The light in Carrie's room was on. Jake parked his car, smiled as he collected small rocks, and tossed them carefully, accurately, against her second-floor window. The light went off, he saw her shadow in the window.

In a few moments she joined him. It was long past curfew for sophomores. She had sneaked out the fire exit that had, for years, and unbeknownst to the administration, been disconnected from its alarm. She wore baggy blue jeans, graphic, comfortable memories of her larger shape, and a sweatshirt. She had been writing.

"I came to apologize."

"No need." Carrie's voice was cool.

"I got a telegram from a friend asking me to do something that I thought was wrong."

"But something you were tempted to do."

Jake cocked his head and sighed. "Yes. Something I had to think about."

"And you solved it?"

"Yes."

"Great." Carrie's voice was flat, almost unrecognizable.

"I owe you dinner."

"You don't owe me anything." Except to trust me, to treat me like a friend.

"Are you free tonight?"

"No. That's what I was going to tell you. I made the varsity tennis team. Starting this weekend we will be traveling to other schools on the coast, for matches, or will be hosting other teams when they come here. So, my weekends are full." Carrie must have been thrilled to make the varsity team; her voice made it sound as though someone had died.

Jake didn't know what to say. Carrie's message was clear. She had spent the evening making a decision of her own. She didn't want to see him. Jake couldn't blame her. And yet the decisions he had made—not to go to Julia, not to be with Megan—had given him, for the first time, hope that maybe someday he and Carrie . . .

"It's cold and late. I'm going back in." Carrie didn't look at him.

"Too late," he whispered and then said to her back as she walked away, "Take care. Caroline."

Carrie made her way through the blur of her tears back to her room.

"Remember last fall when I told you that I was going to be a millionaire?"

"Multi!" Beth corrected. John smiled. Of course she remembered. Beth ignored nothing and remembered everything. That was the way her mind worked.

"Well, I'm ready to tell you my idea, because I want your reaction. Your honest reaction."

Beth's cool brown eyes widened with surprise.

"Oh, right. I forgot. I don't need to worry about tact with you. Honesty at all costs. I have it all written down here, the proposal, but basically the idea is this . . ."

Small computers for the home, computers for small businesses, computers as learning tools for children, maybe even computers for games.

"Portable computers, John? Computers you can carry?" Beth asked, curious but not skeptical.

"Yes. Look Beth. We're already in the computer age— you, me, the technical sciences, big business. We're already there. But in five, ten, twenty years everything will be computerized. And every business, everybody will want one. It's going to be very big business. I'm sure of it."

"Who's going to operate these little computers?" Beth asked, skepticism now clear in her voice.

"Beth, you are such an intellectual snob. I—we—can make computers that are simple to use. We write the programs. Different types of programs for different needs—

budget planning, data processing, writing, calculating. The intellectual snobs write the programs, the simple, clear instruction manuals, and they earn the money."

"Who makes the computers?"

"That's the problem. The best would be to have your own company. If I go to Xerox or IBM or Memorex with this idea, even if I patent it, they'll pay for the idea and then they'll make the millions. That's why I wrote the proposal, to try to entice investors with vision who are not already in the computer business. I've made a list of names. The trouble is, when you give somebody the idea, even just the outline, you're taking a risk that it will be stolen, patent or no patent. It's not as if I'm the only person who has thought of this. I bet the big companies are already working on it."

"I don't know. It's pretty visionary."

"Do you really think computers are a flash in the pan?"

"No." Beth was silent, her large eyes squinted slightly. It was a signal that she was thinking. It was an expression that John had seen often, usually preceding one of her insights.

"Do you know people who could actually build a computer?"

"I could build a computer." John paused. "So could you with a little coaching."

"How much would it cost? How much are you asking these people for?"

"It's all in here. Pre-production, production, marketing. It's all a guess. But if I could even just make one and then sell the patented product . . . That wouldn't cost too much. It wouldn't be my own company, but . . ."

John was discouraged. Beth hadn't responded the way he had hoped. He wanted her to like the idea. He trusted her opinion. Her response had been neutral to negative. He watched her look through the proposal that represented years of plans and dreams. She was scrutinizing the budget page.

"I don't think you should aim for anything less than your own company," she said finally. "And I think your estimates

216

here are unrealistically low. I think you need at least a hundred thousand to make it work."

John was disheartened. His maximum estimate had been twenty-five thousand and that had seemed hopeless. He shrugged and reached to retrieve his proposal, his pipe dream, from her. She didn't let go.

"Is this your only copy?"

"Yes!"

"May I take it with me?"

"Why?"

"To read it, of course."

"I don't think reading it will change your mind. I've explained the idea to you. And you seem a lot this side of impressed."

"Maybe you've never seen me be impressed before. I think this is the most sensational idea I have ever heard. I just don't want you to lose it. Or have it stolen. We—you—really have to be careful. Have you told anyone else?"

"No."

"Good. Promise me that you won't go to any of these potential investors until I've had a chance to read it carefully."

"Don't worry. You have the only copy."

Can I trust her? he wondered. It was a moot point. Beth already knew enough of the idea to steal it if she wanted to.

Three weeks later Beth walked into the coffeehouse. She hadn't mentioned the proposal, or returned it. And she had, uncharacteristically, missed four days of class. She stood at the door until John came over to her.

He saw the sparkle in her eyes and smiled, curious, relieved to see her.

"What's up?"

"What are you planning to name your company?"

"What?" He could barely hear her above the guitarist.

"Can you get off early, like now? I have to talk with you."

"Are you okay?"

"Yes. Great. But if you need an excuse, I can faint or something."

"Wait here."

In four years John had never missed a day of work, and, even during finals week, he had never asked to leave early. The manager saw Beth and recognized her as the woman of the mysterious tête â têtes of last fall. He nodded. "Sure, kid. It's slow tonight."

"What's up, Beth?" John asked anxiously.

"We need to talk in a private place. Where do you live?"

They had known each other for seven months and Beth had no idea where he lived, or with whom.

"In the gardener's cottage at Professor Franklin's house."

"Does anyone else live there?"

"Only my wife and our three-week-old baby," John answered hotly.

"Oh! I didn't know you were married." Beth paused and shrugged. "I think your wife needs to know about this, too. Can we go there now?"

John nodded, bewildered, annoyed. Beth had barely missed a beat when he had mentioned a wife and baby.

They drove in silence to the tiny, one-room cottage that John rented for almost nothing. There were no lights; even the porch light was out.

"They must be asleep," Beth whispered and quietly shut the car door.

"Who?"

"Your wife and baby!"

"There's no wife and baby, Beth."

"Why did you say so then?"

"For a brilliant woman . . . Why are you playing games?"

"I'm not. Why are you?"

John led the way into the tiny, messy room. A single

mattress was shoved against one wall. John hastily pulled the cheap bedspread over the old, rumpled sheets. Magazines and books cluttered the floor and the cinder block and plywood makeshift bookshelves. There was no telephone, no television, no stereo.

Beth noticed the clutter but was more amazed at the obvious poverty. She remembered John's reaction to the five hundred dollars she had given him. No wonder! How would he respond to her current offer?

Beth looked around for a place to sit. There was a single, battered aluminum and plastic chair pushed carelessly under a matching kitchen table with a stained linoleum top. The table was cluttered with books and sheets of paper.

Beth set her briefcase on the floor and removed John's proposal, a legal-sized folder, and a bottle of champagne.

"We have to go over this together."

John pointed to the mattress on the floor. "It doubles as a couch."

"Okay. Here's your proposal. And here is a long legal document that gives you one hundred thousand dollars to create your own computer company . . . and here's a bottle of champagne to celebrate this and my twenty-first birthday."

John's hands trembled as she handed him the legal folder. The document was eighteen typed pages, single-spaced. He didn't even try to read it, but as he scanned through its pages, two names were typed in at frequent intervals: his and Beth's.

"I don't understand, Beth."

"On my twenty-first birthday my inheritance from my grandfather, which has been kept in trust for me since his death five years ago, became wholly mine. I have decided to use some of it to back a new—as yet unnamed—small computer company of which you are the company president. When the company is a success, you'll pay me back, without interest. My lawyer nearly died at that, but your lawyer loved it."

"My lawyer?"

"I knew you'd never get a lawyer to look at this, so I got one for you. Anyway, we're more partners than borrower and lender, because there's profit sharing. If—when—you get rich, I get rich. I think it's a fair contract."

"Fair! I can't believe it. Beth, you are making it happen."

"No, you are making it happen. Although I don't intend to be a totally silent partner."

"I don't want you to be! I need your ideas. See that stack over there?" John pointed to one of several precariously stacked piles of folders and paper. "That is all drawings, circuitry sketches, and program ideas."

"How about a name for the company?"

"I hadn't gotten that far."

"That's the only blank we have to fill in on this contract. Plus signing and initialing our own names."

John was silent for several minutes, looking at the contract but not reading. Finally he said, very quietly, "I didn't know that you had money, you know."

"I know. Anyway, we both benefit from this."

"What if it fails?" John asked uncomfortably.

"It *won't*. But, if it did, I would be really angry with you, but I couldn't get any money from you." Beth smiled, a rare, beautiful smile. "You had a really shrewd lawyer."

"I just can't believe this." He wanted to touch her, hold her, kiss her. He had wanted to so many times. But even now it wasn't possible.

Beth blushed. "Let's just open the champagne, go through the contract, and sign it. I want it to be official as soon as possible. Daddy and my financial advisors call me every day trying to get me to reconsider and get my money back into oil."

When they were finished, Beth left, leaving John with the signed contract.

"Think of a name and get this in the mail as soon as possible."

The next morning during their computer seminar, John passed a note to Beth.

BOARD MEETING
BETHSTAR COMPUTERS
Tonight—Student Union Building
John Taylor, President

"Don't you dare!" she hissed across the room.
John smiled and mouthed the words, "Too late."

Chapter Fourteen

In May, one month before the wedding, Megan telephoned Carrie to invite her to a dinner party.

"Who else is coming, Megan?"

"Just Jake."

"I don't think I can make it."

"Dammit, Carrie, I need to have you both here. It's important. Please."

Megan's temper had grown shorter in the past two months. Everyone attributed it to overwork—her lead role in *Night of the Iguana,* preparation for the wedding and the move to Boston, and her course work. But it was more than that. The headaches had recurred and were continual. Megan told no one, but her energy was consumed by the constant battle with pain and her determination to remain cheerful around Stephen.

"Megan, what's wrong?" Carrie countered.

"Nothing. I'm sorry, Carrie. Lots of pressure, that's all. Has something happened between you and Jake? Is that why you don't want to come?"

"No, I haven't seen him since February. I guess I'm just feeling pressured, too. It will be nice to have a relaxed evening with friends. Of course I'll come."

That evening, Jake telephoned Carrie. It had been three months since that February evening when Carrie had made her decision to stop seeing him altogether. In those months she had vacillated between regret at such impulsive behavior over a small thing like a canceled date and confidence that perpetuating the relationship, even the infrequent dinners, would ultimately bring her more sadness. Her mind balanced the joy she felt when she was with him, when he laughed at her teasing, when he talked to her seriously, with the anger and frustration at the secrets he kept from her. And the physical distance he kept. He had said in the beginning that all they could be was good friends. Carrie knew that, eventually, that would not be enough for her. No, her decision had been the right one—she had to protect herself.

But she missed him.

"Caroline? It's Jake."

"Hello."

"I would like to give you a ride to Stephen and Megan's party. I understand we are the only guests."

"Oh, that's not necessary."

"I didn't realize you had a car."

"I can use Beth's."

The pause was so long that Carrie thought that Jake might have hung up.

"I'll be by at five-thirty Friday night to pick you up." Then he hung up.

They drove in silence for several miles, through the lush mountain roads that crossed from Stanford to the ocean. The May evening was warm, windless. The smell of damp hay and spring flowers drifted into the open car windows. Carrie had decided to accept Jake's offer because, beginning with that evening, they would have to be together several times in the next month, witnessing the marriage license, dinners with their families before graduation, the rehearsal dinner, as best man and maid of honor in the wedding. Carrie had to be happy, civil, and indifferent to Jake for those occasions. She had to be certain that her feelings were under control.

As soon as she saw him she realized how difficult it would be for her.

"How's the tennis?" Jake asked finally.

"Great. Time and energy consuming, but I enjoy it."

"You're very good."

"Yes, so far we're undefeated. But we meet UCLA next weekend. That will be the acid test."

"I mean, *you* are very good. Much stronger than you look."

"You've seen me play?" Carrie asked weakly.

"Sure, I've gone to the matches you've played here."

But I've never seen you, Carrie thought. During a match Carrie concentrated totally on her tennis. She never looked at the crowd. Could she play if she knew Jake was watching?

"Why?" she asked reflexively, then realized she didn't want to hear the answer.

But Jake just looked at her.

"I have never played tennis, but it is a beautiful game to watch. Control, power, grace. I enjoy watching."

Jake the spectator, Carrie thought. One step removed from the action, observing, analyzing. Then she remembered his leg and the nagging, unsettling thought that something serious was wrong with it.

"What is your sport? What do you play?" She had never seen him in shorts, even in the hot spring weather. And he hadn't skied at Tahoe.

Jake blushed; she had caught him off guard. Another direct, unanswerable question from Carrie.

"None really. I used to run and swim." His voice sounded far away, remembering something. Then he said flatly, "But not anymore."

Why? Why? Why? Carrie wanted to ask, but knew she wouldn't get an answer.

* * *

"Something wonderful has happened!" Megan began as they sat watching the sunset from the deck of the beach house.

Carrie looked at her friend; she was tired, pale, strained. Megan didn't look as if anything wonderful had happened. Even her voice was unconvincing. Carrie glanced at Stephen. He looked surprised.

Whatever the news was, Megan had not yet told Stephen. And she had carefully chosen her audience—Carrie and Jake—for the performance. Megan was performing, Carrie realized. Even her enthusiasm was an act.

Carrie looked at her brother. Please don't hurt him, Megan. Beth's relentless predictions that the marriage would never happen pounded in Carrie's head.

"What, Megan?" Carrie asked anxiously.

"Well, when I was in New York over Spring Break, Ian offered to have me join his summer tour. This year he is taking a troupe to Europe, to perform and study. It is really a handpicked group."

"That's wonderful, darling," Stephen said, genuinely pleased for his fiancée. "I'll miss my new bride, but maybe I can join you for part of the tour."

"Oh, I hope so! That would be so much fun. I'm sure you can talk those lawyers into at least a week off." Megan was smiling, but that was all. There was no radiance, no sparkle.

It's not even a very good acting job, Jake thought. What the hell's the bottom line? He thought he could guess.

"When does the tour leave, Megan?" he asked quietly.

Megan stared at him, half glower, half relief.

"Well, that's the problem. It leaves in two weeks. And we travel until mid-September." She didn't look at Stephen, but she felt his eyes on her.

"Two weeks!" he whispered. Then, angrily, "Had you given any thought to the impact of this on our wedding?"

"Please don't be angry, Stephen." Megan's voice was weak, tired, close to tears. And it was not an act. "Of course I have. That's why I wanted the four of us here." Megan swallowed and came up with a smile that quivered. "I thought we could postpone it until October. And then have a romantic, Cape Cod wedding."

Silence.

"Of course we could get married now, before I go. Or I can tell Ian no. I just thought you would be busy working this summer, Stephen. It seemed like such an opportunity. We agreed that I would have my career, too!"

It was Stephen who finally broke the silence.

"I don't think we should rush into this marriage. You three can plan all the weddings you want, but I have already made my wedding plans." Stephen left.

"Stefano!" Megan whispered. Then she started to cry.

"What could you possibly have been thinking?" Carrie asked, bewildered, and left to catch Stephen. By the time she reached the top of the path to the beach, she could already see him in the distance, running on the sand. Stephen ran seven or eight miles a day. This evening he would probably run farther.

Carrie stopped at the top of the path, then reluctantly returned to the cabin. She wished she had driven Beth's car. Then she could leave without seeing Megan again.

Jake watched Megan cry for a few minutes, then got up and put his arms around her trembling body.

"I suggest that you tell him the truth, whatever it is."

Megan looked up at him, startled.

"You're not that great an actress. I know you were lying. Stephen and Carrie don't know how to lie, so maybe they believed you. But whatever it is, Megan, tell him."

"I was telling the truth. I am telling the truth."

"Don't play him for a fool, Megan." Jake ignored her protestations. "He may be kind and gentle, but he is not a fool. And he is very proud."

"Leave me alone, Jake," Megan snapped, pulling herself free.

"Okay. It is your mess. I just hope you can get yourself out of it."

Jake saw Carrie standing in the doorway. She had been there the entire time.

"Let's go," he said, walking toward her.

"You don't believe her?" Carrie asked as soon as they were outside. Jake opened the car door for her and waited until he got in the car before answering.

"No."

"Why would she lie?"

Jake smiled. He started to reach to touch her face, then withdrew his hand. Carrie blushed.

"I heard what you said about me and Stephen not knowing how to lie."

"It was a compliment."

"Why would Megan lie?"

"For the reason that most people lie—because the truth would be more painful."

"More painful for whom? Nothing could cause more pain than this for Stephen. It seemed painful for Megan, too, didn't you think?"

"Yes."

"Do you think she's in love with someone else?" Carrie asked anxiously. Did Megan want Jake back?

"No!"

"Do you think she's ill?"

"Maybe."

"Do you think," Carrie asked slowly, painfully, "that she really doesn't love him? That this is her way of getting out?" Like Beth has been predicting.

Jake shook his head slowly. "I don't know, Caroline. I just don't know."

Miraculously, Megan and Stephen resolved the problem. Once Stephen's anger subsided, he found less argument with her plans than with the manner in which she had presented them.

"There's madness in her method!" he teased.

227

Stephen agreed that it was an opportunity of a lifetime. They had already discussed the importance of her career. They knew that there would be times apart; she planned to do theater in New York and London. And he planned to practice law in Boston. They knew that their love was strong enough to survive time and distance.

In the week before she left, in addition to everything else, Megan and Carrie made plans for the Cape Cod wedding in October.

The week before Jake graduated from Stanford, he received another telegram from Julia.

Divorce from Jean-Phillipe final. Now will you meet me? Julia

Jake thought about the telegram for two days. Then he made two phone calls. The first was to the villa in Monte Carlo, where they had spent Christmas eighteen months before. Julia had given him the number as she had stood, crying, at the airport in Paris, just before he had flown back to Palo Alto. And just before she had gone into Paris to spend New Year's Eve with Jean-Phillipe.

He stared at the number written by Julia on the crumpled piece of paper that he had saved as he waited for the overseas operator. It still made him angry. But he was calling her.

There was no answer at the villa. On a whim he dialed the private number in Washington. It rang. He wondered who owned the number now.

"You got my telegram," Julia answered.

"Yes." Jake had forgotten about her voice. Soft. Fragile. He hadn't heard it for eighteen months, but it was the same. And the memories rushed back.

"How are you?"

"Well. Graduating soon."

"I know. I'd like to be there."

"Be my guest, but I won't be." Jake realized how harsh his voice sounded. The memories were good and bad. The recent memories were bad. His anger was still near the surface. He wanted to control it. He wanted to see her, to be with her.

"Oh!" Julia reacted to the roughness of his voice.

"I'll be in Washington. In training."

"Training? Washington?" Julia echoed hopefully.

"I am going to work for the State Department."

"Doing what?"

"Whatever they say. I want to work abroad. Diplomatic Corps. I won't be in the Armed Services officially, of course."

Of course, Julia thought, because of your leg. Because of what happened last time you were in the army. What the hell is he doing this for?

"Why don't you just manage your estate? That would be a safe, full-time job."

There was a long pause. They both knew the answer. Finally Jake said it.

"Because of Frank. Because I owe him something. Because I need to do something for what he believed in."

Julia's worst fears were confirmed. Jake wanted to do something that would have an impact on the safety and supremacy of democracy. Jake didn't want to work in an embassy in England. He wanted to be on the front lines, negotiating with terrorists, negotiating for peace. It was the same compulsion that had driven him into battle that day in Vietnam on a day he was off duty. He wasn't doing it for Frank; he was doing it for himself. But it was the same compulsion she had seen in Frank. Patriotism. Jake and Frank were both patriots; Jake could have been Frank's blood son. Julia admired their patriotism with a contempt that was half for herself, for not feeling the way they did, and half for them, for being so obstinate.

"Who will you be working for?"

"Stuart Dawson," Jake said nonchalantly, knowing full

well that Julia knew him and the area of diplomatic relations in his charge—the most dangerous missions, the most sensitive world targets. Frank had introduced Jake to Stuart before he died. It all made sense now, the foreign languages, the political science and history courses. Jake had created an undergraduate degree that would prepare him for this.

"Oh, Jake," she said quietly, silently mourning.

"I want to do it, Julia. I am excited about it. I think I can do it well, be of use."

"I know you can. What about your leg?" A tiny part of Julia's mind even wished his leg would get worse, to prevent him from doing this.

"It has a few good years left in it. I go in for my yearly check next week. I'm not going to be a secret agent, you know. Nothing requiring anything more than mental agility." His voice softened. He realized how much he had missed her. "And remember who taught me that!"

Julia was silent. That topic of conversation was over. Where next?

"My last final is over at noon next Friday. I'll take the evening flight to National, so I'll arrive about two. I still have a key if I have permission to use it."

"I'll meet your flight." Darling.

As he got into his car to drive away from the Stanford campus for the last time, after four years, Jake made a subconscious decision. He would drive through campus—a sentimental last look—past the post office, the student union building, the fountain in White Plaza, the theater, the lake, winding slowly through the narrow streets to the opposite side of campus. As he drove toward Lagunita Hall, he made another decision. He would not stop; he would not try to find her. He would just drive past.

Then he saw Carrie, obviously returning to the dormitory after a game of tennis. She swung the racket easily, happily lost in thought. Jake hesitated, then drove up beside her.

"Hi."

Carrie spun around, startled, then suddenly self-conscious about her damp shirt and sweat-curled tendrils of hair. Jake wore gray slacks, a pale blue sports coat, a white long-sleeved shirt, and a tie.

"Jake."

"I thought tennis season was over. You won, didn't you?"

"Yes. We actually beat UCLA. I was just practicing. It's a good study break."

"I was just leaving . . ."

"Leaving?"

"Yes. My last final was today."

"You aren't staying for graduation? I thought your family might want to watch you graduate."

Carrie's parents had canceled their plans to watch Stephen graduate when the wedding was postponed. It was money they could save and use toward the wedding festivities in Boston in October. But money should not have been a consideration for Jake's family.

"No. I am eager to get into the real world."

"What are you going to do?"

"Joining an international corporation. Lots of foreign travel."

"Sounds glamorous."

"We'll see." Jake paused. "I still owe . . . no . . . I would like to take you out to dinner again, sometime."

"For old times' sake?" Carrie asked as lightly as she could. It was a safe offer; they might never see each other again. Then she remembered the wedding. "Will you make it in October, to the wedding?"

"I wouldn't miss it," Jake said distractedly. A flicker of worry crossed his face.

What is it? Carrie wondered. Is he worried that he won't make the wedding? Or is he worried that there won't be a wedding?

"I'll see you then, I guess," she said.

"Take care, Caroline."

Jake got back into his car and drove toward San Francisco Airport. He ached with a sadness that he couldn't define, a feeling of loss and emptiness. He wished he had told her again how sorry he was about everything. He wished he had told her a lot of things.

Jake and Julia lapsed effortlessly into the comfort of living with each other. For four weeks, Jake spent the days, often sixteen-hour days, at the State Department and the nights with Julia. The training was intense—customs, rituals, history, politics, jargon of the languages he had mastered in their purest forms in the classrooms of Stanford and Berkeley. Then there was interrogation training, psychological testing, memory tests, fatigue stress. Often, he returned to Julia's too tired to speak. They would wordlessly sit on the veranda in the white wrought-iron furniture, sipping wine, feeling the welcome coolness of the evening breezes, listening to the music of Mozart.

"I think they're grooming you to be a spy."

"No." Sometimes he wondered. They were training him to eavesdrop; to hear words spoken in the native tongue that the interpreters chose not to translate; to read the visual clues and body language. They were training him to be invisible yet omnipresent. A two-way mirror. And, they were training him in how to cope if he were captured.

Jake's first assignment was in Saudi Arabia, in Riyadh and Jeddah. It was hardly an assignment; it was a test run, a dry lab. Saudia Arabia had been rock-steady for years; politically almost inert. But culturally, it was a safe learning place.

Jake and Julia flew to Nice together. The eight-hour nonstop flight was the first chance they had had for uninterrupted, nonfatigued conversation since Jake's return from Palo Alto. They held hands and drank champagne in the first class cabin. It was a trend that Jake would establish early in his career with the State Department. He would fly first class at his own expense and stay in luxury hotels of his choosing en route to assignments.

"Do you want to talk about us?" Julia asked. "We've avoided that topic so far."

"You know how I feel. How I've always felt. I haven't changed."

"Yes, you have."

Jake raised his eyebrows. "Really?"

"Yes. You're more distant—even than usual. Pre-occupied, restless. Moody."

"Maybe it's because of my new job, Julia. I'm anxious about it, I don't deny it."

"No, it's something more. Or someone more."

"Aha! Is the lady jealous?"

"Maybe. Should I be?"

"Jealous enough to tie me down? The offer is still open, although I don't know why. You really are getting so old!"

"You've totally evaded my question and are throwing in the diversionary tactic of marriage. Clever, but transparent."

"And you are evading my question."

"What, will I marry you? Someday, Jake, I may say yes, just to call your bluff."

The conversation had deteriorated into half-teasing, half-serious banter. Julia decided to let it drop. But she wanted to know what—who—had happened to Jake in the past two years. Someday he would tell her.

Jake left Julia in Nice and continued on the Air France flight into Riyadh.

Jake joined the rest of the American delegation in Riyadh, the capital city of Saudi Arabia. There, the role that had been carefully created for him during the weeks of training in Washington was put to the test. Jake was the underling, the lowest man on the totem pole. It was a position that the Saudis knew well—the invisible, unimportant servant, like the Bedouins or the Pakistanis, meant to serve and to be ignored.

Jake liked the role because he knew its purpose and its

importance; he was, in fact, the eyes and ears of the delegation. He reported to the leader of the delegation, the principal negotiator. Jake told him what the Saudis had said, off the record, for Saudi and Jake's ears only. And he offered opinions about what the negotiator should say. For weeks Jake had been trained to pretend that he didn't speak Arabic; not to respond to test phrases such as "Watch out," "He has a gun," "Assassin," and "Fire."

The cover was perfect not only because of Jake's ability to seem uninvolved and subservient, but also because of the way he looked. Tall, blond, blue-eyed, handsome. Typically American, all-American. Incapable of speaking or understanding any foreign language. Like a woman—beautiful, but, essentially, decorative; of no substance and certainly no threat.

The other reason Jake liked his position so much was because he was allowed to be alone. While his supervisors were entertained in the homes of their Saudi hosts, Jake was free to explore the cities; first, Riyadh and then the Red Sea port of Jeddah. The two were essentially the same—lean white buildings with dark, wood-carved trim, white sand, streets over crowded with cars, horns blaring. The noise was incessant. The Saudi drivers drove with one hand on the horn. And they drove fast. Jake watched the women, covered in black, some with veiled faces, all free from worry. They were free to walk the streets without fear. They were protected by religion in a nation where religion was law. A crime against a woman was punished swiftly and severely, just as all crimes were punished.

Jake strolled along the docks in Jeddah. The historic Red Sea sparkled clear, blue, peaceful, under the scorching equatorial sun. And he browsed in the *souk,* the marketplace. In Jeddah he made the first of many purchases that he would make during his travels. It was an antique Oriental rug woven in all shades of blue laced with green and ivory. It reminded him of something, but he couldn't remember what. A dream maybe. A dream of a time and a place in the future where he would put the rug and the other treasures he would collect. A dream of a home, his home. Jake smiled. It was a happy thought.

At the gold *souk* Jake bought a necklace for Carrie. Why? he mused as he paid the shopkeeper. Because it would look so lovely on her young, graceful neck. The necklace was like the rug. Part of a dream. Again, he smiled. Someday he would see her again and give it to her . . .

The day came quickly. The mission in Saudi Arabia was completed, successfully, in ten days. Jake's role had been a success. He would serve them well. The next assignment would be the real test—Damascus, Syria in September. Until then he was to return to Washington for more training.

Chapter Fifteen

The letters from Megan arrived frequently in June. They were eager, passionate, loving letters: "My dearest Stefano, I love you so much. I miss you so much. But this is the right thing for me to be doing." Megan wrote long descriptions of plays she'd seen, actors she'd met, places she'd visited. Each letter bore a different postmark: London, Paris, Tours, Vienna.

Early in July, a new theme appeared in the letters: "I am so busy. I don't think it will work to have you come visit. We'll just have to suffer until September. But think of the reunion!"

Then, in reply to Stephen's letter, she wrote:

> . . . You wouldn't be in the way. I just wouldn't be able to spend time with you. It would be such a conflict. It might make Ian angry and I have managed not to antagonize him so far. I would hate to lose all the progress when we're so near the end of our tour. He can get me a job on Broadway, darling. Or he can prevent me from working anywhere ever. Please don't be angry.

In the next letter, dated July fourteenth, Megan wrote: "You are being unfair. If only you really knew how much I love you and how hard this is for me. Please don't do this to us. It is only eight weeks."

Stephen answered that letter with a loving, forgiving, understanding one. He would not come visit. He would suffer through the next eight weeks. But, he warned her, he was counting the days.

Then the letters from Megan stopped. Stephen didn't know where to reach her. Her itinerary had been free-form. She had told him in each letter where to send the next. A week passed. Then two. At the beginning of the third week, in desperation, Stephen called the only possible link—Ian's home in Connecticut. A woman answered the telephone. Stephen identified himself.

"Oh, Stephen, how nice to hear from you. This is Margaret." Ian's wife. She had met Stephen the summer before, when Megan had been living at Pinehaven. "How are you?"

"I'm sorry to bother you, but I haven't heard from Megan for two weeks. I have no idea where she is and I am concerned that something has happened."

"Happened?" Margaret echoed.

"An accident. Something . . ."

Margaret laughed. "No. Don't worry. I spoke to Ian two days ago. Megan is fine. Probably too busy to write. Or it could be the mail. They've been in Italy and that country is notorious for mail strikes."

"Do you know where they are, where I can call her?"

A pause. "Uh, no. Let's see. I believe they were going to Naples. But Ian will call me in a day or two. I'll tell him to have Megan get in touch with you. But don't worry, she'll be fine."

"She'll be fine?"

"As always," Margaret said firmly.

"Thank you very much. I'm sorry to bother you, but I was awfully worried."

That evening, Jake phoned Carrie at the club.

"Hi, Caroline."

"Jake?" Carrie couldn't believe it. From their last conversation, as Jake was leaving Stanford, Carrie had gotten the clear impression that Jake would miss Megan and Stephen's wedding. She hadn't expected to hear from Jake or see Jake ever again. She'd convinced herself of it. It made things easier. "You sound far away."

"Only Washington. I have been far away. I've just returned."

"Do you like your new job?"

"Very much." Jake paused. "Listen, I wondered about one of our famous dinners. Would you like to?"

Carrie was too surprised by his call, too happy to hear his voice, to remember her resolve of last February: he will only hurt you; stay away.

"Yes, I would like to." It was the truth.

"How about this weekend? Your place or mine?"

"What?"

"Shall I come to Boston or shall I fly you down here?"

"Have you finally gotten yourself an airplane?" Carrie teased, stalling for time. Her parents would never approve of the trip to Washington. She could go, but not with their approval. And there was Stephen, frantic with worry about Megan. It would help him to be able to talk to Jake.

But she wanted Jake to herself, for those few private hours that they could share and that she could remember.

"No, but you have a choice of airlines."

"There's a bit of a problem here. Stephen hasn't heard from Megan for awhile. She's okay, because he spoke to Ian's wife. But he's getting a little anxious. Lots of crazy analyses of the situation."

"So I should come up there?"

"I think he could use some reality testing. And who better? You don't sound too surprised that she hasn't written."

"Actually I hadn't thought about it. But surprise is one of Megan's things."

"I know. That's what worries us all. Remember her last surprise?" Her announcement that she was leaving for four months and that the wedding would have to be postponed.

Carrie thought about the other surprises the vanishing head-aches, going to Tahoe with Jake and coming home, in love, with Stephen.

"Shall I come to Boston, then?"

"I guess so." Carrie sighed.

"No?"

"Yes, but . . ." She couldn't say it. Stephen needed Jake much more than she did. In fact, it would probably be best if she didn't see Jake at all.

"I should spend time with Stephen while you're working, but you and I will dine alone, as always. Okay?"

Carrie smiled, nodded, and whispered into the receiver, "Okay."

Jake arrived in Boston two hours after the day's mail had brought a letter from Megan, postmarked in Amsterdam three days before. Stephen had come home to check the mail, as usual. He tore open the thin envelope.

Dear Stephen,

I haven't written because of what I have to say. What I must say. I have thought a lot about us in the past two months. I realize now that it's over. Our goals and values are too different. This separation was lucky be-cause it has prevented us from making a terrible mis-take. You may not have come to this realization yet, but it doesn't really matter. I know how I feel and what's right (and what's wrong) for me. Please don't try to get in touch. There is really nothing to discuss.

Megan

Stephen stared at the letter in disbelief. He was alone in the house; his parents and Carrie were at work. The feeling of uncontrollable anger—a feeling that he had only known since meeting Megan—welled up inside him. What did he want? To throw something? No. To hurt himself? No. To hurt Megan? Yes. To make her feel the same kind of pain he was feeling. Because he hated her for doing this. And for being so cowardly.

Stephen drove to the club and watched Carrie give a tennis lesson. When the lesson was over, he handed her the letter without speaking. Carrie knew from his eyes that the news wasn't good.

"I don't understand," Carrie said quietly after she had read it.

"No. And she certainly doesn't bother to explain." It was difficult for Stephen to speak. Anger alternated with grief. He couldn't think clearly.

"I'm glad that Jake is coming today," Carrie whispered almost to herself. She glanced at the large clock at the end of the center court. Jake's plane should have already landed. He was probably on his way to the club. It was a lucky coincidence.

Carrie moved Stephen to a white table with a pale blue umbrella in the corner of the club's outdoor lounge. She ordered an iced tea for him.

"I have to give a lesson, Stephen. It's my last one for the day. If you sit here, you'll see Jake when he arrives." Carrie put her arms around his proud, broad shoulders and squeezed him. "I am so sorry."

Carrie blinked back tears and returned to the court. How dare she do this to him, Carrie thought. Megan was her best friend, too. She did it to both of them.

Halfway through her lesson, Carrie saw that Jake had arrived and was reading Megan's letter. Finally, the lesson was over and she joined Jake and Stephen. Jake stood up and smiled as she approached. For a moment she forgot about her brother's pain, Megan's betrayal, the pain that Jake had caused her. She forgot about everything as she looked into his eyes. In two months, he seemed older, more serene, and definitely happy to see her. He held a chair for her as she sat down, touching her lightly on the cheek with his hand.

"Why did she do this, Jake?" Carrie asked. She was

240

drinking iced tea. Jake was drinking bourbon on the rocks. It was two o'clock.

"Who knows?"

"The letter sounds as if she hates me. As if I have done something to her. I am racking my brain for anything that I might have written that could make her feel this way . . ." Stephen's pain was palpable and contagious. Carrie ached watching him. And it was just the beginning; he was still numb. The full effect, the loneliness, the rejection, the bitterness, would come later.

"You've done nothing wrong," Jake said emphatically. "This is just foolishness. She's not thinking clearly."

"About what? Have you heard from her?" It was a direct question and Jake avoided a direct answer.

"She is so impulsive. She doesn't think about consequences. I wish she had never sent this letter."

"Meaning what?"

"Meaning I can't believe this is really what she wants. She'll regret it. She'll want to come back to you." But how much destruction can a relationship take? he wondered. The damage caused last spring had almost been irreparable. But they had survived that. It was amazing how much forgiveness one could find if the love was strong enough. Jake's thoughts wandered, for a moment, to Julia.

"If I could count on that. If I knew she would change her mind."

"I don't think you can count on anything with Megan," Carrie said, startled by the bitterness in her own voice.

Jake started to object but stopped. He took a large swallow of the bourbon and emptied the glass. He spotted the cocktail waitress and signaled, almost imperceptibly, for another glass.

"I think," Jake said slowly, "that this has all happened too quickly for Megan. She's confused. In her confusion, she has squandered the best thing that has ever happened to her—that's you, my friend. And the best thing that ever *will* happen to her. As *her* friend, I'd plead with you to wait

241

for her and to forgive her. As *your* friend, I'd say forget her. Don't spend much time trying to guess what happened. Just pick up the pieces and get on with your life."

It was a speech coming from Jake, a speech based on some hidden knowledge. Did he know something specific, or did he just know Megan? Carrie wondered. She also wondered how he could drink so much without seeming drunk.

Jake took her to dinner that evening. Stephen didn't even want to join them. Already he had found what would get him through this, through life without Megan—work.

Carrie wore a simple ivory dress with long sleeves and a sash belt. The color was stunning against her tanned skin. She piled her strawberry blond curls on top of her head.

"My God, Caroline, you are beautiful."

"I wish you didn't sound so surprised."

"You just look more mature, womanly."

"Good! I'm really not a baby, you know."

"I know."

The heat of the day was subsiding, leaving in its steamy wake a pink-blue haze, a soft, pastel memory of a too bright, too harsh, too painful day. It could have been a peaceful softness, but Carrie still churned with anger.

"I hate Megan for doing this," she blurted out.

"Don't hate her. She is going to need you to be her friend."

"How can you expect me to be her friend after this?"

"Because you *are* her friend. And you are fair."

"She hasn't been fair to my brother."

"No, but she will suffer much more from this than Stephen."

"How can you say that?"

"Because he's like you, a survivor. Because you both believe that life is good. You'll both find someone deserving of you, someone who will make you happy." Jake was serious.

"Megan made Stephen happy! He had never been that happy before," Carrie protested and wondered, Who is he talking about? Stephen? Megan? Or me? And him?

"Not today she didn't. And not last spring, either."

"So she's not worthy of him? I thought you were her friend."

"I am her friend. We are very much alike."

Carrie and Stephen, deserving. Jake and Megan, undeserving.

They drove in silence.

"I got something for you." Jake smiled slightly. He removed a long, slender cardboard box, without wrapping, from his pocket. "From my travels."

"Why?" Carrie asked without thinking.

"Because when I saw it I thought of you. That it would look nice on you. Open it."

It was the gold necklace, delicate links of polished gold alternating with links of brushed gold. Carrie had never seen anything like it.

"It's beautiful. I can't believe it. It's so beautiful. Thank you."

"You're welcome. Put it on."

"I can't with the car moving." I can't because my hands are trembling.

"We're almost there anyway. Then I'll help you."

Jake parked the car and reached across the seat. She handed him the necklace and moved toward him. He quickly secured the clasp around her neck and backed off to assess the result. It looked the way she looked simple, elegant, pure. Her blue eyes glistened with joy and her full, sensuous lips trembled slightly.

He leaned toward her and kissed her lightly on the lips. They were warm and moist and soft. She responded to his lips the way she had responded once before. And he broke the vow he had made then: I must leave her alone; she is too good, too precious.

And now he couldn't help himself, because she was so

precious. Because she kissed him back. Because her lips made him feel good and precious; she infused herself into him, just by the touch of her lips. Because she was healthy and wholesome and untainted. Because he had drunk too much bourbon that afternoon, all afternoon. A million reasons to break his vow.

After several minutes he pulled himself away and looked at her. Her healthy cheeks glowed with a faint pink flush; her carefully pinned hair fell in silken strands down her neck; her eyes glistened with pleasure.

"Well . . ." he murmured softly. "We'd better go in. These elegant restaurants take a dim view of their clients lingering too long in the parking lot."

Jake ordered champagne cocktails while Carrie rearranged her curls in the powder room.

"I think you'll like this."

"I think the restaurant could lose its liquor license." She giggled after the first sip.

"My God, aren't you twenty-one? Yet?"

"In September."

"Happy Birthday." He touched her crystal glass gently with his.

"Where will you be in September?"

"Probably back in the Middle East."

"Is that where you bought my necklace?" Carrie touched it carefully as she spoke. It was still there. It was real.

"In Saudi Arabia."

"Really? What were you doing there?"

"Consultant work."

"For what?"

"Different things. Whatever needs consulting. Different companies need different types of work."

"In other words, you do this and that, here and there?" Carrie giggled. The champagne was going to her head, quickly.

"Exactly!"

"Will most of your consulting be overseas?"

"Yes."

"And you will be gone for long periods of time?"

"It will vary. This trip was only for two weeks. But the next one will probably be six months to a year."

"A year? You'll be gone for a year?" Carrie's heart sank. When would she see him again? In a year, for dinner somewhere. "I can't believe it. I'll miss y . . . our dinners."

"I'll miss you, too. And I think you'll have no trouble finding people to take you to dinner. Of course, they'll all want to marry you."

"Marry!"

"Of course. Just be careful not to pick someone like me." Jake had gotten serious. He was telling her something: that kiss didn't mean anything. Forget about me. Like Megan and Stephen, it won't work.

"Why not?"

"I'm not the marrying type. Too restless. Too unreliable." Jake was trying to sound casual, but he continued to make his point.

"I'm not the marrying type, either," Carrie said. Then she looked seriously into his deep blue eyes and said, softly, "But if I were going to marry someone, he would be exactly like you."

Jake looked at her thoughtfully. If only it were possible. Maybe, someday. Someday in a faraway dream. He touched her cheek gently.

"Then it's lucky you aren't the marrying type. Except when I close my eyes I can see you, surrounded by wonderful, happy children in a country estate, writing novels and tending your prize-winning roses."

"What would my husband be doing?"

"Admiring you."

"You don't see me on the professional tennis circuit?"

"No, not that you aren't capable."

"How about as a cub reporter on a newspaper somewhere?"

"Not really. Except, again, you are capable."

"Michael says he can get me a job in New York when I graduate. In journalism. He thinks I need to be in New York if I am going to 'make it.' "

"I didn't realize you were still in touch with Michael."

"He has always been interested in my writing."

"And in you."

Carrie narrowed her eyes. Did Jake care? "He still wants me to marry him, speaking of marriage. How does that fit into the country estate image?"

"It doesn't. I like Michael, but . . ."

Carrie waited. Jake wasn't going to say it: you can do better.

"I like Michael, too. But not to marry. Even if I were the marrying type."

Jake smiled. He felt relieved. Maybe he didn't want to know the man that would marry Carrie.

Stephen was in the living room when they returned. It didn't occur to him that they might want privacy. Carrie knew that Jake wouldn't kiss her again anyway. It was obvious that Stephen needed to talk with Jake. Carrie looked at them both. They looked exhausted.

"I think I'll go to bed. It's been a long day," she said, then added softly to Jake, "Thank you for my necklace." Carrie kissed Stephen on the cheek, and then Jake. "Good luck with your consulting," she whispered. She couldn't force herself to say good-bye.

Several hours later she awoke. She looked at her bedside clock: five-thirty. She heard a car start outside and went to the window. It was Jake, leaving. For six months, or a year. She touched the precious metal necklace still around her neck. A memory. And a reminder.

Part Five

Chapter Sixteen

Stanford, California . . . September, 1972

Beth and Carrie decided to room together their junior year. It was a decision born of inertia rather than choice. Beth didn't care where she lived. She planned to devote her time to graduating at the end of her junior year and to BethStar. She had stayed in Palo Alto that summer, taking classes and working with John on the company. For three months, she hadn't thought about Stephen or Megan. She had gloated last spring when the wedding was postponed, but had lapsed into silence again as the plans for the Cape Cod wedding unfolded. The news Carrie brought back with her from Boston that fall gave Beth yet another project for her final year at Stanford.

"When is the wedding?" Beth asked idly.

"No wedding, Beth. You were right," Carrie said sadly. For the past eight weeks, she had watched her brother shrivel from loneliness, hopelessness, and an obsession for his work. She could only imagine the rigor with which he would attack law school. He had lost weight, smiled little, and was very quiet. His anger subsided quickly and was replaced by remorse. Carrie knew that he had tried, unsuccessfully, to find Megan. She had even withdrawn her acceptance to begin at Radcliffe as a transfer student.

"What?"

"No wedding. You were right. Megan backed out."

"For what reason?"

"No reason. No apparent reason. Whim, maybe. You predicted it, Beth. You always mistrusted her and I defended her. You were right."

"How's Stephen?"

"Despondent. That's what makes me so angry, what she had done to him."

"Has he started law school?"

"This week. It's all he has left. I hope it's enough."

"Do you have his address? I would like to write to him."

Carrie hesitated. She knew how Beth felt about Stephen. In fact, it had been Carrie who had thought that they would make a perfect couple. They had seemed that way, for awhile. But when Carrie saw how much in love Stephen was with Megan, she realized that his relationship with Beth had not been really serious. Carrie knew how much Beth hated Megan.

"Okay. But a warning. Don't write anything negative about Megan, or any 'I told you sos.' He's not ready for it."

"I don't want to antagonize him! I am his friend. I am sorry that she hurt him."

After Carrie told Beth about Stephen and Megan's broken engagement, Beth retreated into her room, closed the door, and sat on her bed. She had to think, to plan.

At first, Beth couldn't concentrate; she was too excited. It was over. Stephen was free, finally, from the incomprehensible spell Megan had cast. *Free*. Available. Not immediately, Beth reminded herself sternly. Stephen had to adjust. But, eventually, he, her Stephen, would be available, again.

Eventually, Beth forced her disciplined mind to focus. She was used to spending hours systematically finding solutions to complex, intricate mathematical problems. Beth was a master at patient, careful, logical problem solving. She had to use that approach now, to control the almost irresistible urge to go to Stephen, now. She had to think of a way that she could make it all work out after all.

Beth sat, immobile, on her bed until dawn. Overnight, she formulated her plan. It could work.

It has to work, she thought as she lay awake, too excited to sleep, even at the end of the long night, still fighting the urge to talk to him. Timing, she knew, was critical. She would have to wait, be patient, a little longer. Still, she was glad that Carrie hadn't given her Stephen's telephone number in Boston.

That fall, Carrie devoted herself to tennis and to her writing. As Jake had predicted, her interest in tennis waned and she focused on her writing. She had spoken to Michael at the end of the summer. He convinced her that she had to move to New York. He had moved from newspaper journalism to television journalism. He was certain that he could find her a job when she was ready. Following Beth's lead, Carrie decided to graduate at the end of her junior year. The campus seemed empty without Stephen, Jake, and Megan. Carrie wanted to get on with her career.

Beth and Carrie truly became friends. They both avoided dating. Carrie learned to turn down invitations for dates graciously. Beth's obvious coolness continued to discourage invitations. The telephone rarely rang, except for the daily, company-related calls from John.

Beth and Carrie developed respect for each other's careers, lifestyles, and privacy. They didn't pry, but were available to talk. Beth noticed that Carrie had become less saccharine; she now had the capacity to be critical. Beth found that refreshing. And Carrie found Beth to be more open, more human, even kind. Now that men left her alone, Beth could relax. Carrie wondered about Beth's relationship with John. It was mid-year before she even met him.

On Carrie's twenty-first birthday, Carrie got a phone call from Stephen, roses from Michael, a bottle of Courvoisier from Beth, and a telegram from Jake from Damascus.

Happy Birthday and Happiness, Caroline. Always, Jake

It was the first of many telegrams and letters that he would send her over the next eighteen months. Reminders that he was alive, that he cared about her happiness, that he was thinking about her. There was never a return address, never a postmark from the United States. Carrie wrote letters to him, carefully saved in a shoe box.

The week after Thanksgiving, the telephone rang. It was the lobby switchboard.

"Carrie, you have a visitor." Carrie's heart skipped a beat. Jake.

"Who is it?"

"I don't know. A woman. Shall I send her up?" The switchboard was run by freshmen in the dormitory. They took turns and were paid for it. But none of them took it seriously. It would not have occurred to this one to find out the name of the woman.

"Okay." Beth was at company headquarters. Carrie knew very few "women," and none that would be likely to visit her.

Carrie stood in the hall outside the door. She watched the woman approach. There was something vaguely familiar about her, but it wasn't until she was close that Carrie recognized her. Megan.

Megan looked like a woman, an old, tired, sick woman. Her gait was slow. Where was the spring that had made Megan seem like a gazelle ready to bound away? The shoulders were slouched; the perfect, arrogant posture had vanished. The spun gold hair was short cropped, sparse, straight, and gray-blond. It had no shine. And she was so thin, so pale.

"Megan!" Carrie gasped. She remembered Jake's words: *she will need you to be her friend.* Carrie forgot all the speeches that she had rehearsed, the tirades she had planned, the recriminations and hatred.

"Hi." Even the voice was weak, the wonderful rich huskiness lost. "I knew if I called you wouldn't see me. So I just came."

"Come in." Sit down, Carrie thought. Megan looked too weak to stand for long. "What happened? You look awful."

"I got the flu about three weeks ago. Worse than the flu, I guess, because they put me in the hospital and gave me antibiotics. I'm actually on the mend now, except that I look like death. I'm on my way to Malibu to bake in the sun for a few days. I feel better than I look." Megan smiled; there was no twinkle in her eyes.

"You mean three weeks ago you were well?"

"Yes, completely. In fact, I just won a part in an off-Broadway play. It's going to open in mid-January. I have to be well enough to start rehearsals in three weeks."

"I can't imagine you'll be well enough to fend for yourself in New York in just three weeks," Carrie said.

"That's the wonderful part. Margaret and Ian have asked me to stay with them until I'm settled. I can commute into the city with Ian." Megan's eyes brightened slightly. She added, "Margaret just had a baby—a little girl. So she and I can recuperate together. And play with the baby."

They sat silently for a few moments, Carrie still reacting to Megan's shocking appearance.

"What happened to your hair?"

"I was too sick to take care of it in the hospital. I kept getting it tangled. So I told them to cut it off. I must have been delirious."

"You look terrible."

"If Stephen saw me he'd probably be relieved that we didn't get married."

That was why she had come, of course. To get it out in the open. To see what had happened after she sent the letter.

"Have you spoken to him, Megan?"

"No. There's no point." She paused. "How is he?"

"His heart is broken." Carrie felt the rage building. She had adjusted to Megan's appearance, had accepted her story, knew that in three weeks Megan would be better. And in the same three weeks her brother would continue to suffer. "How could you do this to him?"

"I had to, Carrie. It just would not have worked. It was impossible."

"Why won't you talk to him? Explain it to him."

"Because he wouldn't understand." Because I'm a coward.

"That's ridiculous."

"I can't even explain it to myself, so how can I explain it to him? It just backfired, that's all."

"What backfired?" Just as when Jake had been talking about "it," Carrie got the impression that there was something specific.

Megan looked confused for a moment. "The relationship. My plan to go on the tour and come back and it would all be the same. It just didn't work out."

"Did you meet someone else?"

"No!"

They sat in silence on Carrie's bed.

"Do you hate me?" Megan asked finally.

"I hate what you did."

"Will you call him and try to explain it to him for me?"

"You haven't told me anything!" Carrie watched her friend. She looked defeated, battered. "I will call him and tell him that at least you are alive. Even if it's just barely. Are you really going to be all right?"

"Yes. I really am. My heart is broken too, you know."

Carrie stared at her. There were tears in Megan's eyes.

"Why don't you go back to him? Why don't you try again?" Carrie remembered something else that Jake had said: *she'll want to come back.*

Megan said, "I can't. It's too late."

Carrie put her arm around Megan's shoulders; there was hardly any flesh, just sharp, fragile bones.

"Let's go to lunch. You can tell me about your play."

"Thank you." Megan squeezed Carrie with a dry, bony

hand. Nothing was forgiven or forgotten. But Carrie and Megan could go on. Perhaps as friends.

John noticed the change in Beth. At first, it was a subtle restlessness. But, as Christmas approached, it was obvious; Beth was totally preoccupied. It wasn't anything to do with BethStar; it had replaced BethStar as the most important thing in her life.

Beth began to smoke. She chain-smoked.

"I cannot believe that you are doing that to your body," John said finally. "Not to mention the casual damage you may be doing to *my* lungs."

"I'm nervous."

"I know."

No explanation. But she stopped smoking and began biting her fingernails.

Finally it came to him: Beth was planning something. And whatever it was, she was uncertain of its success. But it was something she had to do.

"I'm thinking about going to Harvard for a year. To do graduate work in aerophysics," she announced casually one day in December.

"Why?"

"Polish off the edges."

"I thought you were desperate to get to Houston. To make your name in the Space Program." John had tried in vain to convince her to spend another year in Palo Alto, to help him with BethStar. But she had refused. She wanted to go to Houston. She already had a job.

Now John knew what she had been planning, but he still didn't know why.

"I have to see the program, of course. I plan to visit Carrie in Boston over Christmas break. To see if it seems worthwhile."

"It won't be. Not graduate school. You don't need any edge polishing."

255

Beth shrugged. John knew her mind was made up, but he still didn't know why. He just knew that it had very little to do with the graduate school. The thought made him sad.

Beth had difficulty packing for her trip to Boston. She had long since given away her frilly, Southern belle dresses. But that was how Stephen had known her. He didn't know the new Beth.

Beth wanted to be pretty for him. How could she make herself pretty for him and still protect her new self, the self that she, at last, was comfortable being? Beth couldn't even act like a Southern belle anymore; she had forgotten how.

Stephen had to want her for what she had become. She had to believe that he would, but it made her very nervous.

During Christmas week in Houston, Beth shopped at Neiman Marcus. She bought a peach-colored cocktail dress with sheer silk sleeves, gently fitted bodice, and a slightly flared skirt. Stylish but not frilly; Beth could live with the look.

Beth confessed to the horrified beautician at Houston's most exclusive beauty salon that, indeed, she had taken to cutting her own hair. When the bangs got too long, she cut them. It hardly mattered, Beth said defensively. Her hair curled to cover the mistakes.

After a full five minutes of scolding, during which Beth almost walked out, the hair stylist wordlessly set to work. In thirty minutes, he created a masterpiece. He shaped her thick, dark hair beautifully around her aristocratic face. The haircut accentuated her high cheekbones, her large brown eyes, her full red lips, and her long ivory neck.

Beth was very pleased. It was all her, nothing artificial, and the effect was beautiful, natural.

Carrie and Stephen met Beth's plane at Logan Airport. It was two days after Christmas. Carrie knew how Beth felt about Stephen, how she had always felt. But she thought it was too soon for Stephen; he had not recovered from the loss of Megan. Beth had insisted that the purpose of her visit was to investigate the Harvard Graduate School. And, after five days of watching her brother suffer through the holidays, Carrie was eager for anything that could possibly be diverting for him.

For a moment, neither Carrie nor Stephen recognized her. Carrie had gotten used to jeans, a tangle of dark curls, and no eyes. Stephen expected shoulder-length hair, perfectly flipped at the ends, white gloves, and pearls.

What they saw was elegance without affectation; simple, natural style. Beth wore a pleated Stuart-plaid skirt, a tailored silk blouse, and a forest green cashmere sweater. On anyone else, it might have looked like a prepschool uniform. But on Beth, it was feminine and appealing. Her short hair softly framed her face; her eyes were large and dark and seductive.

"Merry Christmas," she said, smiling. In an instant she noticed the change in Stephen, the pale skin, longer hair, dark circles from restless nights. But his smile gave her confidence. He likes how I look, she thought.

Carrie saw very little of her roommate during the five-day visit, and very little of her brother. For the first time since July, Stephen was genuinely distracted from thoughts about Megan. He was intrigued by Beth, as he always had been, by her soft prettiness, her sharp tongue and quick wit so incongruously wrapped in the gentle Southern drawl. Most of all, he was intrigued by her mind. Stephen had thought he knew her, but he realized, he had only seen glimpses, before, of her true intelligence; she had artfully, demurely, hidden it. But now, the artifice was gone. Stephen was dazzled.

At first, when she asked him about law school, his answers had been superficial. But her curiosity wasn't idle; it was genuine interest. What do they teach you in law school? Do they teach you how to reason? How to think? How to argue logically? How do they teach you those things?

Beth really wanted to know, and Stephen took great pleasure in her interest. He hadn't really talked to anyone about law school, about what he liked or what he disliked. About what made sense and about what worried him.

"They teach you to find the loopholes, to ferret out the errors in logic. To find the technicality."

"Mass murderer free on technicality," Beth murmured.

Stephen smiled at her. That was what had worried him. What about right or wrong? Could he defend someone who he knew had committed a murder? Not only defend, but try, by whatever technique, to get him freed?

"I guess, when you're a lawyer, your commitment is to the system, the system that allows innocence until guilt is proven. And the system that allows due process. The judgment is not yours to make," Beth said.

Stephen nodded. That was what he had decided. But it had taken him months.

Beth loved the Harvard campus, an epicenter of the early seventies, pulsing with youth and energy and commitment. Stephen guided her along the paths carved out of the snow. He touched her then, and he kissed her briefly when she left. In the five days, they never mentioned Megan or the possibility that Beth might move to Boston. Alter she left, Stephen missed her for a few days; then the dreams, the nightmares about Megan, returned and the easy, happy days of Beth's visit were forgotten.

Beth returned to Stanford undecided about her plans. It was too soon, now, for Stephen. But, maybe, in nine months it would be their turn. What if it never worked out? What if Megan decided to come back? That was the blackest thought of all. And what if Beth sacrificed her dreams, the dreams that could become a reality in June with the job at NASA, for nothing?

But what if it worked? What if Stephen fell in love with her? Then it would all be worth it.

John had hoped Beth would return from the trip to Boston as her old self. But she was worse—edgy, tense, irritable. With her new hairstyle, he could see her beautiful eyes. They were brown-black, sometimes blazing, sometimes troubled, sometimes seeing their own vision—a scene in the future somewhere else with someone else.

BethStar was progressing ahead of schedule, but he had lost Beth's enthusiasm. It was destined to be the great, revolutionary success they had hoped. Beth knew that, and was "pleased."

But she wouldn't tell him what was troubling her.

Stephen approached his course work at Harvard Law School with a one-mindedness and dedication that would have been offensive and threatening to his classmates had he not been so likable, and, at the same time, so obviously sad. His veneer of manners and good humor was impenetrable, but he was a loner. His classmates guessed correctly that his guise of cheerfulness disappeared the moment he was alone. He pleasantly declined invitations to parties, to weekends at Cape Cod, to study sessions that were largely social. It was painfully obvious that Stephen, the undisputed and unbegrudged top student in the class, was in mourning. But for what? For whom? That was his secret.

It made Stephen angry that even after six months his stomach ached and his eyes misted when he thought about her. He hated her for what she had done to him, to them. He wanted to see her, to speak with her, to try to understand. Carrie had told him that Megan would be staying with Ian and Margaret for awhile, recovering from her illness. Carrie strongly advised Stephen against a surprise visit, until Megan was well. So, he wrote to her instead, but his letters, sent in care of Ian, returned unopened. It was as if he had done something unforgivable to her.

Stephen enjoyed law school. It was the only part of his life that he enjoyed. Law would become his whole life. There were times that he was almost happy. The stimulation and energy in his life was all intellectual. He studied law, read books on politics, economics, history, the local newspapers and the *New York Times*. And he ran seven miles a day, every day.

He realized how alike he and Carrie were—the central

core of discipline. If their lives could not be run by love and emotion, they could be run by discipline and dedication. They could fall asleep at night, physically exhausted from exercise, too tired to think about the emptiness. They became creatures of habit, nonadventuresome, nondaring, because habit was safe.

Megan's play opened in January. The Sunday *New York Times* dedicated one-and-a-half columns of rave review to the play and another half column to its "captivating, talented, magical" young star, Megan Chase.

So she was in New York City. And she was well. And doing well. It was time.

The next Friday, Stephen went to New York to see the play and to see Megan. She had obviously recovered from the illness that Carrie had described to him. He had never seen her look more beautiful, strong, and healthy. She had matured in the past eight months. Her acting had matured; it had a new, rich, emotional quality. Megan commanded the stage and the audience. Stephen watched in awe, his eyes blurred with pride and sadness.

Stephen waited at the side stage door after the play. Unless she had changed, Megan would leave by this door, long after everyone else had gone, after she had wound down, exhausted, when she could be assured of her privacy. He waited for an hour in the cold, his face whipped by the wind until it was numb. Perhaps he was wrong. Perhaps the new Megan walked out the front door of the theater surrounded by her fans. Perhaps the new Megan was not frightened by crowds like the old Megan, his Megan.

He heard a click at the door and watched it open, slowly, tentatively. From inside the door, the street would look empty; she couldn't see him. In fact, she didn't see him at all and started to walk toward a cab.

"Megan." His voice was dry, parched by the cold wind and his own emotion.

She stopped, her back toward him. She didn't turn around, but she stiffened. She knows, he thought, and she doesn't even want to turn around. He walked toward her. She didn't move, but she sighed and moved her gloved hands to her face. Was she crying?

"What?" she whispered back. What was the emotion? Not anger or curiosity. Just exhaustion, as if it took great energy to speak.

Stephen walked around and stood facing her. The wind made her eyes water; he couldn't tell if there were more. Now there was anger in her eyes, and something else unmistakable—fear.

As if I have done something to her. She's afraid of me. He wanted to hold her, reassure her, but, instead, he asked weakly, "Can we go for a drink?"

"Why?"

"Because I want to talk to you"

"I can't. It's . . ." Too soon, she thought, but said, "Late."

"Will you see me tomorrow then, for lunch or dinner?"

She smiled wryly. He knew it was an excuse. He knew her too well and she knew him. He wouldn't give up until she agreed. "No."

"Then now," he said firmly.

"Yes, I guess, now." She sighed.

By the time they reached the bar, Megan was calm. She had decided on her role—friend of the family. She had even rehearsed her lines. But Stephen had a different script and she was afraid.

"How's law school?"

"Fine." He glowered at her. It always angered him when she hid behind acting. She was acting now.

"You've got what you wanted. I'm glad."

"So did you."

"Yes." Pause. "How's Carrie?"

"I'm not here to talk about Carrie." Megan looked away. "Megan. Tell me what happened. Tell me the truth." His voice wasn't gentle, but it was pleading. He had to know; he had a right to know. But she couldn't tell him.

261

"It just wasn't meant to be. Maybe there wasn't as much love as we thought."

"Meaning you didn't love me."

Megan shrugged. "Most relationships don't work out in the long run. Ours was good for awhile, but it didn't last. It happens." Megan tried to sound casual and was amazed at her success.

"Did you meet someone else? Is there someone else?"

Megan couldn't lie about that. She shook her head.

"How about you?"

Stephen looked startled. "Me? My God, Megan, you don't seem to understand. This relationship of ours that 'didn't work out,' as you say, meant a great deal to me. I am still feeling the aftershocks. And I am trying to make sense of it, so that, maybe, next time . . ."

"Next time," Megan repeated, shook her head, then smiled. "I wonder how many chances one gets."

"You sound so bitter. You left me, remember? You ended it without bothering to tell me why. Tell me why, dammit." Stephen's rage was surfacing.

"I told you. It just didn't work. Wrong place, wrong time. We were too young and ambitious."

"Megan, those are clichés, right out of some corny play."

"Clichés are simply boring truths. You just don't like to admit that our relationship was just another, unspectacular, unsuccessful love affair."

"It wasn't and you know it." Stephen was angry and defeated. Megan wasn't going to talk. She was going to hide behind platitudes.

And he was troubled by the change in her. On stage, he was impressed with her strength, her maturity, her confidence. Now she seemed frail and tired and frightened. He had remembered her as a fighter. Now he couldn't even provoke her, and he almost felt guilty trying.

"I have to go now." She stood up. "Thank you for coming to see the play. Did you like it?"

"It was wonderful. You were magnificent."

Megan smiled. His opinion still mattered to her.

"Megan, don't leave."

"I have to, Stefano," she whispered, then looked embarrassed that she had called him Stefano, her private, intimate name for him, so naturally.

Then she was gone. And he was too stunned to follow. He took a late-night train back to Boston.

Beth stopped at the Stanford Post Office on her way over to John's. It was February fourteenth, Valentine's Day. She was reminded of it by the silly poster in the lobby of Lagunita Hall. She had to get out of this place!

There was a letter in her post office box. The postmark read "Cambridge, MA." Stephen! Her delicate, tapered fingers became clumsy. She tore open the envelope. "Dear Beth, I think it would be very nice to have you in Boston next year . . ." It was a short letter with short news items. It ended with: "Let me know if you're coming and when. I can help you find an apartment, et cetera. Stephen."

It wasn't much, but it was enough. He had given her the nod.

Beth burst into the tiny gardener's cottage that John referred to as BethStar Control. It was where he and Beth spent many hours a week, sitting beside each other on the lumpy mattress, planning, sketching, filling every corner of the room with ideas, and where he worked, alone, for unending hours on the computer he was building.

"I'm going to Boston."

John looked up. Her cheeks were flushed, rosy, radiant. The anxiety and tension had magically vanished.

"They accepted you into graduate school there a month ago," John observed calmly. He was going to find out, now, all of it. But he wasn't sure he wanted to know.

Beth told him. About Stephen. About Megan. She really hates Megan, he thought, worried. About what Megan had done to Stephen. Beth told him a theory that she had never told to anyone else. John listened carefully to the whole story. It saddened him, angered him, and, most of all, worried him.

"I thought you hated men."

"Except Stephen." Beth paused. "And you." And the men at NASA.

"You're chasing him. You're giving up everything that matters to you for him."

"I am spending a year getting an advanced degree in my chosen career. Hardly a waste!"

"And then you plan to move to Houston? And he'll go with you? Transfer in his last year of law school?"

"If things work out, I may modify my plans a bit."

"Modify?"

"I have my priorities, John."

"You had your priorities. Now you're giving everything up for some dumb jock who may not care a bit about you. It's beneath you, Beth. Where's your pride?"

"He's not a dumb jock. And he does care about me."

"He just doesn't know it yet, right? Jesus, Beth, you *are* chasing him."

"I expected you to be happy for me."

"If I really thought this would make you happy in the long run, then I would be," John said evenly.

"Well, it's really none of your business anyway, is it?" Beth asked coldly.

"No." John sighed. "None."

Chapter Seventeen

The telephone rang. Carrie was stirring spaghetti sauce.

"Shall I answer it?" he asked.

"Sure."

"Hello?"

"This is Jake Easton calling. Is Caroline there?"

"Jake! This is Michael."

Carrie stopped stirring and slowly removed the saucepan from the burner. It had been eighteen months since that evening in Boston. He had sent her cards, telegrams, and letters every few months, but she hadn't spoken to him.

Carrie watched Michael. He was obviously enjoying talking with Jake. They had been friends during Carrie's first year at Stanford. It seemed so long ago. Carrie sat on the edge of the sofa in her tiny apartment, waiting for her chance to speak to Jake. Finally, Michael handed her the phone. He sensed that Carrie wanted privacy and gestured that he would go for a walk.

"Hi," Carrie said after Michael had gone.

"Hi."

"Where are you?" Long distance, that much she could tell.

"San Francisco. I had a plan to take you out to dinner. In my day, everyone spent four years at college."

"Better educated for it, I'm sure. But you know us kids,

eager to plunge into the real world." Carrie tried to sound casual, cheerful. But, at that moment, she would have given anything to be spending a fourth year at Stanford. "Are you heading this way?"

"No." His voice was almost bitter. He had just flown in from Washington. He had spent two weeks there. It would have been so easy for him to have seen her in New York. But his plan, his dream for the past year, had been to surprise her at Stanford. How arrogant of him to assume that she would be there.

"Oh." So after eighteen months a long distance phone call. It was hardly worth the effort. Carrie fought back tears.

"It took me a little while to find you. I finally found Stephen and got your number from him."

"Did he tell you the news?"

"Yes." That he and Beth were to be married.

"You sound . . . what . . . unenthusiastic?"

"Concerned. Beth has never been my . . . type."

"I know." Carrie, and now Stephen, were the only people who had truly cared about both Megan and Beth. Most others felt they had to take sides.

"Is he happy?"

"He's content. He will never have the kind of happiness he had with Megan, but, of course, that didn't last. Maybe that kind of happiness doesn't."

"Does Megan know?" It was more than an idle question. Something in Jake's voice made it seem important that she know.

"I haven't told her."

"Don't you see her? I would think that you would, with both of you in New York."

"She's in Los Angeles. She's making a movie. She's become a bit of a star. A celebrity, in fact." Carrie paused. She was glad that he didn't know where Megan was. And that she was the one that he had called, at least, first. "Where have you been?"

"A million worlds away."

"I know. I've been collecting the most exotic postcards."

"Even this year, since you've moved?"

"Yes, I've trained them to forward everything. But let me give you my address." She gave it to him. Then she said, "I have answered every one, you know. Well, you don't know, because I have the letters."

"Really?" Jake sounded pleased.

"Yes," Carrie said, but her voice cracked. She was crying.

"What's wrong?"

"I want to see you."

"I want to see you, too. I need to talk to you. I even have a present for you. I've been trying to figure out a way to fly there tonight and be back to catch my noon flight to Hong Kong tomorrow. It's not possible."

"It's a lovely thought though."

"You're not living with Michael, then?"

"What? No! You and I discussed that eighteen months ago. Nothing has changed. Or will change. Michael is my boss. He got me a wonderful job, although now he's trying to coerce me into doing an interview show on television. Anyway, he comes over for dinner sometimes, because every so often I get tired of him acting pathetic about having to cook for himself."

"Oh."

"Will you come to Stephen's wedding?" It was mid-January. The wedding would be in August in Houston.

"I will try."

"Even though you don't approve."

"I will come to see you."

Carrie started to cry again.

"Are you there?"

"Yes. What did you need to talk to me about?"

"I'll tell you in Houston."

"Okay. Do you want Megan's number?" Carrie gave it to him.

They talked for a few more minutes.

"I'll see you in August, Caroline."

Jake replaced the receiver slowly and cursed himself again for his stupidity. He had planned this for so long. He had thought he had planned it so carefully. But he had made one fundamental, incorrect assumption. He should have known better.

By the Christmas after their dinner in Boston, Jake had made a decision that he would marry Carrie. He had told Julia about her then. He had had to explain why he could no longer make love to her.

"She doesn't know you're being faithful to her? She doesn't know you plan to marry her? Does she know you love her?" Julia had asked.

"I think she knows that. But she's so young, Julia. And I will be tied up with this work for the next couple of years. It's not fair for me to ask her until I can be with her. And it will give her time to grow up, have more experience."

"She's probably not being faithful to you."

"Maybe not." Jake hadn't told Julia that it wasn't even a matter of being faithful, that he and Carrie had never made love.

"She must be a pretty remarkable young woman," Julia had said, half jealous, mostly pleased for Jake.

"She is. You liked Stephen, didn't you?"

"Very much. I hope it works out for you, Jake, I really do. Aren't you worried that you may lose your sexual touch with what may be a year or two of abstinence?" Julia had teased, her violet eyes flashing.

"It's just what I have to do, Julia," he had said so seriously that she had vowed not to tease him about it again.

Jake had bought a wedding band for Carrie the next month. It was a beautiful ring. From a distance it looked like a simple gold band. But it was an intricate intermingling of white, rose, and yellow gold. Not three distinct bands, but the three colors, melted together, intertwined.

Jake had bought it in Amsterdam. It had sealed the decision he had made. He had conquered his past before; he would do it again. He would spend his life making her happy.

He had bought the ring and had sent her a postcard.

Dearest Caroline, In Amsterdam. Thinking of you. And us. Love, Jake.

Three days later, he had been sent from Amsterdam to Damascus, then Cairo, then Calcutta. A year elapsed. Jake had carried the ring with him. He had sent postcards and letters to Carrie.

He had had the ring in his pocket that day in January when he had flown from Washington to San Francisco. He had planned to show it to her that night, to ask her to marry him when he returned from Cambodia. Instead they had spoken long distance on the telephone. Afterward, Jake had flown to Los Angeles to have a late dinner with Megan.

The next day, he flew to Hong Kong and then to Cambodia.

The negotiations in Cambodia were difficult. Jake assumed his obsequious, unobtrusive role, listening to the hybrid Chinese-Cambodian dialects that he had learned in the past two weeks in Washington—two intense weeks, during which time he had only been an hour away from Carrie. Not that he could have left during his training. But she could have flown down. Or he could have, so easily, flown to New York and then to Hong Kong.

The thought haunted him during the intolerably hot, humid days and lonely, humid nights in Cambodia.

Two months passed. The negotiations encountered obstacle after obstacle. The negotiating table was steeped in tension, deceit, and distrust. The streets outside the building were patrolled by men with submachine guns and bloodied with remembrances of past violence.

One evening, Jake was awakened from his usual light,

restless sleep by noise and movement in his tiny room. The intruders—two young men—had intended to awaken him.

They spoke to him in the most common Cambodian dialect. It was a test; they wanted to know if he understood. They had been sent by their government to see if Jake knew their secrets.

Jake's training had prepared him for this. Under no circumstances would he reveal that he understood, even if—

One of the men held a knife to his throat. Jake trembled and looked scared—it wasn't all an act.

"I will count to ten and slit your cowardly throat unless you give me all your jewelry." He almost spat in Jake's face. It was a test. Jake had to make offers, pleas in English, but he could not mention jewelry. If he did, they would know he was a spy and they would kill him. It was likely that they would kill him anyway. His hands were pinned under the sheet. The knife was at his throat. The second man had a gun.

"One." The assailant said quietly in Cambodian. The steel blade pressed into Jake's neck.

"Say. What do you want?" Jake sputtered. "I have money."

"Two."

"Take the money. It's in the top drawer."

"Three."

"What do you want?" Beads of sweat dotted Jake's forehead. He knew it was a test, but he could pass with flying colors and still die. Or fail and die. He thought about Carrie.

"Four. Five. Six."

Jake gave no sign that he understood that the man was counting. His face revealed only fear, cowardice, and bewilderment, as it had been trained to do.

"I have clothes. I can get alcohol. Please don't hurt me." He couldn't say kill; they would know he had understood.

The knife pressed deeper. Jake felt a trickle of blood slide down his neck. He couldn't move. The bed sheet and

270

the men on top of him were like a straitjacket. In four counts his throat could be slashed. He wanted to be with Carrie.

"Seven. Eight." The man who was counting glanced at his colleague. Jake understood the glance; they had agreed that Jake didn't understand the language, that he wasn't a spy. But would they kill him?

"Nine. Ten." On ten the man raised the knife and watched Jake's eyes. He saw fear but not understanding.

"I guess we'd better rob him, to cover," one said to the other in Cambodian. The other man nodded.

"Okay American coward. Where is your money?" he asked in English.

Jake's mind reeled. The last question had been in English, hadn't it? Or had it been in Cambodian? Jake's special talent for languages was a potential liability. He understood foreign languages as well as English. The languages became interchangeable. He had to pay careful attention. And now when his life depended on it, was he sure?

The man waited. He wasn't going to repeat.

"M-my m-m-money is in the top drawer. P-please take it."

The men emptied the drawer. They took the fifty dollars in Jake's wallet and his watch. And they found the small wooden box that held Carrie's ring. They took the box and the ring.

The next day, several things happened. Jake told the leader of the delegation about the events of the previous night.

"I'm not surprised. They don't trust us. We don't trust them. The negotiations are almost useless." He looked at Jake. "You'd better get a weapon, son. Better get a knife. I'm going to try to get us out of this hellhole as soon as possible. But, until then, protect yourself."

In the middle of the afternoon's negotiations, one of Jake's assailants entered the room. He was wearing the full military dress of the Cambodian Army and had ribbons and medals signifying that he was a captain. He stared pointedly at Jake.

Jake showed no outward sign of recognition.

The captain-assailant raised his right hand to touch his face. There was a point to the gesture. It was to show Jake what he wore on his little finger—Carrie's ring.

Jake ignored him and tried to decipher the meaning.

It was, at least, another test. If Jake recognized the man, then it meant that Jake would know who had sent him. But even if he didn't recognize the man, he would recognize the ring.

It was more than a test. It was a message. It was a message that Jake had to be killed. He knew too much. They had made him know too much. Be killed, or what?

Cooperate with them. They must have decided, after all, that Jake was the spy. That he alone in the delegation understood Cambodian. They could tell him what to say.

The message was painfully clear: cooperate or be killed.

Jake bought a stiletto—thin, razor sharp, with a mother-of-pearl handle inlaid with sapphires. It had to look as if he was purchasing a souvenir, not a weapon. The shopkeeper wrapped it in a purple silk cloth, to protect the craftsmanship and the blade.

The military assailant returned that night, alone. Again he made his presence known. This time he spoke in English.

"I know you are the spy. You did well last night. Good nerve. But it has to be you."

"I don't know what you're talking about." Jake looked blank. Under the sheets his hand was wrapped tightly around the stiletto. The assailant held his curved knife in his right hand. He still wore Carrie's ring.

"You are very good at this buffoon role, Easton. Cooperate with me or I'll finish what I started last night."

He gestured casually at the cuts on Jake's neck.

"I don't understand." Jake moved slightly. He had to be ready.

The man lunged at him, the knife pointed at Jake's throat. Jake turned and caught the knife in the flesh of his shoulder. He slid onto the floor and was standing when the assailant

272

lunged for the second, surely lethal, time. The man didn't see the stiletto.

As he lunged at Jake, Jake shoved the stiletto under his sternum—*upwards and to the left. Then, when you're in the heart, pull the knife toward you a bit. That makes the hole in the heart bigger. They die more quickly.* It had all been part of Jake's training—how to murder, quickly, quietly.

Jake had never asked, How do you know when you're in the heart, because he hadn't believed he would ever need to know.

But it was obvious. The violent agonal pumping of the young, dying heart was transmitted vividly through the stiletto into Jake's hand. It took great energy for Jake to hold the knife in place, and even more to make the quick, finally lethal slice to the left.

The man's heart pounded frantically but, ultimately, hopelessly. Jake felt every beat. He felt it in the movement of the stiletto and in the hot blood that spilled onto his hand.

God help me, he thought, overcome by repulsion. At that moment it would have been better if the other man's knife had found its mark in Jake's carotid. Kill or be killed. Which, really, was worse?

Finally the heart stopped beating, reluctantly vanquished. The body slumped, heavy, warm. Jake lay him on the floor and removed the stiletto. He went to the bathroom, cleaned his hands and the knife, and vomited.

Jake stayed in the bathroom for thirty minutes, trying to recover from the horror of what he had done, knowing that he had to make rational decisions about the body, thinking about the other men he may have killed.

Jake didn't know if he ever really had killed anyone before. In combat, in Vietnam, it had been a matter of firing bullets at unknown targets in the distance. Watching them fall, wounded, maybe dead. Watching your friends, your buddies beside you, fall from bullets fired back. Falling yourself.

It had been a horror, a source of nightmares and sleeplessness over the past years. But it had been a horror of fear and hopelessness and senselessness. Anonymous and frightening.

It was nothing compared to the horror he felt now. Feeling life—struggling valiantly to the end—drain from another man's body. Making that life end. Calculated, premeditated murder.

But he was going to kill *you,* a voice inside him reminded him. That was indisputable. He thought wryly of the college campus doctrine: if a man wants to kill you, talk to him, brother to brother. He will understand.

Jake thought of Carrie. Maybe it would have been better, after all, to try to talk to the man, to sign his own death warrant. Maybe it was better to be dead than to feel the way Jake felt, was doomed to feel forever.

Jake shuddered, vomited again, and, finally, returned to the bedroom.

There wasn't much blood. That, Jake had been taught, was the beauty of the stiletto. The bleeding was internal. The heart ruptured into the chest cavity. Very little mess. A patch of blood the size of a butter plate was drying on the man's chest. Very neat.

Jake had devised a plan, not original, but time tested. He would tie a weight to the body and sink it in the dirty, polluted river that flowed slowly through the city. It flowed, in fact, outside Jake's window, twelve feet below Jake's balcony. Jake would bury the man in his own backyard.

It was three-thirty. Jake walked the deserted dirty streets in search of weights. It was a long search but, finally, a successful one. He found two cinder blocks, already loosened from a decaying wall. He worked them free. It was stealing; but that was a small crime by comparison. A tiny sin. A mere blemish.

Jake secured the blocks to the man with the man's own belt. He dragged the weighted body onto the balcony and carefully worked it over the balcony railing.

Something glittered in the tropical moonlight—the gold band on the dead man's finger. Carrie's band. The symbol of a dream, a foolish, unattainable dream, Jake thought bitterly.

He shoved the body, the weights, and the ring into the muddy river. He watched it sink, swallowed in an instant by the dark, depthless water.

The ignoble end of a young life.

The ignoble end of a dream.

Two days later the delegation returned to Hong Kong. The negotiations had reached a standstill. They would wait in Hong Kong until Stuart Dawson arrived to discuss the value of returning to Cambodia.

Jake telephoned Julia from Hong Kong.

"I need you, Julia."

"Where are you?" Julia was in Washington.

"Hong Kong."

"How awful for you!" she teased. Their voices were delayed. There were pauses. Then they would both talk at once.

Like their friendship. Delays, pauses, then flurries of intense activity.

"Will you join me?" From halfway around the world Julia could hear the sadness, the defeat, in his voice. Carrie must have refused him and he was devastated.

"Why don't you come here? Or we can meet in Monte Carlo?"

Jake explained briefly about the negotiations in Cambodia.

"We may have to go back." The dread in his voice was palpable. Maybe it wasn't Carrie; maybe it was something else.

"I have trouble making long trips for platonic relationships," Julia said. It wasn't true. If Jake needed her, she would be there, no matter what the rules. But she was trying to find out what was wrong.

"I know."

Jake booked a suite at Hong Kong's most expensive hotel for himself and Julia. For five days, he spent the days in meetings with Stuart and the nights with Julia. He told her

275

what had happened in Cambodia, what he had done. How it had made him realize he could never ask Carrie to marry him.

"Remember the 'I love you too much to marry you' line?" he asked. It was what Julia had said to him four years before.

"You understand it, finally?"

"I understand it for myself and Caroline. But not for us," he said seriously and pulled her closer to him. "Why don't we get married?"

"Because I know I'm your second choice! Because I want you to marry Caroline. You love her so much, Jake. Because that bastard would have killed you. Because I know Caroline will understand."

"You sound as if you know her," Jake said idly.

"No, but I feel that I know her because of what you have told me. I know she would understand." Julia hesitated. "I have seen her. She has an interview show on television. It's a sensation. In fact, I have been asked to be on the show."

"As what?"

"Don't act so surprised. I do involve myself in worthy projects between trips, you know. I think this is about the historical homes restoration project."

"Are you going to do it?

"I actually was considering it, before this. I wanted to meet her. She doesn't know about me, I assume."

"No." Jake could imagine the interview. He could imagine Carrie finding out about Julia, because of her uncanny intuition. The Jake Easton restoration project would make interesting copy. How many times have you made love with Mr. Easton? Is he really the best lover you have ever had? How many times has he asked you to marry him? Why don't you?

"I'm not going to do it, especially not now."

Jake nodded.

Julia worried about Jake's moodiness. The episode in Cambodia had damaged him deeply. He could only take so much battering—his leg, Vietnam, his shattered dreams about Carrie. If this was the price of patriotism, the price was too high. He had already paid enough, repaid any debts that he felt he owed.

Julia telephoned Stuart. He had a small room in the same hotel, twenty floors below. Jake was asleep in the bedroom.

"Stuart, this is Julia."

"Julia? Where are you? You sound so close."

Stuart didn't know she was there; Jake hadn't told him. Why should he?

"I'm here. With Jake." Julia paused. The tone of her voice made it clear that her presence was as Jake's lover, not as his mother or Frank's widow.

"I'll be damned." Stuart whistled. And he thought, That kid. It was envy mixed with pride.

"We all will be. Listen Stuart, Jake has to get out. He's had enough."

"I know."

"You do?"

"Sure." It's just that he's so damned valuable to us, Stuart thought. In response to her question, he said, "I can tell."

"Do you know what happened in Cambodia?"

"With the captain? Of course."

"He actually wishes that he had let the other fellow kill him. Jake's dead and in hell as it is."

"I know, Julia." Christ, she was beautiful, but she could treat men like idiots sometimes.

"So he's off the hook?" she pressed.

"He's never been on the hook. It is, and always has been, Jake's decision."

"You won't send him back to Cambodia?"

"No. No one's going back. Even if we were, I wouldn't send Jake." They'd kill him.

"So?"

"So what?"

"So why are you sounding so coy? I know you, Stuart." You don't know me as well as I wish you did, Stuart

277

thought. At least, you don't know me the way I want you to, the way you know the kid. Stuart sighed.

"There's talk of a Middle East peace treaty. It's at least six or eight months off, if it happens. I've already told Jake. Nothing until then. And if it doesn't happen, nothing else, ever. He's retired. But Julia, I may need him for this. He's the best we have."

"What does Jake say?"

"Jake says, 'I'll do it if Stuart needs me.'" It was Jake's voice. He stood at the bedroom door, half frowning, half smiling. He liked the fact that Julia had told Stuart that they were together, that she didn't want to hide it.

"Oh-oh, Stuart. Guess who has just found me out. Your star spy. Ta-ta." Julia hung up and looked tentatively at Jake. He could be angry. She remembered her surprise visit to Stanford. Jake's rules. Julia's rules.

"What the hell are you doing?" He walked toward her, but he was smiling.

"Are you really going to quit?" she asked.

"Yes," he said firmly. He began to undress her.

"What about the Middle East thing?" Julia was having trouble concentrating. He was kissing her breasts, stroking her thighs. And she was naked.

"The Middle East thing?" he murmured into her chest. Julia sighed softly.

Jake and Julia flew from Hong Kong to Papeete, Tahiti. They spent three days at the Hotel Taharaa, walking slowly on the black sand beach, silently watching the pink-orange sunsets over the island of Moorea, speaking little, making love. They drove around the small island of Tahiti, visiting the isolated beaches, the Gauguin museum, the tiny French restaurants.

Julia watched Jake's torment helplessly. He slept little. He was afraid to go to sleep. He awakened drenched in sweat, gasping, terrified. He apologized to Julia.

"I'm sorry, darling. This can't be much fun for you."

"Tell me about your nightmares, Jake. It might make them seem less real."

Jake had finally told her about the ones that he had had after Vietnam. And it had helped. They had almost disappeared by the time he had been assigned to Cambodia. That was part of the reason that he had dared to dream about marrying Carrie.

He shook his head. "I can't. Not yet."

They were too horrible, too unspeakably horrible. In them, Jake, the murderer, brutally murdered people that he loved: Carrie, Julia, Megan, Stephen, Frank. The murders were vivid, brutal. The victim pleaded for their lives, pledged their love to him. And still he murdered them.

There was nothing mysterious about why he had the nightmares; they were an obvious reaction to what had happened in Cambodia. Even Freud would have found them boringly simple. Jake understood them, but he couldn't make them stop.

They sailed from Tahiti to Bora Bora and spent a week in an overwater bungalow. Their bungalow was private and secluded. From it, Jake could swim unobserved. No one, except Julia, could see him or his leg. They snorkeled from their bungalow, in waters where thousands of splendidly colored reef fish swam just below the surface.

Swimming was a new freedom for Jake, and the snorkeling a welcome escape. For those moments he lost himself in the soundless undersea world. He forgot his own torment. He focused, without thinking, on the peaceful, natural, silent beauty. He spent hours every day in the warm, clear water.

Julia sunbathed, topless, on the deck of their bungalow. Watching, worrying, wondering.

There was so little Jake could do to escape his thoughts. Snorkeling, making love, drinking.

They made love often, with an energy and intensity that left her breathless. In those moments, Jake was able to forget about everything, to concentrate only on their lovemaking, and to find pleasure in it. It was a different kind of lovemaking than theirs had been before. Jake seemed almost driven. And he was more demanding.

Jake's intensity didn't frighten Julia; it was exciting. But it made her worry even more about the turbulent, violent, restless emotions that plagued her lover.

Jake drank too much in those weeks in French Polynesia. Unlike the hours in the lagoon and the hours in bed with Julia, in which his senses were heightened and directed, the alcohol made him forget, momentarily, by dulling his senses and blunting his emotions.

Julia knew that Jake hated himself for drinking. He had blamed the morphine that he had asked for when he had been wounded in Vietnam for the damage that had been done to his leg. If the pain hadn't been blocked by the narcotic, he might have known sooner; they might have been able to save more muscle; he might not have had to live with the inevitable loss of the leg. Since then, despite the pain that the leg had given him during the years of rehabilitation, he had refused medications. And he had tried to avoid alcohol.

When Jake drank, when the hopelessness of his life became oppressive, he drank to excess. Julia knew that he could control it with the same rigid control and rules that directed his life, but in those weeks he didn't even try.

They flew from Papeete to Nice and spent the summer at the villa in Monte Carlo.

Gradually, Jake's hope returned, in tiny bits, careful, precious fleeting moments of optimism. He drank less. He laughed a little. Their lovemaking became more gentle and sensual—and less frequent as Jake's restlessness grew.

"It's almost time for you to leave," Julia said one day in late July.

"You know me so well."

"I'm glad you're restless. It's a good sign. A sign of health. What are your plans?"

"I'll go to the wedding in Houston. Then I think I'll

move to New York, wait to hear from Stuart, make plans for life after spying." Jake sounded almost happy.

Julia looked at him meaningfully. Caroline would be in Houston and in New York.

"I don't know if I can tell her, Julia. Now or ever. I won't know until I see her."

Part Six

Chapter Eighteen

Houston, Texas . . . August, 1974

Carrie watched Jake arrive. She was trapped in polite conversation with the mother of Beth's best friend from high school. About whom, Carrie thought, Beth had never said a word in all the years they had been friends. The woman was one of two hundred guests—close family friends—invited to the garden party. Stephen and Beth would be married in two days, the wedding itself capping a week of parties given and attended by Houston's wealthiest citizens. Each party had been more spectacular, the food more gourmet, the band more renowned, the clothes more expensive, and the guests more select than the last; an elaborate crescendo that would culminate in the wedding itself.

Carrie had been in Houston for four days and had not yet tired of the glamour and the parties. At times, she became so involved in the celebration that she almost forgot what they were celebrating: the biggest mistake her brother had ever made, and the most irrevocable. Stephen looked happy, calm, untroubled. He seemed pleased with himself, as if he knew he was doing a sensible thing. To everyone else, they seemed the perfect couple; but that was because no one else, except her parents, had seen Stephen with Megan. Maybe, Carrie thought, Stephen could never find that brand of happiness again. Maybe he was too battered to even look. Damn Megan. Why had she done this to Stephen?

Carrie's heart pounded when she saw Jake. He was across the perfectly manicured lawn, being greeted enthusiastically by Stephen. They spoke for a few moments, then, in response to a question from Jake, Stephen nodded, looked around the crowd, and, finding Carrie, beckoned for her to join them.

Carrie excused herself and weaved through the guests. Slowly, her heart racing. No one had known until that moment whether Jake would be coming. No one had spoken to him since that evening last January. He hadn't written to Carrie for seven months. She had gotten a long letter from Hong Kong postmarked three days after the call from San Francisco. And then nothing. She had spent hours worrying about him. Was he safe? Had there been an accident? Was he ill? Would she ever see him again? Had he fallen in love with someone?

She had not seen him for over two years.

"Jake! We're so glad you made it!" Carrie stood across from him and extended her hand. She had on her gracious Southern garden party manners. She wanted to throw her arms around him with joy. Maybe later. Many eyes were on the new arrival.

Jake's presence had always commanded attention—the white-blond hair, clear blue eyes, handsome, aristocratic face. Now there was something more compelling than simply good looks. In a crowd of the wealthiest, most powerful men in Houston, Jake's presence, Jake's power, Jake's importance, was felt and appreciated. No one knew who he was or what he did; but they sensed that he was powerful.

The effect was dazzling—golden tan, fashionably long, sun-bleached hair, tailored blue silk suit, and the demeanor of power. Except, Carrie thought, something is very wrong.

"I'm glad I made it, too."

"Where were you?" Stephen asked.

"Eighteen hours away by plane. You'll have to excuse a little jet lag." Jake smiled.

He didn't tell us where he has been, Carrie thought. And he doesn't plan to.

"Would you like to go up to your room now and rest?" Beth's mother asked.

"No, thank you. I think after all those hours of sitting on planes and in airports, what I need is a walk through your beautiful gardens. Caroline, will you join me?"

"Of course," Carrie said quietly. Maybe the dark circles and troubled eyes were just fatigue.

"You look magnificent," Jake whispered as they left the group.

Carrie knew that she looked better, more womanly. Her new job had given her confidence. Her red-gold hair fell in soft curls to her shoulders, pulled gently away from her slender face by gold barrettes. She wore a blue silk cocktail dress that matched her eyes. And she wore, as always, the gold necklace.

"You look rather dapper yourself. I had never pictured you in a three-piece suit. But I should have; it makes a nice picture."

Jake got a bottle of champagne opened for them by the bartender and two crystal champagne glasses. They walked slowly away from Houston's social elite, through the prize-winning rose garden, toward the woods beyond. Two miles away, thunder rumbled through the hot, humid August air.

Twenty minutes later, warm, heavy drops of rain pelted the steaming earth. Jake and Carrie had been oblivious to the impending storm.

"Welcome to Houston," Carrie giggled, but realized that, in a matter of moments, they would be drenched and chilled by their soaking clothes. They were too far from the main house to run for cover. And she had never seen Jake run, just as she had never seen him wear shorts. Because of his leg.

Carrie remembered the guest house. As she and Jake had strolled aimlessly, she had paid very little attention to where they were. When the rain made her focus on something other than Jake, she realized that she had been here before.

Two days before, she and Beth had gone for a walk. Beth had shown her the guest house.

"I thought Jake and Megan might like to stay here," Beth had told her, adding, "if they come." Carrie had suppressed her anger—at what Beth had said and the way she had said it. At the stupidity of inviting Megan. Carrie had been startled by Beth's casual allusion to Jake and Megan as lovers. How had Beth known? Because Beth noticed things. How had Carrie known? Because when you love someone, and he is with someone else, you notice, you ache and you remember. Carrie guessed, though, that Beth had never told Stephen. She wouldn't hurt him.

"There's a guest house nearby. I think it's just around the trees over there."

The cottage was unlocked, and in the two days since Carrie had been there, it had been made ready for guests. There were fresh-cut roses in every room, plus towels neatly stacked in the bathroom, a fire laid in the brick fireplace, liquor and glasses on a tea tray in the living room. Apparently, Beth had given the order to prepare it, just in case.

"It reminds me a little of the cabin in San Gregorio." The cabin—Jake's cabin, Stephen and Megan's love nest. Jake and Megan's love nest, too, she guessed.

"Just a little. That cabin was true rustic. This cottage is expensively created rustic."

"I liked that cabin. Is anyone living there now?"

"I don't know. I sold it," Jake said flatly, as if he had sold the memories with the real estate.

Carrie shivered, from her wet, cold clothes and from some old, painful memories—memories of Jake building walls around himself. What had he said last January? *I need to talk to you.*

"I think I had better light the fire. And you had better get out of your clothes. I'll pour us both a drink. Something warmer than champagne. What will you have?"

"Brandy."

"It's a myth, you know, about brandy being good for you

288

when you're cold," Jake said, smiling, as he poured an ample amount of brandy into a snifter.

"Surely all those Saint Bernards can't be wrong!" Carrie was already giddy from the champagne and from being with Jake, but she took a large swallow of the brandy. Physiologic or not, it made her feel warm and confident.

Jake poured himself a large glass of bourbon.

"You're shivering. There must be blankets or something."

Carrie found blankets and two terry cloth bathrobes, unused, hanging in the bedroom closet. The robes were identical. Carrie undressed and put one of them on. On her, the length was below her knees. On Jake it would be about mid-thigh. She wondered . . .

When she returned, Jake stood in front of the fire, still dressed in his three-piece suit. Carrie handed the second robe to him.

"It may be a bit short on you, but still decent." What am I doing, she thought. Taunting him. Probing, as usual, for his secrets.

Jake took the robe and shrugged. "The fire is actually drying my clothes pretty quickly."

He looked at his still-drenched clothes and was dismayed by the obviousness of his lie.

Carrie sat on the sofa and looked at him thoughtfully. What now? How far should she push? She had been so hopeful that this time they would be able to talk. That was what he had said. But that had been seven months ago. And something had happened. Another secret in their way.

She drank the brandy hastily. A new wave of warmth and confidence rushed through her. And anger. She sat in front of him, unglamorously clad in an overlarge bathrobe because he had ordered her out of her wet clothes, while he intended to remain fully dressed because of some secret.

"I know about your leg." She watched Jake's face tense and he paused in the middle of a swallow of his bourbon. He stared at her, curious. He's calling my bluff, she thought. "I know there's something wrong with it. No one has ever told me about it, but in all these years I've never seen you run; I've never seen you wear shorts. Sometimes you limp a bit. And . . ." She stopped.

"And?"

"And." Carrie took a deep breath. The memory was so personal. But it was their memory, not just hers. "And I felt it that day that I made such a fuss about the antiwar rally." And you held me and kissed me.

"What did you feel?" he asked carefully.

"A hardness. Like steel." Carrie looked at him, wide-eyed. She didn't want to tell him that she lay awake at night worrying that he had bone cancer and that they had removed his leg. She didn't want to tell him that in the past few months her greatest fear had been that the tumor had spread. That sometime since January he had developed a cough and the X rays had shown spread of the tumor to the lungs. She didn't want to tell him that she was afraid he was dying.

He read the unspoken worry in her eyes and was angry with himself that she had worried about him.

"Caroline, I have an ugly leg. From an accident when I was a child. It's ugly. It doesn't work awfully well. But"— he stood in front of her and gently touched her cheek—"it's not terminal."

He smiled wistfully. He hadn't wanted her, of all people, to know about his leg, until and unless he decided to tell her. But she had noticed, because Carrie would notice. And she had cared. And she had worried needlessly.

"Then get out of those wet clothes," she whispered. It was a challenge: prove to me that I don't have to worry.

Jake poured himself another glass of bourbon, refilled Carrie's brandy, and left the room. Carrie prepared herself to see the "ugly" leg. When she saw it, she was startled, alarmed. Then she furrowed her brow. Finally she spoke.

"It wasn't from a childhood accident." Even in the midst of war there were physical examinations from the army. Jake could never have passed.

"No."

"It happened in Vietnam."

"Yes."

"Tell me."

"No."

"My God, Jake. I am a grown woman. I'm not little Carrie who we all need to protect from the cruel world anymore. I am so tired of this halfway friendship that you and I pretend to have. How can you allow people to care about you and reward them with lies and coyness? How can you live with yourself?" Keep angry, Carrie. Don't cry.

"Maybe," Jake said slowly, carefully, "I am afraid that if the people who care about me really knew me, they wouldn't care anymore."

"That's stupid and childish." Except, at first, she hated knowing that he had been in Vietnam.

"Or, maybe, I don't really want people to care." Jake sounded defeated.

"Worse yet. More stupid and childish."

"Maybe I have never lived any other way."

"Or maybe you have and it didn't work?" Carrie guessed. They were playing word games, but at least they were talking.

"Or maybe I thought I had tried, before, and it didn't work because it was all an illusion." It was cryptic, but it was honest; it was something about himself that had mattered to him.

Jake smiled. "Too much bourbon, Caroline. Too much jet lag. Too many memories." He looked carefully at her; the old, familiar look of pain flickered across his face and was gone.

Carrie waited.

"If it matters that much to you, if you feel that you can't really know me unless you know about my past, then I'll tell you," Jake said quietly. His expression mixed reluctance with relief. He agreed with her; there were things she needed to know. He didn't know how much he could, or would, tell her.

"Tell me," Carrie said softly and curled tightly against

the corner of the overstuffed sofa, like a child snuggling in anticipation of a favorite story. Carrie was certain that she already knew the story: spoiled rich boy, bored, defiant, who, perhaps emotionally wounded from a failed high school romance, ran off to war. Ran off to an imagined adventure that backfired miserably, leaving him crippled, disillusioned, and bitter. That story was enough to explain his moodiness and his detachment.

But the story that Jake told her was entirely different; he told her the truth. He told her about his childhood, his dying parents, his nameless brothers and sisters, his illiteracy, and the hopelessness of that life. It was the same story that he had told Julia ten years before, but now eloquently, emotionally.

"How many brothers and sisters do you have?"

"I don't remember."

"Haven't you gone back?"

"No!" Jake said vehemently. "Why would I?"

Why indeed, Carrie thought. To see the graves of his parents. To try to speak to the brothers and sisters who wouldn't understand his words or his clothes or his life. No, he could never go back. But how had he gotten here?

Jake read her look and continued the story. He told her about meeting Julia. He modified the story a bit; the chauffeur had been "injured"; the assassin, "captured". He told her about Julia's agreement to teach him to read and write and speak. He told her the truth about that weekend—why he went back to the barracks, why he went into battle, the sound of the shrapnel tearing his leg.

"And you decided that what happened to you was punishment for what you and Julia felt for each other?" Carrie guessed.

"I toyed with that idea. We both did. But who was doing the punishing? Frank? Sending his wife's would-be lover to almost certain death? No, not possible, of course. God? If there is a God, he had washed his hands of Vietnam long before that battle. Or, he is an unimaginably despicable God. No, what happened to me that day happened without sense or reason. Like most of the events of one's life, Caroline." Jake smiled faintly and shrugged.

Jake told Carrie about the gas gangrene, the year he spent as an inpatient at Walter Reed Hospital, the rigorous, painful physical therapy and the equally rigorous tutoring provided by Julia and others.

"She was merciless!" Jake said, the gentleness in his voice betraying his feelings about Julia, his bittersweet memories of that time in his life. "But we accomplished a lot—a high school diploma, admission to Stanford . . ."

"You must have felt very lonely arriving at Stanford." Carrie remembered how she had felt, and she had had Stephen and Megan. And Jake.

"I was very lucky to have Stephen as my roommate."

"But you never told him any of this!"

"No."

"Why not?"

"I wanted my life to stop being different. I didn't want to be different. I was tired of being a specimen to be stared at and admired. I didn't want to be noticed. I wanted a chance to create my own identity, to be and do whatever I chose. I guess I was scared more than lonely."

Jake sat quietly for a few moments. Weary, thoughtful. Finally he lifted his shoulders and turned toward Carrie.

"So, there. You know the rest."

It wasn't true. He knew, and she sensed, that there was much more. But the effect of the effort it had taken him to tell her this much was evident on his tense, tired face. It had been an ordeal for him, because the retelling recalled the memories, the memories that accounted for the haunting looks of pain. Jake had told her the facts of his past, but not the feelings; a skeleton without meat or heart or brain. It was a beginning.

"Do you still see Frank and Julia?" Carrie asked lightly. What had become of a seventeen-year-old boy's yearning for the older woman? And what of Julia's desire for him? And Frank, who had become like a father?

"Frank died my sophomore year." Jake hesitated. Then he said, slowly, "He left me half of his estate." Jake's voice choked with emotion.

The money, which was obviously a fortune, meant little to Jake. Frank's true legacy to Jake was his love and his pride.

"And Julia," Jake said finally, his voice strong and slightly amused, "is between marriages, as usual. I think whatever patience Julia had was spent trying to teach me."

"Trying? My goodness, Jake, succeeding. She must be a remarkable woman."

"Remarkable. Spoiled. Not even very nice, sometimes. But remarkable, yes."

And you are still in love with her, Carrie thought, remembering the letter she had seen on Jake's desk that day: *My darling Jake.*

"But all that time she spent with you. That seems so unselfish," Carrie protested. She had imagined a selfless, naive, motherly, gentle woman.

"I was the greatest project of Julia's life. The only thing she has ever achieved through her own talent and energy. For once, she couldn't just buy the result; she had to create it. It was hard work, but she enjoyed having her own personal Pygmalion. It was a new kind of power for her, power money couldn't buy—the making of a man."

"Her ideal man? A man created in her own image?" Carrie asked, amazed by Jake's words, a mixture of love and resentment and pride.

Jake laughed. "Neither, I think. But it was fun for her once I was presentable and could walk. My love for art, theater, literature, and opera is as instinctive as hers. And, since Frank disliked the arts, I became her companion. I think that Frank was her ideal man," Jake said seriously.

"She must have missed you when you left. Must still miss you," Carrie pressed, urged on by the warmth of the brandy.

"In Julia's circles, men of culture are a dime a dozen. If Julia misses anyone, it is the illiterate, sensitive, untamed

294

seventeen-year-old waif that she found in Vietnam. And he doesn't exist anymore."

Yes he does, Carrie thought. Somewhere under that splendid veneer of culture, education, and elegant clothes, he still does exist.

After a few moments, Jake stoked the dwindling fire and walked to the window.

"The rain has stopped," he said. His voice was natural, confident. He turned and looked at Carrie, huddled under a blanket. She looked small and fragile and shaken.

"Are you cold? Do you need another blanket?"

"No, I'm fine. It's the brandy." She smiled weakly. The brandy hadn't helped; it had made her mind foggy and her body warm. But that wasn't why she was shaken. It was because she felt, more than ever before, peripheral to Jake's life. And she had never wanted him so much. They had shared so little—a few dinners, a few letters, brief moments of touching, two kisses. Nothing of substance. Nothing, Carrie realized, compared to the years with Julia; nothing compared to the emotion he felt for Julia and Frank. Nothing even compared to what he had shared with Megan.

There were people in Jake's life, people that he loved deeply, people that he made an effort to see. Carrie wasn't one of them; she never had been. It was, as Megan had said once, so many years ago, a silly schoolgirl crush. Jake had never deceived her; she had deceived herself.

Carrie tried unsuccessfully to blink back tears.

"Caroline, what's wrong?" Jake sat beside her. He looked worried, concerned, like a brother would, like Stephen would.

"Nothing," she whispered. "Nothing of substance. Just foolishness." She tried to smile, but the tears didn't stop.

"My God, Caroline, why do I make you cry?" Jake sounded angry with himself.

"It's not your fault, Jake. It's me. I'm just a silly little girl, after all."

"Hardly a silly little girl," he said gently.

He kissed her then. Not a brotherly kiss. A lover's kiss—warm, probing, tender, endless. Carrie closed her eyes and her mind and followed the commands of her senses. A minute, an hour, a lifetime later, the kiss ended. They lay on the sofa, entwined but modestly and securely wrapped in their robes. Jake looked at her, gently running his finger along her cheek, around her mouth.

It was a thoughtful look, loving but troubled.

He wants to tell me something, Carrie thought, trembling. He's trying to decide. She held her breath.

Jake didn't speak but pulled her close to him, pressing his body into hers. Then he felt the pounding of her strong young heart. Like another young heart he had felt. But that had been a different kind of heart, a dying heart—the heart of a Cambodian captain. Jake tried to banish the thought, to focus on Carrie and their future.

"Make love to me, Jake," Carrie whispered.

Carrie felt his body tense and his breathing stop for a moment. Her heart pounded restlessly against his chest. With each beat the memory of the agonal moments of the life he had taken became more vivid. Irrepressible, taunting memories: No, you can't have her. No, you can't tell her. No, you are unworthy of her. *Lub dub*.

"No!" Jake pulled free and sat on the edge of the sofa.

"No?" Carrie asked weakly, startled, unsure. She retreated to the corner of the sofa and stared at Jake's back.

"No."

"I don't understand," Carrie said helplessly. But she did; at least, she had understood before he had kissed her; she wasn't part of his life. But then he had kissed her.

"It would be wrong." His voice was firm, flat. "I can't feel that way about you."

"Can't?" Carrie whispered.

Jake's shoulders slumped. He stared at the floor. When he spoke, finally, he hissed under his breath. The words, almost inaudible, were clear. And their meaning was even clearer. Carrie would never forget them.

"Can't. Don't. Won't. Not ever, Caroline."

Thank you, Julia, for teaching him the subtle, devastating meanings of those words.

"What did your letters mean, Jake? What did the postcard from Amsterdam mean? Why did you call me and tell me that you needed to talk to me and that you had something to give me? Were those all lies, Jake?" Carrie hissed back, angry. The fog of the brandy was clearing. Their relationship had not all been in her mind. Jake had written those words, had given her the necklace. And he *had* kissed her. Had he intentionally misled her? Or had something changed?

"No." There was a long pause. "I had something for you. It was stolen." His voice was bitter, defeated. More had been stolen than the ring. What had been stolen were his hopes and his dreams.

"Stolen?" Carrie echoed softly.

"Things change, Caroline. I have never intended to lie to you or to cause you pain." Jake left the room and returned five minutes later, fully dressed. He waited for Carrie to dress.

They walked wordlessly through the soggy woods. The sky was gray and flat and sulky. The warm earth steamed. The scent of damp roses filled the summer air.

Carrie tried to make sense of her feelings—anger, humiliation, regret, frustration. And that other one, the one she had learned years ago from Jake and Megan—hatred.

"I am sorry, Caroline." Jake's voice broke the stillness as they approached the house.

"Why should you be?" she countered. It wasn't a question; it was a shot. Jake said nothing.

The garden party had moved inside when the storm had come, but that had been hours before. The last guests were just leaving. But a new guest had arrived.

"Megan is here," Beth announced to Jake and Carrie as soon as she saw them. Beth had insisted on inviting Megan, but now she sounded less than enthusiastic. Stephen looked uneasy for the first time in the week of pre-nuptial festivities.

297

Damn Megan, Carrie thought. This is so tasteless. But, she was invited.

"Where is she?" Carrie asked.

"Her room is next to yours. And Jake's is at the far end of that hall. If you're going up to see Megan, maybe you could show Jake the way to his room. You look exhausted, Jake," Beth said critically.

"Jet lag. I could use some rest. When is the next major function?" Jake asked politely without enthusiasm.

"Supper at ten. Cocktails in the living room at nine."

Jake nodded and followed Carrie up the broad, banistered staircase. They had to pass Megan's room to get to Jake's.

"Megan?"

"Carrie!" Megan appeared in the doorway. Carrie was struck, as she had been the first time they had met, with Megan's natural, healthy beauty. "And Jake! You two look like soggy, unhappy kittens. Come in!"

Megan hugged Carrie tightly and kissed Jake briefly, because of his reluctance.

"I wasn't sure you'd be here, Jake. I am so glad."

Megan had debated seriously the wisdom of attending the wedding. But at the last moment, spurred by excellent reviews of her recently released movie, she decided to come. Still, it was a relief to have Jake here, too.

"I wasn't sure either. I've been out of the country."

"And incommunicado, as usual. Carrie, what do you suppose Jake really does on these mysterious business trips abroad?"

Carrie shrugged. She didn't care anymore.

"I'm going to find my room and take a nap. See you later," Jake said tiredly and left.

"What's wrong with him?"

"Jet lag."

"And you? What's wrong with you?"

"Life lag," Carrie quipped and forced a smile. "In fact, I need a nap, too. Sorry to be a sad sack, but we can visit this evening."

Megan and Carrie walked down to dinner together.

"You're angry at me for coming, aren't you?"

"It depends on how you behave," Carrie answered truthfully.

"I was invited, you know."

"I know."

"I had to come."

"Why?"

Megan hesitated. "Because I couldn't stand the thought of Beth thinking that I had stayed away because she got Stephen after all. To think that she won and I lost."

"Megan! You didn't lose Stephen. You threw him away," Carrie bristled. She would never be able to forgive Megan for what she had done to Stephen.

"Well, whatever. Anyway, it's really past history. I was a bit surprised they invited me."

They didn't, Carrie thought. *Beth* did.

It was a small dinner party, just the house guests: Beth's parents, Stephen and Carrie's parents, Beth, Stephen, Jake, Carrie, and Megan. Small enough to be very awkward.

"When do you graduate?" Jake asked Stephen.

"Next June."

"Do you have plans?"

"Yes, I will join a firm in Boston. After I spend the summer studying for the Bar," Stephen said and smiled quizzically at Beth.

"As if he needs to study for the Bar," she said softly, teasingly. Stephen always worried about exams; then, he always got the top grade. It was a standing joke; Beth teased him about it. But she was careful not to bother him when he studied. She continued, proudly, "And the firm Stephen's joining is the best, the best in Boston."

"What kind of law will you practice?" Megan asked, carefully, trying to be casual. It was a subject they had discussed often, while watching the sun set over the blue Pacific from their porch at San Gregorio, over a leisurely dinner in San Francisco, in bed, after they had made love.

"Contract law," Stephen answered flatly. He looked at Megan almost defiantly. It was a different answer; they both knew it. His plans to be a public defender, to practice grass roots law, had, apparently, been abandoned. Stephen knew that Megan would assume, smugly, that it was Beth's doing; that she had convinced him to make a more lucrative, socially acceptable path.

But it wasn't true. Beth had had nothing to do with it; she was supportive of whatever he chose. It was Megan, not Beth, who had influenced his decision. Because when Megan had abandoned Stephen, Stephen had abandoned the plans that, together, they had made.

"Contracts," Jake mused, almost to himself. He might need a good contracts lawyer, someday, in the future, when he tried his hand at business. If . . .

A silence followed, everyone at the table painfully aware that there were unspoken, uncomfortable depths to the exchange between Stephen and Megan.

"Jake, did you see Julia this trip?" Stephen asked finally, searching for a neutral topic. He explained to the others, "Julia is a friend of Jake's family. A jet setter *par excellence.*"

Jake glanced uneasily at Carrie. She gave no sign of recognition or concern. Megan arched an eyebrow; she had never heard of Julia.

"I did see her. She is living in Monte Carlo at the moment."

"Have you met her, Stephen?" Carrie asked politely.

"Only once. But she's quite memorable," Stephen said.

"Speaking of memorable," Megan said, pausing perfectly until she had everyone's attention, "I would like to hear about Carrie's new show. The reviews are marvelous and the segments I have seen are wonderful."

"I hear you are a star," Jake said quietly.

Carrie stared at him. How had he even heard about the show? Hadn't he been away? Who could have told him?

300

Then, in a horrible instant, it all crystallized: Julia Spencer was Jake's Julia. The same Julia that Carrie had invited to appear on the show. The beautiful, wealthy widow of the distinguished general who had founded the historic homes restoration project after her husband's death. The same Julia who had at first responded enthusiastically and then, at the last minute, with no explanation, had changed her mind. Jake had known that, too.

Perhaps Jake had insisted that Julia cancel.

I hate you, Carrie thought.

"It's a great show, Jake. Carrie is the host and each time has one or two guests, celebrities, politicians, newsmakers, and so on. And she just talks to them, in her typical, un-assuming Carrie way, and they tell her all sorts of things that they probably have never told anyone before. It's really an art that Carrie has," Stephen said proudly.

Carrie blushed. She hadn't been practicing for her show this afternoon, or any of the other times she had tried to get Jake to tell her about himself. What did Jake think of her? Then she remembered that it didn't matter anymore.

"Stephen, I'm not a gossip monger!"

"Of course you aren't. That's the point. That's why the show is so good. It's honest and open and sensitive, like you are. It's not entertainment, it's communication. That's why it's so unique."

"We're really proud of you, Carrie," Megan interjected enthusiastically.

"Thanks. Now that you'll be in New York for awhile . . ." Carrie smiled at Megan.

"No way, my dear. But speaking of New York, I have some bad news. I spoke with my director, Ian Knight, just before I came down for dinner. I'm afraid I have to take the first plane to New York tomorrow morning. There are some last-minute rewrites for the new play, and they have to be done this weekend. I'm very sorry."

The instant Megan had seen Beth and Stephen together, she had realized how happy they were. And she had known she would have to leave; it would be too painful for her to watch them. Megan had felt safe in coming, had believed that seeing them together wouldn't hurt her, because of what Carrie had told her. Because as much as Carrie liked Beth, she was convinced that Beth and Stephen's marriage was a big mistake.

Megan had accepted the invitation, expecting that she would be able to take some small comfort in the obvious fact that, despite what had happened to them, Stephen would never love anyone the way he had loved her. *But it wasn't obvious at all!*

Carrie was wrong. Perhaps because Beth and Stephen had looked so different from the way Stephen and Megan had looked when they had been in love—so much more quiet and reserved. No obvious displays of affection, no exuberance, no ecstasy. But Megan knew Stephen. Better than anyone. As soon as she saw him, Megan knew that Stephen was happy, genuinely, honestly, happy. She saw a peace and contentment in his handsome, slightly older face. Megan watched the way Stephen and Beth interacted, exchanging glances, gently teasing, the unspoken communication. Megan saw it in his eyes. Stephen was in love.

In love with Beth. It might not be obvious to Carrie, but it was painfully clear to Megan. Stephen respected and admired Beth. And he loved her.

When Megan saw Beth, she knew why. Beth, the Beth Megan had known and taunted, had been transformed, her Southern belle frilliness replaced with a mature, natural, honest beauty. The hostility and icy contempt that had always lurked menacingly beneath the veneer of manners had vanished. Beth no longer needed to conceal her intelligence. She was loved by a man who was proud of his bride to be in every way—her beauty, her wit, her mind, her sexuality.

In another time, another place, another situation, Megan would have liked and admired the new Beth very much. But not here. Not at a celebration of the marriage between Stephen and Beth.

Megan had come to quietly gloat. To pity them for the mistake they were making. To reassure herself that what she and Stephen had shared was enduring and irreplaceable, even though it was over. But, Megan realized the moment she saw them together, there was no one there to feel sorry for. Except herself.

Everyone politely expressed their alleged regret that Megan could not stay for the wedding; but no one, except Jake, could hide the relief. Even Jake believed it was best for Megan to leave, but he would be sorry to see her go.

Carrie excused herself immediately after dinner. She sat at the antique desk in her room and wrote. She wrote as furiously and beautifully as she had written that November night four years before. But this time, no one else would read it. But she would keep it as a bitter reminder, to read and reread whenever she felt herself lapsing into fantasies about Jake or trust or honesty.

Hours later, Carrie heard a nearby door close. It had to be Megan.

Carrie crossed the hall and knocked gently on Megan's door. Megan opened the door partway. She wore an emerald green silk robe.

"Carrie!"

"I just wanted to say that I'm sorry you felt driven away."

"You don't buy the script rewrite business?" Megan smiled wryly.

"No. But I suspect the others bought it. Anyway, you've proven your point; you're doing fine. It's the rest of us who are trapped in the past. Anyway, it was nice of you to take us all off the hook. I'd give anything to get on that plane with you tomorrow morning."

"Why? Listen, come on in. Jake and I . . ." Megan opened the door.

Jake stood by the window, his face in the shadows. He wore tan slacks and an open-collared shirt; he had changed out of the formal evening wear into something more comfortable. The situation was obvious. Megan and Jake had arranged to meet, secretly, privately, after the rest of the household was asleep. In the name of discretion.

This is so awful, it's almost funny, Carrie thought. Almost, but not quite.

Jake acknowledged her presence with a taciturn nod. Carrie gave no response. Her goal was to get out of Megan's room as soon as possible.

"I was just telling Jake about the penthouse. I have been totally unsuccessful in convincing Carrie to move in with me," Megan explained to Jake.

I can't afford it, Carrie thought. And I like living alone.

"Is Jake going to be your roommate?" Carrie asked flatly, as if Jake weren't even in the room. Why not? she thought. Megan had been her roommate, then Stephen's. Why not Jake's?

"No," Jake answered, looking at Carrie, who didn't look back.

"I want him to buy the other penthouse on the same floor. It's a mirror image of mine. It would be nice to have someone there who I know."

"Is Jake moving to New York? I didn't think he lived anywhere."

Megan stared from Carrie to Jake. The hostility was palpable. What was going on?

"I am going to live in New York," Jake said flatly.

"That's wonderful," Carrie answered sarcastically. Then she said to Megan, "It's been a long day. I'd love to visit with you, but I'm really tired. Let's get together, soon, in New York."

Carrie slept fitfully. Several hours later, as the first light of yellow dawn filled her room, Carrie heard the door across the hall open and shut again.

Chapter Nineteen

The idea of his own home appealed greatly to Jake. It had been part of his dream, too; perhaps now the only part he could still salvage. Beginning with the green, ivory, and blue Oriental from the *souk* in Jeddah, Jake had collected rugs, furniture, paintings, sculpture, and vases from all over the world. With each purchase, as he had carefully provided the merchant with the name and address of a storage company in Washington, Jake had promised himself that someday he would create a quiet, peaceful home for his treasures.

The other part of that dream, he knew from what had happened in Houston, was impossible. He would have to be content to find a separate peace.

The penthouse was new and had a commanding view of New York City. Jake had debated the wisdom of being Megan's neighbor. It was a brief debate; the positives outweighed the negatives.

Megan watched Jake's selection of draperies and rugs with interest and skepticism; the thick, cream-colored carpets, heavy silk drapes in muted pastels.

"How do you plan to make cream and pastel look masculine, my friend?" she teased.

"Just wait. Suspend criticism until you see the final product," Jake insisted confidently.

A month later, he invited her over for the unveiling. Filled with his rugs, his vases, his furniture, his paintings, it had been transformed into a retreat that was unmistakably Jake.

"I love it!" Megan exclaimed. "Wait until Carrie sees this. It's enchanted. It makes you never want to leave."

Jake smiled. He was pleased. It was a perfect home for him. It was what he had dreamed.

But Carrie will never see it, he thought.

In the next three months, Jake left the penthouse twice; once, with Megan, to the Knight's estate in Connecticut to celebrate their daughter Stephanie's second birthday and once to see Megan's play. Other than that, he had no need to leave, nor was he lonely. The flow of visitors to his apartment was constant: attorneys, financial advisors, corporate presidents. He bought and sold stock. He consolidated his holdings. He made a new will. He listened politely to job offers from huge companies to manage their overseas concerns. They "had heard" that he was a talented consultant. It worried Jake, and it worried Stuart, that these men "had heard." But it didn't surprise them; big business and government and politics and the military had been intricately entwined throughout history. Some of the offers appealed to Jake; he would let them know.

Julia visited for a week. During that time, Jake had no other visitors.

Megan visited frequently. She always called first. Those were the rules. Sometimes Jake called her. And sometimes she would spend the night.

"What the hell are you doing with your life?" Megan demanded the week after Christmas.

"Resting." It was true. His leg had hurt him ever since Cambodia. But with the enforced rest of the past few months, it hurt less. He was optimistic. If Stuart needed him for the Middle East peace negotiations, he would be fit; he could go.

"More than that."

"Planning." And waiting. Waiting for Stuart's call. Waiting to know if they needed him. He couldn't make any other plans until he knew. And then, the plans would have to be for after. If there was an after.

"You seem remarkably complacent."

"I am." His fate, for the moment, was out of his hands.

"Do you watch Carrie's show?" Since Houston, Megan had been unable to sustain a conversation with either Jake or Carrie about the other. And Carrie repeatedly refused invitations to come to Megan's penthouse.

"Sometimes." It was true. Jake made a point of neither watching every show nor avoiding every one. Subconsciously, he was rationing himself.

"Sensational, isn't it?"

"Uh-huh."

"What is going on between you and Carrie?"

"Nothing!"

"Do you want to tell me what happened?"

"No." End of conversation.

Stuart called on February sixth.

"We need you, son."

"Okay."

"It's dangerous, Jake."

"I understand."

"Can you be here on Monday?" It was Thursday.

"Yes."

Jake hung up the phone slowly and found the telephone number that he had copied out of Megan's address book. It was an unlisted number.

He dialed slowly, thoughtfully.

"Caroline?"

Carrie recognized his voice immediately. It had been six months since that rainy afternoon in the guest house in Houston. Six months during which Carrie had trained herself to forget about Jake, and, if she remembered him, to

307

focus on his cruelty, his arrogance, and his deceit. Six months of wondering when he would call again, and, when he did, if she could refuse to see him without emotion or regret. As time passed, Carrie started to believe that he might never call, that she would never have the chance to say no to him, that he would leave her life as he had entered it—enigmatic and inscrutable.

"Yes." Carrie was angry that her heart still pounded, reflexively, when she heard his voice, that in a moment she might have forgiven him if she hadn't conditioned herself so well. Part of her, most of her, wanted to say, "Jake, how are you?" But the sensible part prevailed: he will only hurt you again. Pretend you don't even recognize his voice.

"It's Jake"

"Oh. Hello, Jake."

"Am I calling at a bad time? You sound preoccupied."

"No, not at all." Carrie felt sick. She was bursting with emotion—how much she hated him; how happy she was to hear from him. But her resolve was strong: be ice-cold, but polite, indifferent. And say no.

"Will you have dinner with me tonight?"

"No."

"Can I see you any time this weekend?" He had already gotten the message; she was unwilling to see him.

"No," Carrie almost whispered. Tears filled her eyes. A gush of explanations and apologies lodged in her throat, but she didn't speak.

Jake didn't speak either, but he stayed on the line.

"Caroline," he began finally, softly, "I am sorry about what happened in Houston. I didn't mean to hurt you. I have never meant to hurt you, of all people." But I always do, he thought. To protect myself, I hurt you.

"Jake. It doesn't matter anymore. It's over. It's all over." Carrie's voice was strained, taut. With great effort she said slowly, evenly, "I have to go now, Jake. Good-bye."

Carrie depressed the button and disconnected the call,

but she clutched the receiver, as if part of Jake was still there. And she cried.

I have to let it go, Jake thought. It was plain that Carrie hated him. He had planned another sort of good-bye. Selfish, because he wanted to see her one last time. Unselfish, he had argued, because he could explain everything to her and free her from any pain. But Carrie had already freed herself—through hatred. It was a hatred born of rejection and self-doubt. Jake couldn't bear the thought of her living with that and never knowing. And this might be his last chance to tell her.

One way or the other. *Dangerous,* Stuart had said. Every assignment was dangerous, but Stuart had never said it before. He had always used words like "tricky" or "touchy." And Stuart's voice had always sounded eager. But this assignment, Jake's last, was classified as dangerous, and Stuart had sounded worried. It didn't frighten Jake, because, even if he survived, he would be facing another kind of death . . .

The pain in his leg that had begun after that night in Cambodia was in a new place, the site of the tendon insertion. It had started gradually, but now there was pain with very little exertion. It was clear that the tendon was beginning to tear away from the bone. It was only a matter of time. By being careful, he could make it through this assignment, but after that . . .

For the next two hours, Jake went through the motions of packing and preparing to leave. He left a note for Megan. He notified his attorneys. He wrote a letter to Julia.

In those two hours he made a decision. Whatever the cost, whatever the consequences, he had to see her. He would see her. He would make her listen.

The sound of the doorbell startled her. It pulled her abruptly back to reality. In the hours since the phone call, she had been in a trance. Empty. Void of thought or emotion. Carrie glanced around her twilight-darkened apartment without recognition. She turned on a lamp, rubbed her eyes to make them focus, and staggered to the door, her legs stiff and cramped from hours of being curled underneath her without moving.

"Who is it?" Carrie asked. She had locks and chains, but she didn't have a peephole. The manager kept promising.

"Jake." He had been in a trance, too. Her voice startled him. Here you are, he thought, and she is home. He didn't have a plan, he realized. No rehearsed speech. It would come. If she would open the door.

Carrie opened the door slowly, as if each bolt she threw, each chain she unhooked to let him in, increased her own bondage.

"Hello," she said wearily, without looking at him. How many times do I have to mourn him, she wondered.

"May I come in?" He leaned against the door because his leg ached from climbing the stairs. He stared at her face—sad, tense, drawn. She wouldn't look at him. Instead of answering his question, she opened the door wide and gestured—a resigned gesture—for him to enter.

"You're limping," she said to his back, but her voice, at last, was alive. With concern for him.

"A little." He turned and their eyes met. Jake extended a hand, but he didn't move. He didn't want to frighten her, to push her.

Carrie walked toward him, slowly, tentatively. She could not ignore, or misinterpret, the message in his eyes. He wanted her. At last. She saw no doubt, no reservations. Carrie was beyond thinking or reasoning. She wanted him, as she always had.

"Caroline," he whispered and took her in his arms. He kissed her, at first carefully, then passionately. Carrie responded, urgently and confidently, as he whispered her name again and again.

Jake led her into the bedroom. Carefully, he undressed

her, then himself. He lay beside her, in the bed, under the warm down quilt that Carrie had made. Jake held her face in his hands and looked at her, his eyes full of love, free of doubt. He knew that tonight Carrie's heart's pounding wouldn't remind him of ghosts and nightmares; he wouldn't allow it to. This night was for Carrie—it had to be perfect.

Her eyes met his. They reflected the love. And the desire.

But there was something else in her beautiful, clear blue eyes, something that looked like fear.

She's afraid, Jake thought, unnerved for a moment. Maybe this isn't what she wants. Maybe it's wrong. She must be afraid that I will leave her again, and she's right. But not until she understands . . .

"Darling, what's . . . ?" Carrie looked away as soon as he spoke.

"I have never . . ." Carrie began, then stopped. She couldn't tell him.

"Never what?" His voice was gentle, worried, totally uncomprehending.

Carrie shook her head. He wasn't going to guess. Why should he? In a few moments he would know. Her answer was barely audible, but she knew he heard it because she felt his body stiffen. "Made love."

"Never?" Jake suppressed a gasp. He had been certain about Michael and had assumed there had been others.

Carrie shook her head. Jake looked carefully into her eyes; her wide, trusting, innocent blue eyes that told him she was his and his alone. And always had been.

"Do you want to now?" he asked gently.

"Yes," she said quietly, confident of her answer. But, still, shy and uncertain about what was to follow.

Jake held her tightly against him, feeling the warmth and softness of her body. And the tension. She was a little afraid. Jake held her without speaking. He loved her so much. He wanted her so much. Above all he wanted her to know his love, to feel it, to be confident of it, before he made love to her. He wanted it to be perfect for her—a wondrous affirmation of their feelings, a lasting memory of love and pleasure—but he knew that it might not be, for her, the first time.

If only they had more time.

"I love you, Caroline," Jake said after a few moments.

He felt the impact of his words on her warm, trembling body. He felt the tension release as she pressed closer. Jake watched the fear vanish from her eyes and be replaced by desire, clear, unafraid, uninhibited. Carrie found his soft, sensuous lips with her own eager ones.

They kissed deeply, passionately, consumed by desire and emotion. Carrie's heart pounded and her entire being tingled with hot, powerful, demanding sensations. Her mind whirled. It was a magnificent dream: Jake—her beloved Jake—in her bed, his strong body touching hers, wanting hers, his warm, gentle fingers discovering her, his lips caressing her, tenderly. She had dreamed this dream a thousand times. It was a dream made of precious memories of their few moments of closeness.

But it wasn't a dream. It was real. And it was more wonderful, more consuming, more demanding than anything she had ever dreamed. Jake lay beside her, the strength of his arms, the pounding of his heart, the warmth of his lips, the passion in his eyes all telling her how much he wanted her. And her body responded, naturally, innately, instinctively. Wanting Jake. Needing Jake. Needing him more and more as he touched her and kissed her. Finally, needing him inside her. Needing all of him, all of his love . . .

Jake whispered her name, over and over. And Carrie whispered his. And he told her, as he touched her, as he kissed her, as his body, finally, carefully, joined hers, how much he loved her.

"I love you, Jake," Carrie whispered, her lips touching his, feeling the warmth and quickness of his breath, her body knowing, at last, the strength of him inside her. They moved together then, a perfect union, sharing the joy of their passion. And the joy of their love.

* * *

Jake held her, with the same closeness, for a long time after they made love, kissing her gently. Carrie returned his kisses. Careful, loving, soft kisses. Kisses that told each other how wonderful it had been, for both of them. Carrie's virginity made the sharing, and the loving, more private, more personal. Uniquely theirs. Forever.

"Did I hurt you?" he asked, finally, begrudgingly pulling away, a little.

"I'm not hurt," Carrie said, smiling at him, pulling him back to her. This new closeness, this intimacy, the look of love she saw, still—*more*—in his eyes, made her bold. She would talk to this man, at last, after all these years. "I'm just happy."

"So am I," Jake said. And there was no doubt about how he felt. If he could live this moment forever . . . holding Carrie, loving Carrie. Maybe it was possible after all. He would pretend, now, that it could last forever. "This is perfect. You are perfect."

"Hardly. But this is."

He held her without speaking for a long time, memorizing the moment; etching it indelibly in his mind. Finally he said, "All these years. My obsession for you. Your . . ." He paused.

"Obsession," Carrie said quickly.

"Obsession for me. I just couldn't have it all end without having you know how I really feel, have felt all along."

"End?" Carrie asked, but she wasn't surprised. She knew, somehow, in his desperateness, in hers. It wasn't a leisurely loving. Not the sleepy beginning of forever. It was the urgent clinging to something precious, but fleeting. She felt it, because she sensed it in him; but she didn't understand.

"I wanted you to know that I have wanted you, wanted to love you, to be with you, to make love to you, from the first moment I saw you. Remember? Your first Sunday dinner with us?"

313

"Fat Carrie."

"Beautiful, sensitive, young, naive, protected Carrie. I felt so old, so jaded. You were so optimistic, so full of hope, so confident that life was wonderful."

"And you knew that it wasn't. That I was floating on air."

"No, I believed that life would be wonderful for you. I wanted that for you. I still do." Jake kissed the top of her head and pulled her closer to him.

"But not with you," Carrie whispered, looking into his eyes.

"My life has been tainted, to say the least. I don't bring a lot of happiness, especially to you. In fact, quite the opposite."

"Only because you have never told me this before. Why haven't you?"

"A thousand reasons, mostly selfish. I knew if we tried to make it work, it would fail. And if I told you, you would want to try. And I would lose you altogether. And I was right, the one time I believed it could work . . ."

"When, darling?"

"You know. The postcard from Amsterdam, the letters. I was living my life for us, then. Foolishly believing that it could happen."

"What destroyed it, Jake? It was destroyed before that day in Houston, wasn't it?"

"Yes, destroyed in all but fact. And that day confirmed the hopelessness and damaged you in the process."

"When did the dream die, Jake? What killed it?"

Jake smiled sadly and touched her face. "I love you so much, Caroline. You know me so well. Too well. And there are parts about me that I don't want you to know. Because you deserve better. Because you deserve someone who believes in life as you do, believes in happiness. You don't need to be awakened by my nightmares or tormented by my moods. Caroline, I am afraid to go to sleep because of the images I see when I close my eyes. I have seen too much horror. And I don't want you to know about it." Jake

314

paused, kissed her lightly on the nose, and added, "You also deserve a man who will walk by your side, play tennis with you, dance with you, run with your children, teach them to ride their bicycles. Very soon, I will lose this grotesqueness in exchange for something even worse—no leg at all."

"I don't care about any of that. How can you possibly imagine that it would matter to me?"

"I care about it, darling. And believe me, it does matter."

"No!"

"Yes, it does," he said firmly. "Caroline, promise me that you will believe that it is over. That it never would have worked. Be content that we had this time. That no matter what happens you will get on with your life. I have to know this. Please."

No matter what happens . . . What wasn't he telling her? He was desperate, again. He had to know. She had to promise.

"I promise," Carrie whispered and cried silently. Jake kissed her tear-damp eyes and held her so that she couldn't see his own tears.

"I love you more than anything in the world."

"Oh, Jake. I love you."

They made love again. And again. And each time, it was even better, more loving, more sharing, than the time before.

They were awakened by the telephone. The apartment was dark; it was dark outside. The bedside clock read eleven. Carrie reached for the phone.

"Hello?"

"Hi, Carrie. It's Megan. Were you asleep?" Megan usually called Carrie this late.

"Just napping. Hi, Megan." Jake reached for Carrie's free hand and held it firmly. Damn Megan, he thought. I want to tell her.

"Are you in the mood for brunch on Sunday?"

"Oh, sorry, I can't." It was only Thursday. Jake might be gone by morning; he might leave tonight. Still, she didn't want to make plans before she knew. Carrie was glad that Jake was holding her hand. "Is it a special occasion?"

"No. Not really. But I just got sort of a sad, farewell note from Jake, and I thought it would be nice to have a farewell party for him. I thought it would be nice for you two to reconcile. I mean, who knows when we'll see him again?"

"It's a nice thought, Megan, but I can't make it. We'll get together soon, okay?"

After Carrie hung up, she took Jake's hand in both of hers. "Where are you going? What are you going to do?" *Are you coming back?*

"I honestly don't know where I will be. I'll find out the details in Washington on Monday."

"Washington?"

Jake sighed. He had vowed not to lie to her. "Since college I have been working for the State Department. I have mainly assisted negotiators overseas." Jake smiled. It felt good to be talking to her. "It turns out I'm pretty good at it."

Carrie knew he was telling her the truth; she knew, too, that it was sugar coated and modest.

"It's not all sitting in embassies sipping tea, is it?"

"No. But I'm not James Bond, either. Remember, I'm not too agile."

"But it can be dangerous?"

"Anything can be."

"And it's almost over, this job?"

"Yes. My leg is getting bad. And I've almost paid my dues to Frank."

No matter what happens. The words rushed back to her and her blood ran cold.

"But this assignment. This final assignment. It's more dangerous, isn't it? That's why you're here, now." *That's why Megan was so worried by the sad, farewell note. You're not coming back.*

"Yes."

"Jake, for God's sake, don't go."

"I have to."

"Why?"

"I told you. I'm a pretty good negotiator. And they really need me on this one."

"But you're also saying good-bye."

"I'm saying I love you." Jake paused. "And I am saying goodbye. Both are long overdue."

Carrie began to cry. "I'm sorry. I just don't understand why we can't be together, like this, forever."

"Darling, this is our forever. Now is the only forever we can have." Jake's voice was stern; he was angry at himself. It was folly to think that this could work, that there would really be less pain this way. He should have let her hate him. A hated thing is forgettable. A loved thing . . .

Carrie sat up and gently touched his face.

"When do you leave?"

"I leave for Washington Monday morning."

"When do you leave here?" Meaning her apartment, her side, her bed.

"Monday morning."

"Good. Then I have three-and-a-half days to make you remember, always, how much I love you."

The next three days were a series of unforgettable moments, moments of talking, moments of making love, moments of being together, punctuated, occasionally, begrudgingly, by sleep.

On Friday afternoon they decided that they would "dine" that evening at New York's finest restaurant. Jake returned to his penthouse to dress and to collect extra clothes. In the two hours that he was away, Carrie trembled with fear that he would not return, remembered that in three days her fear would be a reality. She spent an hour dressing for their dinner, carefully arranging her red-blond curls on top of her head and wearing a dress that accented the gold necklace Jake had given her.

Jake returned at seven. He was wearing black silk evening clothes.

"You are so handsome!"

"And you are so kind." He took her hand. "And you are so beautiful."

"Do you know how much I have missed you?"

"In two hours?" he teased. He had missed her, too.

"We have a problem." Carrie's eyes sparkled. She began to unbutton the pearl buttons of his silk shirt.

"Hmmm." Jake reached casually for the zipper of her dress. "A big problem. With a marvelous solution."

"Should we call the restaurant?" Carrie asked, giggling, between kisses. "I'll cook dinner for you . . . later."

"You're insatiable."

"So are you."

"Because of you."

"Darling, we're not using anything to prevent pregnancy," Jake said one evening.

"Why would we want to prevent having a baby? I would love to have your baby." Carrie watched his reaction. He looked worried, for a moment, and then pleased. "Unfortunately, I think it's the wrong time. I think we've missed the chance by about a week. Oh, did I tell you that Beth is pregnant?"

"Already?" Jake grinned. "How pregnant?"

"Only four months. But they did an ultrasound because she is so big. She's going to have twins!" Carrie was excited. Someday she will be a wonderful, loving mother, Jake thought, momentarily jealous of the unknown husband and father to be.

"I didn't think Stephen wanted children."

"What makes you say that?" Carrie asked, surprised.

"Oh." Jake fumbled for a fraction of a moment, wishing that there could be no more secrets between them. "I guess that's how he felt in college. He probably doesn't feel that way anymore."

"I never knew he felt that way at all. Did he tell you?"

"No, Megan told me." Jake remembered the conversation vividly. Megan had told him what Stephen had said the day they had watched the two children playing tag with their mother at the beach. Jake had tried, then, unsuccessfully, to convince Megan that Stephen's comments only reflected how deeply he loved her, how happy he was with her, and that it did not mean he didn't want children. Jake remembered, sadly, that he had not been able to convince Megan.

Jake realized that Carrie was watching him, wondering what had prompted his thoughtful, serious silence. Jake smiled and said quickly, "I'm surprised that Beth wants children. She doesn't really seem like the motherly type."

"I don't think Beth is any type. I admit that she sounded a bit reserved. But Stephen is excited. Maybe their marriage will work after all."

"I think Stephen still loves Megan."

"Really?" Carrie asked, but she wasn't surprised. "Why shouldn't he?"

"Because of what she did to him, because she hurt him so much . . ." Carrie stopped and smiled. "Oh, yes, the fatal Richards family flaw; tenacious loving despite pain and rejection."

"Careful, darling. Hardly a flaw." Jake smiled at her.

"When you look at me like that I can't think!" Carrie closed her eyes. "Do you think that Stephen knows he is still in love with Megan?"

"If he would allow himself to think about it, he would know. But that is not Stephen's style."

"What good would it do anyway? Megan doesn't love him." Carrie's eyes were still closed. She didn't see the look of surprise on Jake's face. She has no idea, he thought sadly. But she should know. And Stephen should know. Jake should have insisted, then. But it was a promise. And now it was too late.

Chapter Twenty

Three months after Jake left, Carrie took a short vacation. As she drove through the rolling spring-ripe hills from New York City to East Town, West Virginia, Carrie was filled with happiness.

Jake had left that Monday morning in February, leaving behind an unforgettable memory of love. And something else; a tiny miracle of love, growing within her womb. Carrie believed that he would return to her and their child. While he was away, she would take care of herself and their unborn baby. And she would learn as much as she could about his life.

She decided to start in his home, in East Town. It was a leisurely two-way drive. Carrie took care to rest, to eat, to sleep. As she approached East Town, the scenery changed. The well-paved highway was replaced by a rutted narrow road. Rolling green hills gave way to barren hillsides studded with dwarfed shrubs and debris.

East Town was marked by a battered sign, a small, battered grocery store, and several decaying houses. Thin dogs, crying, dirty children, and haggard young women populated the dry, dusty side streets. Carrie parked in front of the general store, took a deep breath, and walked in.

The inside of the store was as oppressive as the town itself. A new group of children and women milled in the store, talking to each other and the store owner. When Carrie entered, all noise stopped and all eyes watched her. She smiled and pretended to look with interest, as a potential consumer, at the dirty, battered sacks of generic flour, sugar, wheat, and corn.

Then she saw her—a woman who looked exactly like Jake. His mother? Carrie remembered Jake's description of his mother, a woman dying at age twenty-five. This woman, although her face was strained and haggard, was young. As young, Carrie realized, as I am, or younger. She had the same sad, pained look that Carrie had seen, in glimpses, on Jake's handsome face. This young woman could have been beautiful, as beautiful as Jake was handsome. Her blond hair could, with healthy food and rest, become silken white-gold; her dark blue eyes could, with a little happiness, sparkle and flash.

Carrie walked up to her, smiling. She had no idea what to say. Pardon me, do you have a lost brother? Yes? Well he is a multimillionaire, the father of my child, a military hero of sorts. No, he has no interest in seeing his family.

"Hello," she said. "My name is Carrie."

"Yes 'um."

"Who are you?"

"Em'ly."

Carrie knew she was talking to Jake's sister. Carrie said that she was a reporter. Emily didn't appear to understand what that meant, but it didn't matter. Emily had no objections to talking to Carrie. It was no threat. Carrie couldn't take anything from her, because Emily had nothing to give.

Carrie asked her about her family. Did they all live in East Town? Yes, but the parents were dead. How many brothers and sisters? Six. All in East Town? Five in East Town, one dead. One dead brother. Dead? Drowned in the river, years ago. It must have been awful for whoever found his body? No, they never did find him. How long ago was that? Ten or twelve years. He was sixteen. She was only nine. What was his name?

Emily's large blue eyes grew wide, then troubled, then untroubled again. She couldn't remember his name. It had been such a long time ago.

Carrie gave Emily the silk scarf that she wore, to thank her for her time. Then Carrie left.

Tears blurted her eyes as she drove away from East Town. Jake was right not to return to his home. It would make him too sad. He could never explain his life to Emily and the others. Carrie vowed that she would never tell Jake that she had made the pilgrimage to East Town.

The next day, as Carrie drove through Pennsylvania, she developed cramps. At first, they were mild, like the beginning of a menstrual period. But they increased in severity and their potential significance suddenly occurred to Carrie.

I should not be having cramps, she thought. For the next sixty miles, she tried to deny their existence.

Then she began to bleed.

No, no, she thought, panic increasing.

She checked into a motel. If she could just rest, the cramps and the bleeding would stop. She would be fine. The baby would be fine.

She spent a restless night in the motel. When the cramps subsided long enough for her to fall asleep, she was awakened by nightmares.

In the morning, she passed tissue—the complete embryonic sac. Within an hour the pain and bleeding stopped. It was all over. She had lost Jake's baby.

Carrie returned to her apartment in New York at ten-thirty that night. Reflexively, she checked with her answering service; maybe there would be a message from Jake. She was not scheduled to return to work for three days.

Megan had called, Stephen had called. Michael had called.

"And Mr. Mark Lawrence called." The operator paused, letting the effect register on Carrie. Mark Lawrence was the network anchorman for the evening news, a celebrity and one of America's most eligible bachelors. Carrie had never met him. "He said it was very important that he speak with you. I told him that I expected you to return tonight. He left a number for you to reach him. He wants you to call, no matter what time you return."

The operator's enthusiasm and curiosity were obvious but not contagious. Mark Lawrence probably wanted to appear on her show, or had a friend who wanted to. It could not be anything important; he could not possibly have news of Jake.

Carrie brewed herself a cup of tea, then lay down on her bed. She would return his call after she had drunk the tea. Or, perhaps, in the morning. She closed her eyes and tried, in vain, not to think about her dead baby.

The telephone rang at midnight. It was her answering service. Mr. Lawrence was on the line. He knew she was home.

"Hello?"

"Hello. Carrie Richards? This is Mark Lawrence."

"Yes?"

"Were you asleep?"

"Yes. I fell asleep before I had a chance to return your call." Carrie sat on the edge of the bed, forcing herself to wake up and concentrate on the conversation.

"I apologize, but I really need to speak with you to-night."

"Okay.

"As you know, I am the anchor for the six o'clock news. I have decided, and the network agrees, that it would be nice to have a second anchor. Providing we can find the right person. In my mind, you are the right person."

"What?" Carrie had not guessed correctly the direction of the conversation. She had assumed that he would want her to interview the new person on her show. "I have no experience!"

"No newscasting experience, but plenty of on-camera

323

time. I think you could make the transition easily. You could still do your interview show, of course."

"Why did you need to speak with me tonight?"

"We are meeting to discuss the candidates first thing in the morning. I need to know if you are interested. I did call last week, about two minutes after you left town." He wanted her to know that this wasn't a last-minute thought. "Are you?"

"What?"

"Interested."

Carrie sighed. She had just lost her baby. She had been in the land of the hopeless and herself had lost hope. She was neither interested nor uninterested; she simply didn't care. She didn't have the energy to care.

"I don't know," she said truthfully, vaguely aware that she had not even graciously acknowledged his personal selection of her. From the little that Carrie knew about him, she suspected that Mark Lawrence would notice.

"You okay?"

"Barely. Sorry. This really is a bad time." Carrie's voice wavered slightly.

"Some vacation." The little that Mark knew about Carrie, other than what he saw on television, was her reputation for good humor, generosity, and honesty. Tonight he was getting the honesty, stripped of her usual enthusiasm. Somehow, it made him more convinced that he wanted to work with her.

"A sentimental journey to a place that I never belonged."

Silence.

"May I at least tell them that you might be interested?" Mark asked carefully.

"Sure!" Carrie said, a slight trace of humor in her voice.

"Care to venture a guess as to when you'll know?" His voice teased gently.

"When I'll know if I'm interested? I'll know in two days. Will they already have made the selection by then?"

324

"No." Because I won't let them. "May I phone you at five o'clock on Tuesday, then?"

"Sure. Thank you."

Mark Lawrence was forty-two years old. In the past year, after a distinguished career as a foreign correspondent and a White House correspondent, he had been awarded the anchor position for the evening news. During the same year, Mark had rid himself of his second wife, cigarettes, and thirty-five pounds. He reduced his alcohol intake from habitual to rare and clad his slender, carefully muscled body in suits, shirts, and neckties of understated elegance.

That year, he had been labeled, in various periodicals and newspapers, one of America's "best dressed," "most eligible," "sexiest," and "most intellectual" men. Ten years before, these accolades and the associated notoriety would have meant more to Mark than anything else; certainly more than his wife, his children, or his health. Indeed, the drive to achieve the status that he now had had cost him dearly. Mark spent little time trying to decide if it had been worth the cost. He knew that, finally, he had what he wanted and he meant to enjoy it.

Mark loved his new life, his success—the challenge and competition of his job, his attractiveness, his popularity, his money. At last, success begat success. Mark worked as hard as he always had, driving himself to excellence, but now the work was fun, not oppressive. His ideas had always been innovative and challenging; now he had the power to actualize them.

The idea of a woman co-anchor occurred to Mark one evening as he watched a tape of Carrie's show. He decided that he wanted a woman, and, moreover, he wanted Carrie. While network agents found possible candidates from local news stations throughout the country, Mark waited impatiently for Carrie to return from her ill-timed vacation. He had demanded ultimate approval of any candidate; he intended to veto every one except Carrie. It had never occurred to him that Carrie might not want the job.

In November, nine months after Jake had left Carrie's apartment on that cold, snowy morning in February, he knocked lightly on a thin plywood door.

"Paul? It's Jake."

Paul Abbott opened his hotel room door and smiled.

"We did it, Jake. They signed the peace treaty an hour ago. Copies are on their way to Washington, Cairo, and Jerusalem right now. There will be a celebration dinner, for all of us, in the embassy in two hours. Then we can go home."

Jake smiled. The long, hard months had been worth it after all. Nine months of political chess; slow, deliberate moves, long pauses between each move, always the fear of an unanticipated mistake that could destroy everything. It had been nine months of intellectual and psychological strain, and, for Jake, nine months of physical pain. The pain in his leg had become constant; the leg, red and swollen. In the past four months, his limp had become so pronounced that he made a point of arriving at the negotiating sessions early and leaving after everyone else had left.

Jake knew that any sign of weakness, including a physical disability, might hamper the strength of their position. Jake had not discussed this with Paul, because he knew that Paul would agree. Paul had learned quickly about Jake's unerring instinct for the appropriate political gesture and about his consummate patriotism.

But, at first, Paul had been skeptical. He had been aghast when Stuart Dawson had told him that Jake, a young man who had spent some time in Vietnam, graduated from Stanford with a degree in political science, and had been "like a son" to Frank Spencer, was to be his counsel to the treaty negotiations in the Middle East.

"Goddammit, Stuart. This is the most important business in years and you're arming me with an unknown, untried amateur. Do you want us to fail?" Paul had smashed his cigarette into an ashtray for emphasis. His face was red and damp with anger.

"He's not an amateur, Paul. And he's unknown because I've kept him that way. He's been behind the scenes, making suggestions, translating, interpreting gestures, and so on, on some of our biggest deals. His instincts are uncanny. I hate like hell to lose him."

"Lose him?"

"This is his last assignment. He'll be right at the table this time, by your side, out in the open. When this is over, he'll return to civilian life. His imagined debt to Frank will have been paid, and then some," Stuart said, thinking about Cambodia. "The kid has a medical problem, too, with his leg. We need to let him go, to live his life. I shouldn't even involve him in this. But, the truth is, Paul, you need him."

Paul grunted. He had never needed anybody, least of all a "kid."

"Sounds like you're in love with him, Stu." Paul winked. "Jesus!"

Now, as Paul smiled at Jake, he knew that Stuart had been right. He *had* needed Jake, his honesty, his fairness, his instincts and insights. And, he had needed Jake, as a friend, through the long, discouraging months. The success of their mission—and, finally, it was a greater success than they had dared to hope—lay in Jake's cool mind and his uncanny sense of timing. It had been a waiting game, and they had won. It had been Jake who had told them when to wait and when to move.

"Your name should have been on that treaty, not mine, Jake." It was a great and rare compliment from Paul. It brought an uncharacteristic blush to Jake's sallow cheeks.

"Thanks," he said. "I'm not going back to Washington with you. I'm going to spend some time in Europe. May I send my notes along with you?"

Jake handed Paul his locked attaché case. It contained succinct summaries of Jake's impressions about the foreign negotiators and about the negotiation process. The summaries might be helpful to Stuart in the planning of future meetings.

"Of course, I'll take it. What about your leg?" Paul didn't know the details and hadn't asked. But he could see from Jake's face that the pain was severe and constant. He knew that Jake had borne the pain, had not taken pain killers, because it was so important for his mind to be clear.

"Rest may help. Maybe I can stay off it for awhile . . ." Jake stopped, smiled, shrugged.

"I hope so," Paul said and meant it. He wanted to help "the kid," but he didn't know how. "I'll see you at the dinner. It should be quite a celebration."

"After nine months of intense negotiations, a peace treaty has been negotiated in the Middle East. Experts are calling this a triumph of gigantic proportions and likening it to the treaty of Versailles . . ." Carrie stared at the red light on the television camera and read the copy. She looked sincere, interested, and beautiful. That look, and her freshness and spontaneity, were keys to her immense and instant success.

At that moment, her mind wandered. Was Jake there? Was that where he had been all this time? No one had heard from him in nine months. It made sense. He had said that his talent was at the negotiating table and that the mission would be dangerous. Carrie's heart pounded. This meant he would be coming home, safe. She believed, despite what he had told her so carefully, that he would return home, and to her.

Two hours later Carrie was called at home and told to return to the studio for a special bulletin. Thirty minutes later they handed her a script; she had no time to read it before the camera with the red light pointed at her.

"Tonight, only three hours after the signing of the historic peace treaty, a bomb . . ." Carrie's voice broke, and she stared as if mesmerized, into the camera, her eyes filled with tears. Months later, she would receive an award for that moment, for the compassion and honesty revealed by her reaction of horror and grief at the news she read to the nation.

"A bomb," she continued, carefully controlling her voice, "exploded in the American Embassy where American and Middle East negotiators had joined for a dinner to celebrate the hope and pledge for peace expressed by the treaty they had just completed. Early reports indicate that there are no survivors."

Carrie put her head in her hands. After a few beats, the director cut to a commercial.

When the telecast resumed, it was Mark Lawrence, who had arrived in the studio moments after Carrie, whose calm, steady voice chronicled the events of the historic, now tragic, day. It was Mark Lawrence who spoke to the network's foreign correspondent who stood outside the bomb-demolished embassy in a rubble of fine bone china, hand-cut crystal, sterling silver, and watched as a crew removed tarp-covered bodies.

"Where is the treaty?" Mark asked, on the air, diverting his colleague, for a moment, from the horror to which he was an eyewitness.

"Unconfirmed reports are that the five original copies of the treaty were sent immediately following the signing to the United Nations Security Council and to the heads of state of the participating nations. This act of terrorism should not undermine the intent nor the enactment of the treaty."

After the emergency telecast, Mark went to Carrie's dressing room. He thought about the four months that they had been working together. His idea of Carrie as co-anchor was an instant success; the ratings, already number one with Mark in the solo position, had soared even higher. Carrie's natural reserve was an appealing counterpoint to the more vocal women activists of the day.

A spontaneous repartee had developed on the air between Mark and Carrie. The unaffected, genuine admiration they

felt towards each other was obvious to the viewing public—a non-sexual mutual respect laced with a perfect
amount of humor. It was refreshing. It made people feel
good, even when the news was bad. Every evening, the
majority of the nation heard its news from Mark and Carrie.
People turned to the show because of its impeccable record
for honest, accurate, professional reporting. They kept
watching, night after night, because they enjoyed having
Mark and Carrie in their homes.

Off camera, their relationship had been all business, pleasant, full of humor, and impersonal. Carrie knew about Mark's
personal life, because she could read about it in any one of
several magazines. Her co-newsman was news. She had seen
pictures of both wives and his two children. She had seen
pictures, almost unrecognizable, from his foreign correspondent days—overweight, dark-circled eyes, and the inevitable
cigarette. Carrie read about his erratic behavior, extramarital
affairs, and overindulgence in alcohol. Nothing she read
about his past reminded her in the least of the Mark that she
knew, albeit superficially. He wasn't the same man.

"Carrie?" Mark knocked on her dressing room door.

"Come in." Carrie sat in the armchair in her dressing
room, her legs curled under her, huddled. "Mark, I am
sorry."

"Don't be. It'll be a hit, a new breakthrough in journalism—real human emotion." He smiled.

"I couldn't help it. I was unprepared. They just handed
me the script." Carrie stopped. Her cheeks drained of the
blush that had come with Mark's compliment. She shook
her head.

"What is it, Carrie?"

She sighed. "It's silly because I don't even know for sure.
But I think . . . I'm afraid that . . . a very dear friend of
mine was in that embassy."

Mark looked through her, suddenly lost in his own
thoughts. He had several friends who were likely to have
been there. He hadn't even thought about it until now. Paul

Abbott, Bruce Lawson, Jeff Simpson. Men he had known in past years, in his years in Washington and overseas. He had stayed up half the night with these men, in dirty bars in foreign countries, sharing dreams and secrets and fears and loneliness. They had talked like they never talked to their wives or their lovers. Yes, he, too, had very "dear friends" who were likely to have been in that embassy. What disturbed him most was that he had not, until then, even thought about them.

"Mark?"

"Who is your friend?" Mark sounded like a reporter. Carrie told him.

"I've never heard of him," Mark said mostly to himself. He was thinking. "But I know who will know."

After fifteen minutes, Mark was finally "on hold," waiting for Stuart. He waited for another fifteen minutes. During that half an hour he and Carrie didn't speak.

"Dawson." Stuart's voice projected exhaustion and anger.

"Mark Lawrence, Stu. Don't worry, this is unofficial."

"Yes."

"Was one of the negotiators Jake Easton?"

"Who wants to know?" Stuart's anger increased. Jake was one of his best-kept secrets. Now the nation's leading newsmen was asking for him by name.

"Carrie Richards, my co-anchor. She's a good friend. She's guessing he might be there, but she doesn't know." Mark already knew the answer. Jake was there.

"I saw the bulletin she did. I didn't know Jake knew her." Another of Jake's women? He had Julia. Most men would kill for Julia. Jake and Julia were perfectly suited. But where did Carrie Richards, so different from Jake or Julia, fit in? She obviously cared deeply about Jake.

"So?" Mark interrupted Stuart's thought.

"Yes. Jake was there. We don't have any positive identification yet, of course. Our team has gone over. It will be a few days." Stuart paused. His voice broke slightly. "Tell Miss Richards that I am very sorry."

331

Stuart felt a kinship with Carrie; they both loved Jake. And Stuart felt guilty. He was the one who had sent Jake on the mission, knowing how dangerous it was. But knowing, too, how valuable Jake could be. From the reports Paul had sent, Jake had been critical to the success of the mission. Jake, Paul. Stuart didn't have time to grieve now.

The identification photographs and dental records had been pulled. Stuart's stomach turned and his throat tightened when he saw the photograph of Jake's leg. He had had no idea. In a day or two someone would look at a mutilated body, identifiable only by that grotesque leg, nod, and declare somberly, "That's him. That's Easton."

Stuart glowered at the blinking lights on the telephone, official calls and calls from wives and sisters and children. All calling him because he had arranged it; he had sent those men to their deaths.

Mark replaced the receiver and looked at Carrie.

"He was there, Carrie."

She nodded.

"They won't know if he was in the embassy for a few days. Maybe . . ."

"He was there. He would be. He saw things through." She smiled sadly. "Some things."

"I'll take you home."

"No, thank you." Carrie started to stand up. She realized that she couldn't possibly get herself home. She was weak, confused, helpless. Like that first day at Stanford when she needed Stephen to guide her. She needed someone now. "Yes."

Carrie handed her purse to Mark when they reached the door of her apartment. Mark found the key chain and, without help from Carrie, sampled several keys and finally opened the door.

"Do you want to tell me about him?" Mark asked. Carrie hadn't spoken since they had left her dressing room.

She looked startled at the sound of Mark's voice.

"Oh, no. Just a friend. My brother's college roommate."

I have to call Stephen and Megan, she thought. But I can't. "We were all in college together. Those were happy times." Carrie touched the gold necklace around her neck, then shivered. "Mark, I'm sorry. This is a big shock."

"Shall I pour you a drink?"

"No. I guess I just need to be alone. Thank you." The words frightened her. Now she really was alone. For the first time since she had met him, Carrie couldn't sustain herself with dreams of a future with Jake. Now, she would have to believe, as he had told her to, that there would be no future, that they had had their forever.

Carrie did not miss any work. Mark's eyes registered surprise when he saw her the next day.

"I'm okay, Mark." She smiled weakly. "Thank you for last night."

Four days later, Carrie received a call at the studio.

"This is Carrie."

"This is Stuart Dawson."

"Oh, yes." Carrie held her breath.

"We didn't find him. We think we found all the bodies and he wasn't there."

"What does that mean?"

"I don't know. We found his briefcase and his notes and summation completed in Paul Abbott's room." Stuart didn't add that Jake's clothes and personal belongings had been left in his hotel room, but his passport and wallet were gone. Of course, Jake was likely to keep those with him at all times.

"Why haven't you heard from him?" Carrie asked frantically. It was the same question that Stuart asked himself constantly. If Jake was safe, he would have contacted them as soon as he learned of the embassy bombing.

"I don't know."

"Do you think he's being held hostage?"

"I don't know." Yes, Stuart thought. That's what I'm afraid of. Better to be dead. "May I ask a favor of you?"

"Yes, of course."

"Please don't tell anyone that he was there. For security reasons—his and ours."

"Of course. Only Mark knows. I haven't told anyone else. I couldn't until I knew for sure."

"Good." Remarkable woman. Remarkable, like Julia. Julia . . . he had been trying to reach her for the past four days. She was somewhere in Europe. A message had been left with her exchange in Paris. He dreaded having to tell her.

The phone rang. Eight times. Nine. Ten. He refused to hang up. She had to be there.

"Allo!" Breathless, annoyed. A wrong number, unless . . . *"Allo?"* she repeated softly.

"Bonjour, ma chère." Relief pulsed through him. She was there. He was home.

"Jake!"

"Mais oui."

"Où es tu?"

"Nice. A l'aéroport."

They continued speaking in French.

"Are you still between marriages?" he asked casually. It was an important question.

"Yes."

"Between lovers?"

Julia paused, then laughed. "There are no lovers on the premises, if that's what you mean. Where have you been, darling? I got your letter nine months ago." A long letter, full of nostalgia and love. And, she feared, a good-bye.

"Business. Dangerous, successful, and, thank God, over." Julia could hear the fatigue in Jake's voice.

"Why are we talking on the phone? Get in a car and come right away."

"My leg's bad. I can't drive. I'll get a driver."

"No. I'll be there. Forty-five minutes."

"Merci. Je t'aime."

She arrived in exactly forty-five minutes.

"You look awful," she said as he got in the car. His limp was marked. His clothes were rumpled and dusty. The skin under his eyes was tight and shiny and black and his eyes were cloudy blue.

She put the car in neutral and he kissed her—long, deep, needful.

Julia returned the kiss and held him tightly. He needed holding. She could see the pain.

The sound of horns, at first amused, then irritated, forced Julia to pull free and put the car in gear.

"How did you know I would be here?"

"I didn't, but I hoped. I was going to call first, but as I was checking into flights, I found one that was leaving in thirty minutes, so I grabbed my passport and left. Right now I am supposed to be at a big diplomatic dinner. But I won't be missed. My work is done. I've been working with Paul Abbott. I guess you know him."

"Of course, he and Frank were close. It must have been very important if Paul was involved."

"It was. I'll tell you later."

"I repeat: you look awful."

"You look beautiful."

"My God, you are charming. I may have taught you a lot, but I never taught you that charm. You were born with it."

"Yes ma'am," Jake said in his longest, deepest Southern drawl. Julia shuddered.

Jake loved Julia's villa overlooking the sparkling blue Mediterranean, with a view from every room, hidden from the road by lush foliage and surrounded by a cheerful blue wrought-iron fence. Private but panoramic, Jake had announced the first Christmas that they had spent there together. It reminded him of the house in Saigon—the pool, the gardens, the privacy, and the emotions. But this place was unencumbered by the horrors of war. And here they spoke French instead of English.

It was Julia's private retreat. Jake was the only man who

335

she allowed there, although she never told him. It was hers and it was theirs.

There were two guest bedrooms and the master suite. The guest bedrooms had never been used. Jake's clothes hung in the closet next to Julia's and lay neatly folded in the dresser drawers.

"I'm glad you didn't throw out my clothes in a cleaning frenzy."

"Let's throw out what you have on, soak you in the jacuzzi, and feed you."

"Are you my mother?"

"No! I am your very greedy, demanding lover and in your present state you are worthless!"

A shadow of worry crossed Jake's tired face at Julia's words.

We are not going to be lovers, Julia thought. Something has happened. She knew Jake would tell her in time. When he was rested.

As Julia watched him undress, throwing his "work" clothes into a pile to be discarded, she saw another explanation for the worried look on Jake's face. She gasped when she saw his leg—red, swollen, pitting with fluid. The pain was obvious; even carefully removing his loose pants caused him to grimace. It was something else that would prevent them from making love. At least, for awhile.

"Jake, what happened?"

"I think the tendons are pulling loose. I haven't been able to rest it. They told us this would happen, eventually."

Told "us." That was right. Julia had been with him. When the tendons pulled loose, as they inevitably would, they would either need to remove the leg or freeze it solid at the knee joint. Amputation would offer the most function, with a good prosthesis. But the leg would have to come off just below the hip. Julia had shuddered then. She shuddered now.

Then she went to him and held him.

"I'm sorry," she whispered. It was a sorry that spanned years. She still felt responsible. If only she hadn't been so attracted to the sexy, illiterate seventeen-year-old. If only he had stayed and made love to her that afternoon. If only she had warned Frank that Jake had returned to the base. If only . . .

"It's not your fault, Julia." Jake's voice was stern. They had argued about this before, many times. "It may not even be the end. If I stay off it, elevate it, put ice on it. They didn't even have ice over there. Maybe it will settle down. It's worth a try."

"What are you taking for pain?" Julia knew about Jake's fear of pain medications since he had developed the gas gangrene while receiving morphine.

"Nothing. But I have been thinking about cognac for about nine months."

"That's easy. I think I'll get you something in the narcotic line, too. It will help you rest."

By the end of the first week, Jake's leg was better, the pain much less. It would have been possible, pleasurable, to make love.

Julia waited. She knew Jake was making a decision, and it was about that.

Eventually he told her about his weekend with Carrie.

"I haven't changed my mind about a future with Caroline. I know that it can't happen. I probably will never even see her again. But it's too soon for me to be with someone else, even you, as much as I love you." Jake paused, then smiled wryly and said, "I'm being faithful to a memory. Crazy, isn't it?"

"Not crazy," Julia said. Jake was so much like Frank; when he gave his heart, he gave it totally. She repeated gently, "Not crazy. Just nice. Very, very nice."

They sat in silence for awhile, gazing at the peaceful blue Mediterranean dotted with yachts and cruise ships.

"Go back to her, Jake," Julia said finally.

"I told you, we made our peace. She's free of me, Julia. It's really best for her."

"And you? What about what is best for you?" Julia

watched Jake's eyes, listened to the tenderness of his voice, whenever he spoke of Carrie.

"It's best for both of us. It can never be."

Three weeks' rest, ice, demerol, cognac, and Julia's constant attention had virtually cured his leg. The swelling and pain had resolved. They had, together, accomplished a stay of execution. The color had returned to Jake's cheeks, the clarity to his eyes, and, for the first time in years, he seemed hopeful. He talked enthusiastically about his future as a civilian. Jake was restless. It was a good sign.

"I'm going to really look at our companies, yours and mine, and see if any need fixing. Or, if any needs a president."

"You think negotiating peace treaties is hard, dangerous work. Just you wait until you get to a board meeting and announce that you plan to take over the company. Controlling stocks notwithstanding, it's tough."

Jake grinned. "What fun!"

"It sounds like we're about to reenter the real world. I had better check with my exchange in Paris. Who knows how many stockbrokers have ulcers waiting for my return call?"

"Won't your exchange call you here?" As he asked, he realized that the phone hadn't rung once in three weeks. It was all part of what made those weeks so peaceful—no telephone, no newspapers, no television.

"No. They don't have the number. Nobody does." Except you.

Jake watched as she collected her messages from the exchange. Her expression changed from curiosity and enthusiasm, as she took messages about financial dealings, to concern. She carefully wrote down one number and repeated it for accuracy. It was a number that she hadn't dialed in years.

"What?"

"Stuart Dawson. An urgent call. Three weeks ago. What time is it in Washington?" It was a rhetorical question. She asked it as she dialed the number.

Stuart glowered at the clock before he answered the telephone. Three in the morning. Then he frowned. Middle of the night calls always meant trouble. He turned on the bed-side light, sat up, and reached for a pencil and the telephone at the same time.

"Dawson."

"Stuart? It's Julia. Sorry to awaken you. I just got your message from three weeks ago. I've been a bit out of touch." Julia waited.

She heard Stuart sigh.

"Julia, it's about Jake Easton. He's missing."

Jake saw Julia's face light with a smile; her violet eyes sparkled.

"No, he's not, Stuart. I know where he is."

"What?" The lead point of the pencil shattered.

Julia handed the phone to Jake.

"Stuart? It's Jake." Jake looked confused but not worried. Then, as Stuart told him what had happened, his shoulders sagged and he shook his head. As Stuart spoke, Jake interjected a few words.

"I didn't know," he said sadly, then continued to listen. After a few moments, he said, "How did she know I was there? Please let her know that I am all right, Stuart."

Julia moved beside him; she couldn't begin to imagine what Stuart could be telling Jake. Something about Carrie?

Finally Jake asked a few questions and told Stuart that he would fly to Washington in the morning. Then he hung up the phone and told Julia.

They flew to Washington together and, together, visited the graves of Paul Abbott and the others. It was too grim, too difficult, for Julia to be in Washington at the graves of her friends, Frank's friends. It reminded her too much of Frank; it brought back the memories and the sadness. After only two days, Julia knew she had to leave Washington, leave the memories. She would return to her villa and escape in the gaiety of the holiday season with the other people, people like her, who chose to spend that time in Monte Carlo.

"Are you okay, Julia?" Jake asked, concerned after she told him of her plan to fly to Nice that night.

"Just okay. Sometimes it's better if I don't have the time to think or remember."

"Better to exhaust yourself with a series of galas?" he teased gently.

"For now it is," Julia smiled weakly. "These maudlin moods are readily drownable in champagne and hedonism."

Jake flinched, then held her. He knew Julia would be all right. Julia was a survivor. And she knew herself very well.

"Okay, darling, have fun." Jake kissed the top of her head. Then he said softly, "I do love you, Julia."

After Julia left, Jake spent a week with Stuart, telling him, in meticulous detail, all the aspects of the negotiations. It was something Paul Abbott would have done, with great pride, had he lived.

Then Jake spent a week in the hospital at Bethesda, undergoing the usual battery of tests for his leg, and some new ones.

"The tendons did tear, but they have partially healed again. So they will hold for a while longer. I have no idea how long. They already have held much longer than I had predicted. Jake, when the time comes to do something about the leg, come back here. I'm not making any promises, but surgical techniques have improved, we have new glues, we can move muscles around. We wouldn't know until we actually took a look, but there might be something."

Jake stared at Dr. Phillips. He was telling him that they might save his leg. But the doctor's expression was uninterpretable, as always—pleasant but noncommittal. Jake couldn't tell if the chance of saving the leg was one in two or one in a million. And there was no point in asking. If Dr. Phillips had known, he would have told him. And Jake knew that Dr. Phillips refused to guess.

"Hi."

"Jake! Where in hell have you been?" Megan exclaimed.

In hell and in heaven, Jake mused. "Away. But I'm back now. How are you?"

"Fine. In fact, I just got a roommate."

Jake waited. Carrie?

"Gwendolyn. Here, she wants to say hi."

Jake heard the unmistakable sound of panting.

"Did you speak to her, Jake?"

"No, I didn't want to interrupt her. Megan, what have you done to the peace and quiet of our floor?"

"You'll love her, Jake. She's a little blond cocker spaniel puppy. Totally charming. When are you coming home?"

"Tomorrow."

"Tomorrow is Christmas Eve!" Megan was annoyed. It was so typical of Jake not to have plans for Christmas. Megan didn't know that, as a child, Jake had never celebrated Christmas, and, as an adult, Christmas vacation usually meant admission to the hospital for tests on his leg.

"I know. Will you be away?"

"Gwendolyn and I are going to the country to spend Christmas with Stephanie and Ian and Margaret," Megan said, then paused, thinking. She couldn't stand the thought of anyone spending the holidays alone. Then she asked enthusiastically, "Why don't you come with us? You haven't seen Stephanie for over a year. She's almost three and a half. She's so grown up. So beautiful. She would be thrilled to see her uncle Jake."

"I'd love to see her," Jake said honestly. He was very fond of Margaret and Ian's daughter.

"Good! Then it's settled. Where are you? I want to leave first thing in the morning."

"I'll fly in tonight then."

"Great. Come over for an eggnog when you get home." Her voice softened. "I'm glad you're okay. I was worried about you. And I missed you."

"See you soon."

As Jake packed, he watched the evening news with Mark Lawrence and Carrie Richards. Stuart had told him about

Carrie's grief, and her relief. Stuart had watched Jake for a reaction but saw none. But inside Jake's head the words had thundered: *All I ever do is hurt her.*

Part Seven

Twenty-one

New York City . . . February, 1976

Two months after Jake's return to New York, Megan gave a lavish cocktail party, in honor of theater patrons and attended by the patrons and Megan's friends. Megan's friends included actors, producers, attorneys, writers, directors, business tycoons, bankers, and, of course, Carrie and Jake.

Carrie told Megan that she would be unable to attend; she did not give an excuse or a reason. The day before the party, Mark invited her to have dinner with him. The invitation surprised Carrie. Their relationship had continued to be one of comfortable camaraderie of successful business partners.

Carrie had been in her dressing room, getting ready to leave for the evening.

"Will you have dinner with me tomorrow night, Carrie?"

Carrie had not been able to think of a reason not to; in fact, she had decided she would enjoy having dinner with Mark. Then she had remembered Megan's party.

"How would you like to make an appearance at a 'Beautiful People Party' with me on the way?"

It had been Mark's turn to register surprise. He had wondered whom Carrie defined as "Beautiful People."

"How beautiful?"

"Megan Chase."

"Do you know her?" Mark had seen all of Megan's plays, often more than once.

Carrie had laughed. "She's my best friend. My college roommate." Carrie had stopped. She could have added: the woman who broke my brother's heart; the woman who virtually lives with the man I love. Instead, she had smiled and repeated, "My best friend."

"Carrie Richards, you never cease to amaze me."

Jake greeted them at the door; he was helping Megan host the party. Megan had told him with certainty that Carrie wouldn't be there.

Carrie stood in front of him. He had not seen her, except on television, since the morning when he had left a year before. She looked at him with blue eyes, ice cold, depthless, like mirrors that reflected but didn't reveal. From the moment their eyes had first met, years ago on a Sunday evening in autumn, those eyes had always sparkled, for him, for life, because they were happy eyes.

But not today. Today they didn't flicker, even for a moment, as if they didn't even see him. They weren't blazing with anger or drowning in sadness. They were without emotion, uncaring, unseeing.

"Caroline!" he whispered.

"Hello Jake." Carrie looked past him. "Oh, Mark Lawrence, this is Jake Easton."

"Jake Easton." Mark repeated the name to jog his memory. Then he remembered. Carrie had told him that his body had not been found. But she had never told him that Jake was alive and well and home.

Mark looked at Carrie quizzically.

Carrie shrugged.

"I guess I forgot to tell you that he wasn't dead after all." Flat, bored, laced with hatred.

Both men cringed.

Megan appeared in the white marble foyer.

"Carrie, I'm so glad you came. And you brought him! You really are bigger than life. Oh, I'm Megan." Megan extended a long, slender hand to Mark.

"I know who you are."

Jake watched Carrie, hoping to find a moment when he could speak with her, alone; when he could try to erase the look of hatred from her eyes. But she was surrounded. They—the anchor team of Carrie and Mark—were surrounded. They were New York's latest darlings; and this was the first time they had ever been seen together off camera.

There were no unknowns at this party. Everyone was, or had been, a sensation, a headliner, a trendsetter, a leader, a celebrity. Everyone, that is, except Jake. Very few guests could accurately identify him: sole survivor of the historic Middle East treaty negotiation, president of one of the world's largest corporations, one of the nation's wealthiest men, coal miner's son. But those who couldn't precisely identify him could, at least, put him in a category that demanded approval—handsome, impeccably dressed, continental manners. Perhaps foreign. Perhaps royal. Obviously wealthy and cultured.

"I can't believe that Carrie brought Mark Lawrence!" Megan was thrilled. They were the perfect addition to the party.

"I thought that Carrie wasn't even going to come," Jake said.

"I didn't think she was."

"Is she dating him?" Jake asked casually.

"Apparently!" Megan smiled knowingly at Jake, kissed him on the lips, and shook her head. She had given up trying to understand the dynamics of Jake and Carrie. But Jake's reaction today was clear. When beautiful, successful Carrie arrived on the arm of New York's most eligible and notorious bachelor, Jake was jealous.

Good for you, Carrie, Megan thought. Carrie had made

the transformation from the pudgy, naive college freshman to the beautiful, successful career woman without, apparently, compromising her sensitivity, her optimism, her beliefs. Carrie had done it in her own, unobtrusive way. She had it all, including, Megan concluded as she watched him watching Carrie, Mark Lawrence. Megan thought about her own life—a great success, too. But at what cost?

Megan shook the thought instantly, reflexively.

From the moment that she had received Stuart Dawson's call telling her that Jake was safe, Carrie had been filled with uncontrollable joy and expectation. He had survived the final challenge. He would return home, to safety, to her.

Carrie had believed that she might never see him again, because she knew that the danger of his mission was real, that he might die.

But she had never believed that he would not come back to her if he could. In the days and weeks since his return to New York, days and weeks that she waited for him to call, the reality of the words he had said to her etched itself painfully into her heart. "It will never work, Caroline. I can never give you the happiness you deserve. This is all the time we can have, and it is selfish of me even to have this time with you. Remember that I love you. Whatever happens, I will always love you."

In those months, Carrie had wondered if there was another reason he hadn't called. His leg, perhaps. Maybe he was waiting for the right time.

But when Carrie saw Jake—handsome, healthy, relaxed—the unanswered questions, the lingering hope, distilled clearly into one simple message: he was not coming back to her. It was over.

Carrie was unprepared for her reaction—a hatred stronger than she had felt after Houston. The hatred was made worse by her desire to hold him and touch him and the knowledge that it was not possible, that he didn't want her. Jake looked pleased to see her, but there was an unmistakable distance.

Jake had moved on to his new life. Carrie was a pleasant memory from the past, the distant past.

Carrie was also unprepared for the effect that her appearance with Mark would have. In the past year, Carrie had been so preoccupied with the wonderful memories of Jake, her grief at the loss of his baby, the news of his probable death, the great relief when she heard that he was safe, and, recently, the waiting, that she was truly oblivious to her own celebrity. She enjoyed her work; she was proud of it. She and Mark had developed a style that felt comfortable and honest to her. Megan had tried to tell her what a sensation she was; but Carrie hadn't paid much attention.

But now, surrounded by famous faces that she recognized, all of whom wanted to meet her, them, Carrie was overwhelmed. She smiled demurely, answered questions politely and shyly, glanced frequently at Mark for support, and had to control the emotions caused by seeing Jake.

Alter an hour, Carrie excused herself and moved purposefully through the crowd to Megan's room. She had to escape, to be by herself, to calm the churning inside before she exploded.

Carrie loved Megan's bedroom, a serene, flowery sanctuary of cream and blue. Forget-me-not blue, Megan announced proudly. The delicate, beautiful wallpaper in the dressing room was forget-me-nots, hand painted for Megan in France. Megan's flower. Megan's room. During the nine months that Jake was away, Carrie had spent many evenings at Megan's, sitting in this room, talking about their careers, reminiscing about the happy moments of the past. There were great gaps in the happy memories, and great gaps in what they told each other. Carrie never told her best friend about Jake. And Carrie guessed that Megan had her own set of secrets.

Carrie entered the room and pulled the door almost shut; the noise of the party was reduced to almost a whisper. It felt like silence to Carrie. She moved across the room to sit on the blue silk chaise longue, when she realized that she was not alone.

Lying on a huge cream and blue pillow on the floor beside the bed was a blond cocker spaniel puppy. The puppy was pressed into the pillow, *her* pillow, looking up at Carrie, the intruder, with liquid brown eyes. She looked as overwhelmed as Carrie felt. Carrie approached the pillow and its occupant slowly, on hands and knees.

"Hello there, little one. Who are you?" Carrie remembered that Megan had mentioned a puppy, about the time that Jake had returned. Carrie hadn't seen Megan much since then.

As she approached the puppy and spoke, the eyes continued to look skeptical, but the tail began to wag.

"You're awfully cute. You don't like this big crowd of people, do you?"

The tail wagged faster. Carrie sat on the floor beside the pillow.

"You can sit on my lap if you want to. Don't be scared. I know exactly how you feel. That's why I came in here. To get away, like you."

The puppy moved cautiously onto Carrie's lap. Carrie patted her gently.

"You are so silky soft, did you know that?"

The puppy nuzzled and Carrie picked her up and held her.

"You're a snuggler, aren't you?" Carrie held the puppy close. Then she started to cry.

"Caroline?" Jake had followed her from the living room. How long had he been there?

Carrie's back straightened, but she didn't turn around. She dried her eyes on the puppy's soft coat. At the sound of Jake's voice, the puppy had started to wriggle.

Jake sat down on the floor beside her.

"I see you've found Gwendolyn."

"Gwendolyn!" Megan had named the puppy after the character she had played in *The Importance of Being Ear-*

nest. Had that been a happy time for Megan? Carrie wondered. Her triumph as Gwendolyn, her affair with Jake, the argument on opening night, the forget-me-not bouquet from Stephen. Happy memories, on balance?

Gwendolyn wriggled away from Carrie and bounded onto Jake's lap.

"She knows you."

"I am her favorite—and only—puppy sitter." Jake smiled. Carrie didn't look at him.

"I didn't realize that Megan was away much."

"She never travels. But this little bundle of joy gets puppy sitting when Megan goes to work."

"Really?"

"Really. Gwendolyn and I spend many evenings together. Reading, chewing leather toys, chasing balls."

"Megan's pretty hooked, isn't she?"

"Yes, she gives Megan what she needs most—unconditional love."

"But Megan is surrounded by unconditional love!"

"From you. From me. From Ian and Margaret and . . ." Jake stopped. Then, he started anew. "But the fans are fickle; the producers are fickle. And this little puppy is not."

Gwendolyn was bounding around the room, a soft, wriggling bundle of energy, chasing toys that Jake casually tossed for her, then running back to him for more patting and playing.

"Besides, Megan is a nurturer. She loves to watch things grow. Just look at her plants."

It was true about Megan; ever since she had ended her relationship with Stephen and moved to New York, there had been a new softness. Megan got attached to things— plants, puppies, places—but she had resisted further attachments with people.

"It all seems like a carefully rechanneled maternal instinct to me. Maybe Megan needs a child."

Jake said nothing but played roughly with Gwendolyn.

Carrie reached to pat her; for a moment her hand touched Jake's. Carrie withdrew it quickly.

They sat in silence. Too many emotions, too many words that could, but shouldn't, be said, too much past history. The silence was peaceful, not restless. They were where they wanted to be. Whatever the future or the past, they both knew how precious and fragile the moment was.

Carrie's hatred vanished. She remembered how she had prayed that he had not been killed: even if I never see him again, please let him be safe. And the prayer had been answered. And now, he sat beside her, safe, whole, and because he wanted to be there. He had followed her into Megan's bedroom to be with her. Did he have a message? Was there something he had to tell her? Something that he hadn't said that long weekend a year ago?

Carrie waited. But Jake had no message. All the important things had been said. But his presence next to her had a purpose—to reinforce what he had said. It is over. This is all we can ever have. I will always love you. Jake was not going to allow her to hate him, nor was he going to change his mind. But he wanted her to be at peace with him, with them.

With the decision that he had made for us, Carrie thought. At that moment, because he was with her, Carrie could accept the decision. Just as she had been able to accept it a year ago, until he left. But what about the rest of her life?

Carrie knew that the minute he left, she would miss him, again, terribly. And, in time, the despair would revert to hatred and anger. That's my problem, Carrie thought. I have to find a way to live with this. Perhaps they could still be friends; perhaps they could "dine" together. I wonder if I can still make him laugh, Carrie thought. She could try.

"Megan says you have your own business." The sound of her voice, strong, pleasant, startled all of them, including Gwendolyn.

"Yes. I sort of took over a company and made myself president." Jake smiled tentatively.

"Just like that," Carrie teased. It felt so good to tease Jake. Because he enjoyed it.

"Just like that!" He grinned and looked straight at her. She met his gaze, her eyes sparkling.

"You rich people!"

Jake laughed. "Don't worry, it was a bloodless coup."

"I guess you got tired of taking orders," Carrie said thoughtfully. "Wanted to be your own boss."

She knows, the way she always knows about me, Jake thought. Because that was precisely the reason. He had taken orders all of his life. The endless chores as a child in Appalachia. The army—Vietnam. Julia's lessons—English, manners, dress, relentless drilling. College—tests, assignments, timetables. And the years since college—he had done whatever and precisely what Stuart Dawson had told him to do. Jake hadn't resented it much; he had chosen to put himself in the position of taking orders.

But now Jake had made the choice to stop taking orders. And only Carrie understood why. It wasn't, as Julia and Megan assumed without asking, because he wanted to give orders, to control others. No, it was simply because he wanted to be his own boss. Carrie knew.

"It's based in New York?"

"Yes. It's based in the penthouse just across the hall. But we have a lot of international holdings."

"So, more traveling?"

"I guess I've gotten addicted to it."

Why? Carrie wondered. Adventure, romance, escape, anonymity. Why did Jake love to travel so much? Carrie could only guess, because she hadn't traveled.

"Do you realize that I have never been outside the United States?" But I have been to East Town, West Virginia, she thought. I have been to that foreign place.

"I can't believe it." How many hours he had spent, during his trips to London, Paris, Vienna, Venice, Rome, Cairo, Hong Kong, thinking about how much he wished she were with him, how much she would enjoy those exciting cities?

Jake suppressed the thought. It made him angry that he would never get to show her those places, but someone else would, someday. His voice changed, stern, bitter. "I would think the network would send its two stars to cover something in Paris or London. Of course, Mark has traveled . . ."

Don't do this! Don't put me in Paris with Mark, or anyone else except you. Don't make it sound like you don't care! Don't spoil this. Carrie realized, again, how difficult it would be for her to live her life without hope of Jake. And she realized, too, how whimsical her emotions were, a delicate balance between love and hate, with nothing in between. Could she ever find a comfortable in-between emotion? She would have to.

"Sorry," Jake said softly.

So am I, Carrie thought. Sorry that you are doing this to us.

"There you are!" Megan said as she entered the room, her bedroom. Gwendolyn dashed to her and was in her arms in seconds. "My three favorite uh . . . people . . . in the world. Carrie, Mark is muttering something about dinner reservations."

Carrie looked at her watch and did a double take. Their reservations had been for an hour ago. How long had she and Jake been in there? She didn't know Mark well, but she guessed this could make him angry.

"I'd better go. Thanks, Megan. Lovely party." Carrie left the room. She didn't say good-bye to Jake. She couldn't. She wouldn't.

Mark was in the living room, the center of yet another crowd. He smiled when he saw her.

"Sorry." Carrie mouthed the words at him.

"It's okay," he mouthed back, then said aloud as he glanced at his gold Rolex watch. "Goodness, Carrie, look at the time. We're going to be late if we don't leave now."

Carrie nodded to her co-conspirator; they had long since missed their dinner but were both ready to leave.

"Interesting party," Mark said as they rode down the private penthouse elevator nineteen floors.

Carrie smiled. "Were you bored?"

"Not a bit. I met people I've been reading about, reporting on, being curious about for years."

"And they wanted to meet you," Carrie said.

"And you."

"Nice people, though, don't you think?" Carrie felt the need to defend Megan and her friends.

"You bet. Interesting, intelligent, talented people."

Funny, Mark mused, for years he would have given anything to be on the guest list for a party like that, to be accepted, to be included. And now he had it, through years of hard work, sacrifice, struggle. And through Carrie. Because as famous and respected as he had become on his own, his celebrity had been enhanced when Carrie had joined the show.

Unpretentious, beautiful, thoughtful Carrie. Carrie would have been on the guest list even if she had been unemployed and unknown, because Megan was her friend, and their friendship transcended pretense or fame or celebrity.

"You have remarkable friends."

"Oh, those people aren't my friends. Only Megan. And Jake."

"I know. Those are the two that I'm talking about."

"Oh, did you speak with Jake?"

"No," Mark admitted. "Did you?"

"Briefly. We hadn't spoken since his return."

Mark registered his surprise. This was the man whose possible death had devastated Carrie. The man because of whom Mark had made a phone call to Stuart Dawson that certainly overstepped the usual bounds of professional journalism and military secrecy. Mark had made that phone call, against his better judgment, because it had been so important to Carrie. And she hadn't even spoken to Jake since his return.

"I'm sorry about dinner," Carrie interjected quickly. Change of subject.

"Are you hungry?"

"Well, yes. I think I sipped away at the same glass of champagne the whole time and ate nothing."

"Me, too. Too awkward to talk with one's mouth full. So, where can we go at nine o'clock on Saturday night in New York City without a dinner reservation?"

"Your place or mine?" Carrie asked innocently. It didn't even occur to Mark that the invitation was for anything other than dinner. And it wasn't.

Mark had barely noticed Carrie's apartment the only other time he had seen it, but tonight, as he sat on the comfortable overstuffed sofa in the small living room drinking champagne, he studied it with his practiced journalist's eye. He thought of adjectives he might use if he were writing an article titled: "Carrie's Apartment." It was a nice list: homey, cozy, small, comfortable, old-fashioned, full of character.

He said aloud, "Very Carrie."

"What?" She was slicing apples and cheese.

"The decor. Very Carrie."

"Meaning . . . ?" she asked idly from the kitchen.

"I like it."

Carrie paused, the knife suspended in midair. She blushed and didn't answer.

"Thanks!" She called back lightly, finally.

"You've probably lived here since you moved to New York. Why don't you find a new place? You know, bigger, with view, modern conveniences, safe neighborhood."

"Because I like it here." It sounded a bit brusque. She continued, pleasantly, "Megan wanted me to buy the other penthouse across from hers."

"Why didn't you?"

"Because," Carrie explained as she returned to the living room carrying the platter of cheese and apples, "I couldn't

356

possibly have afforded it then. And it's not really my style, do you think?"

"Is the other penthouse still for sale?" He could afford it.

"No."

"Oh. Do you know who lives there?"

"Jake does," Carrie said in an end-of-conversation tone, for the second time that evening.

They drank champagne and talked, exchanging safe, humorous anecdotes from their respective lives. Mark glossed over the struggle it had been for him, a war correspondent in Vietnam, a foreign correspondent in the Middle East and northern Africa, in danger, under the pressure of deadlines and competition, away from his family. He made the transition from combat zone correspondent to the nation's leading anchorman and commentator seem effortless and inevitable. But Carrie knew better. She knew that very few made it, starting, as he had, from the bottom.

Carrie also knew the price he had paid. She had read about him, and his life, in magazines, and she had heard the inevitable talk around the studio. She could see the cost, sometimes, in his eyes and in the lines carved in his face. And she heard it in his voice when he reported a story that was tragic or happy or full of pathos. His sensitivity showed, as much as hers did. That was why they were such a natural team, without script or rehearsal. They felt the same way.

"Are you just starving?" Carrie asked, staring at the second empty plate of cheese and apple slices. "I'm resisting the offer of an omelette . . . it seems so unimaginative."

"And trendy. Of course, being the trendy New York bachelor that I am, I can, and do, make wonderful omelettes."

"Then, sir, be my guest. Frankly, mine usually fail." Carrie laughed.

Mark followed her into the tiny kitchen. She collected the ingredients, then stood aside and watched.

"I have even mastered the one-handed cracking technique." Mark demonstrated. Mark made omelettes the way he did most things, without apparent effort but, in fact, the result of patient practice and meticulous attention to detail.

"Marvelous!" Carrie applauded him with her bright sapphire blue eyes, wide, innocent but, also, knowing and appreciative. "Would you like coffee? Or tea?"

"Tea, please. I don't drink coffee."

"What is it that you drink twenty cups a day of at work, then?" she asked.

"Tea. Just like you. Only I bring it pre-made in a thermos, because I don't have the patience to boil water every time I want a cup, the way you do."

Huge urns of hot, thick coffee studded the studio, supplying the employees with hundreds of cups a day. There was a small stove in a corner of the studio and a saucepan. Carrie made her tea there, one cup at a time.

"I've thought about buying a hot plate and a kettle, so that there would always be hot water." Carrie shrugged.

"But you didn't want to do it just for yourself."

"For whatever reason." But that had been the reason.

"You just don't have the 'star' mentality," Mark teased.

"Unlike you, who boils water in the privacy of his own home and brings tea to work cleverly disguised as coffee!" Carrie's eyes sparkled back.

"Touché. I'll buy the hot plate. You get the kettle."

They drank their tea in the living room. Carrie watched Mark's face become serious.

Finally he said, casually, "So, are you the least bit tempted to tell me about you and Jake?"

Carrie smiled. "Not the least."

"From my perspective, it seems unusual," Mark ventured.

"What happened to *remarkable?*" Carrie's voice was sharper than she had intended. But the hint was made for the third time that evening: Carrie would not talk about Jake.

Mark was annoyed. He had a right, albeit a slim one, to know something. He had gone out on a limb for her, because of Jake. Mark sighed. The evening with Carrie had been too pleasant to make an issue of it, tonight.

"Hrumpf!"

"Hrumpf, yourself!" Carrie responded. They both laughed.

Megan, Jake, Ian, and Margaret went together to a late supper after the party. Megan left the penthouse in the capable hands of the cleanup crew hired by the caterers. There would be no trace of the party when she returned. They had spent an hour playing with Gwendolyn before leaving for their midnight reservation.

"It was a great success, Megan. You've set a new precedent—a pre-production patron's party given by the leading lady."

It was true. It hadn't been done before. The new play, *Rainstorm,* wasn't scheduled to go into production for four months and wouldn't open for eight. But the backers had committed the money, the principal cast, the producer and director named.

Megan had given them a thank-you party.

"It was Jake's brainchild. He said it was good business to thank your investors in advance. It shows confidence."

"Extreme confidence. But, we *are* confident about this play." Ian was producing the play, but he had relinquished his usual role as director to a talented director that he had had picked—because he had directed Megan enough, because this role was so important for her, because he knew that this man, Alec Matthews, could direct her with an impartiality that he, Ian, no longer could. Ian yielded the directorship reluctantly, but he knew his decision was best for Megan and for the play. And, as producer, he would be there every day.

"It was sensational to have Carrie and Mark there," Margaret said.

"A sensational surprise. When I invited Carrie, she said she couldn't make it."

"Are they an item?" Margaret asked.

"You mean in addition to being *the* team? I haven't a clue, except that it looked like it. Jake talked to Carrie." Megan looked at Jake.

"I have no idea." Jake shrugged.

"Well, the patrons loved them. Talk about confidence! It was really the perfect touch to a perfect party."

Jake and Megan returned to the penthouse at two-thirty. Jake walked her to her door.

"What are your plans?"

"I thought I'd go to bed!"

Jake looked at Megan thoughtfully and made a decision. It was time for him to get on with his life, just as Carrie had obviously gotten on with hers. For a year, Jake had lived with, and been sustained by, the memory of their four days of love. Jake believed what he had told Carrie then: that they could never have any more. That they never would have any more. No matter what happened, that was their forever. Still, the precious, private memory of Carrie had prevented him from making love—from wanting to make love—with Julia or anyone else.

But tonight, seeing Carrie with Mark, Jake realized that he couldn't live forever on a lovely, loving memory. He had his life to live, too.

"Would you like some company?" he asked, finally, definitively. He had made his decision.

Megan didn't answer but opened the door and led him to her bedroom.

Chapter Twenty-two

At the end of the eighth week of rehearsals, Alec invited Megan to have dinner with him.

"We won't discuss work," he promised.

"It's fine if we do."

Megan had great respect for Alec's ability as a director. He was unrelenting in his insistence that things be done his way, but he had the genius that Ian had promised. Alec made Megan perform at an entirely new level. He pushed, and she responded. Then, he pushed harder.

Ian was dazzled; a masterpiece was unfolding, being created, before his eyes. Alec's genius, Megan's apparently limitless talent, and the brilliant script merged magnificently. Each day of rehearsals was thrilling. The entire cast and crew felt it. This would be the play of the year. Megan's would be the performance of the year. Alec's reputation as a distinguished director would be guaranteed.

As far as Ian could tell, there was no personal relationship between Megan and Alec; respect for each other's talents and nothing else. They didn't chat during breaks. There was no teasing or pouting; there were no power struggles. This time, Megan was all business; she knew the importance of this role, the role of a lifetime.

It was how it should be—all business, no nonsense. It was why he, Ian, could no longer direct Megan. He was too involved; he cared about her too much. He couldn't place demands, push her, argue with her the way Alec could.

It would have worried Ian had he known that Alec and Megan had a date. They were scheduled to open in one week. The play was virtually ready, but the fine tuning, the perfection of detail that separated the mundane from the great, was left to be done. Why risk everything now? Ian would have asked Megan had he known. Wait until after we open. Wait until after it's a great success. Then get involved if you want.

But Megan didn't tell Ian, because it seemed so inconsequential to her—a dinner with a business associate. It was perfectly safe, because Megan knew that she wouldn't get involved with Alex or anyone else.

Alec Matthews was an attractive man, brown-black hair, deep-set dark eyes, thin lips, pearl white teeth. His movements were sleek, catlike, sensual. He spoke precisely, articulately, with a slight accent that lingered from his childhood in Wales. If Megan was neutral about a date with Alec, the other female cast members, and, at least two of the men, would not have been.

But Alec had kept his distance. It was necessary. He had to be in control, absolutely. That was why he had to see Megan, alone.

During dinner, Alec charmed her, mesmerized her, and he made her want him. His sensual, sultry eyes sent a message that was unmistakable and irresistible. And Megan's body responded, instinctively. How long had it been since she had wanted a man like this? The college days of frantic notes to Jake: *we must meet this afternoon; we must.* She had been so young then; it had been a fun, lovely, harmless game.

And with Stephen. It had never been desperate and it had never been purely sexual. There had always been so much more.

And now Alec was finding in her desires that she had long since forgotten, in the same way that he had found talent from emotions that had been locked deep within her soul.

They left the still-full plates of gourmet food and returned to Megan's penthouse. Once inside the door, Alec kissed her, pressing her against the wall, pressing his strong body against hers. His kiss was hot and demanding and promising. His hands reached under her dress and deep inside her, pulling their bodies even closer. Megan found his belt buckle. They kissed for several minutes.

Then, without warning, Alec pulled away. He walked to the wet bar and poured himself a full glass of Scotch, neat. He didn't offer to pour her a drink. Without looking at her, he sat down on the living room couch.

"Come here, Megan." Alec's voice had changed; it was his director's voice, only rougher. What was he doing? What game? Megan, annoyed, followed his command.

"Now, take off your clothes, slowly. And when I tell you to touch yourself, I want you to pretend that I am touching you. Show me how it makes you feel to have me touch you. I want the real thing, Megan. Don't forget, I know when you are acting."

Megan laughed and applauded with several slow claps.

"Very nice, Alec. Next time I hear of a part for a sexual sicko I'll recommend you. You're really quite convincing. Now get the hell out of here." Megan began to leave the room.

In an instant Alec caught up to her and grabbed her arm, roughly.

"I said get undressed."

"No!" Megan's anger battled with a new emotion—fear. Alec's eyes were glazed, his lips curled and ugly. It wasn't a silly game. He was serious. "Let go of me, Alec."

His hands wrapped more tightly around her arm and his nails dug in until they drew blood. Alec was a strong man, and his power was fortified now by uncontrollable rage.

"You will do what I tell you, Megan. I am the director," he snarled between his perfect white teeth.

"Alec, for God's sake, let go of me. Please."

Alec sensed her fear and it strengthened him. She would do whatever he wanted.

"You want me, Megan." His voice softened, the way it had been in the restaurant, charming, seductive. He took her hand and pressed it against his pants.

"Feel that? You can put it anywhere you want inside you. Your mouth . . ."

Megan pulled her hand away.

"Megan," he said gently, tenderly. He released her. His eyes stared at her the way they had in the restaurant. Megan relaxed a little. Alec seemed reasonable now. If he would just leave.

He traced her lips gently with his finger. His touch was electric. He was right; she had wanted him to touch her. Even now. Megan shook away the thought. She had to be careful and she had to get him to leave.

His fingers traveled down her neck to the V in her black silk dress. Lightly, expertly, his fingers moved under the dress to her breasts. With his other hand he reached under her dress and forced his fingers deep inside her, again.

"Megan," he whispered. "You have to do as I say. Then you can have me." His fingers probed even deeper. "I will help you."

Alec took Megan's hand and with it unzipped the dress. It fell loosely around her, exposing her breasts. He guided one hand to her breast and the other to join his hand, still inside her.

"Now, just do what I was doing," Alec removed his hands. Megan withdrew her hands and shook clenched fists at him.

"Get out," she whispered fiercely.

"Don't you dare defy me." Alec tore the dress off her and she stood before him, naked, trembling.

"Please go away."

"Get on your knees."

"No!"

Alec slapped her face. Megan shrieked. He held her by the arm and slapped her repeatedly.

"Stop, please." She was crying.

Alec stopped.

"Are you ready to do the scene?" he demanded.

"Get out. Get out," Megan pleaded, shaking her head.

Megan's scream had awakened Gwendolyn. She bounded into the living room, tail wagging. When she saw Alec, she started to bark. Gwendolyn had never barked at a stranger before, but she barked and growled. It was a pathetically brave gesture for a small dog.

Alec kicked Gwendolyn brutally, hurling her across the room. When she landed, she lay motionless.

Megan's rage as she saw what Alec had done to Gwendolyn gave her power. She lunged at him. He smiled briefly, then overpowered her. He forced her to the floor in front of him, unzipped his pants, and using one hand, quickly removed his belt.

"I'll give you what you want, whore. Open your mouth."

Megan shook her head. He struck her with the belt. She screamed.

"Open your mouth. And do this right. Your best performance." Alec paused. "Or I'll kill you."

Megan obeyed. Once he pulled her head away, viciously, by her hair.

"You are in too much of a rush. Slow it down." Those were words he used during the day to direct her. Words of a genius. He was directing her now. And she would do whatever Alec wanted; she had no choice.

"Slowly, slowly. You love this, Megan." His voice was soft again. Smooth, seductive. "Now faster. Now touch yourself, Megan. Do it."

As Megan followed his directions, she thought, please don't kill me.

Alec climaxed in her mouth, then shoved her onto her back on the floor.

"Now it's your turn. I'll watch. When you're ready, I'll join you."

He spread her legs wide apart. Then he traced the inner parts of her thighs with his belt buckle. She trembled with fear. He began to rub her with his hand, massaging and probing deep into her.

"I'm helping you, too much, Megan. This is not my job. This is your role." Megan had heard those words a thousand times in the past eight weeks. Those same words had made her perform as she never had before.

He put her hands between her thighs and sat back. Megan saw that he was already erect again.

"Ready? Now pay attention to my directions." Alec emphasized his words by running the belt over her belly.

He told her what to do with her fingers, where to put them, how to move them. And he told her what to do with the rest of her body.

Megan followed his instructions, mechanically. It gave her a moment to analyze the situation. The analysis always resulted in the same, grim, inevitable thought: he plans to kill me. He has no choice. If I tell anyone what he's done, he'll be ruined. Can he possibly believe that I won't talk? No, he has to kill me.

Megan knew she couldn't overpower him. Perhaps she could scare him away. Jake! Where was Jake? Megan had called him earlier to see if he would check on Gwendolyn while she was out. *Gwendolyn.* But Jake hadn't been home. Even if he were home, he wouldn't hear her scream. The penthouse was too well built, too solid.

But maybe, she could scare Alec.

"I'm getting impatient, Megan. And bored." More everyday taunts from the master.

Those taunts. That was how he got her attention. He would say things like, "The audience is yawning, Megan. The women are making their grocery lists. Their husbands are fantasizing about their secretaries. Get them back, Megan. Make them think about nothing, no one, but you."

Suddenly Alec grabbed her ankles, forced her legs, knees flexed, against her body. Then he thrust himself into her rectum. Megan felt her flesh tear; and she heard it tear. She screamed.

"Jake! *Jake!* Help me!"

Alec covered her mouth with his hand.

"Nice projection, Megan," he sneered, half laughing.

Her mouth closed on his hand. She tasted his blood, but his hand didn't move. His thrusts continued, painful, violent, determined.

At the same time, he moved his hands from her mouth to her throat.

Carrie touched Mark's unshaven cheek gently. She could almost feel the strain and fatigue that were written so clearly on his face. He hadn't slept . . . since when? Night before last—forty hours ago.

Forty hours of waiting and worrying. And now, they were waiting, again, in the visitors' area of the Intensive Care Unit. Every time the door opened, every time busy footsteps scurried past, every time the page operator called a doctor "Stat to ICU" they came to attention. "They" were Carrie, Mark, Mark's ex-wife, Sheila, and his other child, his son, Andrew. They waited there, together, because this was the place that the news came, when it came. They rarely spoke. The glowering and hostility had ceased hours ago; it seemed petty and inconsequential compared to the reason they were there.

The reason: a little girl who was dying. Or surviving. They didn't know. The chances varied: fifty-fifty, sixty-forty, forty-sixty. All it meant was that no one knew. But she might live, or she might die. The doctors were trying. And Becky was trying. She was a strong, healthy twelve-year-old.

Or had been, until she had awakened in the middle of the night two nights before with severe abdominal pain. It had hurt her to breathe, to move, to speak. If she curled into a tight ball, it hurt the least, but even then the pain had made her cry.

"Mommy. Mommy," she had cried softly. It had hurt to raise her voice. Everything hurt. "Mommy!"

Sheila heard her. Or, she awakened because of the sense that a mother has when her child needs her. Sheila called an ambulance and Mark.

It took the doctors no time to determine how ill Becky was. She had a high fever, low blood pressure, and a rigid abdomen. It was an acute intra-abdominal catastrophe with septic shock.

"We have to operate immediately."

"What is it?"

"We won't know until we get in."

Get in, Mark thought. Get into his daughter by cutting through her young skin. He had seen surgeons "get in" and "explore" and "close" enough times in Vietnam. But this was his little girl.

"I need to ask you a few questions," the doctor said.

Sheila and Mark nodded.

"Was she well when she went to bed? Did she eat a normal dinner, for example?"

"Yes to both. Absolutely fine," Sheila answered firmly, with a tone that the doctors had heard so often: but she was fine six hours ago, so she can't be that sick now. Denial.

"Why?" Mark asked.

"Acute appendicitis. Usually begins with mild belly pain and loss of appetite, then localizes, in a day, to the right lower part of the abdomen. It can present like this, as a ruptured appendix with no prodrome, but it's rare." The doctor paused.

He looked at them, and, for the first time, recognized Mark. A V.I.P., he thought. I'm going to treat him exactly like any other worried father, but he'd damned well better not get pushy or I'll push back. The doctor knew that patients who demanded special treatment, and, by so doing, directed their care, often fared less well than others. I give all my patients the same care, he thought, the best care that I can. It doesn't matter who they are.

But it put him on edge. He took a deep breath before he asked the next question.

"Is she pregnant? Or has she ever been?" Ruptured ectopic and septic abortion both had to be considered, no matter whose child she was.

"What?" Mark roared. "She's twelve years old!"

The doctor looked at Sheila, who said quietly, "She's not sexually active." Sheila glowered at Mark. The look said: she could be sexually active; twelve-year-old girls whose fathers abandon them sometimes are. But Becky's not. She has a mother who loves her.

Sheila signed the consent for surgery; Sheila was the legal guardian. The doctor wrote in the risks for her to understand, "including death." Sheila nodded and signed.

That had been yesterday morning. Becky was in surgery for four hours. They found a ruptured appendix with acute peritonitis. Intestinal contents had spilled throughout the abdomen, causing infection and inflammation. They removed as much pus and debris as they could, but her vital signs were too unstable to risk further "exploration," then. They would have to "take her back" after she'd "stabilized."

Becky was taken from the operating room directly to the surgical intensive care unit. She was too ill to go to the recovery room.

Because she might not recover, Mark thought.

She was given three types of antibiotics, two drugs to maintain her blood pressure, and they kept her on the ventilator with a tube into her lungs, because "there might be lung damage from the septic shock." Becky was unconscious. Mark and Sheila stood at her bedside and held her tiny, cold, purple-blue, lifeless hands.

At three-thirty the first afternoon, Mark realized that he hadn't telephoned the studio. He dialed Carrie's direct line.

"I can do the show myself."

"No. I'll be there."

"That's ridiculous."

"I need to get away from here. We don't get to see her much. It's mostly sitting in the waiting room."

"Why don't I come over and wait with you, after I do the show?"

"Okay. That would be nice."

Mark had not called because he was worried about the evening news. He had called because he wanted to see Carrie. They both knew that he didn't really want to leave the hospital. Carrie would come to be with him. He didn't even have to ask.

In another setting, a casual encounter at a party or in a department store, Sheila would have directed her notoriously sarcastic tongue at Carrie's age, at Mark's age—a father fixation?—at Carrie's feigned innocence, and so on. But in this setting, she came to depend on Carrie.

Carrie kept Sheila supplied with coffee and Mark with tea. She unobtrusively forced food on them, which they ate without remembering having ordered it—they hadn't. Carrie entertained Andrew; they played cards and board games and word games. Carrie's apartment was within walking distance of the hospital; they all used it for naps, showers, escape.

When Mark and Sheila were too tired, or emotional, to think clearly, in those precious moments when the doctors came to them with progress reports, it was Carrie who asked the questions that needed to be asked. Somehow, Carrie was able to ask informed, necessary questions in an unoffensive way; it was her talent.

"Will you need to re-explore her? Is she still requiring blood pressure support? What are her chances?" For Carrie, the doctors answered these questions, patiently and carefully.

They operated again Thursday night, at midnight, and, again, Friday afternoon. Carrie left during the surgery to prepare for the Friday evening newscast. By ten o'clock

Friday night, Becky had been out of the operating room for four hours. Carrie, Mark, Sheila, and Andrew kept their vigil in the tiny room outside the ICU.

They all stood, as they always did, when the doctor walked in. A team of doctors took care of Becky. The progress reports came from different team members at different times. This doctor was Carrie's favorite. He found her anxious eyes first when he walked into the room, and he winked. Tears came immediately to Carrie's eyes. The doctor smiled; he blinked back a moment of wetness in his own eyes. Then he looked at Mark and Sheila.

"She's better."

"Better?" Sheila whispered.

"Much better."

Overcome by emotion, Mark and Sheila couldn't speak. Carrie knew that there were questions that, later, they would wish they had asked. As usual, she asked them.

"Is she conscious?" Carrie asked.

Mark and Sheila nodded, as if to say, Yes, we want to know, is she conscious?

"Yes. She's responding to commands. Like hand squeezing. It's a very good sign. I think you should go see her, speak to her. She may not look too different to you; she's still terribly weak. But all the signs are better."

"Is she off pressors?" Carrie had learned, quickly, the medical term for the blood pressure agents.

"Yes. Totally off. We've been weaning her slowly all day. She's been off now for two hours, and her pressure is fine."

"So you think she'll make it?" That was, of course, the question.

"Yes." He smiled at Carrie. "I think she'll make it." He didn't add his usual "not totally out of the woods, but it looks good" comment. These were sophisticated people; they knew that life had no guarantees. And he believed that Becky had turned the most critical corner.

Carrie waited with Andrew while Mark and Sheila visited Becky. Neither Carrie nor Andrew had been allowed to visit.

"I don't care *who* she is, if she is not that child's parent, she does not go in!" the doctor had said.

"They want us to go home!" Mark announced jubilantly when he and Sheila returned. It was more proof that Becky was better. "They want her to be undisturbed, so she can rest."

"I think they know that sleep would be good for all Becky's family," Carrie said gently. The fatigue still hung heavily on Mark's face, but the strain was less. "Did you leave my telephone number?"

He nodded.

By eleven, Mark was asleep in Carrie's bed.

Chapter Twenty-three

Jake had planned a quiet Friday evening at home. But that afternoon, one of his attorneys had invited him to the opera.

"I have two tickets for tonight. Will you join me?"

"Of course." *Aida* at the Met. It appealed to him very much. And he enjoyed JoAnn Brenner. She was a shrewd, tough corporate attorney because she had to be, and an aggressive but surprisingly soft sexual partner because she wanted to be. Jake liked her, except for the part of her that reminded him of Beth, an unyielding, ruthless core of determination that was sometimes almost blind.

JoAnn was a smart, quick, effective, successful attorney. She liked being seen with handsome, wealthy men. And she liked the way Jake made love.

Sometimes he called her. Sometimes she called him. It worked out nicely.

Jake sensed that something was wrong with JoAnn in the second act. He touched her hand. Clammy. Then he looked at her in the dim light of the Opera House.

"Let's go," he whispered.

"At the end of the act," she whispered back miserably.

"You won't make it." Jake knew the opera well. The act had at least fifteen more minutes. "There's a good time in about two minutes. We'll leave then."

He led her out and pointed her to the ladies' room. She reappeared in ten minutes. She looked green, pale green. She tried to smile.

"Shall we find a doctor?"

"No. I'm sure it's just food poisoning. I had something for lunch that tasted bad at the time. How infuriating!"

"I'll see you home."

"I'll catch a cab. You should stay."

"Nonsense."

Jake didn't stay long at JoAnn's apartment, just long enough to make certain that she seemed all right and would call him if she got worse.

It was eleven-fifteen when he put the key into the front door of his penthouse. As he closed the door behind him, he heard a noise. It was distant, brief, but unmistakably a woman's scream. Jake walked back into the foyer between his penthouse and Megan's. He held his breath. There was only silence. He walked to Megan's front door and listened. Nothing.

Jake returned to his penthouse, worried. He telephoned Megan, but there was no answer. Odd. Megan didn't go out much, even on a Friday night. He dialed again and let it ring fifteen times.

Jake's worry made him restless. If Megan were out, she would want him to check on Gwendolyn. He took the key to Megan's front door from a drawer in his kitchen. He rang the door bell and knocked.

"Megan, it's Jake."

No answer.

He put the key in the doorknob and turned. The door didn't open. The dead bolt had been thrown. *Megan never used the dead bolt lock.* They lived in a security building. The penthouse had its own elevator, key operated from the ground floor or activated by code from the penthouse. When not in use, the elevator stayed at the penthouse level.

"Why do we even lock our doors at all?" Megan had asked.

"Privacy," Jake had answered.

"From each other?" Megan had teased.

"No. Privacy for me from whomever you happen to be entertaining."

"And vice versa!"

But she never used the dead bolt. A cold sweat chilled Jake. He pounded on the door and called her name. Did he have a key to the dead bolt? He would have to look. He rushed back to his kitchen. In the same drawer, there was a shiny key, unused, unlabeled. Megan had probably put it there. Good girl. Jake was about to try the key when the bolt was thrown and the door opened.

"Alec!"

"Jake. Good evening." Alec looked as he always looked, calm, unruffled. The way that Jake himself usually looked.

"Where's Megan?"

"Inside."

"Did you hear me?"

"Of course. We were . . . uh . . . busy." Alec smiled.

"Oh, sorry. I just thought I heard a scream."

Alec smiled, a mean, arrogant smile. Jake didn't like it. "Is Megan all right?"

"She will be. Frankly, she disappointed me tonight. She knows it and she's upset. Tell her it was only a rehearsal, will you? And that I'll call her tomorrow."

Alec walked unhurriedly, confidently, to the waiting elevator and was gone.

The panic that had seized Jake earlier hadn't dissipated. There had been a scream. He saw Alec's sinister smile. He pushed open the heavy oak door.

"Megan?" he called softly.

Then he saw her. Huddled on the living room floor. Naked, bruised, bleeding, clutching the torn dress that Alec had thrown at her before he left—"Get dressed, whore. You have company." Her head was bent; her tangled blond hair covered her face.

Jake's mind wavered for a moment. Should he go to Megan, or should he follow Alec? If he caught Alec, Jake knew that he would kill him. Jake had killed men who had deserved it less. Men who had done nothing other than be born in a country at war with Jake's country.

Jake went to Megan. He sat on the floor next to her and touched her very gently. She looked at him, and through the tears and bruises Jake saw something much worse than pain or humiliation or anger. He saw, in her eyes, a look of total defeat and hopelessness.

"He murdered Gwendolyn," she whispered and gestured with her head toward the little golden heap of fur.

Gwendolyn lay, quite still, but her chest moved.

"Gwendolyn," Jake called softly. The tail moved.

Jake walked over and touched her. Gwendolyn sprang into action. Jake gently squeezed her body, but nothing seemed to hurt. Gwendolyn wriggled excitedly as he carried her over to Megan. Megan clutched the wriggling body. Gwendolyn licked Megan's tear-stained face but could not keep up with the shower of tears.

"He kicked her so hard. And then she didn't move."

"Dogs play dead. It's instinct. She's okay. What did he do to you?"

"She could have internal injuries. She could be bleeding. Jake, will you take her to a vet tonight? Please?"

"If you like," he said, watching a normal Gwendolyn bounding around the living room.

"Megan, what did he do to you? What did Alec do to you?"

Megan stared at Jake with blank, hopeless eyes, but she didn't speak.

"Honey, I think we should call the police."

"Why? You got here in time."

"He didn't rape you?"

"What? Yes. *But he didn't kill me.*"

Megan collapsed into Jake's arms, trembling, sobbing, inconsolable. He stroked her hair and her back. His hand touched a sticky liquid on her back—blood. Jake's anger flared, but he couldn't leave Megan. And he couldn't kill Alec. Because of the rules. In many other countries it would have been so simple. Somewhere in the back of Jake's mind a thought nagged: but that's what makes this country so good . . .

"I'm going to take a shower," Megan announced.

"Megan, listen to me. That animal beat you and raped you. You cannot let him get away with that. I . . . we . . . have to call the police. They will have to collect evidence. The sooner I call them, the sooner it will be over and you can take your shower. Okay?"

It was like reasoning with a child. Megan listened to him amiably and then said, firmly, "No!"

"Okay. Will you tell me what happened?"

"Why?" She stared at him. Added to the hopelessness and defeat, there was a new look—distrust, betrayal.

By God, Jake thought, if he's made her lose her trust in me I *will* kill him.

"Because maybe it would help to talk about it."

"No. I just want to take a shower. I'll do that and you take Gwen to see the vet. When you get back, maybe we can talk."

"Megan. Look at her. She's fine."

"You promised!" The look said: I knew I couldn't trust you. Jake suppressed his anger with great effort.

"Okay. Negotiation time. I will take Gwen to a vet, but I will not leave you alone. I think I'll call Ian. There's no time like the present to let him know about this."

"No! Don't call Ian."

"Why not?"

"He will be so angry with me."

Jake looked blank.

"Because of the play," she said.

"Megan. You are being totally irrational. I know what you've been through, but . . ."

"No you don't."

"Okay. You're right. I don't know. Because you won't tell me." Jake said patiently. "Anyway. You're confused and upset. I can't leave you alone. Who do you want me to call?"

Don't say it, Jake thought. But, of course, she did.

"Carrie," Megan whispered.

Jake drew a deep breath. "Tell me her number."

It was twelve-thirty. Mark answered the phone midway through the first ring. Carrie sat up.

"Yes?" Mark said.

Jake paused.

"Mark?" he guessed.

"Yes!"

"Mark, this is Jake Easton. I apologize for bothering you so late, but I need to speak with Carrie."

"Is it about Becky?"

"Becky? No. It's about Megan. Is Carrie there?"

Mark handed the phone to Carrie without explanation.

"Hello?"

"Caroline. It's Jake." His voice was steeped in apology: I'm sorry to do this to us, to intrude in your life, to open the wounds. It had been seven months since Megan's patrons' party, seven months since they had seen each other. Obviously, Carrie had found a new love.

"Megan has been . . . uh . . . assaulted."

"Oh, no! Is she all right?"

"She's okay physically." Jake looked at Megan. Her bruises were turning red-black and swelling. "Badly bruised, but okay. But she's awfully upset. Confused. Doesn't even want to press charges, call the police . . ."

"Does she know who did it?"

"Yes. Alec, the fellow who's directing the play."

"Did he rape her?"

378

"Yes." I don't want to involve you in this, believe me, he thought. "She won't really talk to me or listen to me."

"Where are you?"

"At Megan's."

"I'll be right over."

"I'll send a limo for you."

Carrie hesitated. That would be safest and easiest. "Okay." She hung up.

"You're not going alone," Mark said. He was groggy from the brief glimpse—an hour and a half—of desperately needed sleep.

"Yes, I am." Carrie smiled at him. He was too tired to argue. "They're sending a limo. I'll leave the telephone number on the table by the phone."

While she waited for the limo, Carrie checked with the hospital. Becky was fine, continuing to improve.

Jake met her at the door. He noted the change immediately, the change that had occurred in Carrie in the past seven months. Carrie projected confidence and independence; she seemed less soft, less vulnerable, less innocent. Why? Jake wondered. But, of course, knew. Carrie was secure, secure with Mark's love—with a security that Jake had never given her. Mark loved her, and that made her stronger, more sure of herself, and, paradoxically, more independent. It should have made Jake happy; it was what he had wanted for her. But it made him sad.

Carrie's eyes met Jake's. She made a brief effort to smile, then looked away. Her heart pounded. She realized how she must look in her old, faded jeans, blue-checked Oxford shirt, V-neck sweater, hand-combed hair, dark circles around her large blue eyes. And Jake, still dressed for the opera, looked elegant.

"Are you all right?" he asked.

"Of course. Stressful forty-eight hours, that's all." She tried the smile again.

"I've never seen you look like this." It wasn't criticism; it was concern.

Something snapped inside her; she didn't want his concern. For the past months she had loved him, hated him, tried to understand, and was carefully building a trusting relationship with Mark. All the energy and emotion of the past seven months focused on this moment.

"You should have seen me the month I spent waiting to hear if they'd found any pieces of you in the rubble." Carrie didn't look at him, but she felt him react to the venom of her words. She walked past him. "Where's Megan?"

Then Carrie saw her. Megan was still sitting in the middle of the living room floor. Jake had forced a blue terry bathrobe on her but had been unable to convince her to move. Gwendolyn lay beside her, asleep. Megan looked up. Carrie gasped when she saw her face, ran to her, held her hands, and looked into her eyes.

"Oh, Megan, I am so sorry." There were tears in Carrie's eyes.

"Don't cry, Carrie," Megan began, then started to cry herself.

In a few moments, Carrie stood up, still holding Megan's hands, tugging gently.

"C'mon, let's get up. I'll make us some tea."

Without resistance, Megan stood up. She immediately swayed, looked surprised, but managed to remain standing. The cream-colored, deep-pile, pure wool carpet where Megan had been sitting was stained red-brown with blood. In the center of the stain was a large clump of clotted blood.

Carrie looked swiftly at Jake and mouthed the words: We have to call the police.

Jake nodded but gestured at Megan and shrugged. It would serve no purpose, and might only cause publicity, to call the police if Megan refused to cooperate.

"Megan, look at all that blood. Where is it from?" Carrie asked.

Megan started to open the front of her robe. But something deep in her brain—a part that was in touch with the

rest of her life—sent a warning: don't show Carrie *that.*
Megan turned her back to Carrie and slipped the robe off
her back. Big welts had been viciously carved into her frail,
slender back. Each was lined with a delicate strip of dried
blood; it didn't explain the blood clot.

Carrie looked at the floor at Megan's feet. She was still
bleeding; every second or two a bright red drop silently
splashed onto the rug.

"You are still bleeding. Megan, where are you bleeding
from?" Carrie wanted to shake her back to reality, to make
her cooperate. Megan was losing a lot of blood. "Tell me.
Are you having your period?"

Megan shook her head slowly. "Think of another ori-
fice." Megan gave a short laugh, a laugh of despair, humiliation, and defeat. "I'm not surprised I'm bleeding.
Virgins bleed, don't they? I was a virgin, there."

Megan paused. Jake and Carrie grieved silently for their
friend's obvious pain.

"Don't they, Jake? Don't virgins bleed from there, too?
You have the most sexual experience. You must know."
Megan's words were fierce.

"Where is that coming from, Megan? How dare you . . ."
Jake's patience was spent.

"Megan," Carrie said gently, "Alec did this to you, not
Jake. Jake would never hurt you."

"No. Jake is always gentle," Megan agreed quietly.

Is. Always. Carrie bit her lip. I don't want to hear about
Jake and Megan's sex life.

Carrie said to Jake without looking at him, "She
doesn't mean it. You're just the closest available male target."

"And it seems to be open season," Jake said coolly. He
had been trying to recover from Carrie's attack: did she
think it had been easy for him?

Carrie sighed visibly. Her eyes were fixed on the steadily
falling drops of blood at Megan's feet.

Megan needs a doctor. Carrie thought of the one doctor

whom she knew. And he was on call tonight, keeping vigil over an angelic little girl. Carrie imagined calling him.

Hello, doctor. Me again. The lady with the questions. Doctor, could you just leave Becky for a minute to check my friend here? Yes, you do recognize her. She's had a little accident. If you could just put in a few stitches to stop the bleeding. What? Well, uh, yes. You know those artsy types. No, I know you'll keep it confidential. That's why I brought her to you.

"We have to get you to a doctor," Carrie said.

"No!"

"You're losing a lot of blood."

"If I put ice and pressure on it, it will be fine," Megan said firmly.

"Okay, we'll give that a try. If it doesn't work, we'll find a doctor."

"Speaking of doctors, I'm going to take Gwendolyn to an emergency animal hospital. As I promised Megan," Jake said angrily. He was eager to get away from both of them for awhile.

When Jake returned two hours later, Carrie sat alone in Megan's living room, drinking tea. She had placed two large towels over the areas of bloodstain. She jumped when the front door opened. What if Alex had decided to come back? From the little that Megan had told her, Carrie knew that Alec was a man to be feared.

"How's Gwendolyn?" She was already scampering.

"Fine, as you can see. Although the vet does think the bastard cracked one of her ribs. No internal injury, though." Jake looked around. "Where's Megan?"

"In bed. Asleep, I hope."

"The bleeding stopped?"

"Yes! With ice and pressure."

"And she took a shower, I suppose. Not a trace of evidence left."

"Right. I tried, but she really couldn't be reasoned with. I've never seen her like this, this stubborn and irrational. Maybe she had too much to drink."

"Megan doesn't drink."

"What? She certainly used to."

"I know. But she hasn't since . . . For a long time. Years."

They were talking about Carrie's best friend and Carrie had just learned something about her that she should have known.

"It's the shock, the trauma of what happened."

"I guess. Did she tell you about it?"

"Not in much detail. But I got the definite impression that she was more worried about what he might have done to her if you hadn't heard her."

"She believes that he would have killed her."

"Yes. She's still very afraid. Do you think it's possible that he might have killed her?"

"No! Megan is so unused to violence. Alec is obviously a violent man. I think she's overreacting. There's probably no real danger." Jake paused, then said, almost to himself, "But can she recover from this emotionally? She has suffered so much."

Carrie stared at Jake, incredulous. Suffered? Megan? Megan, the golden girl. Everything Megan touched turned to gold. She got any man she wanted—Jake, Stephen. She had the career she wanted, leading roles on Broadway, critical acclaim. Megan had caused suffering, Stephen's suffering. But Megan had never suffered. Until now, Megan's life had been charmed.

What was Jake talking about?

Moments passed. Carrie didn't have the energy to ask him. She didn't have the strength to tease secrets out of him anymore. She wasn't even supposed to care.

"Would you like some tea?" she asked finally.

"No, thank you. Would you like some bourbon?" Jake poured himself a glass.

"She really doesn't want Ian to know," Carrie said.

"Christ! What does she plan to do? The show must go on? What does she think she'll do the next time she sees Alec, act normally?"

"She's an actress."

"Do you really think she can act her way through this? She doesn't have your control."

"She wants this play."

Jake shook his head. "Ian has to know."

"Everyone will know when they see her face."

"I'll tell Ian in the morning," Jake said with finality. He had made the decision for Megan. He looked at Carrie. "You really look exhausted, Caroline."

"Long day's journey into night." She smiled wryly.

"And miles to go before you sleep, to mix genres. The limo is downstairs. He'll drive you home. I'll be here, if she wakes up."

Carrie stood up. Jake walked with her to the elevator. He wanted to hold her, but he didn't even touch her.

Instead, he whispered, "I'm sorry."

It was five-thirty when Carrie returned to her own bed, next to Mark. He awakened at eight and went to the hospital while Carrie slept. He returned at eleven. Carrie woke up when he entered her bedroom.

"Becky talked to me!" There were tears in his eyes.

Carrie held out her arms. Mark came to her. "I am so glad, darling."

Seven months ago, nothing could have made Carrie forget about Jake, not even for a second. Now, with Mark, she forgot about him for days. And when she remembered, because her stomach would ache or she would feel, unaccountably, sad, she would confront the pain, and its cause, and force it away. She would not allow it to fester. She thought of the lyric from a popular song: "I haven't got time for the pain . . . not since I found you."

The wounds had reopened last night, the minute she had

seen Jake. But now, with Mark's arms around her, she felt them healing.

"What shall we do on this glorious autumn day?"

"Let's just be here, together."

Mark joined her in bed.

The telephone rang at noon. Megan rolled over in bed and picked up the old-fashioned ivory and gold receiver.

"Hi, Megan. It's Margaret. We've been expecting you. Are you all right?"

Megan had planned to spend the weekend in the country with Margaret and Ian and Stephanie.

"I was ill last night. I finally fell asleep very late. I'm still in bed. I'm sorry, Margaret. I don't think I'll make it this weekend." Megan glanced up. Jake stood in the doorway.

"Tell Ian," he whispered. Megan shook her head emphatically.

"Is there anything we can do?"

"No, thank you. It's just a flu. Give Stephie a hug for me, will you?"

Megan hung up the phone slowly, thoughtfully.

"I'm sorry about what I said to you last night. You of all people." Megan's eyes filled with tears.

"I don't understand why you did it," Jake said quietly.

"I didn't know what I was saying."

There was a long silence. Jake thought about what to say next. He had seen the distrust in her eyes. Jake believed that Megan had been truly devastated by what had happened, and very frightened. But he also knew, well, Megan the actress and her love of theatre.

"You weren't totally confused. You remembered not to let Carrie see your scar." Jake wasn't going to let her off; she had to know that she had hurt him.

"Why are you doing this to me?"

"Why did you do that to me? It was cruel and unnecessary."

Megan stopped crying and looked seriously at him. What would she do if she lost Jake? Why had she attacked him? She tried to find the answer.

Finally, she said, "I don't know why I said it. I was angry and frightened. And for the first time in my life, my instincts about a man had betrayed me. I trusted Alec. Jake, I was very attracted to him. And I was so wrong about him. I guess I was just doubting myself, wondering if I was wrong about my friends as well." Megan spoke slowly, honestly.

"Like me."

"I guess. I really don't know. Except that I would give anything to take it back. Please forgive me, can you?"

"I can try," he answered flatly. "You provoke men, Megan. You say things, maybe without even thinking . . . You have a talent for unleashing rage."

Megan's eyes widened. Perhaps it was true. Megan thought of Stephen and Ian and now Jake. But it was unintentional! Surely, Jake knew that. Then she realized that Jake was talking about Alec.

"I did not provoke Alec!" The distrust was returning to her eyes.

"Darling, he assaulted you. A vicious, brutal assault. I'm not saying that any provocation justifies what he did. It doesn't. But he didn't just do this out of the blue."

"But he did, Jake. I told you. I was attracted to him. I wanted to make love with him."

"Was he drunk?"

"No, I don't think so. He just became mean, without warning. I couldn't reason with him. He was out of control."

How dangerous is he? Jake wondered. Megan's fear, as she spoke about Alec, was obvious. Megan was experienced sexually. What Alec had done to her was humiliating and painful, but Megan's usual reaction would be anger, not fear. And Megan was still very afraid.

"I want you to call Ian, now, Megan. Tell him what happened."

Jake was in control. Megan couldn't stand having him angry with her.

She reached for the phone. Before she lifted the receiver, it rang.

"Reprieve." She smiled at Jake. "Hello?"

"Megan. Good morning."

"How dare you!" Megan's face drained of color; her hands began to tremble.

"I always call to thank women after a date." Alec's voice was velvet smooth.

"Even when you've beaten and raped them?"

"Those are ugly accusations, Megan." The velvet was gone.

"Not as ugly as the facts."

"You're boring me with your pettiness. I'll see you at the theater on Monday. Remember, it all has to be perfect this week." It was a warning. As Megan hung up, she knew that she couldn't face him. Not Monday. Not ever.

Without looking at Jake, Megan dialed Ian's telephone number. Ian insisted on driving to New York to see her that night. He would leave as soon as Stephanie went to bed.

Carrie telephoned at four. Jake answered.

"I'm answering the phone," he explained quickly. "Alec called earlier."

"What unbelievable nerve!"

"He may have wanted to know whether to worry."

"And?"

"Megan said enough to make him nervous. He may call back to see if there is any substance to what she said."

"Which there isn't, without the police."

"Ian knows."

"Good."

Silence.

"Can I speak with her?" Carrie asked finally.

387

"Oh. She's showering, again. Shall I have her call you?"

"No. Only if she wants to."

Ian arrived at nine. He saw Megan's swollen, bruised face and put his arms around her. He didn't realize how much his embrace hurt her, physically. She didn't flinch because she needed his support.

"Something to drink, Ian?" Jake asked.

"Anything."

"Jake made me call you," Megan began. She had already told him that on the phone. But she hadn't told him the next part. "Jake was right. You need to know. I can't work with Alec any more."

Ian didn't look surprised, just serious.

"Why in God's name did you go out with him?" Ian roared. Ian always roared; it was from being a director. Megan often teased him about it, but not tonight.

"Why not?" she roared back. "I assume if you'd known your genius director was a sexual deviant and a murderer, you wouldn't have hired him. Or at least you would have warned me!"

Ian blinked and squinted his eyes.

What is he remembering, Jake wondered. *Something.* Something buried deep. It made Jake nervous.

"You're both under contract," Ian said slowly, trying to solve the problem that tugged at his memory while at the same time focusing on the problem at hand. "Alec's contract goes through the first two weeks of performances, with an option for renewal. Of course, I could take over then. That's three weeks from now. Your contract is for eight months."

"What are you saying?" Megan demanded.

"I can't fire Alec."

"Let me guess—he hasn't done anything wrong."

"He hasn't broken his contract. And we don't have any evidence to prove wrongdoing," Ian said evenly.

"Look at me! Look at my face! What more evidence do you want?" Megan hissed.

"You know what I mean."

"I know that for some reason you and Jake think this is no big deal. And that it's my fault."

Ian looked accusingly at Jake.

"Neither of us believes that, Megan," Jake said.

"But you both act so skeptical."

"It is just hard to imagine why Alec would do something as stupid as this. To you. Now. It's insane."

"I think insane just about sums it up," Megan said. The realization was not comforting.

The three sat uneasily for a few moments.

"Okay, Ian. I'll put you out of your misery. You don't have to fire your precious director. I will quit. Find yourself another lead."

"If you quit, I'll sue you for breach of contract," Ian replied calmly.

"What do you want me to do?" Megan asked helplessly. There was no solution.

Ian held his head in his hands for a few moments. It was a familiar pose; it meant he was making a decision.

"I want to meet with you and Alec, together. To talk this over."

"What's the point?"

"A lot of points. Mostly, he'll know that I'm watching him if we have to go on for the next three weeks."

Megan finally, reluctantly, agreed to the meeting.

"But I want Jake to be there," she said.

"No!" Ian bellowed. He was hurt. He would be there to protect Megan. Jake was not needed.

Monday morning, Alec and Ian arrived at the theater simultaneously.

"Megan won't be here today. I want you at my apartment at noon. You, Megan, and I need to discuss the situation."

389

"The situation?"

"You know what I'm talking about."

Alec muttered something under his breath.

Ian leased an apartment in the city. He stayed there often during the week, when the rehearsal schedule was heavy. He always spent the weekends with Margaret and Stephanie at his estate, Pinehaven, in Connecticut.

It was noon, but there was no food. It was not a social occasion. It was business. Serious business.

Megan sat on the far end of the sofa, her legs curled under her. The bruises on her face were yellow and purple. The swelling had diminished with constant icing.

"Hello, Megan." Alec stared into her eyes, amused, and smiled. "Haven't you ever heard of makeup?"

"Cover-up, you mean."

Alec looked at Ian and shook his head.

"I assume we're here because Megan is behaving like a *prima donna* about our date."

"Megan says that you beat and raped her. The beating is obvious," Ian said evenly, watching Alec intently.

"Am I allowed to speak directly to the injured party?" Alec's tone conveyed amusement and mild annoyance, like dealing with a spoiled but charming child. There was no trace of fear, guilt, or remorse.

Ian nodded. Megan reflexively curled more tightly into the corner of the sofa.

"Did you—at any time—want to make love with me Friday night?"

"Yes, but . . ."

"Answer the question," Alec directed.

"Yes."

Alec raised an eyebrow at Ian and assumed an expression that said, clearly, I rest my case. Ian looked unconvinced, so Alec continued.

"This is a style question, Ian. I like to have sex one way. Megan, apparently, likes it another. I admit to having misjudged Megan. I expected her to be a bit more . . . sophisticated. I admit I was a bit rough. Some women like that. In fact, most do. Even Megan might, in time."

Alec paused. He had their attention.

"But the point is this: Megan wanted to have sex with me. We had sex. We played by my rules. Next time, we'll do it Megan's way. And I promise you, I won't cry rape."

Ian was glad the police hadn't been called. Megan would have been destroyed in court.

"You bastard," Megan whispered.

"Megan isn't comfortable working with you anymore," Ian said.

"Well, it's short notice, but I think the understudy could fill in. What a career break for her!" He paused, then said significantly, "I plan to honor my contract."

Ian waited. Megan fought back tears but said nothing. Alec looked impatiently at his watch.

"All right," Ian said finally. "We open in one week. And Alec will continue to direct for the first two weeks. May we have peace and professionalism for the next three weeks?

To Megan it sounded like: can you be good children?

"Alec?"

"Of course. As always."

"Megan?"

If she nodded, only Ian saw it. But he accepted her silence as agreement.

"Good. Megan will return to work on Wednesday."

"Ian, we open Saturday." Alec was annoyed.

"I know that, Alec."

After Alec left, Ian sat beside Megan on the couch.

"Do you want some lunch?"

"I hate you. You betrayed me. You didn't defend me for one second. I expect you and Alec will have a good laugh over this one. Silly Megan, can't take a little good sex! Doesn't even think rape is funny!" The bitterness in Megan's voice made Ian cringe.

"You know I love you with all my heart, Megan. Like a

daughter." More than a daughter, Ian thought, but that was *his* problem. "I've given it a lot of thought."

His plan, when he had left Megan's Saturday night, was to fire Alec. Grounds or no grounds, contract or not, Ian had the power to ruin Alec's career forever. Ian could force Alec to leave the play, no questions asked.

But, on Sunday, he had remembered. The memory had nagged and finally come clear. It had been a small thing. No one had even talked about it. In fact, he only knew because he read the newspaper compulsively and didn't miss small items buried toward the end. And he had remembered because he had a photographic memory.

It was an off-off-Broadway production. Two years ago. An unknown actress, but the lead, had been murdered. Ian recalled the specific words: brutally beaten, sexually molested, sodomized. Ian remembered the name of the production, *A Small Black Kitten*. He had seen that name again, recently. It was on Alec's *curriculum vitae*. Ian double-checked to be certain. Alec had been the director.

Of course, there had been nothing to suggest that Alec had been involved. If he had even been a suspect, Ian would have known. That sort of gossip—true or unfounded—spread quickly and thoroughly, especially since, even then, Alec was recognized as a talented new director. But it had worried Ian anyway.

"I think he's a very dangerous man, Megan. I can't prove it. Neither of us can. But we both believe it. I think it is safest not to provoke him. You must try . . . No, Megan, you must succeed for the next three weeks. Will you?"

Megan nodded. "You believe that he wanted to kill me?"

"I think it's possible. Promise me that you will never be alone with him. *Ever.*"

"I won't."

"I'll be with you at the theater every day and for all the performances. I'll take you home each night. Perhaps I should stay with you . . ."

Megan smiled and touched his cheek.

"You are a dear. The security in our building really is impenetrable. I'll be fine." Jake had already moved in. Megan didn't think Ian needed to know that.

Despite her accusations that neither Jake nor Ian took the situation seriously, their behavior proved otherwise.

Rainstorm was an instant success. The opening night review in *The Times* projected Tonys for Best Actress, Best Director, and Best Play. The three weeks passed without incident, as if that night had never happened.

After the final performance under Alec's direction, Alec approached Megan.

"Would you like to go out for a drink, for old times' sake?"

Megan smiled sweetly and declined.

Alec seemed unperturbed. The next day he flew to London to begin a new production. His success with *Rainstorm* had resulted in numerous job offers. He was recognized as a great talent.

The night he left, Jake, Megan, Ian, and Margaret celebrated Alec's departure and the play's success with an elegant dinner at Sardi's.

Chapter Twenty-four

"How are the twins?"

For the year and half since their birth, John always began his calls with that question. In the middle of the conversation he would ask, casually, "How are you, Beth?" He never asked about Stephen.

Beth and John spoke to each other every week. They always spoke on Wednesday morning. It was one of the times that Beth set aside for BethStar, which she and John continued to manage together, despite the three thousand mile separation.

John always asked Beth about the twins, because he loved to hear the softness in her voice when she talked about them. Every week she would proudly report a new milestones—a smile, a tooth, a step, a word. It was a softness in Beth reserved for her baby sons. That voice, and the emotion it expressed, had been born the day that they were.

John always pressed her for every detail about them. Too quickly their conversation would shift to business and Beth would change into a shrewd, calculating businesswoman.

"They are incredible, John! Little miracles. Every day something new. Did you get the pictures I sent?"

Beth enclosed photographs with every piece of correspondence that she sent to John. Mixed in with sheets of "ideas for future software," cost analysis calculations, reactions to ideas he had sent her, were wonderful color photographs with descriptions written by her on the back. *Jamie understands relativity, age 16 months; Robbie's first football.*

They were identical twins. Robert was two minutes older than James. They had totally different personalities. Jamie was thoughtful, cautious, careful, like Beth. Robbie was all action, eager, energetic, like Stephen. They had curly brown-black hair and green eyes. They were beautiful, happy babies.

"Yes. I got the pictures. They look exactly like you." Beautiful, intelligent.

Beth laughed.

This is a good time to tell her, John thought.

"Beth, I think we should move BethStar to the East Coast."

"Really. Why?"

"First, now that we're going into marketing, I think we need to be there. Second, I think you and I need to be able to meet regularly. This long-distance brainstorming isn't as creative or innovative as we need to be. We're not the only toy on the block, you know."

"But you don't want to leave Palo Alto."

"It doesn't matter. This is more important. In fact, necessary."

"We did get a lot accomplished sitting on that old mattress in the gardener's cottage, didn't we?"

"Yes." He was glad that he hadn't had to remind her.

"So, does that mean you're moving to Boston?"

"It makes sense. Where do you think I would like to live?"

"How should . . . no, wait. I think you'd like the Cape. A nice beach cottage. Lovely scenery, privacy. Rustic, but expensive."

"Sounds perfect."

Beth was glad that John had decided to move to Boston. It would be nice to see him again. Although they spoke on the telephone frequently, Beth had not seen John since before her marriage to Stephen. Prior to that, for the first year after she had left Stanford, Beth had accompanied John to important meetings—in Chicago, Denver, Dallas, Los Angeles, and New York—with marketing analysts, software manufacturers, and wholesale distributors. They had made an effective team; John's enthusiasm, his ability to promote and sell their computers had been balanced nicely by Beth's shrewd business sense.

John was right. They needed to be able to discuss ideas, to brainstorm.

Having BethStar, and John, only two hours away would add the perfect touch to Beth's already perfect life. Beth thought about the past three and a half years of her life—her move to Boston that June after graduation, the careful rebuilding of her relationship with Stephen, the challenge of the PhD program in aerophysics at Harvard, Stephen's marriage proposal that December, their lovely wedding the following August, their honeymoon in Barbados, her pregnancy. . . .

Beth had become pregnant in November, three months after their wedding. Stephen had told her he wanted children. There was no rush to start their family, but there was no reason to wait, either. They decided not to use birth control, to, simply, let nature take its course. Beth had no idea she would get pregnant so quickly. In fact, Beth was certain that "nature" would somehow see to it that she never got pregnant, because of the kind of mother she would be. Or wouldn't be.

Beth was afraid of becoming a mother, afraid that her perfectionism, her intolerance of clutter and turmoil, her inability to indulge in make-believe, to pretend, would make her a cold, impersonal, unloving mother.

Stephen was thrilled by the news of Beth's pregnancy; Beth was frightened by it.

As her pregnancy progressed, as she felt the babies grow and move inside her, Beth felt herself changing. But, was it only wishful thinking? Was she changing? Could she change?

Beth really didn't know until the first moment she held her tiny warm infant boys to her breasts. Then she knew. She could be, would be, a wonderful mother to her precious little sons.

Two weeks after the twins were born, Beth notified the aerophysics department that her three-month maternity leave would be extended, indefinitely. Her PhD dissertation could wait, would have to wait. Nothing was important to Beth except being with her baby boys and her loving, delighted husband.

Stephen was a loving husband, a devoted father, and a trusted companion. His sexual attraction to Beth was strong before, during—he told her repeatedly, proudly, how beautiful she was, pregnant with their twins—and after Beth's pregnancy. Stephen enjoyed being with Beth—making love to her, playing with their children, talking to her. Beth's agile, analytical mind, her sense of humor, the range of what Beth knew, perpetually intrigued Stephen. He valued her opinions.

Beth and Stephen talked about everything—openly and honestly. Everything except Megan. They never discussed Megan, or the hiatus in their relationship caused by Stephen's affair with Megan. There was no point. Beth knew Stephen loved her. She didn't need to test it. She didn't need to hear him say that he loved her more than he had ever loved Megan. Beth knew he couldn't say that. But Beth knew he loved her deeply and truly, even if differently from the way he had loved Megan.

It was enough. It was plenty. Beth's world was perfect.

Stephen's life was happy and stimulating. He loved his wife and his sons. His job was challenging and fulfilling. Stephen didn't think, much, about the past. He focused on the peace and happiness of the present.

Stephen worked very hard; his job, with one of Boston's top legal firms, demanded it. Stephen's expertise in contract law, his remarkable success in negotiating difficult corporate mergers, quickly earned him partner status in the firm. It was obvious that Stephen's success, and the demands it placed on him, could monopolize his life, if he let it. Stephen made a vow to himself and to Beth: there would be time for his family. He would make time—protected, inviolate time—every evening between six and eight and all day Sunday. Stephen kept his vow, even though it meant that sometimes he stayed up working most of the night.

When the twins were one year old, Stephen and Beth moved from their modest apartment in Cambridge, to a roomy, renovated townhouse with a small, private garden, on Beacon Street. While she was unpacking boxes that had been sealed since her move from Stanford to Boston three years before, Beth discovered a copy of the eighteen-page legal contract between herself and John, the contract that symbolized the birth of BethStar.

Beth smiled, remembering how thrilled and surprised John had been.

She showed the contract to Stephen.

"What do you think of this, counselor?" she asked, smiling.

Beth watched Stephen as he read the contract. He frowned. Then he shook his head in disbelief.

"You gave John Taylor one hundred thousand dollars," Stephen said quietly, realizing how little he knew about Beth's "company" or its president, John Taylor.

"I lent John the money," she said.

Stephen arched an eyebrow.

"Okay," she admitted, laughing. "Okay, I gave it to him."

The contract that Beth had convinced two skeptical attorneys to write did not contain a penalty clause. John could have done whatever he wanted with the money, including losing it all, and Beth would have had no recourse. Beth had known it. The attorneys had known it—hers and the ones she had hired for John—and, now, Stephen knew it.

Beth wondered if John had ever known it. If he had ever even read the fine print.

It didn't matter anymore. BethStar was a tremendous success. John had already repaid the initial investment and he and Beth were sharing the not-inconsiderable profits.

"Why? Why did you just give it to him?"

"It was an investment, an investment in something I believed in, something I could be part of. It really wasn't as much a gamble as investing the same money in offshore oil leases, which is what my father wanted me to do," Beth said, almost defensively.

"It's such a lot of money," Stephen replied thoughtfully.

Beth's wealth was staggering. It made them both uncomfortable. Beth knew that Stephen wanted to, and could, provide for his family. He didn't want to use Beth's money. It remained in her name, managed by financial advisors in Houston, except for the profits from BethStar. Those went into trust funds for the twins.

"I know, Stephen. But it has been a very good investment already and it has a spectacular future."

Stephen was silent for a few moments. Beth wondered what he was thinking. She wished she hadn't shown him the contract. She had thought he would simply have been amused to see what a terribly unorthodox contract it was. She hadn't thought about the money when she showed it to him.

"How well did you know John when you gave him the money?" Stephen asked finally. He had never even met John.

Not well, Beth thought, but said, "Well enough to feel comfortable about doing it."

"What's he like?" Stephen asked. It was a question he had never even considered asking before.

Beth looked blank.

"John? I don't know. He's a genius, I guess. A kind of genius with no business sense." It was the best Beth could do. She had never thought about it. John was John.

"I'd like to meet him," Stephen said.

"Why?" Beth asked, surprised. She couldn't imagine that John and Stephen would have anything to say to each other. They had nothing in common. She remembered John's inexplicably hostile and inaccurate comment about Stephen, whom he had never met: "a dumb jock."

"Curious, I guess," Stephen said.

Six months later, when Beth told Stephen that John planned to move BethStar to Boston, Stephen said, "Finally I'll get to meet him. Good."

"I don't want a party in my honor!" Megan said.

"But you're the one who won the Tony. Besides, Ian and Margaret really want to do this. It gives them a reason to have a party at Pinehaven in the spring." Jake smiled at Megan and shook his head. "If you are going to be famous—and there's no turning back from that now—you have to graciously accept the celebrity expectations."

"But I want to be famous for me. It's my accomplishment."

"But they make you famous."

"You win, you win," she said, laughing.

As the weekend approached, the idea of the party appealed to her. Megan looked forward to a weekend in the country with her friends. A weekend with wonderful meals, tennis, horseback riding, long walks through the springtime gardens; a weekend of laughter and escape from the work and the city. Time with Stephanie.

When Megan thought about Stephanie, which she did often, it made her happy. Stephanie had the kind of childhood a beautiful little girl should have—the kind of childhood Megan herself had had, until her mother left her. Stephanie had loving, interested, devoted parents. Stephanie's life was free and untroubled. She would never have to worry about being abandoned or forgotten. Stephanie was loved. It made Megan happy. She always looked forward to the weekends at Pinehaven.

Megan and Carrie shopped together for Megan's clothes for the weekend. Once Megan got into the spirit of the party, she decided that an entire new wardrobe was in order. They took a shopping break for lunch at the Plaza.

"Will Jake be going with you?" Carrie asked casually.

Megan squinted her eyes. "As my date? I don't know. In the same car? Probably. Unless he's taking someone . . . Why? Do you care?"

"Not really." That she still even cared enough to ask annoyed her. She and Mark were happy. It was mostly curiosity, she told herself and Megan. "Just curious. I guess I am still trying to figure out what makes Jake tick."

"Don't waste your time. You two are my best friends in the world. And I don't begin to understand either of you. I think I understand parts of him, but when I try to put the parts together, they don't add up to Jake. There are missing pieces." Megan's voice was soft, loving, when she spoke of Jake. Her dear, trusted friend.

"Does he date?"

"Date? That's sort of an archaic term. Jake has a lot of women—all smart and all beautiful. Corporate types he meets through his company—lawyers, business executives, architects, computer programmers. He's quite a catch. Handsome, rich, powerful and sex . . ." Megan looked at Carrie. For years she had been so careful about discussing Jake with Carrie. But they were older now. So much had happened. Carrie was living with Mark, in love with Mark. No need to protect Carrie any longer. "Sexual, sensual."

"Sensual?"

"I think so. He lives through his senses, but he has too much control to really be a hedonist. But he loves fine food, fine music, fine alcohol, fine sex. But he doesn't allow himself to drink much, or smoke, or overeat. So . . ."

"Sex is his main release?"

"I guess so," Megan said. He certainly enjoys it, the art of it, the feel of it, the beauty of it.

"Does he have anyone special?"

"No. Safety in numbers, I guess. I think Jake transmits a fairly clear message that he is not looking for involvement."

"What about his leg?" Carrie asked.

"His leg?" Megan looked startled. She hardly thought about Jake's leg anymore. Then she looked curious. How did Carrie know? "His leg is a conversation piece, that's all. Nothing to dwell on. Nothing that matters. He told you about it?"

"Yes," Carrie said softly. Nothing that matters to Jake or his beautiful, sexual women.

"I'm surprised."

"Why?"

"Because he always wanted to protect you, and Stephen, from anything that wasn't perfect. Especially something that was unpleasant or ugly. He never told Stephen, you know." And Megan hadn't told Stephen either. Stephen . . .

Carrie paused a beat. She had gone this far. "What about you and Jake? Do you make love with him?" Carrie knew the answer.

"Carrie, you've really got this interview technique down, don't you? Yes. Sometimes Jake and I make love." Megan didn't make love with anyone except Jake. She remembered how, carefully, gently, he had brought her back to life after the incident with Alec. Night after night, he stayed with her, held her, and, when she was ready, made love with her.

"Do you love him?"

"Of course I love Jake, like I love you. A dear, cherished friend. But we're not *in love.*"

"Maybe he's in love with you." Why am I doing this? Carrie wondered.

"I know he's not. I don't know if Jake could ever be 'in love.' It could be because of his control, or it could be that he was in love once and was terribly hurt. Anyway, I don't think he's the 'in love' type."

"What about you, Megan? Are you going to fall in love"—Carrie paused—"again?"

"No," Megan said seriously. "I think my relationship with your brother cured me of that!" Megan looked down at her food. She didn't want to discuss Stephen with Carrie. Carrie had never really forgiven her. And Megan was afraid that someday Carrie would force her to tell her the truth. "Enough about me! What about you and Mark?"

Carrie smiled. "We're happy. In fact, we plan to be married."

"Really? Congratulations! When did this come about?"

"He gave me the engagement ring night before last. I was surprised."

"Where's the ring?"

"At the jeweler's, being sized. But I'll have it for the party this weekend."

"I still can't believe you aren't bringing anyone, Jake." Megan gave Jake a sidelong glance as they drove to Pinehaven.

"I'm bringing you."

"No. There's something more. You are acting mysterious."

"I told Ian that I would help him play host. Besides, if Ian has anything to do with it, the place will be teeming with beautiful, unaccompanied women."

"And men. He does that for us, you know. Ian is a born matchmaker. He's finally given up on you and me as 'the' couple, so he's trying to find mates for each of us."

"Admirable of him."

"But futile."

Jake drove in silence.

* * *

The guests started arriving at seven Friday evening. They drank champagne and feasted at the hot buffet dinner that was ever-replenished throughout the evening.

Carrie and Mark arrived at nine.

"Congratulations, Mark," Megan greeted them at the front door.

"Thank you. Same to you" Mark waved at Ian, who beckoned to Mark to join him. Mark kissed Carrie briefly and worked his way through the crowd.

"Let me see the ring," Megan whispered.

Carrie blushed, extended her left hand, and glanced uneasily at Jake, who had joined them. He looked bewildered, then comprehending, then interested.

It was a ring of diamonds and sapphires set in eighteen carat gold. It had obviously been especially designed for Carrie—delicate and elegant. Megan thought it was perfect and said so.

"I think it's perfect, too," Carrie said, her sapphire blue eyes sparkling.

"Congratulations. It's a beautiful ring," Jake said, then added, softly, almost to himself, "I always thought you would just want a plain gold band."

Carrie heard it and Megan heard it. Carrie withdrew her hand and clenched her fist until her knuckles turned white. She was trying to control the anger and the aching and the pounding of her heart.

"You don't have to try to make me hate you anymore. You succeeded at that a long time ago." Carrie, white with rage, rushed past him, through the living room, to the antique French door that led to the garden. She had to get out.

Megan stared at Jake, bewildered. Clearly she had missed a few chapters in the saga of Jake and Carrie. Megan had never seen Carrie so angry. And she had never before heard that soft tone of voice from Jake.

Jake looked at her, helpless, confused.

"What happened?"

"Don't ask me. But I don't think Carrie just made it up. What games are you playing anyway, Jake?"

He looked at Megan, then turned to follow Carrie.

Carrie stood at the end of the dock on the small lake. It was a perfect spring night: full moon, balmy air perfumed with lilacs, the melody of busy crickets. The scene was reminiscent of that day in Houston. The world was perfect, but their world was a shambles.

Jake approached her slowly. Carrie was staring at the shimmering moonlight reflected off the softly windblown lake.

"Caroline, I am sorry."

Carrie spun around. She looked straight into his eyes. Hers were tear free and angry.

"Don't call me Caroline! Don't tell me you're sorry anymore. And don't pretend that you didn't mean it."

"I didn't mean to make you angry."

"No, I suppose you didn't expect anger. I suppose you meant to see if you could still hurt me, make me sad. Well, you've lost your touch." Carrie laughed bitterly.

"It was a careless comment," Jake admitted hastily.

"Brought to me by the man who negotiated the most celebrated Middle East peace treaty in history. The man whose great value is that he only makes careful, considered, well-planned statements. No, Jake, words don't slip carelessly from your lips."

"This time they did." He hated the way she was looking at him. "Caroline, please . . ."

"Don't call me Caroline," she repeated instantly. "For years I believed you called me that because you thought I was special. And that made *us* special. But we're not special, Jake. We never were."

"Have you forgotten the promise we made?"

"The promise I made to a man who thought he was going to die? No, I haven't forgotten. You came back, Jake, healthy, alive. You came back to Julia and Megan and a lot of other women. But you didn't come back to me."

"I told you I wouldn't."

"And I didn't believe you. Because even then I knew that people who love each other make plans to be together, no matter what." Carrie looked down thoughtfully at her engagement ring. It reflected the springtime moonlight. "People who love each other don't stay apart in the name of love."

"I thought you understood," Jake whispered.

"I do understand. Now, after all these years, I understand that I was the naive idealist everyone accused me of being. An innocent believer in love and trust and honesty." Carrie stopped abruptly.

When she spoke again, Carrie's voice had a bitterness that made Jake ache.

"That must have been a terrible four days for you, Jake. Someone of your experience trapped with a wide-eyed virgin. I didn't know, then, about giving pleasure, or having it. It must have been awfully boring for you. Maybe, at least, an amusing anecdote for Julia."

Meaning that she had learned from Mark about love and sex and pleasure. Things that she hadn't learned from Jake. Jake seethed with self-recrimination. *What have I done to her? So much bitterness. So much hatred.*

"Carol . . . Carrie. Those four days were wonderful. Perfect. Don't you remember?" he pleaded gently. *The four happiest days of my life,* he thought. A happy memory that had sustained him, nurtured him, for those months in the Middle East. It was a memory that had continued to sustain him, until now. What had made the memory so lovely was knowing that Carrie shared it, too, and that they would have it, always.

And now, Carrie denounced it. It was a sham. The memory was bitter.

Carrie didn't speak. She had thrown away all the memories one by one. On a dreary February evening, she had burned all the letters she had written to him but had never shown him. Then, the postcards and letters he had sent to her from all over the world. Finally, she had thrown the matchbooks she had saved from the restaurants where they had "dined" into the fireplace. The next day, Carrie had returned the gold necklace to its original box and had put it in a safe deposit box, all but forgotten.

But the hardest memory to relinquish had been the memory of those days in February, two years before. It hadn't mattered, then, that she was a virgin, technically unskilled at lovemaking, because Jake had been so gentle, so delighted that she was his alone. Carrie had had to force herself to forget that despite her love and affection for Mark, what she had felt then with Jake remained unsurpassed. But it was all an illusion, she told herself. A time and a memory to be discarded, forever.

Because if he loved me, he would have come back to me, Carrie reminded herself often.

Carrie looked at Jake. She had never seen him look so hurt or so helpless. For a moment, she almost relented. But the bad memories were too strong.

Why does he do this to me? Her anger returned.

"Did you buy me a wedding band?" she whispered.

"Yes," he admitted reluctantly, painfully.

"When?" Carrie was drenched in sadness; tears were threatening.

"In Amsterdam, that autumn."

Carrie remembered the card he had sent her from Amsterdam, the card, long since burned, but the words etched indelibly in her memory: *Dearest Caroline, In Amsterdam. Thinking of you. And us. Love, Jake.* That was the gift he had bought for her. The gift he would have given her that night in January had she still been in Palo Alto. The gift that, somehow, had been stolen, with the dream. If only . . .

"What happened?" Her voice was shaking. He had refused to tell her before what had happened in Cambodia.

"Too much. Too much ugliness. Too much to make the gap between us bridgeable." He wasn't going to tell her.

"More murders?" Carrie hissed.

She saw the pain in Jake's eyes. Where did I learn this cruelty? The answer came to her swiftly—from Jake. I learned it from Jake.

"My God, I hate you," she said.

Carrie turned and walked toward the shore. Jake didn't try to follow her. When she reached the house, a man emerged from the shadows. Mark. They didn't speak, but he put his arm around her, held her, then guided her back to the house.

Jake trembled with anger, grief, horror, all directed at himself. His damned foolishness for ever thinking, even for a moment, that he and Carrie could have a future. If he had only had the strength to leave her alone, from the beginning. She would have been spared the pain. And he would have missed the joy of the cherished moments that they had shared. And now, he, too, would have been spared the pain and remorse.

Why *had* he mentioned the ring? Careless, stupid nostalgia. A sentimental thought spoken aloud. If only he had kept the thought to himself. As Carrie said, he didn't make careless remarks. Why had he slipped this time?

"Jake?"

Megan's voice interrupted his thoughts. For a moment he stared at her, vaguely.

"What happened between you and Carrie?"

"A terrible misunderstanding. I have to try to explain it to her." He would tell her everything. About Cambodia. The dead captain. Her ring. His dreams. Then she would understand.

"She and Mark have gone. She seemed awfully upset." Megan looked at him. His eyes looked wet. Was it possible?

"So do you."

"It doesn't really matter, does it?" he asked flatly. It was just as well that Carrie had left. Even if he told her everything, she would never understand. The only thing he could do for her now was to leave her alone. Forever.

Megan and Jake walked in silence back to the house.

Megan rested her hand on Jake's shoulder. The lights from the house hurt Jake's eyes, but the party jogged another memory. He glanced at his watch—ten-thirty. Maybe he wouldn't come. It would probably be best. Jake had caused enough misery in the name of love for one night.

The door bell rang. Jake went with Megan to answer the door.

Stephen.

"I'm sorry I'm late. I had a meeting with some clients in New York. It ran pretty late. Congratulations, Megan. These are for you."

Stephen handed a shocked but smiling Megan a bouquet of white roses and forget-me-nots.

"Thank you. They're lovely. I'll just find a vase for them." Megan vanished, trembling, into the kitchen.

"How are you, Jake? You look tired."

"Long day." Jake had almost said, Long day's journey into night. That's what Caroline had said to him that night eight months ago. Caroline. Carrie. "You look good."

"I am good. Happy to be here." Stephen glanced beyond Jake toward the kitchen door.

"Why don't you go help her? She probably has no idea . . ."

Stephen nodded and moved toward the kitchen before Jake could finish his sentence.

Megan sat at the carved oak kitchen table in the huge, cheery country kitchen. The bouquet lay on the table. She held her head in her hands.

"Megan?"

She looked up at him and he knew, instantly. She had not invited him. She had had no idea that he would be there.

"Oh." He sat down across from her, a bit deflated but still smiling.

Megan smiled, a somewhat shaky smile. She hadn't seen him since the wedding, almost three years. He looked older, more serious, dignified, in his three-piece grey suit. But his green eyes twinkled. He was so pleased to see her. He had been thrilled to get the invitation. It had been delivered to his office and addressed to him, only. Beth had been excluded; it seemed like something Megan would do.

"Your friend Jake . . ." Megan said.

"I'm afraid so. I'm sorry, Megan." The disappointment in his voice was obvious.

"I'm not. These are lovely flowers, Stephen," she said softly.

"I'm not in trouble for the forget-me-nots?"

"No!" Megan laughed. *Why am I trembling?* "Of course not. I should try to find a vase."

"I'll help."

They opened and closed cupboard doors in the cheery blue and white country kitchen with the red brick floor. Megan found a crystal pitcher.

"They'll be perfect in this."

Megan set the flowers in the middle of the table.

"Do you want something to drink?"

Before Stephen answered, they were interrupted by the sound of cocker spaniel paws on the brick floor. Gwendolyn was followed, slowly, by a sleepy-eyed child with black curly hair and huge blue eyes.

Megan held her breath.

Stephen laughed.

"Who's this?" he asked, patting Gwendolyn as she put her paws on his legs. "And who are you?" he asked of the little girl as she crossed the kitchen and cuddled into Megan's lap.

"This is Gwendolyn. Would you let her out? And this . . ." *Calm yourself.* "This is Stephanie."

"Hello, Stephanie."

The child curled against Megan and smiled tentatively at Stephen.

"Stephanie, this is Uncle Stephen." Megan raised her eyebrows questioningly at Stephen. Stephanie had a string of uncles and aunts: Uncle Jake, Uncle Mark, Aunt Megan, Aunt Carrie.

410

"Hello Stephanie," Stephen said again.

"Hello Uncle Stephen." Stephanie giggled. She was waking up.

"I thought you and Gwendolyn were asleep, little one." Megan's voice was gentle, loving.

Stephanie nodded.

"What happened? Was it too noisy to sleep?" Megan winked at Stephen.

Stephanie considered this, then nodded vigorously.

"And Gwendolyn was very hungry."

"Really?"

"Uh-huh."

"Are you hungry, too?" Megan asked, then added an explanation for Stephen. "Stephie and 'Dwendolyn' have remarkably similar metabolisms!"

"Yes. I would like a tookie, please, Aunt Meg."

"Okay. Hop down and let's go find one. Want a tookie, Uncle Stephen?"

"Sure."

"And milk? Coffee?"

"Coffee would be great." Stephen moved beside Megan, helping her, talking with Stephanie.

They ate cookies and talked about Stephanie.

"She's gorgeous."

"Yes. Ian and Margaret are very proud. She's also smart. Aren't you, Stephie?"

"How old are you?" Stephen asked.

"This many." She held up four fingers. "But almost this many." She added the thumb.

Gwendolyn returned after ten minutes. Stephanie's energy began to wane. Stephen offered to carry her to her bedroom. They tucked her in. Gwendolyn slept on the bed beside her when Megan visited. In the hallway outside Stephanie's room, Stephen touched Megan lightly on the shoulder.

She was crying.

"What's wrong, honey?"

411

"Nothing. You know me. I cry easily."

"The Megan I knew never cried," Stephen said firmly. That Megan had the world by the tail. She wouldn't waste time even thinking about tears.

"Oh, well. The new Megan cries easily." The Megan that lost you cries easily.

He pulled her gently toward him. To his amazement she moved willingly, closer to him. In another moment she was in his arms, crying soundlessly, her head buried in his chest. Stephen stroked her silky blond hair, smelled her wonderful freshness, and rocked slowly with her.

Finally, with a theatrical sniff she pulled away and dried her eyes. They were no longer touching.

A curious look came over her face—perplexed, then provocative, then confident. The old Megan.

"Do you want to know something, Stefano?" she purred.

"Yes." He held his breath.

"I can't stand being this close to you and not being in your arms."

Stephen held her then and kissed her. Years of passion and desire were released, and all the pain, for the moment, forgotten.

"Megan, I have missed you."

"Hold me!"

"Where can I take you, darling? Where can we be alone?"

Megan led the way to her bedroom.

"I have to say good night to my guests. To tell them I'll see them in the morning. Will you wait?" Megan was afraid to let go of him, afraid to leave him, afraid that he would vanish.

"Yes."

"Promise?"

"Yes."

It took Megan thirty minutes. When she returned, Stephen was there, sitting, fully clothed, as she had left him, on the poster bed.

"You're still here!"

Megan curled instantly into his arms.

They didn't make love; they didn't talk, except to whisper each other's names. They lay, entwined, until dawn. As the earliest rays of the spring sun shined insistently through the lace curtains, Stephen stirred purposefully.

"I have to go."

"No!"

Stephen smiled, sadly. "Yes, my darling, precious forget-me-not."

Stephen left. Confused, happy, sad, celebrating, grieving. He had learned nothing. He had asked nothing.

And he didn't tell her that he loved her.

It had been a dream. As he drove his car into the ever-brightening harshness of the day, the dream became dim—a night mirage; a trick of darkness, vanishing with daylight.

He had a wife, two wonderful sons, and a night of holding Megan. His life and his future were with Beth and the boys. Megan was in his past and in his dreams.

I should have told her that I still love her, he thought as his car sped inevitably home, to Boston, to Beth.

Chapter Twenty-five

In June, two months after the party for Megan, a message was received at the theater box office for Ian. The play was in its ninth month. Ian only attended one or two performances a week. But he made a habit of attending the Saturday night performance. Afterward, he and Megan would drive to Pinehaven to spend Sunday and Monday with Margaret and Stephanie.

The message was urgent. It was from Margaret. It took the usher forty-five minutes to find Ian. He had a habit of pacing during a performance, sometimes backstage, sometimes sidestage, sometimes in the lobby. He telephoned Margaret within a minute of receiving the message.

She answered on the first ring.

"Margaret? What's wrong?"

"Stephanie's gone!" Margaret was crying.

"What do you mean?" he demanded. Gone. Missing? Runaway? Lost? What?

"Someone has taken her."

"Margaret, tell me what happened."

"I took Stephie to the club this afternoon, for her swimming class. She was supposed to have dinner at the Carson's afterward, so Eva Carson said she would pick her up at the club and bring her home after dinner. It was getting late so I called Eva to see if I should come get her."

"And?"

It took Margaret a few moments to speak.

"She never went to the Carsons. After the class she told Susan Carson that she couldn't go to dinner after all. That she was having dinner at home because 'Aunt Megan' would be here."

"My God. Did Susan see anyone? Or Eva?"

"Neither of them saw anyone."

"Have you telephoned the police?"

"I telephoned you. I've been waiting for your call."

Ian heard the applause in the background. End of the first act. It was intermission. Ian made a decision.

"Call the police. Keep them there until I get there. I'll be home in an hour."

Ian knocked lightly on Megan's dressing room door.

"It's Ian."

"Come in! It's going well tonight—" Megan stopped when she saw his reflection in the mirror. She spun around. "What's wrong?"

He took her hands in his and sat down beside her. There were tears in his eyes.

"I think someone has kidnapped Stephie."

"Noooo! No. No. No."

Ian held her for almost five minutes. It had no effect on her tears or her trembling. Then he let go and said, sternly, "Get changed. I'll be right back."

Ian instructed the stage crew to blink the house lights, signaling the end of intermission. It had only been ten minutes, instead of twenty, but no one ever argued with Ian's orders.

"Give me the stage lights."

Ian stood in the center of the stage, an imposing figure with his arms raised for silence. The audience stood, still, silently, in the aisles.

"Ladies and gentlemen. I am Ian Knight. Tonight there will be no second act. I will give you rain checks, or return your money, or both. Believe me, I would give anything not to have to cancel this performance."

There were two police cars in the gravel driveway when Ian and Megan arrived, and a station wagon belonging to the Carsons.

The police officers, Eva and Susan Carson, and Margaret sat in the living room. A silver service of coffee and tea sat on the living room table. The police officers drank carefully from the Limoges china cups.

The officers stood up when Ian and Megan entered.

"They think we should call the FBI—set up surveillance on our phones as soon as possible." Margaret sounded calm, but she was avoiding looking at Megan.

"That's right, sir."

"What if the kidnappers say 'no police'?" Megan asked.

"They always say that, ma'am. But the outcome is much worse if the police and bureau aren't involved; the statistics show it."

"I'm sure you're right," Ian said. He had already made that decision. "How do we get the FBI?"

"We can handle that, sir. If I could use your phone."

The officer made two phone calls.

"An agent will be here by midnight."

"What if we get a call before then?"

"You won't hear from them until morning, at the earliest," the officer answered definitely.

Because whoever it is wants to make us suffer, to make us crazy with worry so we will pay any price, Megan thought. We would pay any price right now.

The police officers left. Eva and Susan left. They had little to add. Except that Susan said that Stephanie seemed fine. And she had the distinct impression that it had been a man who had come to get Stephanie. No, she hadn't seen him.

Ian and Margaret and Megan sat, numbly, in the living

room. After an hour the silence became more oppressive than the waiting.

"I need to let Jake know. He has friends in the FBI."

"Call him."

Megan started to dial Jake's number. Then she depressed the button.

"Damn," she whispered. "He's in Europe."

"Do you know where?"

"No, but he usually leaves an itinerary with me. He usually just puts it on my desk. I suppose he did this time."

"Shall we go get it?"

"No, I'll call Carrie. If she can't get it, I'll see if I can convince the doorman to leave his post." Someone needs to check on Gwendolyn anyway, she thought.

It was eleven-thirty. Mark reached for the phone, but Carrie answered it.

"Megan!" Carrie whispered to him.

Carrie had been on edge since the eleven o'clock news had announced the mysterious canceling of the second act of Broadway's number one play, *Rainstorm,* and the rapid departure of the producer and lead.

"I am so sorry, Megan. What can we do? Okay. Sure. You'll tell the doorman to let us in? Yes, I'll find Jake. We'll take Gwendolyn home with us tonight. I'll bring her to you in the morning. Okay. Call us the minute you hear anything."

Carrie found the itinerary, neatly typed by Jake's secretary:

ITINERARY FOR MR. EASTON
June 21st to June 28th

Carrie glanced down the sheet to find Jake's location for June 24. *June 23-25*: Hotel George V, Paris. The telephone number was provided.

While Mark gathered dog food, toys, and Gwendolyn, Carrie placed the call. It would be six-thirty in the morning in Paris. He should be there.

After fifteen rings to his room, the hotel operator returned to the line.

"Il n'est pas ici maintenant."

"May I leave a message? It is urgent." Carrie hoped the hotel operator could speak English.

"Un moment, madame."

Carrie was transferred to the front desk. The concierge spoke perfect English. He repeated Carrie's message back to her.

"Stephanie has been kidnapped. *Quel dommage, madame!* Please return if possible. Leave message for Carrie Richards at (212) 474-3000." Carrie gave the number of the studio's answering service. She would notify them to contact her as soon as the call came through.

"Do you think we need a dog?" Mark asked, handing the wriggling animal to Carrie while he carried the heavier sacks of food, toys, and blankets.

"I don't want you to cancel your plans to be with Becky and Andrew. Today, of all days, you should be with them."

"I worry about you."

"I know you do. But, basically, I'm going to spend the day chauffeuring. I'll take Gwendolyn up this morning. Then I'll pick Jake up at two-thirty at Kennedy . . ."

"I really don't like that."

"I know. But it's unavoidable. Megan needs him. I want to help Megan if I can. Maybe she'll go with me to meet him."

"You're really more worried about Megan than Margaret or Ian. Stephanie's their little girl, after all."

"Yes. But Stephanie is so important to Megan."

It was nine Sunday morning. There had been no news. The telephone hadn't rung, except to give Carrie the message about Jake's arrival time. It appeared Jake had returned to his hotel shortly after her call.

"I'll call you this evening," Carrie promised. "Or I'll leave a message sooner with the service if there's news."

"All right, darling." Mark hated the thought of Carrie spending the day immersed in the sadness and worry that he knew was consuming Pinehaven. But, more, he hated the thought of her being forced to see Jake Easton. She had made it clear, without giving any details, that it would be best if she never saw him again. And that had been only two months ago.

Carrie arrived at Pinehaven at eleven. She was screened briefly by an FBI agent. He knew that she was expected.

"We don't want the news media to have this story yet, Miss Richards."

Carrie silently communicated her astonishment at his remark and entered the house.

They had not heard from the kidnappers; it was apparent from their faces; palpable strain and fatigue, raw nerves and emotions. They all claimed to have had a little sleep, but Carrie doubted it.

Megan was cheered somewhat by the news that Jake was on his way.

What can Jake do? Carrie wondered. She was amazed that Jake symbolized such hope and power to Megan.

Megan refused to accompany Carrie to the airport. She had to be there when the call came.

Part Eight

Chapter Twenty-six

New York City . . . June, 1977

"Pan American Flight 167 from Paris is now arriving at Gate 34."

Carrie's heart began to race when she heard the announcement. It was the same, uncontrollable feeling she always had when she saw Jake—an excited, eager feeling. But this time, she told herself sternly, surprised by the familiar reaction, her heart didn't race with excitement. This time it pounded, uncomfortably, because of dread and apprehension, and the still-vivid memory of the bitter, hateful words.

As Carrie waited, near the door, but off to the side, away from the rest of the crowd, she remembered that spring evening, only two months ago. And, she remembered other times, happier reunions, unencumbered by pain.

Carrie's mind searched the memories of the past seven years, trying to find the happy ones. There *had* been lovely, happy memories: the first Sunday dinner at Stanford, when she had met him—and fallen in love with him; "dining" together, laughing and talking, at San Francisco's most celebrated restaurants; the evening in Boston, when he had given her the gold necklace and kissed her; the cards and letters from him, from his travels around the world; the telegram from Amsterdam; their weekend that snowy February. . . .

But for every happy memory, Carrie's mind firmly countered with an unhappy one: Jake and Megan; the canceled dinner date; the dreadful, soggy afternoon in the guest house in Houston; Jake and Julia; Jake's secrets; his safe return from the Middle East, but not to her; Megan's patrons' party; and, finally, the angry, hateful words—her words, her anger, her emotions—two months ago. Words that erased the happy memories. Words that should have marked the end, finally. She should never have seen him again.

And now she waited, her heart pounding reflexively, as it always had in anticipation of seeing him. Her mind flooded with memories and questions. Could she, could they, forget the pain and remember the friendship, the moments of happiness, long enough to get through this final ordeal? They had to. One last time. For Megan. For Ian and Margaret. For Stephanie. No matter how difficult it would be for them.

The door from the customs area opened. As Carrie had expected, Jake was the first one through. He looked as if he hadn't slept. Of course, Carrie thought. He was out all night. In Paris, the City of Love. With whom?

It was true that Jake had been awake most of the night, awakened by a nightmare. Unable, unwilling, to try to sleep again, he had gone for a walk. But he couldn't walk far. In the past week that familiar, tearing pain in his leg had returned. The tendon was pulling loose, again. He had spent the night, until sunrise, sitting on the bank of the Seine, across from Notre Dame.

As soon as Carrie saw him, felt the rush of unsummoned emotions, she knew how difficult it would be. He paused at the door, his eyes calmly searching the crowded area for her, finding her almost immediately. He looked at her, over the row of lively children, beyond the eager families and busy tour guides. Their eyes met, and held, tentatively, for a moment.

In that moment, looking across the room into the tired,

worried blue eyes she knew so well, Carrie realized that they could—would—do it. It would be difficult, but they would do it, together. She saw in Jake's eyes an acknowledgment that he knew how hard it would be, for both of them. And she saw a promise that he would try.

Before his eyes left hers, before he started to move toward her, he smiled; a tired, awkward, inquiring smile; a smile that asked a question and required an answer: will you try, too?

Carrie smiled slightly in return, controlling the rush of emotions with difficulty. Yes, she would try.

When Jake reached her, finally, he said gently, "Hello Caroline."

"Hello, Jake," she answered quietly, surprised by the softness in her own voice. And by the control.

"Thank you for coming to meet me," he said, the careful gentleness still in his voice.

He waited a few moments before speaking again. When he did, his voice had hardened slightly as he forced his thoughts away from Carrie, their careful, guarded reunion and their unspoken truce, and onto what had brought them together. He asked, "Any news?"

"No." Then Carrie told Jake all the details that she knew. There weren't many. She was finished by the time they reached her car. She had noticed his slight limp, had slowed her pace to adjust to it, but hadn't mentioned it.

"How's Megan?"

"Terribly upset. Hysterical, really. Almost more upset—"

"Than Ian and Margaret?" Jake completed her sentence.

"Yes. In fact, they seem very worried about Megan."

"Can we stop at my place? I'd like to pick up some things. Phone numbers and so on."

So, he intended to be part of it. He intended to pull strings. Just as Megan had said he would.

"Sure."

* * *

Carrie had never seen Jake's penthouse. She had assumed it would be similar to Megan's. But she was wrong.

Jake's penthouse was a different place—exotic, foreign, mystical—a tasteful potpourri of art objects, rugs, furniture from around the world. It was a home made of the memories and dreams of a man who felt comfortable living anywhere. It was the home of a man who had had to make his own home, his own identity, from scratch.

"Jake, this is wonderful!" For a moment, they were back to happier times. The past years hadn't happened. Carrie lapsed, for an instant, back to the wide-eyed, optimistic girl she had been when they had met.

"I'm glad you like it, Caroline . . . uh . . . Carrie," Jake corrected himself quickly, grimacing slightly as he remembered her words of two months before, prohibiting him from using his special name for her. Because they weren't special. They never had been.

It's yours, he thought. In the will he had written before he left for the Middle East, he had given the penthouse and its contents, with clear title, to Carrie. Jake had no intention of changing his will.

To Carrie, the penthouse was enchanted, full of treasures and beauty and free of the ugly memories. She and Jake had no ugly memories here, because they had never been here, together, before.

But somewhere, in all these treasures, was there, perhaps, a gold wedding band purchased in Amsterdam? He had said it had been stolen, along with the dream, but maybe that was merely a figure of speech. The memories began to return, good and bad, reality and fantasy. Who would she be hurting if she asked to see the ring? Herself. Perhaps both of them. For a moment of indulgence in an old dream.

Carrie started to ask, then stopped.

"What?" he asked quietly.

She shook her head and forced a smile. Her eyes were moist.

"It's very lovely, Jake."

Carrie sat in the rich pastel and cream living room listening to Mozart while Jake showered and changed. He packed a small suitcase with clean clothes and his address book. Before they left, he opened the safe in the living room behind a Matisse original. He removed a long, slender object wrapped in a purple silk cloth. Carrie had no idea what it could be and Jake didn't explain.

Halfway to the estate, Jake asked casually, "Has Megan called Stephen?"

"Stephen! I doubt it."

Jake nodded.

A mile later. *"Why?"*

"Emotions. You know Megan."

An hour after Carrie had left for the airport to meet Jake, Megan *had* telephoned Stephen. She had debated all night, tossing and turning. She thought about discussing it with Ian and Margaret, but she didn't dare. Besides, it was her decision and she had made it. The FBI agent listened to the call, in amazement, and recorded it.

Beth, Stephen, and the boys were playing in the living room. It was a lovely, lazy family afternoon. Sunday was their family day. No matter how busy he was, Stephen always spent the entire day with Beth and the twins.

Beth answered the phone.

"Beth, this is Megan. I need to speak with Stephen."

Beth froze. Please, no. For years, she had feared a day like this. But, as time had passed, she had forgotten that fear, because everything was so perfect.

"Is something wrong with Carrie?"

"No. This is personal, between me and Stephen."

"There is nothing personal between you and Stephen."

"Let me talk to him, Beth."

"No!"

Stephen stood beside Beth. He had heard Carrie's name and observed the expression of horror and fear on his wife's face. He took the receiver from Beth's trembling hand.

"Who is this?" Stephen demanded.

"It's Megan."

"Oh." Why had Beth been so hostile and protective?

"Stephanie has been kidnapped."

"How awful. Ian and Margaret must be frantic. How can I help?"

There was a long pause.

"Stephanie is *my* daughter."

"I didn't know. I am so sorry."

Another long pause.

"Stefano, you don't understand. She is my daughter. And she is *your* daughter. Darling, she is our little girl. Someone has kidnapped our little girl." Megan's voice broke and she began to cry.

The color had drained from Stephen's face. Beth watched in horror: it was true, her worst fears had been confirmed. Except, what was awful?

Finally Stephen whispered, "Megan, I have to hang up." And he did. Beth waited.

"You knew, Beth?"

"Knew what?"

"That Stephanie is my daughter."

"No, I didn't know. But I wondered. I thought Megan was pregnant that spring. I even asked her. But she denied it. I didn't know she had had a child, or who she was. I still don't. Except the name . . ."

The name, Stephen thought. They had named his daughter after him. But, of course, they had never intended to have him meet Stephanie, or even know about her. No wonder Megan had seemed so anxious at the party.

"Stephanie is Ian and Margaret's child. Only she's really my child," he said numbly.

Beth wondered how and when Stephen had met Stephanie, but now was not the time to ask.

"What could have made Megan tell you now?"

"Stephanie has been kidnapped."

"Oh, no." Beth's heart sank. She thought about her boys, how she would feel if anything happened to them. Stephen would feel the same way. And now his daughter, a daughter he had never known, had been kidnapped. Beth put her arms around her husband. He stood still, stiff.

"I have to go to Connecticut," he whispered finally.

Oh, no. Beth thought.

There still had been no news by the time Jake and Carrie reached Pinehaven. It had been twenty-four hours. They all ate a dinner of cold cuts and spinach souffle. They ate in silence. Afterward, Ian and Margaret went to their room.

Jake, Megan, and Carrie sat on the veranda. It would have been a peaceful, perfect, balmy June night. The moon was full, the crickets whirred energetically.

One of the FBI agents walked onto the patio.

"Stephen Richards is here. Frankly, we've been expecting him, but since no one told us to let him through, I thought I'd better check."

Jake glowered at Megan. Carrie watched Jake and remembered his question: has Megan called Stephen?

Megan ignored Jake's glare and nodded to the agent.

Stephen walked onto the patio. He had already learned from the agents that there had been no news. He had practiced a hundred different speeches—angry, sad, indignant—on the drive from Boston to Connecticut; but now, face to face with Megan, he forgot them all. He only wanted to know one thing.

"Why?"

Megan didn't answer.

"Why what, Stephen?" Carrie asked anxiously, afraid that she already knew the answer.

"Don't you know? Maybe Jake doesn't know either. I'll

tell you. Stephanie is my child. Mine and Megan's. I found out a few hours ago."

Carrie looked at the others—her brother, Megan, Jake. They had all been friends, once. They had loved each other. And yet, Megan had kept this secret from them. Megan had not trusted any of them enough to share her secret. Carrie looked at Jake and her heart sank. Megan had shared the secret . . .

"Jake has known for a long time, haven't you?" Carrie asked quietly. She remembered his words, spoken so long ago: *Megan will need a friend. Megan has suffered enough. Megan hasn't had anything to drink since . . .*

Jake nodded.

"How long?" Stephen demanded.

"Since the night after the dinner party that spring at Stanford. When I told you about my plans to go on the tour," Megan answered.

"And you didn't tell me?" Stephen asked Jake.

"I promised Megan."

"I think we should hear it all now," Carrie said.

"I didn't get pregnant on purpose," Megan began. Her voice was strong. It was a relief to rid herself of this secret. "I couldn't take The Pill. It was what had given me those horrible headaches. I tried to be careful, to always be prepared. But, sometimes . . ." Megan's voice wavered. She was remembering how much, how often, Stephen had wanted her, then. How it had made her forget everything else. "I knew you didn't want children."

"Didn't want children?" Stephen echoed, bewildered.

"You said so."

"I wanted you. I might have said I didn't want to share you, not then. But I don't remember saying that I didn't want children. I wouldn't have said that," Stephen said, thinking about his beloved twin sons and about the beautiful little girl who was missing, who was his daughter, whom he had never known.

"Well, *I* remember," Megan said defiantly. Had she been

430

wrong? Jake had tried to convince her even then that she had misinterpreted Stephen's feelings about children. No, she couldn't have been wrong. The price she had paid—losing Stephen, abandoning her baby—had been too high to have been the result of a misunderstanding.

"Ian and Margaret wanted a child desperately, but they were unable to have one of their own. I knew what wonderful parents they would be. How I would trust them to raise our child," Megan continued, then paused, searching her memory for why she had made the decision that she had made, still shaken that it may have all been made in error. It could not be. "So, I decided to have the baby, give her to Ian and Margaret, then return to you in the fall and be married, as we had planned."

"There was no European tour?"

"Ian was in Europe that summer, on a tour. I was here, with Margaret. We sent letters to him to mail from Europe." Megan's voice weakened as the memories of that summer returned.

"What happened, Megan?"

Megan couldn't speak. She was crying.

"Megan was very ill," Jake continued for her. "The hormonal effects of pregnancy were like being on the Pill, only worse—the headaches began, again, even before she left Stanford. Her doctor put her on bed rest, here, as soon as she arrived. Toward the end of July her blood pressure increased, she retained fluid, had protein in her urine . . ."

"Eclampsia," Carrie said quietly.

"Yes," Megan said. "I felt so sick. I began to hate the baby and I began to hate Stephen."

"So you wrote me that letter."

"Yes," Megan said softly.

Carrie watched the muscles on her brother's jaw ripple.

"Your visit to us, Jake. It coincided nicely with the arrival of the letter," Carrie said sadly.

"When I telephoned you I had just returned from Saudi Arabia. I hadn't spoken to Megan. I didn't know what was

431

happening until I spoke with you. I wanted you to fly to Washington, remember?" Jake's voice was stern: let the record be clear.

Carrie nodded. "But then you talked to Megan."

"It worked out for the best that you and I had planned for me to come to Boston," Jake said firmly.

"I was admitted to the hospital on August first. Stephie was born August twenty-seventh," Megan continued.

"They gave Megan intravenous fluids for that month, strict bed rest, no salt, medications to keep her blood pressure under control. She had her first seizure on August twenty-fourth. They put her on a ventilator. They had to paralyze her with curare to keep her on the ventilator. Megan was unconscious."

"They thought that my brain might have died on the twenty-fourth, but they wanted to keep me alive so that the baby could mature as much as possible before birth. Jake and Ian and Margaret had to make all the decisions."

"Jake was there the whole time?" Stephen asked. "And *I* wasn't?"

"If we had to do it over, Stephen, we would never have done it this way. From the beginning, it was wrong. We know that, now." Jake looked at Megan; she looked down at her clenched hands.

"On the twenty-seventh of August, Megan developed septic shock from an infection in her uterus. They did an emergency Caesarean section. They removed the baby, and Megan's uterus."

"And the rest is history." Megan tried to sound light. "I surprised them all by recovering, eventually. And Stephanie . . ."

"You gave the baby my name, but you gave her away. What you did is illegal, you know."

"So sue me!" Megan regretted the words instantly. She didn't want to make him angrier. She knew how hard this all was for him. It had been so hard for her. She continued, softly, "It backfired, Stephen. I was young, remember? I had the world by the tail. I was happy and in love. I believed that I could control things, everything. My life, your life, our baby's life. It seemed like a perfect solution. It would have been, but it backfired."

"And somewhere along the line, we weren't in love anymore.

"I was sick and confused when I wrote you that letter."

"And later? How about on October fifteenth? You didn't make it to our wedding, remember?"

"I was no prize then. Carrie saw me a month later, when I was just beginning to return from the dead. I still have a big, ugly scar on my stomach and no uterus. Too much had happened."

"Is that when you stopped loving me?"

"I nev—"

Megan stopped abruptly at the sound of the telephone ringing. They all rushed to the living room. Ian had answered it in the bedroom. The FBI agent was recording the call. He turned the amplifier on. They listened in horror.

"I have Stephanie." It was a male voice, muffled. "So far, she is well. I have some demands. They all must be met. Once I make them, they must be met quickly. I get bored easily. I leave you to consider what she is worth. Oh, about the police and the FBI. Very annoying. It makes the price go up."

He hung up. They heard footsteps rushing downstairs.

"Alec!" Megan whispered.

"Who, ma'am?" the agent asked.

"I think it's Alec Matthews."

"You recognized his voice?"

"Not really. It was disguised. I recognized his words and his style. Things like getting bored easily."

Ian walked into the living room then and said, "I think it's Alec."

"So does Megan."

"What will he do to her?" Megan shuddered, glad that she hadn't shared the details of what he had done to her with anyone but Jake. "My little girl . . ."

433

Ian heard Megan's words and noticed Stephen.

"We all know, Ian," Carrie said. "Including, I assume, the agents."

"Well, let's just get her back," Ian said firmly. He turned to the agent. "It makes sense that it would be someone Stephie knows. She knows Alec. He spent a few weekends out here last summer. She wouldn't be afraid of him."

"Who is he?"

Ian told him. "The last I knew he was directing *Canterbury Tales* in London. But that was a few months ago." For awhile, Ian had kept track of Alec's whereabouts. But, as time passed, he had relaxed his vigil.

"Why would he do this?"

"Revenge," Megan answered bitterly. Ian explained briefly. He also told the agent about the actress who had been murdered in a production that Alec had been directing.

"How long have you known about that, Ian?" Jake asked brusquely. Ian should have told him.

"I remembered it after the incident with Megan. I don't think Alec was even a suspect. If he had been, there would have been talk."

"But that's why we treated him with kid gloves," Megan said. Ian hadn't told her, either.

"Right."

"All right," the agent began. "If he's our man, it sounds as though you two know him pretty well. We'll call in our psychologists; see if we can piece together a profile. It may sound a bit farfetched, but sometimes it pays off. You may know something about him that could provide a clue, and you may not even know it."

"Jake should be involved. He has experience with this sort of thing," Megan said firmly.

The agent looked at Jake critically.

"I don't have experience with exactly this sort of thing. But I have some experience that might be useful. And I know Alec and Stephie. When it's time to pick her up, I could help."

The agent eyed Jake skeptically. Jake knew not to push. The agent would make a few phone calls. Then Jake would be part of the team. There was no reason that the agent should accept his offer of help without knowing his credentials. It was no \place for an amateur.

Margaret had not come downstairs after the phone call. Ian looked at his "guests."

"You are all welcome to stay. We can keep the vigil together. But please, let us all remember that the only thing that matters is our little girl's safety. Find yourselves a room; we have plenty. Make yourselves comfortable. You are welcome to stay, Stephen."

"Thank you."

Chapter Twenty-seven

An envelope arrived in the Monday afternoon mail. It was postmarked 10:00 P.M. Saturday, June 23, in Southbury, a small town near Pinehaven.

The envelope contained a Polaroid snapshot of Stephanie, sitting on a chair, smiling brightly. It was a natural, happy smile. She was making a picture with a friend for her mommy; she was, then, still unafraid, unsuspecting.

Jake studied the photograph carefully. It had been taken in a wallpapered room, probably in a house rather than a hotel. The doorknob was unusual—ornate, carved. Distinctive? Jake wondered.

Moments after the mail arrived, Alec called.

"We know it's you, Alec," Ian bellowed. The FBI agents had been divided about the wisdom of confronting Alec. The psychologist was of no help. The police had confirmed that Alec had been the prime suspect in the assault-murder of the actress. But there had been insufficient evidence to press charges.

"Bravo, Ian. That makes it easier. I don't have to explain my demands. You'll understand."

"What are they, Alec?"

"I want Megan. And two million dollars. And the usual guaranteed escape. I won't kill Megan. We just have some unfinished business. If she cooperates, she'll be perfectly safe. If I don't get Megan and the money, I'll have to substitute the child for Megan. Don't make me do that, Ian. It's your choice. You have until Wednesday morning."

Alec hung up.

Megan sobbed. Jake held her. Stephen looked questioningly at Carrie.

I can't tell him, Carrie thought. I can't tell him what that man did to Megan and what he might do to a child. Someone else would have to explain it to Stephen. But no one would. Not really. They all loved him too much. They all knew how much he was suffering for his daughter.

"He's in the area," Jake said. "He plans to make a switch. Megan for Stephie. He's probably very close. And he's given us thirty-six hours to find him."

The FBI agents nodded, waiting.

"Any ideas where he might be?"

"No. But this photograph may be a clue. We need enlargements of it."

The agent looked again at the snapshot, with interest. The message had come from Washington: count Jake Easton in. He was described as a top agent with a brilliant mind. They had been instructed to follow his leads, pay attention to his ideas.

"Why, sir?" the agent asked politely.

"The wallpaper and the ornamental doorknob may be distinctive enough that someone might identify the place. Maybe not, but it's worth a try."

Wordlessly, the agent nodded, took the photograph, and handed it to another agent.

Three hours later, twenty-eight ten-inch enlargements of the doorknob and twenty-eight ten-inch enlargements of the wallpaper print had arrived.

Both the doorknob and wallpaper looked expensive and unusual. Ian and Margaret did not recognize either.

"What now, Jake?" Carrie asked.

"I think we need to show these to every real estate agent, hardware store owner, and interior decorator in the area.

Maybe someone will recognize this room. We are operating under a few assumptions that may be wrong. We assume that he is nearby. We assume that he is still at the place where this photograph was taken."

"But at least it gives us something to do," Stephen said.

"Wait a minute . . ." the FBI agent interjected.

"I think if we set up I few ground rules . . ." Jake said, anticipating the agent's concern.

"Maybe. But if he is nearby, watching, and if he guesses what we're doing, he may move. If this gets into the news . . ." He looked pointedly at Carrie.

"It won't," Carrie said flatly.

Carrie's presence, her twice-daily televised reports from the estate, protected them from the usual intrusion of the press. In addition, it allowed them to carefully control the facts that were made public; facts that Alec might use to gauge the activities and progress of the authorities trying to find him.

The agent's instinctive mistrust of Carrie was learned behavior from years of investigations undermined, criminals freed, victims killed, because of the meddlesome First Amendment rights of the press. He liked Carrie, personally. Her concern for her brother, her friend, her niece was undeniable; but, still, she was a reporter.

"Here are the ground rules. We don't tell anyone what we are really looking for. Pretend you're decorating a house, saw the photograph in a museum, whatever. If you get any leads, tell me or Agent Preston. Do not try to find him. Do not even drive by a possible house, understood?" Jake's seriousness was obvious.

They all nodded, solemnly.

"Okay. We work in pairs." Jake paused. "Stephen and Megan and Carol . . . uh . . . Carrie and I. Ian and Margaret need to stay here in case Alec calls."

Ian moved to protest, but Jake raised a hand.

"Ian, you can't do this anonymously. People know you; they know what's happening. You have to stay here."

"Carrie and Megan are pretty recognizable, too."

"Yes, but we'll do something with hair and hats."

"It's just so damned hard to wait," Ian said, resigned.

"I know."

I wonder if this is just a wild goose chase, Carrie thought, created by Jake to save us from going crazy. If so, they were grateful for it. They all, especially Megan, needed something productive to do. For the first time in two days, there was hope in the eyes of Megan and Stephen. Maybe they could help their daughter.

The agent looked at them, worried. They all nodded when Jake emphasized the importance of reporting all information to himself or the FBI. But, could they stick to it? The agent wondered. Megan, the emotional, guilt-ridden mother. Stephen, the successful, aggressive attorney, the child's father. Carrie, the star reporter. The only one he trusted was Jake. Jake was a proven team player. Jake knew the importance of playing by the book, especially in life and death situations.

They studied a map of the area and carefully divided the territory within a thirty-mile radius. Carrie and Megan wore hats that totally concealed their hair, and large dark glasses. They were convincing as interior decorators. Jake and Stephen wore pagers; they could be in contact with each other and with the agents at the estate.

It was late Monday afternoon. There were only a few hours left before the shops and agencies closed for the day, but they were eager to start.

Their questions drew little curiosity and no results. Discouraged, they returned to Pinehaven by seven.

The conversation at dinner turned, inevitably, to Alec.

"He doesn't know Stephie is Megan's child."

"Thank God."

"He really is grandiose."

"What does that mean?" Megan asked weakly. "Delusions of grandeur. Manic. Omnipotent."

"Crazy," Megan uttered disconsolately.

Abruptly, Jake left the table and walked through the French doors toward the lake. Without thinking, Carrie followed him.

She watched his silhouette at the end of the dock—tormented, in pain. What is he doing? she wondered. Blaming himself?

She walked to him.

"Jake?"

Her voice startled him. He stared at her, through her, his eyes blazing.

"I should have killed the bastard when I had the chance."

"Jake!" Carrie pleaded. "Don't blame yourself. This isn't your fault."

"I should have killed him. It would have been so easy . . ."

"You can't just kill people, Jake," she said quietly. She wanted to touch him, to hold him, to stop the torment.

"Oh?" He laughed harshly. "Of course you can. It's very simple."

"No, Jake. I mean *you* can't." Carrie touched his hot cheek with her cool hand. *"You* can't, darling. It damages you too much."

Jake drew her to him, carefully. He held her gently, lightly, kissing her silky hair.

"Oh, Caroline . . ." he whispered.

As he held her, Carrie felt his agony. She guessed that he was punishing himself for past decisions that he now regretted: the decision not to tell Stephen about Megan's pregnancy; the decision not to deal with Alec—to, at least, frighten Alec. Carrie wondered if there were other decisions Jake regretted. Did he regret his decision that he and Carrie could never have a life together?

Carrie thought about decisions she had made. The decision never to tell Jake about their baby, the unborn baby that they had lost. She knew, now, as he held her, that she would never tell him. It would hurt him too deeply. She still grieved for the baby, but her grief was tempered by

440

her own optimism and hope. For Jake, it would be one more sign that his life was destined to bring pain to those he loved, that he had no right to dream his dreams.

Carrie thought of another decision she had made, the decision to marry Mark. She sighed and gently pulled away from Jake. She looked into his eyes.

"We'll just have to find the bastard, Jake. Tomorrow, you and I will find him."

Monday evening, Beth drove from Boston to Wood's Hole. It was an impulsive decision, made shortly after a phone call from Stephen. She left the twins in the capable hands of Mrs. Pierson, their live-in housekeeper, left the telephone number where she could be reached, and started driving.

Beth had to talk to someone. The past twenty-four hours had been the worst of her life. Stephen had called twice, his voice full of pain and worry for his daughter. Beth ached for Stephen and his child.

But there had been something else in Stephen's voice, something new. Underneath the worry, underneath the pain, there had been relief, almost joy. Something Stephen had learned had set him free, given him hope. It was obvious Megan had told him something that, in spite of the tragedy of the kidnapping, had made him happy. When he spoke of Megan, his voice had been gentle, concerned, loving. It was no longer the angry, bitter voice that Beth had known so well from the rare occasions when Megan's name had been mentioned.

Beth could only draw one horrible, painful conclusion: Megan had told Stephen the truth, and he had forgiven her.

I hate her, Beth thought as the car sped toward the Cape. For what she has done before. For what she might do again. For what she might convince Stephen to do.

But, as much as Beth hated and feared Megan at that moment, Beth also knew how much Megan was suffering for her daughter. The mother in Beth, the part of her that knew how she would feel if anything happened to either of her boys, shuddered at the thought of what was happening to Megan and ached with her. And with Stephen.

It was nine-thirty when Beth drove into the gravel driveway of John's secluded house near Wood's Hole. Beth had found the house for him. It was not a rustic cottage. It was a large, beautiful, wood-plank house, painted teal blue with white trim, with large, sunny rooms and a commanding view of Nantucket Sound.

John loved it instantly, its four brick fireplaces, its hardwood floors, the separate wing for BethStar, the music room. John never knew that Beth had spent hours carefully inspecting every available home at the Cape, finally choosing this one, because it seemed perfect for John.

"Oh, John," Beth said offhandedly during their weekly conversation, "by the way, I found a house for you. It's really the best property on the Cape and the price is fair. I've actually given them an earnest money agreement on it."

"What does my lawyer say?" John had asked, laughing.

Beth loved working at John's house. She spent every Wednesday there, working with him. Occasionally, he drove to Boston to meet with attorneys and marketing consultants. Twice, he and Beth had traveled together to New York on business. But, just as the creation of BethStar had come from a gardener's cottage in Palo Alto, the brains and headquarters of the company stayed in the sunlit dayroom of the house overlooking Nantucket Sound.

Beth hadn't telephoned John before she left Boston. As she entered the drive she was relieved to see that the lights were on and his car was there. His car, and another one.

Beth knocked lightly on the heavy oak door. She waited, then knocked again, more loudly.

John opened the door.

"Beth!" John looked startled. He was wearing a Pendleton bathrobe and held a half-empty glass of white wine.

"Hi, John," Beth said uncomfortably. Why had she come? A few hours earlier it had seemed clear—she needed to talk to someone. No, she needed to talk to John.

"Why are you here, Beth?" John asked flatly.

"I wanted to talk to you."

"About BethStar?"

"No. It's something personal."

John opened the door. Beth walked in, then pulled up abruptly as she took in the scene: a roaring fire, a woman curled on the sofa wearing a bathrobe identical to John's. It was obvious what she had interrupted.

"Oh!"

"Beth, this is Marilyn. Marilyn, this is Beth."

Marilyn raised her wineglass. "I've heard a lot about you, Beth. You and the company."

I've never heard about you, Beth thought. Beth was puzzled. Marilyn was obviously not a casual date; she was part of John's life.

"I guess this is a bad time, John," Beth said weakly.

"Unless you want to talk to both of us." John's voice revealed his annoyance at Beth's intrusion. "Is my phone out of order?"

"No . . . I . . . guess I was so upset I just started driving," Beth said honestly.

"Upset?" Marilyn asked, staring with open bewilderment at John's coldness toward Beth.

"Yes. Something's happened. I thought I would talk to John about it since he knows the other people involved." Beth's awkwardness was apparent; so was her helplessness. She looked uneasily at John and said, "I can see you are busy. Would . . . would it be possible for me to see you tomorrow?"

John stared at Beth. It was impossible to interpret his expression. Anger? Concern?

Marilyn stood up. "Don't be silly, Beth. You've driven all the way from Boston tonight. John, I have a long shift starting at seven in the morning. I really should be going . . ."

"No, Marilyn," John said firmly.

"Yes," Marilyn whispered back, half-glowering, half-mocking. Why was he being so obstinate? It was so unlike John. Another perplexing item—Beth obviously needed John's help and he seemed unwilling to give it. Marilyn had always assumed that they were close friends.

John shrugged.

"Beth, give us an hour, will you?" John's tone was one of condescension. It wasn't lost on Beth, but she was too astonished to say anything.

She nodded. "I'll go to the workroom. Please don't rush. Thank you, Marilyn. It was nice to meet you."

Beth turned quickly and walked toward the separate area of the house that contained the BethStar workroom and the music room.

"What was that all about, John?" Marilyn asked as soon as Beth had left.

"My attitude? She has no right to burst in, unannounced, and assume that I will drop everything for her."

"But she's upset. If she came into the Emergency Room looking that tired and frantic, we'd triage her into a treatment room immediately."

"She did look bad, didn't she?" John asked, his voice indicating concern for the first time.

"Yes. Do you have any idea what happened to her?"

"I think I know." John's voice became hard again. "It's a problem of her own creation."

"But a problem, nonetheless." Marilyn paused, then added, "I had the idea that you two were close friends."

"Friends?" John laughed. "No. We are business partners, period. You are my friend."

John moved to her and kissed her. Marilyn returned the kiss eagerly, then pulled away.

"I feel a little uncomfortable."

"Meaning we're not alone."

"Uh-huh."

"She's managing to cancel our plans anyway, isn't she?" John asked bitterly.

"Yes . . . but we're the lucky ones. For whatever reason, she's miserable. I feel sorry for her. I hope you'll be nice to her."

"Did anybody ever tell you that you're one fine, compassionate doctor?"

"Only you, when I sewed up your finger."

Beth paced in the workroom, idly glancing at sketches and project ideas, trying to make sense of John's reaction. Nothing in the past twenty-four hours made sense. She was too exhausted and confused even to try to analyze his behavior.

Restless, she walked into the music room. Beth usually avoided the music room because it contained an old, untuned baby grand piano. It had come with the house. John had shown no interest in having the piano restored, despite Beth's urging.

Beth stopped still at the doorway of the music room. The piano had been moved into the center of the room and it had been completely refinished. Beth slowly ran her hands over the beautifully polished wood.

It had been so long, so many yearn, since she had played.

Beth touched the keyboard tentatively, then gently depressed one of the new white keys. The tone was perfect—rich and clear. She sat down and began to play. She closed her eyes. The direct pathways between her brain and her fingers still existed. Automatically, without conscious thought, without looking, without effort, the vast repertoire of concertos and sonatas returned to her.

Beth played, as she always had played, with great feeling and emotion and peace. She played for thirty minutes without stopping, without opening her eyes, unaware of the time, or of John's presence.

When she paused, finally, John said, quietly, "Beth?"

She spun around and stared at him. He leaned casually against the far wall of the room. He wore a plaid shirt, sleeves rolled to his elbows, and tan slacks. His hair was wet; he had showered and dressed since she'd left. How long had it been? How long had he been watching her?

The spell, the peaceful moment, was broken. All the realities bombarded her mind at once: Stephen, Megan, Stephanie. And, most recently, John's hostility.

"I had no idea you played, Beth!" John's enthusiasm was genuine. He was a musician himself. He had great respect for talent like Beth's. It was a passion they had in common but had never shared.

"There are a lot of things we don't know about each other," Beth answered coldly, avoiding his eyes.

"That's right, Beth."

"For example," she continued quietly, "I thought we were friends."

"Really? What could possibly have made you think that?" John said sarcastically.

Beth shrugged. She stared at the keyboard. John didn't move or speak.

"Everything we've shared, all the time we've spent together . . . BethStar . . ." Beth shrugged again. "I just thought we were friends, that's all."

"It's not enough to have thought it. You have to do something to be a friend, Beth. You have to interact with your friend, share things. Care." John paused, then added angrily, "Don't you think it's amazing that, knowing how much I love music, and how much you apparently do, you have never told me that you play the piano? In all these years, you've never mentioned it!"

"You never told me about Marilyn!" Beth countered defensively.

"But I would have told you, if you had cared enough to ask. I have tried to be your friend, Beth. I've tried to learn about you. Over the years, I've teased out bits and pieces."

John stopped. Then he said, slowly, bitterly, "Do you realize that you have never asked me one question about me, my life . . . Not even a 'how are you'?"

Beth shook her head. No, she hadn't realized that. She had believed that she knew John. She had believed that they were friends. In the past twenty-four hours, she had lost confidence in her beliefs. And in herself . . .

Large tears tracked down her cheeks. One splashed onto the shiny white keyboard. Beth wiped it quickly with her trembling hand.

John watched with amazement, then regret. He had been too hard on her, pushed her too far. She was in pain. And she was fragile. John walked across the room and sat beside her on the piano bench, helplessly wanting to touch her, comfort her.

"Now you're going to be mad because you didn't know that I could cry." Beth smiled weakly.

"I didn't know. But I'm sorry, not mad."

Beth turned toward him, her huge brown eyes glistening with tears, and smiled, hesitantly. "To tell you the truth, John, I didn't know I could cry, either. This has been a night of revelations."

"I'm sorry I was unkind."

"But you were being honest." Beth and John had always prided themselves on their directness and their honesty.

"Yes. It struck me as a bit . . ." John paused, searching for an honest, but not hurtful, word.

"Presumptuous?" Beth offered.

"Presumptuous." John nodded.

"I guess it was. I did *presume* that you would be here, and that you would be willing to talk to me," Beth said, apologetically and stood up and started toward the door.

John caught her arm. It surprised them both. He let go quickly. Beth waited, confused.

"I know this must be very difficult for you, Beth," John said.

"What must be difficult?"

"The kidnapping."

Beth drew in a breath.

"How do you know?" she whispered.

"I read newspapers. I even watch the news on television."

"What do you know?"

"Nothing. But I guess that the child is Stephen and Megan's. Why else would Megan be at the estate?" Why else would you be here? he wondered.

"How?"

"You told me that Valentine's Day a million years ago. When you told me about Stephen and your plans to move to Boston. You told me, also, that you thought that Megan might have been pregnant."

"And you remembered?"

"How could I forget?" John asked softly. He remembered how much it had worried him at the time. And how sad it had made him.

Beth started to cry again.

"I feel so sorry for that little girl. I desperately want her to be safe. I know how unspeakably awful this is for Stephen . . ." Beth said.

"But?"

"But something else has happened."

"What?" John's voice became more gentle with each question.

"I am so afraid . . ." Beth couldn't say it, as if putting her fears into words might make them real. But John could guess.

"You are afraid that this will bring Stephen and Megan back together? Is he with her now?"

Beth nodded in answer to both questions.

"Have you spoken with him?"

"Yes. But not about that, of course. But there is something in his voice." A hope in the midst of hopelessness. It could only be because of Megan.

Beth shivered, a shiver of fear and fatigue. She still stood, awkwardly, between the piano bench and the door, an arm's length from John. He moved toward her. She looked weak and helpless.

"Are you cold? Do you want some coffee? Or wine?"

"I am a little cold. I probably should be going."

John was not going to let her go, not looking the way she did. It would be dangerous for her to drive. He stood beside her and touched her lightly on the arm, guiding her.

"I'll make some coffee. Let's go upstairs by the fire."

Beth watched in silence while John brewed the coffee and stoked the fire. She sat, curled, in a large chair by the fire.

"Do you sing, too?" he asked.

"Sing? No. Well, I do sing to the twins," she mused.

"Why don't you have a piano?"

"I don't know. I didn't realize how much I missed it until this evening."

"Maybe you should get one."

"Maybe." Her thoughts were elsewhere. Finally she said, barely controlling the panic in her voice, "John, what if he leaves me? What if he goes back to Megan?"

"Then you pick up the pieces and carry on. You're a strong woman, Beth."

"No, I'm not. I don't think I could go on if he left."

"Don't be ridiculous!" John was annoyed.

"Oh, I forgot. You don't like Stephen."

"That's not true. The one time I met him, the one time in all these years that you've invited me to your home, I did like him."

It was true. John had liked Stephen. They met, for the first and only time, at a party three weeks after John moved from Stanford to the Cape. It was a formal dinner for the partners in Stephen's law firm, given by Beth and Stephen. John had no idea why Beth invited him. At first he declined; he didn't really want to see Beth with her husband. But Beth pushed—because Stephen was pushing her—and John finally agreed; he was curious to meet Stephen.

John was glad that he attended the party. He had never seen Beth look more beautiful. She wore a long black silk dress, closely fitted, and a necklace of diamonds at her ivory neck. She had her hair brushed away from her face and had artfully accented her large, sensuous eyes with mascara and eye shadow. John watched with amazement the woman he knew—the woman with the brilliant mind, sharp tongue, and brooding sensuality—transform into the perfect Southern hostess and wife she was bred to be.

It didn't make John change the way he felt about her; it only made him more certain about his feelings.

John studied Stephen carefully. Like Carrie, whom John had gotten to know in their last year at Stanford, Stephen was kind, generous, uncritical, and genuine. It was hard not to like Stephen. Stephen's pride and respect for his wife were obvious. They smiled at each other frequently during the evening; good friends, enjoying each other, understanding each other, admiring each other.

But, John realized, not in love with each other.

John had suspected that Stephen might not be deeply in love with Beth; he knew enough of the story about Stephen and Megan to wonder. But he had not expected to conclude that Beth was not in love with Stephen. And yet, watching them, the conclusion was inescapable. There was no softness, no gentleness. Stephen and Beth behaved like successful business partners and close friends, not lovers. John wondered if Beth even knew. Or if she knew the difference. It was a revelation that made a lot of difference to John; he was glad that Beth had forced him to come to the party.

"I do like Stephen," John repeated. Beth was staring into the fire.

"But you don't think it would matter if Stephen left me."

"It would matter a great deal. It would give you a chance to make a choice about your life. To decide what you really want, what's important to you, what makes you happy. I bet you don't even know."

"Really?" she asked sarcastically.

450

"Really. What makes you happy, Beth? What do you look forward to?"

Beth continued to stare into the fire, thinking about John's question. Finally she answered.

"Sundays with Stephen and the twins . . . except for yesterday. The twins, all the time. I guess I've rediscovered the piano. I feel happy when I'm playing. I'd forgotten how happy." Beth stopped. She was obviously debating whether to say the next. It was honest, it surprised her, and she didn't know what it meant. She sighed.

"And Wednesdays," she said quietly.

Wednesdays she spent there with John. They worked on ideas and plans for BethStar. She left Boston every Wednesday by six in the morning and often didn't return until ten at night. In warm weather, she sometimes brought Jamie, Robbie, and Mrs. Pierson. She and John would play with the twins during breaks. Sometimes, they would all have lunch on the large porch that faced southeast toward Martha's Vineyard and Nantucket Island. They laughed and played in the warm spring sun and the soft sea breeze. Those were happy, perfect days.

Even when she left the twins in Boston, Beth looked forward to Wednesdays. She was always a little sad as she drove home each Wednesday night.

Admitting that Wednesdays made her happy was admitting that being with John made her happy.

They sat in silence while the realization settled.

Finally, Beth spoke.

"Are you planning to be my friend in the future?"

John smiled. "Maybe. Why?"

"It seems that your definition of friendship includes knowing about the other person's personal life."

"It's caring about the other person's life."

"Okay. Tell me about Marilyn, then."

"What do you want to know?"

"Who is she? What does she do? Are you going to marry her?"

John laughed.

"Do you care?"

"John, stop teasing. I won't die if you don't tell me. But as your friend I am interested."

"She's a doctor. Yes, I am thinking about marrying her."

"Oh." Beth didn't know what to say. A friend would say, That's wonderful. I am so happy for you. But Beth felt no urge to say that. It wasn't honest. Just as John hadn't told her he was happy that she was marrying Stephen; it hadn't been true.

"Do you want some more coffee?"

Beth looked at her watch. It was one-thirty.

"I had no idea it was so late. I really have to go."

"Beth, you can't drive home tonight. You're too tired. It would be dangerous," John said sternly. "If you need to get back, I'll drive you. If not, you should stay here."

"Oh."

"The guest room is made up."

"Okay."

"Now, do you want some more coffee?"

"Sure. I doubt it will keep me awake."

"Do you want to go to sleep now?"

"Not really. Do you?"

"No. Something else you don't know about me. I usually stay up later than this, playing my guitar."

"I'll just have one more cup of coffee, then."

Beth cupped her hands around the fresh mug of hot coffee that John handed her. "Tell me more about Marilyn."

"Well, there is a problem about marrying her." John looked at Beth. "I'm in love with someone else."

"What a problem! Why don't you marry the one you love?"

"Not possible. It's complicated. She's married."

"Oh. Won't she leave her husband?"

"No. I doubt it. I would never ask her to. I don't believe in breaking up marriages."

"But you're having an affair with her!"

"No."

John watched Beth. Her expression hadn't changed.

"Is she in love with you?"

"I don't know."

"Have you told her how you feel?"

"No."

"Does Marilyn know?"

"No."

"What are you going to do?"

John hesitated. What was he going to do? Finally, he said, "I'm going to marry Marilyn."

"Oh." Beth held her mug to her lips, feeling the warmth, not drinking. She said quietly, "Tell me about the married woman."

John smiled, then sighed.

"The married woman. Let's see. She's very smart. Very beautiful. Very sexy. She's not very nice, sometimes, on the surface. But, inside, she's warm and loving. She's a little out of touch with herself. She always has been."

"Have you known her long?"

"Long enough."

"Have you always been in love with her, since you met?"

"Yes."

"She must know how you feel. She must sense it."

"One would think so. But, I told you, she's a bit out of touch."

"Maybe you should tell her directly."

"No. She's had enough clues. She's smart. She can figure it out."

"And what if she does?"

"I told you. I don't want to be responsible for breaking up a marriage. She would have to come to me. She would have to make the first move."

Beth stood up abruptly. She finished her coffee in a large swallow.

"I am very tired. I think I'll go to bed." Beth didn't look at him.

"There are clean work shirts in the closet," John said to her back as she left the room.

After he heard the guest room door close, John began to play his guitar. He sat in front of the fire and sang. The songs recalled memories, mostly bittersweet. John tried not to think about the most recent memory—what he had just told Beth. But it was unavoidable; it was all he could think about. She had heard his words. She had understood their meaning. Her reaction had been to leave, quickly, without looking at him.

He should never have told her.

Beth sat on the bed in the guest bedroom, in darkness. Her mind reeled. What had John said? Had she understood him correctly? Was he really talking about her? What did it mean?

What does any of this mean? Beth wondered, struggling to make sense of the events of the past twenty-four hours. None of them made sense; they were just things that had happened. Things she had to live with.

The most irrevocable thing that had happened, the event that she *had* to deal with, was Stephen's reunion, and his apparent reconciliation, with Megan. Whatever the outcome—Beth hoped desperately that the little girl would be safe—everything had changed. Stephen had a new knowledge—something Megan had told him or something that he sensed—that made him happy.

Megan had taken Stephen away from her once. Could she do it again? The answer was yes. She had already done it. Even if Stephen returned home to live with Beth and never mentioned Megan's name again, everything still would be changed, different. Because Beth had already heard it in Stephen's voice—he was still deeply in love with Megan.

How could Beth live with Stephen, knowing that?

Years before, when she had learned of Megan and

Stephen's broken engagement, Beth had sat up all night on her bed at Stanford, carefully planning how she could rebuild her relationship with Stephen. Now, she had another decision to make as she sat in the darkness of the night that was silent except for the distant sound of John's low, gentle voice singing softly and playing his guitar.

Beth had to decide, carefully, if and how she could now let Stephen go.

Finally, after an eternity of memories and emotions, all conflicting, all bombarding her already fatigued mind, Beth decided. She could let Stephen go. He would want to leave; she knew that. But he might not even mention it, because he wouldn't want to hurt her and because of the boys. Because Stephen was, above all, a kind, loving, considerate man.

But he would want to leave, to be with Megan, to try to reclaim that happiness. Beth couldn't live with him, knowing that he would rather be with Megan. It wasn't possible. Beth knew her marriage to Stephen was over.

She and Stephen would talk about it, when the horrible ordeal with Stephanie was over. They would decide, together, how to arrange to live the rest of their lives, apart. The twins would live with her, but Stephen could see them whenever he liked, because he loved them, too.

Beth couldn't make herself hate Stephen. He had never intended this to happen. Beth loved him, would always love him. Stephen had given her so much! He had given her confidence in herself as a beautiful, bright, loving woman— loving and loved. Beth had no doubt that Stephen had loved her. But, she realized, Stephen had never been in love with her. Stephen had only, and always, been in love with Megan.

As Beth listened to the distant sound of John's voice, her heart pounding and her body tingling as she remembered what John had told her, she wondered, Was I ever in love with Stephen?

Beth didn't answer her own question, but her thoughts drifted involuntarily away from Stephen, to John. John. . . .

* * *

Later, Beth walked into the living room. John was still playing the guitar, singing quietly. The fire had died. He didn't know she was there until she stood in front of him. She was wearing one of his denim work shirts. He stopped playing and put the guitar down.

"Hello," he said.

"I've been thinking about your married woman." Beth's voice was small, uncertain.

"Good," he said gently.

"Sexy?"

"Very." John looked at her. "Even in a rumpled work shirt."

Beth shook her head slowly.

He waited, but she didn't move. Her eyes were hidden by her tousled hair.

"What have you been thinking, Beth?" he asked carefully.

"I've been thinking about Wednesdays. Sometimes, except for the twins, I live for Wednesdays. I never even realized it." Beth looked at him then, her eyes large, dark, sensuous.

"I live for Wednesdays, too." John was helping her. She had to make the move, but he could help her.

"When I'm not here," she continued, her eyes not leaving his, "I find myself thinking, John would like this; I must tell John about this . . ."

"John, not Stephen?"

"John, not Stephen." Beth looked down and said, "But I did love Stephen."

"I know." John's heart leapt. Did love.

"But I think about you. I look forward to seeing you."

"For the great relief of having you to talk to," John murmured.

Beth looked at him again.

"John, I don't know how to do this!"

"Do what?" he asked gently.

"To make the first move," she said, almost inaudibly. "To touch you."

"Yes, you do. Try."

Slowly, tentatively, she reached to touch his cheek.

He took her hand and kissed it. Then he pulled her to him and kissed her lips. Beth's lips were warm and soft and responsive. In all the years of wanting her, John had wondered if she would be as cool and distant sexually as she could be emotionally.

But now, as he kissed her, she was warm and sensual. He sensed, in the blur of his own elation, that Beth was surprised by her passion. Her body responded to his touch instinctively and confidently. Her body was no longer her enemy. Her emotions and her lust surfaced naturally, without inhibition. The feelings were nothing that she could, or wanted to, control.

"Are you interested in making love on the living room floor?" John whispered into her mouth.

"I am interested in making love . . ." she answered immediately, surprising herself.

John's mind reeled. He couldn't take her to his bedroom. He and Marilyn had spent too many nights, too recently, there.

"How about the guest room?" he asked, between kisses.

"We can try. It may be too far."

They stopped four times between the living room and the guest room, kissing each other, undressing each other, touching each other, each moment wanting each other more, delighting in each other, prolonging the delight until it was almost unbearable.

"Make love to me now!"

"We're not there yet."

"Then don't kiss me there."

"I have to. I want to."

"I want you to." I love you.

457

Chapter Twenty-eight

At two, Tuesday afternoon, while Ian was meeting with his bankers to arrange for the ransom money, Jake discovered where Alec was. Or, at least, where Alec had been.

"Sure, I recognize that doorknob. The whole house has them, every door. Custom made in Italy, I believe." Mr. Dunworth of Dunworth's Hardware Store was a soft-spoken man of about sixty. It was obvious that his small store was barely surviving the competition of the chain hardware store half a block away. The store, like the man, conveyed a pride and honesty that seemed irreplaceable. Mr. Dunworth reminded Jake of Frank.

"Do you think that the owner would remember where they were made? Perhaps I could visit."

"Well, the owner moved out about three years ago. They keep the house and farm as a rental. Brings a good income, because city folk like to rent it out for spring and summer, so their children can see something other than asphalt and crime, I guess."

"Oh." Jake feigned disappointment. Actually he was thrilled. It increased the likelihood that Alec was there, that he had rented the farmhouse, that he would still be there. Jake's brain reeled, but he looked calm.

"I reckon the real estate agents would know how to contact the owner."

"That's a good idea. Do you know which agency handles the property?"

Mr. Dunworth knew and told Jake. He also, without prodding, gave Jake clear, precise instructions to the farmhouse and a description of it. It was two miles north of town.

When this was all over, Jake would tell Mr. Dunworth the truth. And he would give Mr. Dunworth some money, a great deal of money, so that Dunworth's Hardware Store could continue to prosper.

The real estate agency was on the opposite side of the street, Carrie's side. She probably hadn't been there yet. Jake walked across the street and into the agency office.

Jake pretended that he had driven past the farmhouse and wondered if it were available. The agent showed him photographs to make certain that they were speaking of the same "property."

"Yes, that's it." Mr. Dunworth's description matched the photographs exactly. "Is it available to rent?"

The agent referred to a card file and nodded.

"Yes. It was rented in March. Let's see, it's a six-month lease, but there's a note here saying that it will be available July first. I expect the present occupant would be happy to sublet it to you for July and August."

"Great! Could you give me a name or a telephone number." Jake paused. Real estate agent. Commission. "Or, perhaps, you could arrange it for me?"

The agent relaxed. "Of course. We don't have a record of a telephone number for him. I'll drive out and discuss it with him."

Jake counted to five. The agent had said "him"; it had been rented by a man and something in the agency records made the agent think he was living there, alone.

"Listen, if it doesn't pass my wife's inspection, that would be a waste of our time. Before we bother the occupant, or get his hopes up, I'd better just drive by it with her. That will be next week at the earliest. So, if you give me your card, I'll call you after that."

It was three o'clock. Jake had already devised a plan. The first step was to get Megan, Carrie, and Stephen back to Pinehaven before they, too, discovered Alec's whereabouts.

Carrie emerged from an interior design store. Ahead of her, on her side, were the real estate agency that Jake had just left and a paint store. Jake beckoned to her.

"I finished my side and went on to yours."

"No luck?" Carrie asked.

"I think we should call it a day," he said, without answering her question.

"But we only have until tomorrow morning!"

"I know. I guess I want to hear what the agents are planning. It's time to concentrate on how to catch him tomorrow."

Carrie agreed readily. She was tired, discouraged, and worried. Megan was steadfast in her determination to meet Alec's demands, to give herself in exchange for her daughter.

Stephen and Megan had already returned. The agents had paged them. They needed to meet with Megan.

"We want to send a woman police officer."

"No! Don't you understand? Alec knows me. If he suspects a trick, he'll run. And he'll take Stephie with him. It has to be me. The real me."

"Okay. Then we have to teach you to defend yourself. Can you use a gun?"

"You want me to kill Alec?"

The agent stared at Megan. Megan raised an eyebrow at Carrie and smiled.

"With pleasure. But, a dead Alec won't tell us where Stephie is. And no, I don't know how to use a gun."

"You have to be armed, Megan," Jake said sternly.

"This is so irregular, Mr. Easton," the agent said nervously. "The agency isn't used to involving . . . er . . . civilians."

"Er, amateurs, you mean," Megan chirped. She was

460

strangely excited about her role. Terribly frightened and nervous, but also eager. Eager because of Stephanie.

The agent put a small revolver in her trembling hands and explained its use. Periodically he glanced at Jake. The look said, This isn't going to work; we're sending her to her death. But Jake appeared calm and unworried.

Alec telephoned at seven to issue final instructions. Megan and the money were to leave the estate at six in the morning, alone by car. He gave directions for Megan. The route, Jake noted, took her within four miles of the farmhouse, then continued north. Presumably, Alec would intercept her at some point. There were hundreds of side roads he could divert her to and she would be lost. A car trailing her would be too far away. The beeper planted on Megan's car would be of little value if Alec forced Megan into his car.

The best they could do was to post unmarked cars and trucks along the route. But Alec could intercept her within a mile of Pinehaven. On the winding country roads, they could too easily lose her.

Jake and the agents knew that if they followed Alec's demands, they stood a good chance of losing Megan and Stephanie.

At nine o'clock, Jake left the estate, quietly, unobserved, by the kitchen door.

At nine-fifteen, Stephen knocked on the door to Megan's bedroom. Megan had gone upstairs at eight. She sat upright in her bed. The room was dark.

"Come in." Megan saw the light in the hallway on Stephen's handsome, concerned face.

He sat on the far corner of the bed.

"I don't want you to do this."

"I have to."

They sat in silence for several minutes.

"Why? Why don't you want me to?"

"Because I don't want to lose you, again."

"But she's our daughter!"

"She was our daughter the last time I lost you."

"Don't hate her!"

"I don't. I love her. I want you both to be safe. If you go, I believe I will lose you both." Stephen's voice was thick with emotion.

"Do you hate me, Stephen?"

"I hate what you did to me, to us. To you and me and Stephanie. But I don't hate you. I just wish that it had been different." He sounded sad and defeated.

They sat at opposite ends of the bed in silence. There was nothing more to say. Stephen knew that he should leave, but he couldn't. He might never see her again.

"Please don't go, Megan," he started again.

"I have to, don't you see?"

Stephen did see. It was Megan's chance to make up for her mistakes. Even though she had given her precious baby daughter to people who would love her as their own, Megan had abandoned her child—just as Megan's own mother had abandoned her. To save her daughter, Megan was prepared to give her own life, if necessary. But the price was too high; the punishment too severe.

"I understand why you have to do this. But I am asking you not to." Stephen's voice was confident. He had made a decision. Megan would not go. He would, simply, not allow it.

"Why?" Megan asked cautiously.

"Because I love you, Megan."

"I love you too," she answered quickly. "I have never stopped loving you."

Stephen pulled her close to him. "Marry me."

Megan giggled—the healthy, happy giggle that had come so easily and so often in their days together at Stanford. It was a giggle that knew no sadness, no fear, no limits. It transported Stephen back to the happiest days of his life.

"Marry me, Megan," he repeated.

"You have a wife!" she teased, her eyes sparkling.

"Beth will . . ." Stephen paused. He hadn't thought this

through. It felt right. He knew, somehow, he had to be with Megan. It was where he belonged, where he had always belonged. But it wouldn't be easy.

"Understand? No, Beth won't understand," Megan said. But she didn't sound worried. It was all just a lovely fantasy.

"Ours hasn't been the easiest relationship in the world, has it? Why should it change now?" Stephen was smiling. He held her tight and kissed her for a long time.

"I have to go in the morning. When this is over, when Stephie is safe, then we can make our plans, okay?" Megan asked seriously. Maybe there was a chance. It was something to live for.

Carrie placed her nightly call to Mark at nine-thirty. He had been unable to get away to join her.

"How are you?"

"Frightened for Megan."

"She's really going through with it?"

"Yes. I don't know what the agents plan, how closely they can follow her. But I know they are worried. I know Jake is worried."

"Jake . . ." Mark murmured under his breath.

"What?"

"Nothing. I miss you. I'm worried about you."

"I'm okay. Honestly. I am worried that the real horror of this is just about to begin."

"I'll try to come up tomorrow morning." Mark was tempted to get in his car right then, but he was "on call." A hostage situation had developed in Damascus. He had to be available for special reports.

Jake arrived at the farmhouse at ten. He had parked his car a mile away and walked across the rutted, uneven pasture, guided by moonlight. The pain in his knee was severe by the time he reached the farmhouse. He rested for a few minutes, surveying the situation.

The farmhouse was small, one story. Jake guessed that there were bedrooms in the back. The back of the house was dark. The lights were on in the front and on the porch.

Jake saw no car, but one could have been hidden behind the barn. The evening was silent except for the chirping of crickets and the sound of his feet, moving unevenly, on the straw-dry grass. As he neared the farmhouse, he heard voices. He paused, straining to hear the conversation. There was something unnatural about it—an even tempo, continuous dialogue. Television, Jake realized. Alec was probably watching the news.

Jake crept quietly onto the porch at the back of the house. He looked through a window into one of the darkened rooms. It was a bedroom. It contained a suitcase, men's clothes strewn over a chair, a pipe, road maps spread on the bed, a camera. It was Alec's room and no one was in it. Jake held his breath and made his way to the next window. Please be there, little one.

At first, the second bedroom looked unoccupied. It contained the chair, the carved doorknob, and the wallpaper of the photograph. The bed was directly under the window. As Jake's eyes adjusted to the darkness of the room, he discerned a shape in the bed, the shape of a small, sleeping child.

Jake blinked back a brief wave of tears and swallowed the emotion that lumped in the back of his throat. She was safe, still. Carefully, Jake tried the window. Locked. The lock was too high for Stephanie to reach, even if he could awaken her. But he could reach the lock if he could find something to stand on. He had a glass cutter.

The porch surrounded the entire house, but the wooden chairs and tables were at the front, brightly illuminated by the porch light. The farm yard was neat, tidy, uncluttered.

Jake walked to the barn. It was a risk. At one point the path to the barn could be seen from the living room. If

Alec happened to be looking . . . Jake kept low and in the shadows, and hoped.

A car was parked behind the barn. Jake checked it for keys. If there had been keys, he could have used it for his own escape, with Stephie. But there were no keys. Jake pulled some wires that would prevent, for awhile, Alec's escape in that car. Jake was making their job easier. It was a small, worthwhile distraction from his own task of saving Stephie.

Jake found an oak crate and emptied its contents, oats, onto the ground. A horse whinnied gently. Jake took a handful of oats and fed it to the horse.

He returned to the bedroom with the crate. Stephanie was still asleep. Jake cut a six-inch square out of the upper pane of glass. He applied a rubber suction cup to the glass to prevent it from falling inward, onto her. He removed the glass and placed it on the porch away from the crate and his planned path of escape. Then he stood on the crate and twisted the window lock.

The angle was poor, the lock old and rusted. It took several long minutes to loosen it, but, finally, it gave with a snap.

Stephanie turned and stretched, then curled and fell back into sleep. Jake pushed the sides of the warped wooden window upward. There was no outside handle. At least the window hadn't been painted shut.

The noise of the wooden window scraping against the window frame awakened Stephanie.

She sat upright, startled.

Don't scream, Jake thought.

He tapped gently on the window. When she looked up, he smiled and put a finger over his lips. It worked. She was silent. She stood up on the bed, looking up at Jake, smiling, waving her hands, gesturing to him to hurry—smiling, but anxious, frightened.

Jake saw her mouth the words: Hurry, Uncle Jake. Please hurry.

He smiled, put his finger to his lips again, then slowly, with great effort, forced the window until the gap was wide enough to permit a slender five-year-old child to squirm through.

"Come head and arms first. I'll pull you. It may hurt a little, or a lot. Let me know, quietly, okay?" he whispered.

The black curls nodded eagerly. Jake grabbed her small hands and pulled firmly.

This has to be hurting her, Jake thought grimly.

But in a few moments, the wriggling child was in his arms, her small arms wrapped tightly around his neck.

"I love you, Uncle Jake. You saved me!" she whispered.

"I love you, honey. Now, hold on tight and we'll go home."

"Hello, Easton."

Jake spun around and faced Alec. Stephanie clung more tightly.

Instantly, Jake saw the revolver in Alec's hand. He slid Stephanie down to the ground and behind him; she was completely protected by him. She clung to his pant leg, but his hands were free. As he slid her to the ground, he took something from the back pocket of his trousers.

"Hello, Alec."

"Nice detective work, Easton. How?"

"Photo of the room. Doorknob, wallpaper. One of a kind around here. Like a fingerprint."

Jake was accustomed to this cat-and-mouse conversation. It was part of the game. Try to get the other one to relax, just for a moment, then attack. Jake had been trained to do it. But Alec hadn't. Alec wasn't a trained agent or even an accomplished criminal. Alec was something much worse— he was insane. Alec didn't play by any rules. His behavior was erratic and totally unpredictable.

At any moment, without warning, he could pull the trigger of the gun that he held aimed at Jake and Stephanie. Jake knew that Alec would soon become bored with the repartee. Then, he would shoot.

Alec shrugged. "My mistake."

"Not a mistake, really," Jake said casually. "It just makes it more interesting."

Alec moved slightly. Jake's muscles tightened.

"Where are your friends? Where is the F . . . B . . . I?" Alec taunted. His voice revealed the obvious fact; he knew that Jake was quite alone. Alec held all the cards.

"Oh, they're out there, behind the trees."

Alec looked anxious for a moment, then laughed.

"Nice try, Easton. But I know you. The lone hero. Wants the glory for himself. To impress Megan, perhaps? Well, this time you made the mistake." Alec's voice got ugly. "Now, give me the child."

"No."

Alec moved one step closer. At the same moment, Alec's finger began to squeeze the trigger and Jake commanded with a yell, "Run, Stephie, run!"

Jake lunged forward. The sound of a shot rang out. Then a thud. Then a man's scream. Then another. Then the sound of a child screaming, men running, sirens blaring.

And in the background, faintly, the crickets chirped and a horse whinnied.

At eleven-thirty the telephone rang at Pinehaven. The FBI agent lifted the receiver a second before Ian did.

"She's safe, sir." The agent's voice broke slightly. He had a five-year-old daughter himself. "Your little girl is fine. We'll be there within the hour."

"Thank you! Thank God!" Ian replaced the receiver. For a moment he wondered if it had been a crank call. It worried him. He depressed the receiver twice to speak with the agent stationed in the living room.

"Yes sir?"

"Was that . . . ?"

"Real, sir? Yes, indeed. That was Agent Preston. They have her, sir, no doubt about it."

With tears in his eyes, Ian went to the bedrooms of his guests.

"Megan. Wake up, dear. She's safe. Stephie's safe."

Megan rushed to the door. "Is it true?"

"Yes. True. Get Stephen and come downstairs. She'll be home soon."

Carrie was awakened by the noise in the hallway.

"I'll get Jake," she said and half ran to the far end of the house, to Jake's room.

The door was closed. Carrie knocked and called his name. There was no answer. She knew that he slept lightly, restlessly. Why didn't he answer? She took a deep breath and opened the door.

The bed was made and the bedside lamp was on. On the bed lay a purple piece of silk. She had seen it before. Jake had taken it from the safe in his apartment. It had been wrapped around something long and thin.

Carrie sat on the bed, trembling. She felt nauseated and inexplicably frightened.

No, please, *no.*

They all waited, impatiently, nervously. Margaret made hot chocolate in the kitchen. Megan held Stephen's hand.

"Where's Jake?" Megan asked.

"I don't know. He's not in his room," Carrie said flatly.

"Then he's with Stephie. And they are both safe. They have to be," Megan said. Her knuckles were white.

At midnight, the front door opened and Stephanie bounded in. Her long black curls were tangled, but she looked happy, healthy, untroubled. She did not look like a child who had been abused.

"Mommy! Daddy! Aunt Megan! Aunt Carrie!" One by one she was squeezed and kissed by the adults who loved her so dearly.

"Did Alec hurt you, darling?" Megan had to know.

Stephanie looked surprised, then shook her head emphatically. "No. But it was so boring. He didn't let me do anything. And he didn't let me come home, even though I kept telling him I wanted to."

Megan held her. "You're home now, Stephie, and we are so happy. We all wanted you to be home very much."

Stephanie nodded and wriggled away. She was excited. She was the center of a great deal of attention.

She stood in front of Stephen and smiled. He squatted down and looked into her blue eyes, Megan's eyes, and at her black curls, like his. How had he missed the resemblance?

"I know you. You are my . . ." Stephanie stopped.

"I am your . . ." Stephen paused, sighed, then smiled. "I am your Uncle Stephen. I met you at the party for Aunt Megan. Remember?"

Stephanie nodded, satisfied.

"Have you seen Uncle Jake, Stephie?" Carrie asked. Agent Preston signaled to her not to press the child on that issue.

"Where is Uncle Jake?" Stephanie looked at Agent Preston. "Uncle Jake saved me. He pulled me through a window, but I did get some scratches. Then Alec came after us with a gun. Then Uncle Jake told me to run and he hit Alec. Uncle Jake saved me. Where is he?"

"He got hurt a little, so he's seeing a doctor. He'll be fine," Agent Preston said unconvincingly and looked pointedly at Margaret. She got the message.

"Stephie, let's go into the kitchen and get some hot chocolate and marshmallows."

Stephanie galloped toward the kitchen, followed by Margaret. The rest stayed to hear what Agent Preston had to say.

"Alec is dead. Jake killed him."

"And Jake?" Carrie asked quickly.

"He took a bullet in the shoulder. Just a flesh wound. But he seems to have injured his leg badly. I don't think he was shot in the leg, but he must have torn something when he lunged at Alec."

"Where is he?"

"On his way to Bethesda. He was very insistent that he be taken to Walter Reed. It's a helluva long trip for someone in that much pain, but he wasn't interested in listening to reason."

"But he's okay?" Carrie asked, again.

"I expect he'll be fine. He really did save Stephanie's life. And he really damn near got himself killed. If he hadn't moved at Alec exactly when he did . . ."

"Where were you?" Stephen demanded.

"We were there, at a distance. But we couldn't do anything until the child got clear. It was too risky. We just had to watch and hope."

"How did you find them?" Carrie asked.

"Easton discovered their location this afternoon, by following his hunch about the doorknob. He found someone who recognized it. It's really lucky, because if we'd had to proceed with the plan for tomorrow, well . . . This is a really happy ending."

They all nodded and shook hands with the agents. Carrie lagged behind as the others went to the kitchen. She overheard the agents discussing what had happened.

"Did Easton really kill him with a punch?" the other agent asked Preston.

"God, no. He skewered his heart with a stiletto. A pearl handled, gold and sapphire one. He probably picked it up in the Orient. It's obviously pretty valuable. We'll have to get it back for him, after the inquest."

"He killed him with a knife, and Alec had a gun?"

"Yessir. A lot of guts, a lot of training. Easton put the knife exactly where it's supposed to go. He's probably done it before. Very slick."

Carrie walked slowly into the kitchen, their words pounding in her brain.

Sometime later she telephoned Mark and the station. The

camera crews were mobilized. They taped a special report at two in the morning. It was broadcast at three and hourly after that until the morning news. In it, Carrie described the heroism of Jake Easton.

They all had breakfast with Stephie on Wednesday morning. Then, they dispersed, to return to their normal lives. Stephen left for Boston "to tell Beth." He assured Ian and Margaret that he would take no action to claim Stephanie. And he told Megan, again, that he loved her.

After breakfast, Carrie made a brief call to Mark. Then she drove to La Guardia and caught a commuter flight to National Airport in Washington, DC.

Carrie walked along the long, shiny linoleum hallways at Walter Reed Hospital. The admitting office had given her Jake's room number. The information desk had provided her with directions to the Orthopedics and Rehabilitation wing. It was only a matter of following colored signs and appropriate elevators.

It helped that she was recognized. They even assumed that she was coming to interview the hero. They had all seen the morning news; at most stations, the report that Carrie had taped was shown. They were impressed that someone of Carrie's importance would fly to Washington to do a personal interview. But then, it had been apparent all along that Carrie was personally involved with the case.

No one knew the real reason that Carrie was in Washington. She herself had only a vague idea.

The secretary at the nursing station directed Carrie to Jake's room.

"Is it all right to go in now?" Carrie asked.

"Of course!" Which meant the secretary couldn't imagine saying no to someone like Carrie. It made Carrie anxious; she wished that someone would check the nurse. Or better, check with Jake. But no one did.

She took a deep breath and walked toward room five-fourteen. The door was open.

Jake sat upright in the bed, his eyes shut. He looked very pale and tiny beads of perspiration dotted his forehead. His hair was damp. He was in a great deal of pain.

Facing Jake, with her back to Carrie, was a woman. She had long black hair, held his hand, and spoke softly to him. The woman heard Carrie enter, turned, and smiled.

"Hello!" Julia purred.

She is beautiful, Carrie thought. Carrie was struck immediately by Julia's agelessness and by her delicacy. Her jet black hair softly framed her small, beautiful face with its translucent, smooth skin and depthless violet eyes. The face was peaceful, graceful, and mesmerizing. No wonder Jake had fallen in love with this woman. Was he still in love with her? Carrie thought of all the hours Julia and Jake had spent together, how much they had shared, how many hundreds of times they had made love.

"I'm Julia." She smiled a warm, welcoming, nonthreatening smile.

"I'm Carrie."

It was an unnecessary formality and they knew it, acknowledging this with smiles. They each knew a great deal about the other.

Jake opened his eyes. "Carrie."

"Hi. I just came to thank you, for all of us. For the family. We owe you so much." Carrie still stood in the doorway. She felt like an intruder. Her words sounded empty, memorized.

"Thanks." Jake smiled an unconvincing smile.

Julia stood up. She still held Jake's hand.

"Carrie, please. Sit here and hold his hand. Mine needs a rest from the squeezing. Maybe you can talk him into some demerol."

"Why won't he take demerol?" Carrie asked, not moving.

"He wants to have his wits about him when he talks to

the doctor." Julia looked lovingly at Jake. Lovingly and proudly.

"Why?"

"Because"—Jake spoke—"they may be able to piece it all back together, from scratch. Much better than last time. Maybe permanently."

"Newer technology," Julia explained. "But Jake, you know that Dr. Phillips will order at least three days of tests before he's even ready to discuss the possibilities. You can't go without pain medications that long. You'll be too exhausted."

Jake smiled. "Julia and I have been through this before. She's right, of course."

"Carrie, just your presence is making him more sensible. I am going for coffee, but, on my way, I am going to give the nurse a verbal order for one hundred milligrams of demerol, stat." Julia held Jake's hand out to Carrie.

Carrie had no choice. She sat in the chair warmed by Julia and held onto Jake's cold, clammy hand. Within minutes a nurse appeared with a syringe of demerol. She injected it intravenously, into the tube that ran into Jake's arm. Carrie wondered if it would put him to sleep or make him groggy. But it did neither. It took the edge off the pain. It made it easier for him to concentrate on something other than the pain. It made it easier for him to talk.

"How is Stephie?"

"Wonderful. I don't think Alec did anything to harm her. She seems pretty unscathed and pretty proud of her Uncle Jake."

Jake smiled. "It was all very lucky."

That was what the agent had said. To Carrie, it seemed to be more than luck. Jake had acted on a hunch and seen it through.

"The lucky part was that you were there." Carrie paused. "I am so sorry about your leg."

"It was pulling loose again. It was about to go." Jake

shrugged. He didn't want to talk about his leg or his heroism. "How's Alec?"

Carrie was surprised. "He's dead, Jake."

Jake nodded, solemnly. He hadn't known. The tendons in his leg had torn completely as he had lunged at Alec; his brain had been reeling with pain. But his well-trained hands had carried out their mission, automatically. The same type of technique he had used in Cambodia. Apparently he had done it this time with comparable success.

Jake looked at Carrie's hand, the one that held his, the one that wore the engagement ring from Mark. He moved the ring idly on her finger, lost in thought. Carrie watched him, trying to decipher his expression.

"When are you and Mark getting married?" he asked, finally.

"In December." Six months. Carrie took a deep breath before speaking. "I don't care about your leg. Whatever happens to it. You are still you." Was he listening to her?

"Are you happy with him?" Jake asked, still looking at her hand.

"Of course!" Carrie answered reflexively. But it wasn't what she wanted to talk about. She said seriously, "Jake, it was best for everyone that you killed Alec. It ends the nightmare. For everyone, except you." *Listen to me, Jake.*

He looked at her and smiled. "What are we talking about?"

"You know perfectly well. We're talking in bottom lines. I'm telling you what is important to me," Carrie said. His eyes were glassy, from pain, demerol, lack of sleep, another murder. It was hopeless to expect him to understand what she was telling him. "Those four days we had together, Jake, that February—"

They were interrupted by the entrance of the doctor. Jake sat upright.

"Dr. Phillips. This is Carrie Richards."

"Miss Richards. I enjoy your show. I enjoyed your news bulletin about Jake this morning."

"Thank you."

"Now, Jake. Let me look at your leg." The doctor exposed Jake's leg. Carrie saw that the mass of muscle, which had reached the length of his thigh before, was now bunched up at mid-thigh. The tendons that had pulled the muscle to its full, functional length had ruptured.

"I think we should plan for surgery in three days. Between now and then you have to decide whether you want the leg amputated or you want me to freeze it at the knee joint. If we amputate mid-thigh, you can be fitted with a prosthesis and maintain very good function. Knowing you, you'd be able to walk without a limp. If we lock the knee joint, your leg is preserved, but it won't flex at the knee. It will always be straight. You'll never walk or sit normally."

"Dr. Phillips has a strong preference, as you can tell," Jake said to Carrie. Jake had known the options for years. "What about . . . ?"

"Revising this? It may be possible. I'll know more after the tests, but I won't know for sure until I get in there and see. If we go that route, we have to transplant some muscles from your other leg, and so on. It would be a long rehabilitative process."

"I'm used to those."

"You know that if I can save it, make you a new leg, I will. But if I can't, I need to have you decide what you want me to do. I'll be back when I get the results of the tests. Oh, I'm glad to see you're taking some demerol. It will work together with the muscle relaxant to counteract the spasm. Nice to meet you, Miss Richards." Dr. Phillips left.

"I like Dr. Phillips," Carrie said after he had gone.

"So do I. He's been on my side since the beginning of this. If it can be done, he'll do it." Jake had released Carrie's hand when the doctor had come in, but now he reached for it again. He held it gently. Not from his physical pain, but because he wanted to touch her.

Carrie realized, sadly, that there was nothing left to say. The crisis with Stephanie was over. They could now return to their real lives—Carrie to Mark and her vow never to see Jake again; Jake, to finally learn the fate of his leg, and to Julia. Perhaps Megan and Stephen could begin again. Time would tell. But for them, for Jake and Carrie, it had all come to an end. Carrie had no need, no reason, no right to be there any longer.

"Are you happy, Carrie?" Jake asked, reading her thoughts.

"Of course," she said again and stood up to leave. "Well, I have to go." She didn't look at him. She couldn't.

"Take care, Caroline," he whispered as she left.

Epilogue

All day the next day, Carrie ached with a sense of emptiness and loss. It was over. Finally over. It was better that it had ended this way, with a quiet farewell in Jake's hospital room, rather than the bitter, hateful words of two months before.

Better, but harder. Sadder.

Carrie knew the aching, the final mourning for a life with Jake that never was to be, would pass. She hoped that Dr. Phillips could repair Jake's leg. Since she would never know, Carrie would choose to believe that Jake's leg would be fixed, and that Jake would be happy, always.

The telephone—her private line in her dressing room at the studio—rang, startling her out of her reverie. It would be Mark, wondering what was keeping her. Their evening newscast was over. They were going out to dinner to celebrate Stephanie's safe return to her loved ones and Carrie's return from Pinehaven, and from Washington, to Mark.

Smiling, Carrie answered the phone, "Hi. I'm on my way!"

Silence.

She sounds so happy, he thought. What am I doing?

But, he had made a decision. He had made it soon after she had gone, when the memory of seeing her, touching her, was most vivid. He had forced himself to wait, to see how the decision would feel in the morning, after some much needed rest, and when his mind was clear of pain medications. He had fallen asleep, thinking about his decision. For the first time in years, he had had lovely, happy dreams. No nightmares.

In the morning, the decision had still felt right. As the day progressed, it had felt even better. He had watched her evening newscast. Then, when it was over, he had called her.

When he had heard her voice, lightheartedly, happily speaking, she assumed, to Mark, Jake had hesitated. But only for a moment.

He had made his decision. He had to give her a chance to make hers.

"Carrie?"

"Jake?"

"Hi."

"Hi," she said tentatively. Why was he calling?

"I have thought about the conversation we had yesterday," he said. "Or whatever it was."

"Whatever," she repeated, her heart pounding.

"I have a bottom line for you." Jake paused, momentarily choked with emotion. How often had he dreamed of this moment? He said, softly, "I love you and I want to marry you."

Carrie's blue eyes flooded with tears. She couldn't speak. She couldn't control her heart.

Jake heard only silence; long, empty silence. He waited, wondering. Had he misinterpreted what she had said to him yesterday? Had his mind been too foggy? Maybe she hadn't meant it, after all. Maybe it was, finally, just too late.

"Carrie?" he asked after several moments.

"The name is Caroline," she whispered, her voice trembling.

"Caroline," he repeated softly, as only he could.

More silence. More tears.

"Do you mean it, Jake?" she asked finally, weakly.

"I mean it, darling."

Difficult, emotional questions raced into Carrie's mind: what about Mark? Her commitment to Mark. Her love for Mark. What about all the pain of the past? Can it be forgotten? Will there be more pain? Is it worth the risk?

The questions were hard, but her answer was easy.

"Yes, Jake, I will marry you."

"You will?" he asked eagerly, wanting to be certain he had heard her answer correctly.

"Yes," Carrie said confidently, "I will."

Now it was Jake who was silent, overcome by his own emotion, his own happiness. When he spoke again, his joy was obvious.

"I love you. When shall we get married?" he asked happily.

"How about now? Or yesterday? Why don't I fly down right now and we'll discuss it."

"That would be wonderful. Can you?" he asked carefully.

"I think so," Carrie answered slowly. They were both thinking about Mark. Mark, who was waiting to take Carrie to a celebration dinner. Carrie thought about Mark's reaction. He would be angry—at Jake, not her. He would tell her, because he honestly believed it, that she was making a terrible mistake. But, he would not be surprised, not really. And he would not try to stop her. Carrie repeated quietly, "I think so."

Several moments passed. Jake guessed Carrie was thinking about Mark. Was she changing her mind? He waited, anxiously. When Carrie spoke again, it had nothing to do with Mark.

"You must have found out about your leg," she said thoughtfully.

"No. Nothing has changed since yesterday," he said slowly, a shadow of worry in his voice. "I thought it didn't matter."

"It *doesn't* matter, Jake." Carrie began to cry, again. He understood, finally, how much she loved him. He had heard what she had said, that the only thing that mattered to her was being with him. "I'm so glad you know it."

"Are you happy?" he asked finally, gently. It was the same question he had asked her twice yesterday.

"I have never been this happy. Ever. I love you, Jake."

"I love you, too, Caroline."